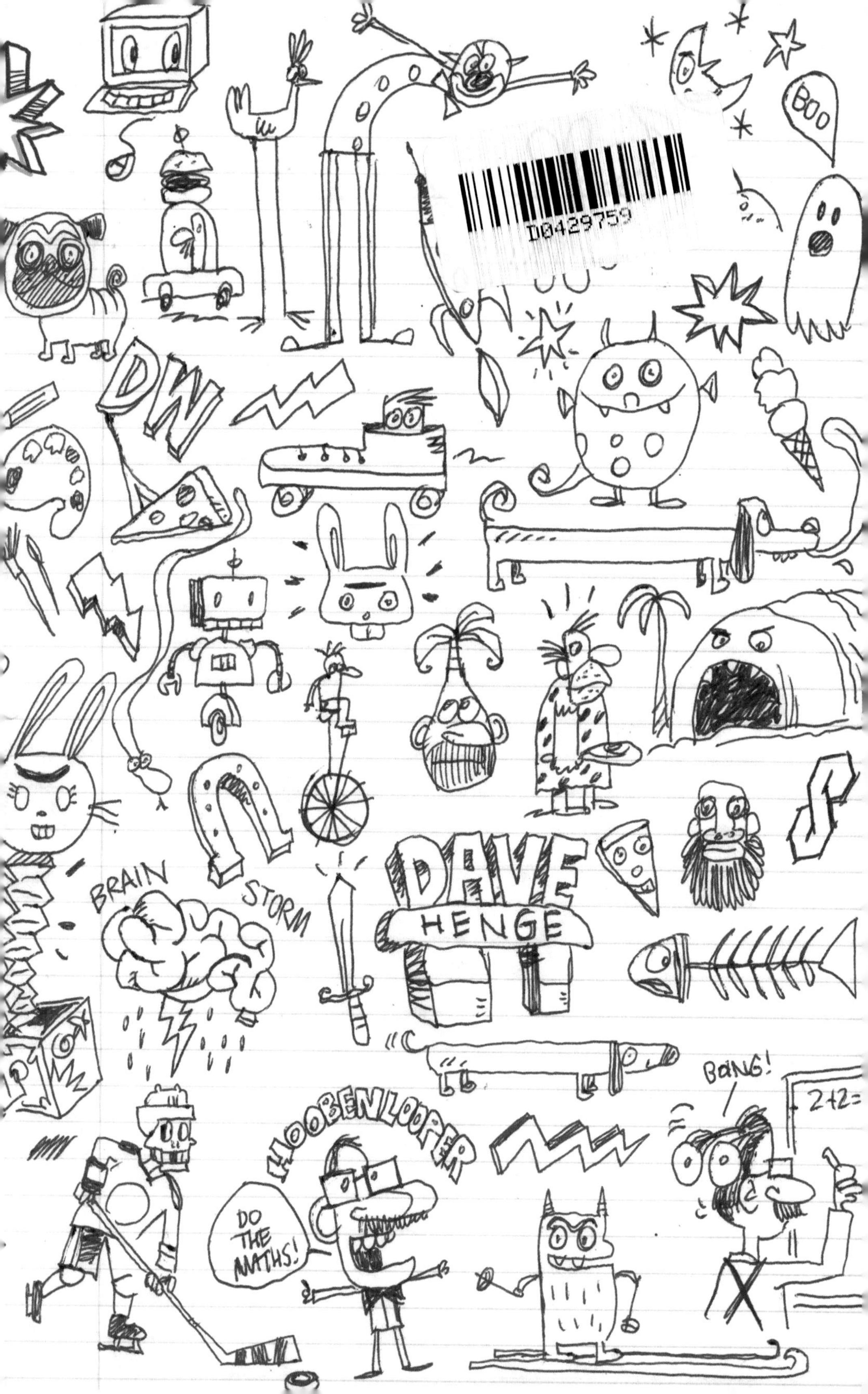
Boo
DW
BRAIN
STORM
DAVE
HENGE
KLOOBENLOOPER
DO THE MATHS!
BANG!
2+2=

TO MY PARENTS AND MY SISTER, WHO HAD TO PUT UP WITH ME DURING MY REAL MIDDLE SCHOOL YEARS.

Published in Canada and the U.S. by Kids Can Press Ltd.
25 Dockside Drive, Toronto, ON M5A 0B5

Kids Can Press is a Corus Entertainment Inc. company

www.kidscanpress.com

The artwork in this book was rendered in pen and ink and digital watercolor.
The text is set in SmackAttack BB, Squidtoonz and Nippon Note.

Edited by Jennifer Stokes
Designed by Michael Reis

Printed and bound in Heyuan, China, in 3/2021 by Asia Pacific Offset

FSC www.fsc.org MIX Paper from responsible sources FSC® C012521

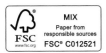

CM 21 0 9 8 7 6 5 4 3 2 1

Library and Archives Canada Cataloguing in Publication

Title: Muddle school / written and illustrated by Dave Whamond.
Names: Whamond, Dave, author, illustrator.
Identifiers: Canadiana 20200365142 | ISBN 9781525304866 (hardcover)
Subjects: LCGFT: Graphic novels.
Classification: LCC PN6733.W43 M83 2021 | DDC j741.5/971 – dc23

Kids Can Press gratefully acknowledges that the land on which our office is located is the traditional territory of many nations, including the Mississaugas of the Credit, the Anishnabeg, the Chippewa, the Haudenosaunee and the Wendat peoples, and is now home to many diverse First Nations, Inuit and Métis peoples.

We thank the Government of Ontario, through Ontario Creates; the Ontario Arts Council; the Canada Council for the Arts; and the Government of Canada for supporting our publishing activity.

MUDDLE SCHOOL

Dave Whamond

KIDS CAN PRESS

CHAPTER 1: NO JOY IN MUDDLE

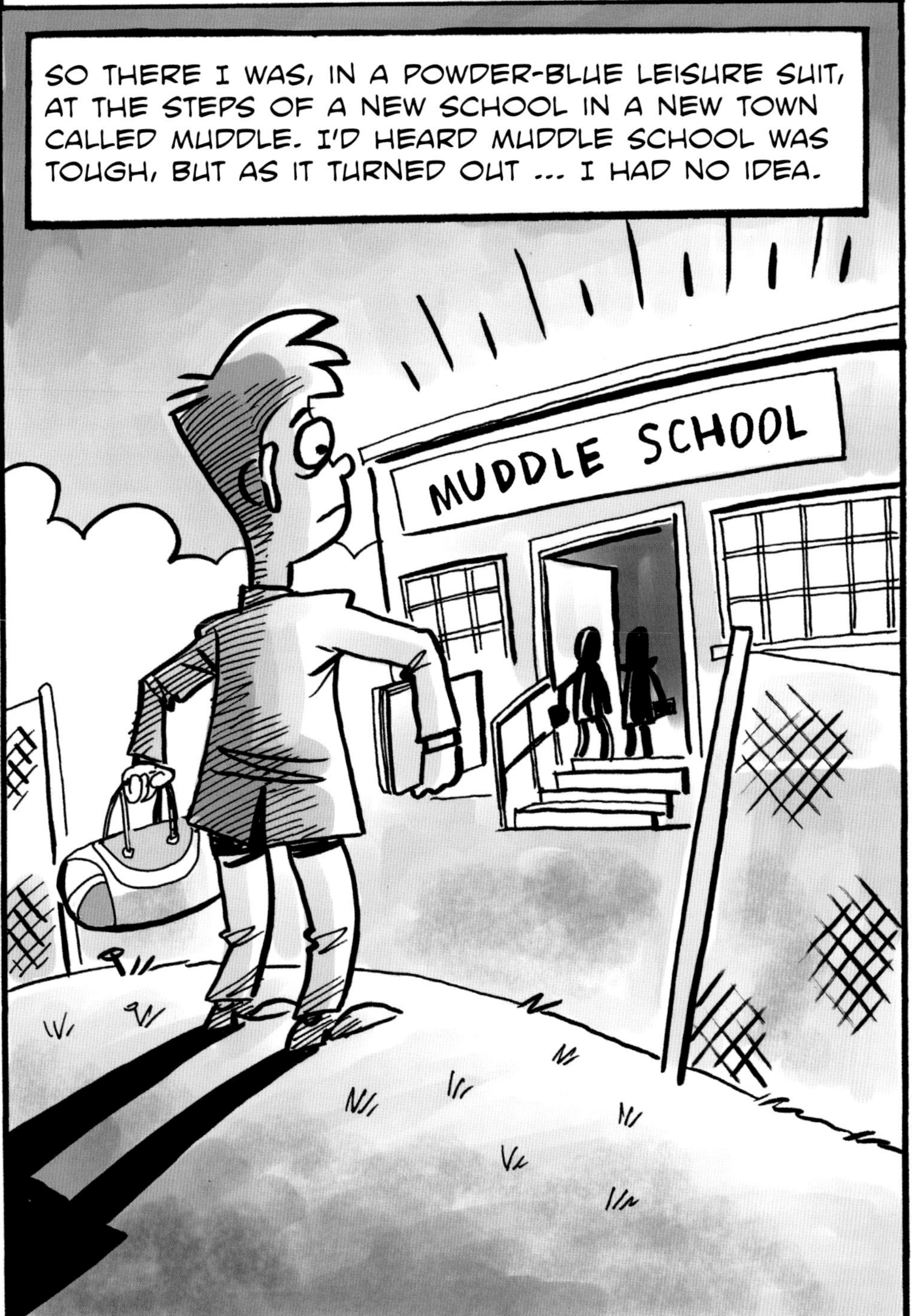
SO THERE I WAS, IN A POWDER-BLUE LEISURE SUIT, AT THE STEPS OF A NEW SCHOOL IN A NEW TOWN CALLED MUDDLE. I'D HEARD MUDDLE SCHOOL WAS TOUGH, BUT AS IT TURNED OUT ... I HAD NO IDEA.
MUDDLE SCHOOL

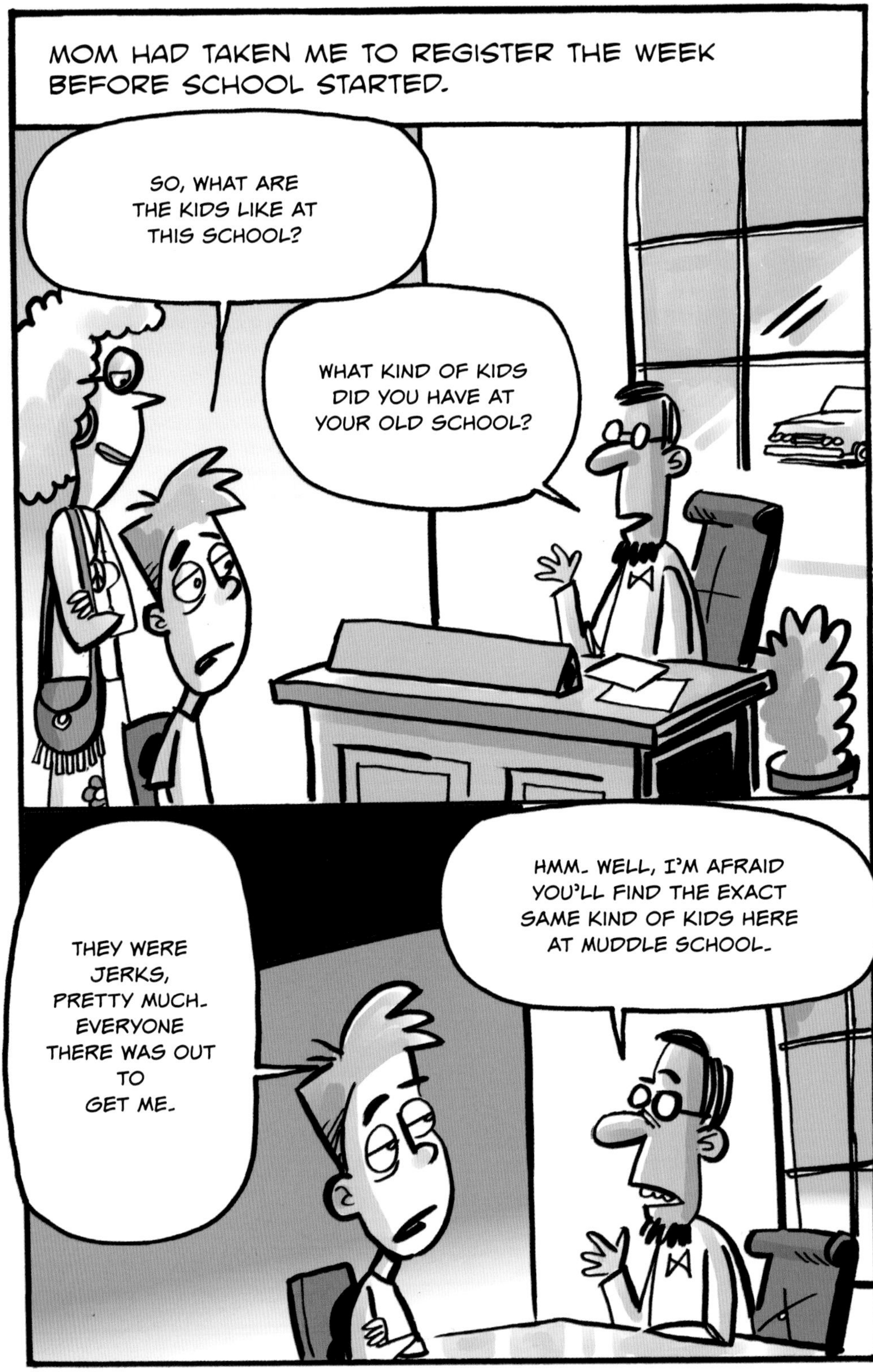
MOM HAD TAKEN ME TO REGISTER THE WEEK BEFORE SCHOOL STARTED.
SO, WHAT ARE THE KIDS LIKE AT THIS SCHOOL?
WHAT KIND OF KIDS DID YOU HAVE AT YOUR OLD SCHOOL?
THEY WERE JERKS, PRETTY MUCH. EVERYONE THERE WAS OUT TO GET ME.
HMM. WELL, I'M AFRAID YOU'LL FIND THE EXACT SAME KIND OF KIDS HERE AT MUDDLE SCHOOL.

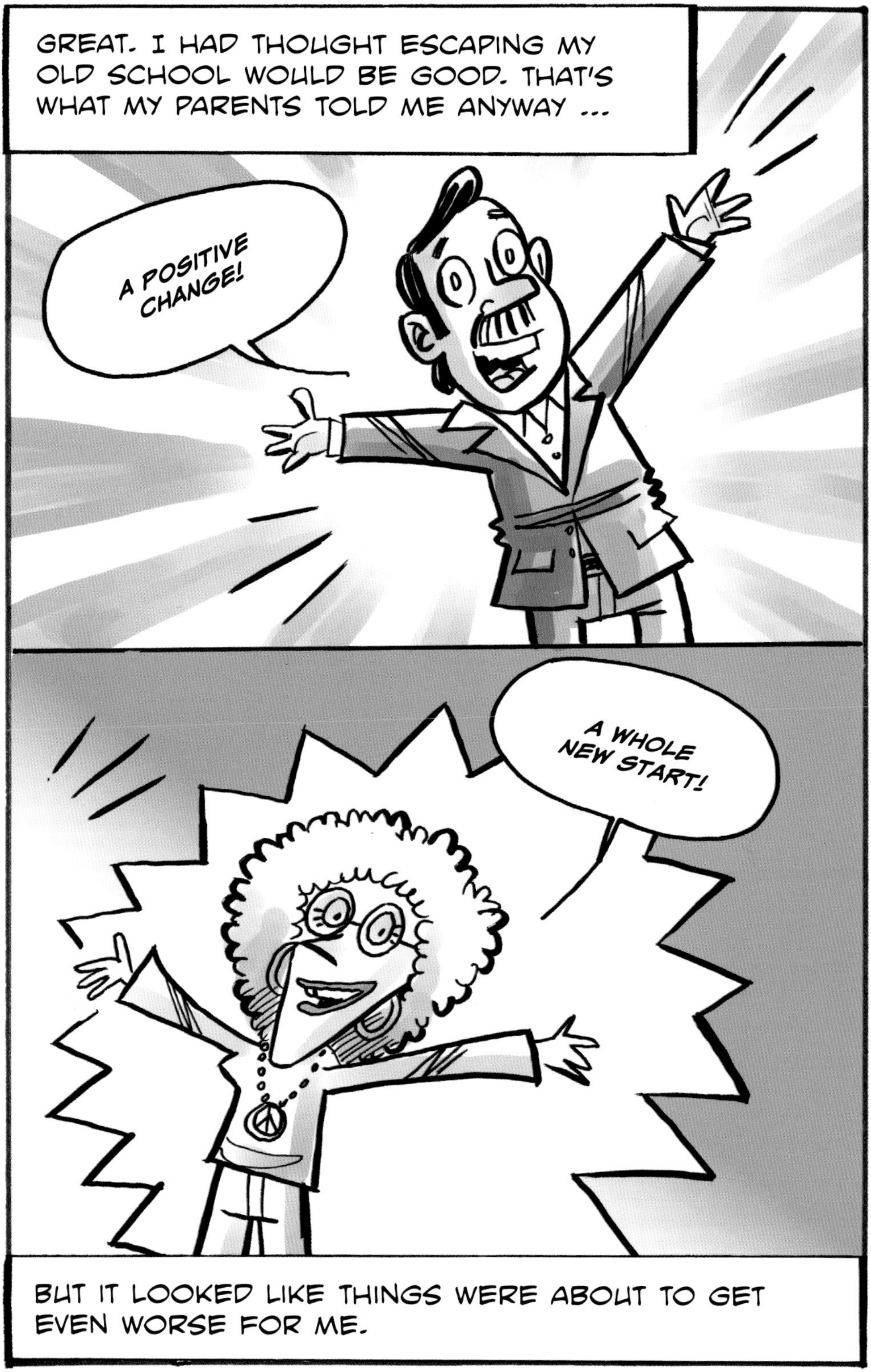
GREAT. I HAD THOUGHT ESCAPING MY OLD SCHOOL WOULD BE GOOD. THAT'S WHAT MY PARENTS TOLD ME ANYWAY ...
A POSITIVE CHANGE!
A WHOLE NEW START!
BUT IT LOOKED LIKE THINGS WERE ABOUT TO GET EVEN WORSE FOR ME.

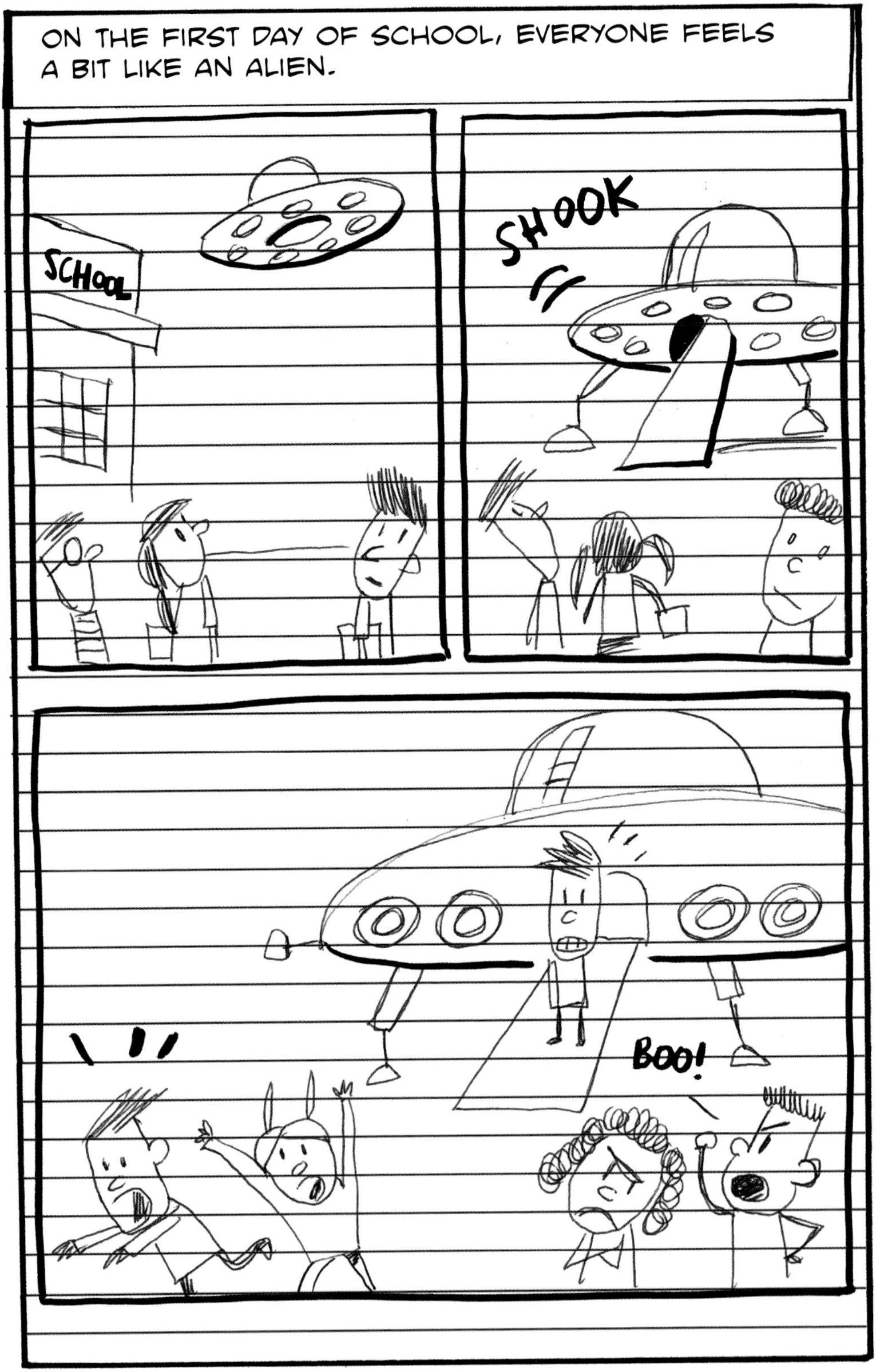
ON THE FIRST DAY OF SCHOOL, EVERYONE FEELS A BIT LIKE AN ALIEN.
SCHOOL
SHOOK
BOO!

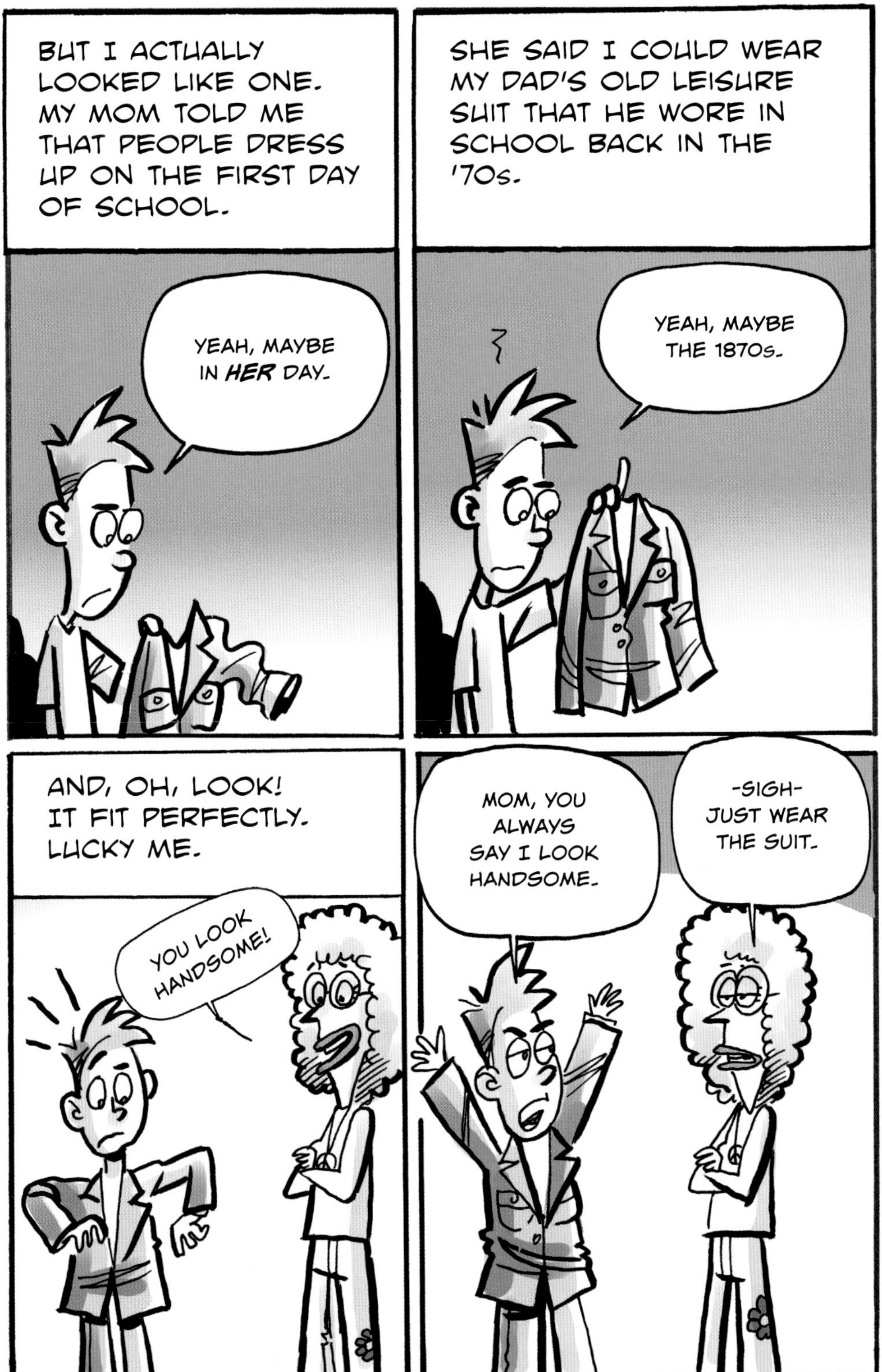

BUT I ACTUALLY LOOKED LIKE ONE. MY MOM TOLD ME THAT PEOPLE DRESS UP ON THE FIRST DAY OF SCHOOL.
YEAH, MAYBE IN HER DAY.
SHE SAID I COULD WEAR MY DAD'S OLD LEISURE SUIT THAT HE WORE IN SCHOOL BACK IN THE '70s.
YEAH, MAYBE THE 1870s.
AND, OH, LOOK! IT FIT PERFECTLY. LUCKY ME.
YOU LOOK HANDSOME!
MOM, YOU ALWAYS SAY I LOOK HANDSOME.
-SIGH- JUST WEAR THE SUIT.

I'VE ALWAYS HAD A PROBLEM WITH AUTHORITY ...

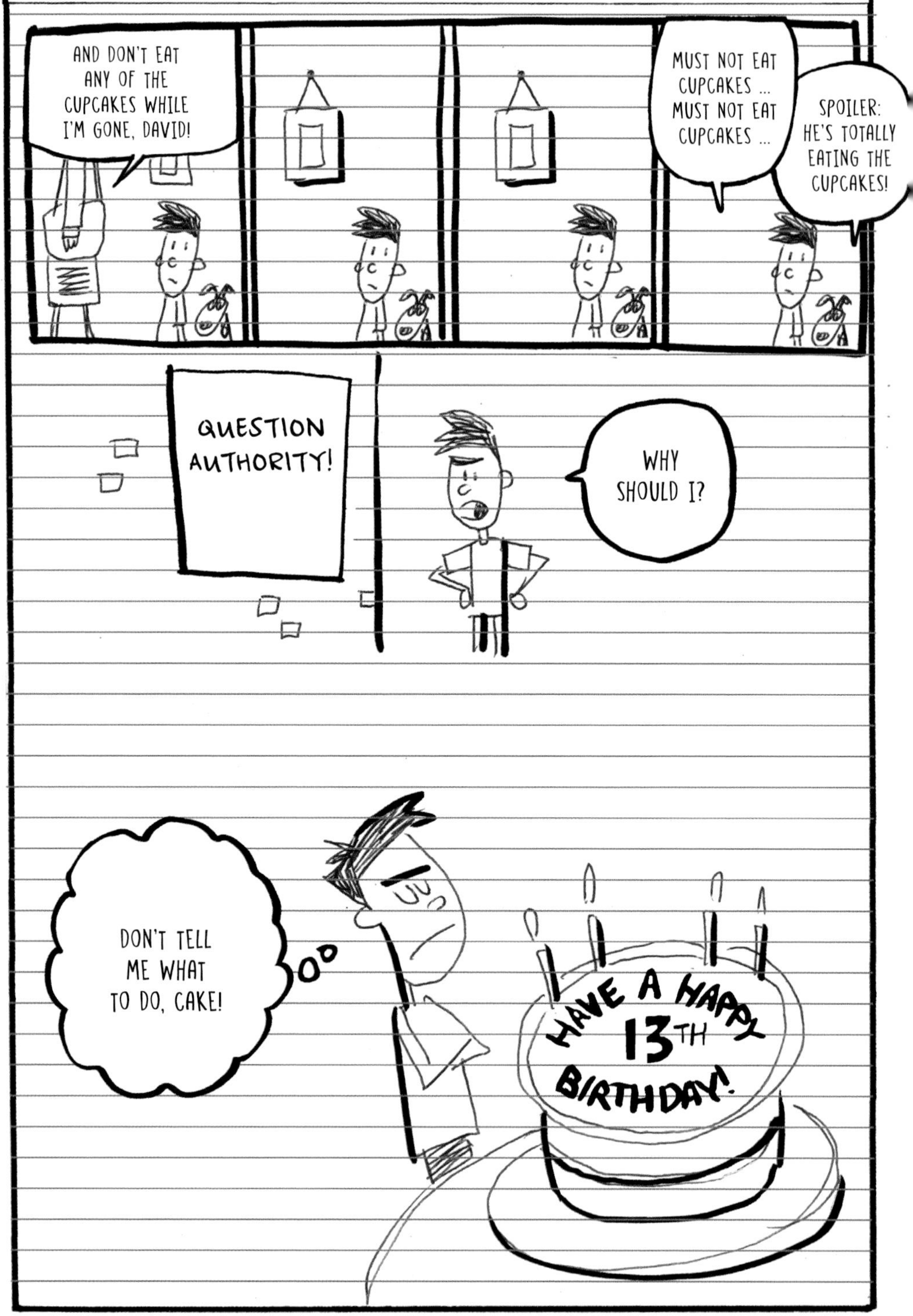
AND DON'T EAT ANY OF THE CUPCAKES WHILE I'M GONE, DAVID!
MUST NOT EAT CUPCAKES ... MUST NOT EAT CUPCAKES ...
SPOILER: HE'S TOTALLY EATING THE CUPCAKES!
QUESTION AUTHORITY!
WHY SHOULD I?
DON'T TELL ME WHAT TO DO, CAKE!
HAVE A HAPPY 13TH BIRTHDAY!

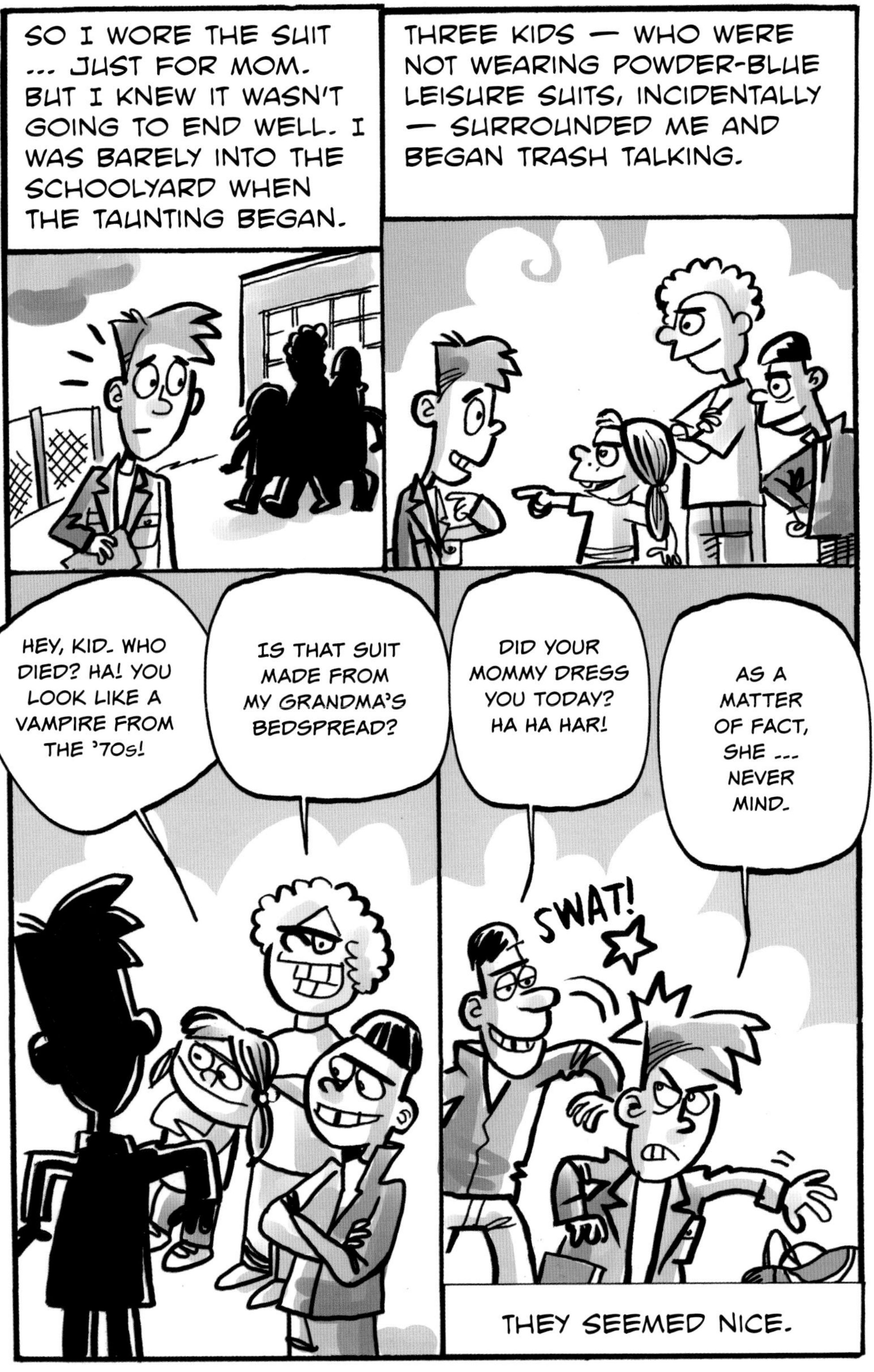
SO I WORE THE SUIT ... JUST FOR MOM. BUT I KNEW IT WASN'T GOING TO END WELL. I WAS BARELY INTO THE SCHOOLYARD WHEN THE TAUNTING BEGAN.
THREE KIDS — WHO WERE NOT WEARING POWDER-BLUE LEISURE SUITS, INCIDENTALLY — SURROUNDED ME AND BEGAN TRASH TALKING.
HEY, KID. WHO DIED? HA! YOU LOOK LIKE A VAMPIRE FROM THE '70s!
IS THAT SUIT MADE FROM MY GRANDMA'S BEDSPREAD?
DID YOUR MOMMY DRESS YOU TODAY? HA HA HAR!
AS A MATTER OF FACT, SHE ... NEVER MIND.
SWAT!
THEY SEEMED NICE.

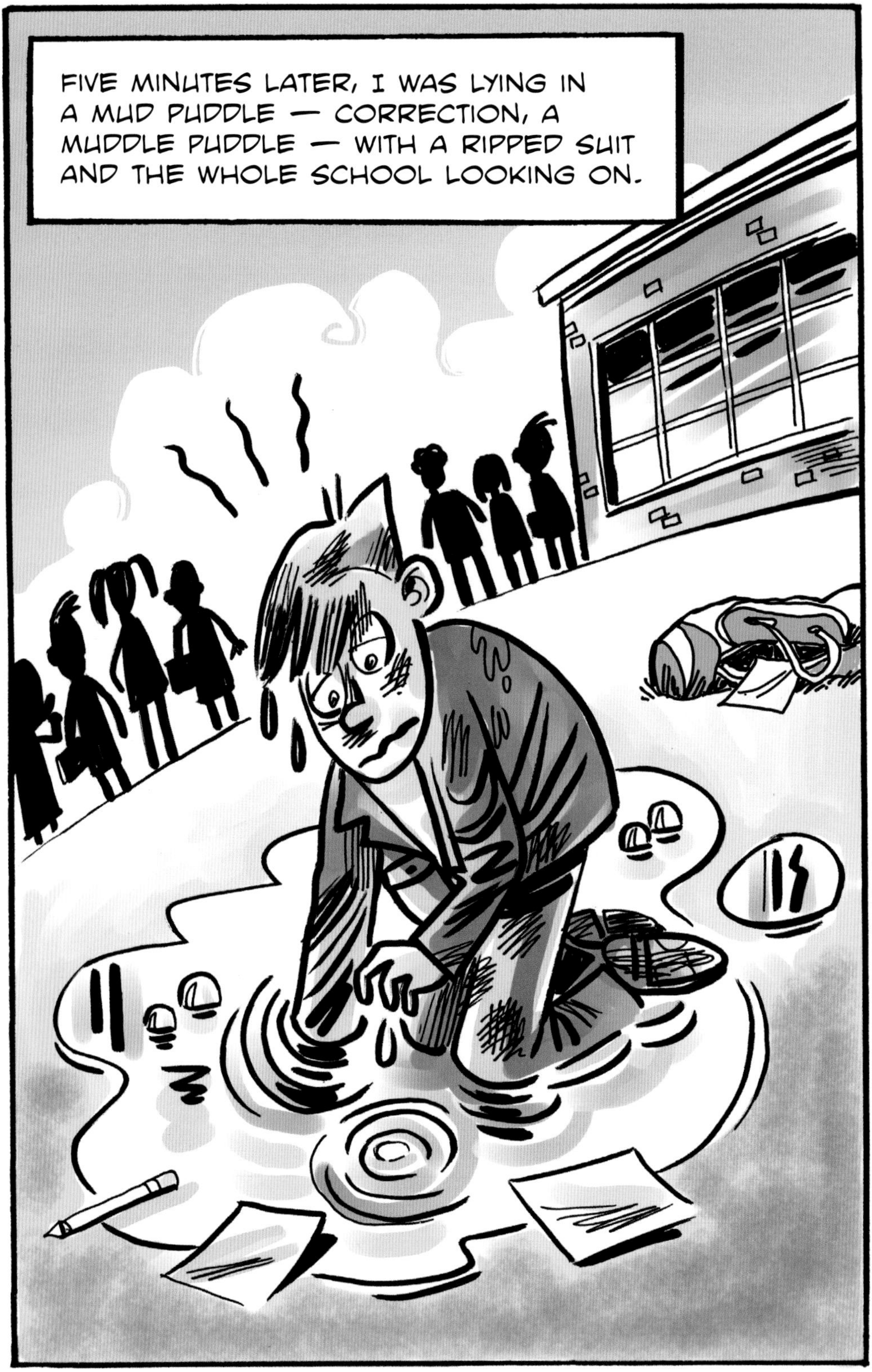
FIVE MINUTES LATER, I WAS LYING IN A MUD PUDDLE — CORRECTION, A MUDDLE PUDDLE — WITH A RIPPED SUIT AND THE WHOLE SCHOOL LOOKING ON.

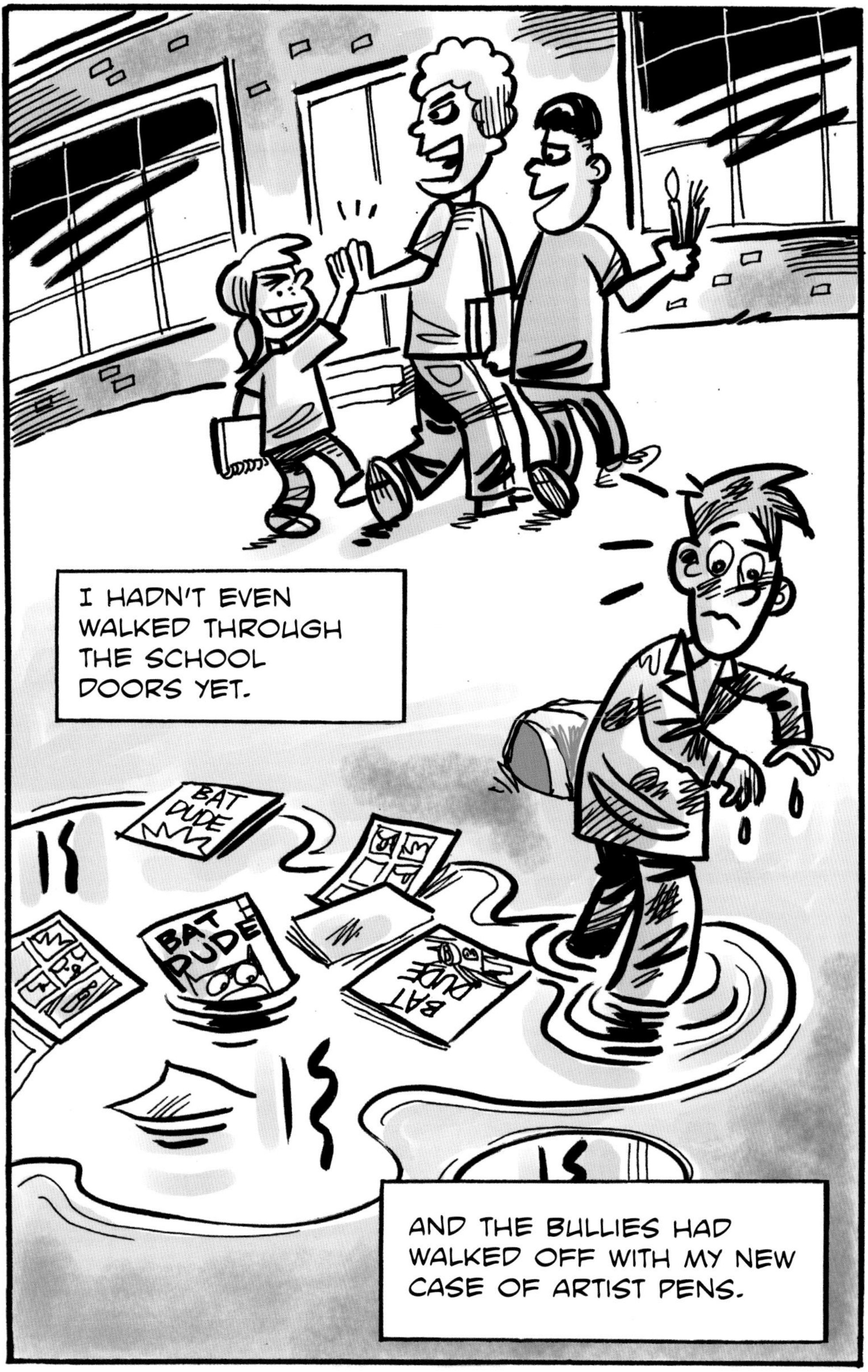
I HADN'T EVEN WALKED THROUGH THE SCHOOL DOORS YET.
BAT DUDE
BAT DUDE
BAT DUDE
AND THE BULLIES HAD WALKED OFF WITH MY NEW CASE OF ARTIST PENS.

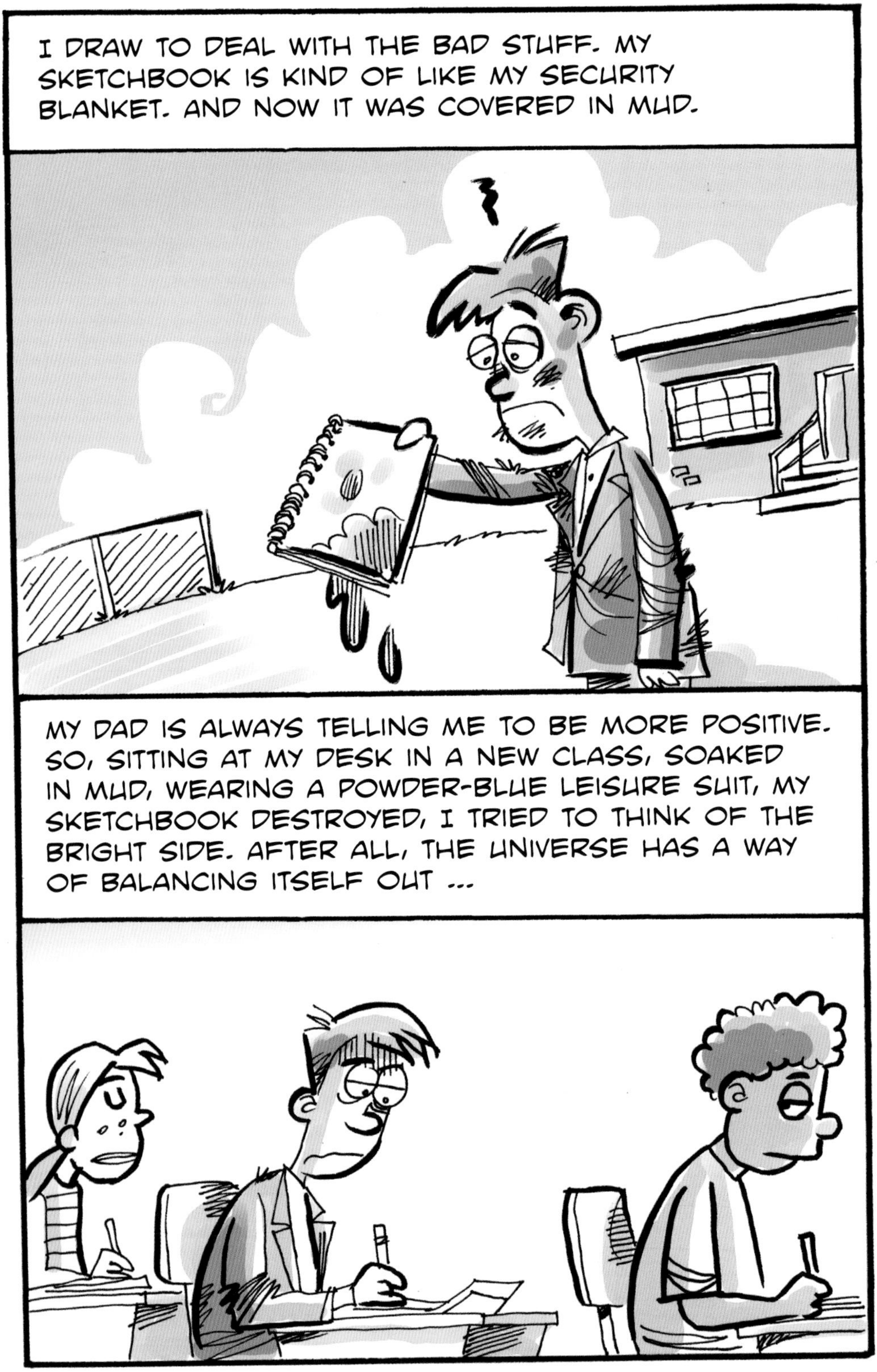
I DRAW TO DEAL WITH THE BAD STUFF. MY SKETCHBOOK IS KIND OF LIKE MY SECURITY BLANKET. AND NOW IT WAS COVERED IN MUD.
MY DAD IS ALWAYS TELLING ME TO BE MORE POSITIVE. SO, SITTING AT MY DESK IN A NEW CLASS, SOAKED IN MUD, WEARING A POWDER-BLUE LEISURE SUIT, MY SKETCHBOOK DESTROYED, I TRIED TO THINK OF THE BRIGHT SIDE. AFTER ALL, THE UNIVERSE HAS A WAY OF BALANCING ITSELF OUT ...

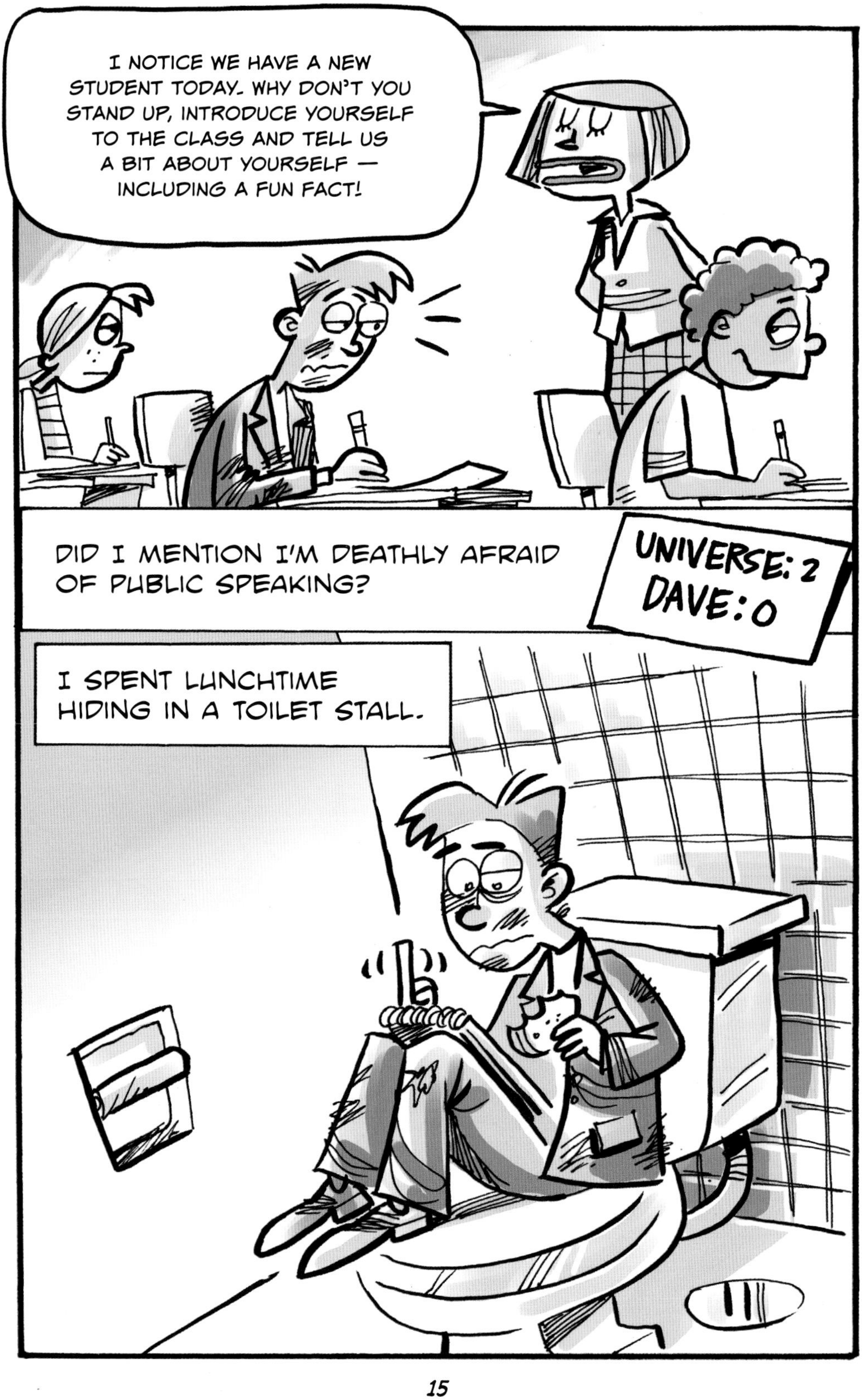
I NOTICE WE HAVE A NEW STUDENT TODAY. WHY DON'T YOU STAND UP, INTRODUCE YOURSELF TO THE CLASS AND TELL US A BIT ABOUT YOURSELF — INCLUDING A FUN FACT!
DID I MENTION I'M DEATHLY AFRAID OF PUBLIC SPEAKING?
UNIVERSE: 2
DAVE: 0
I SPENT LUNCHTIME HIDING IN A TOILET STALL.

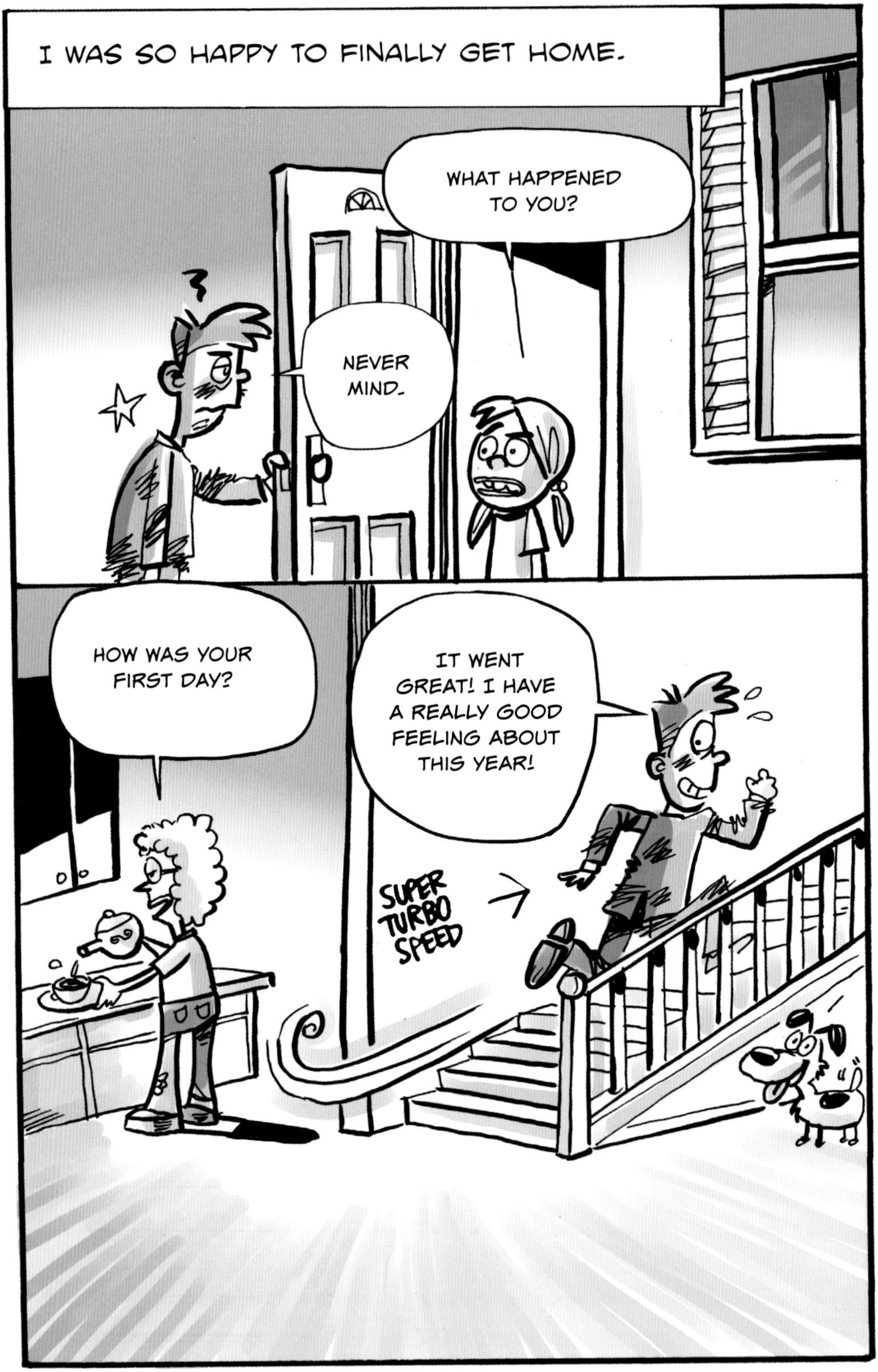
I WAS SO HAPPY TO FINALLY GET HOME.
WHAT HAPPENED TO YOU?
NEVER MIND.
HOW WAS YOUR FIRST DAY?
IT WENT GREAT! I HAVE A REALLY GOOD FEELING ABOUT THIS YEAR!
SUPER TURBO SPEED

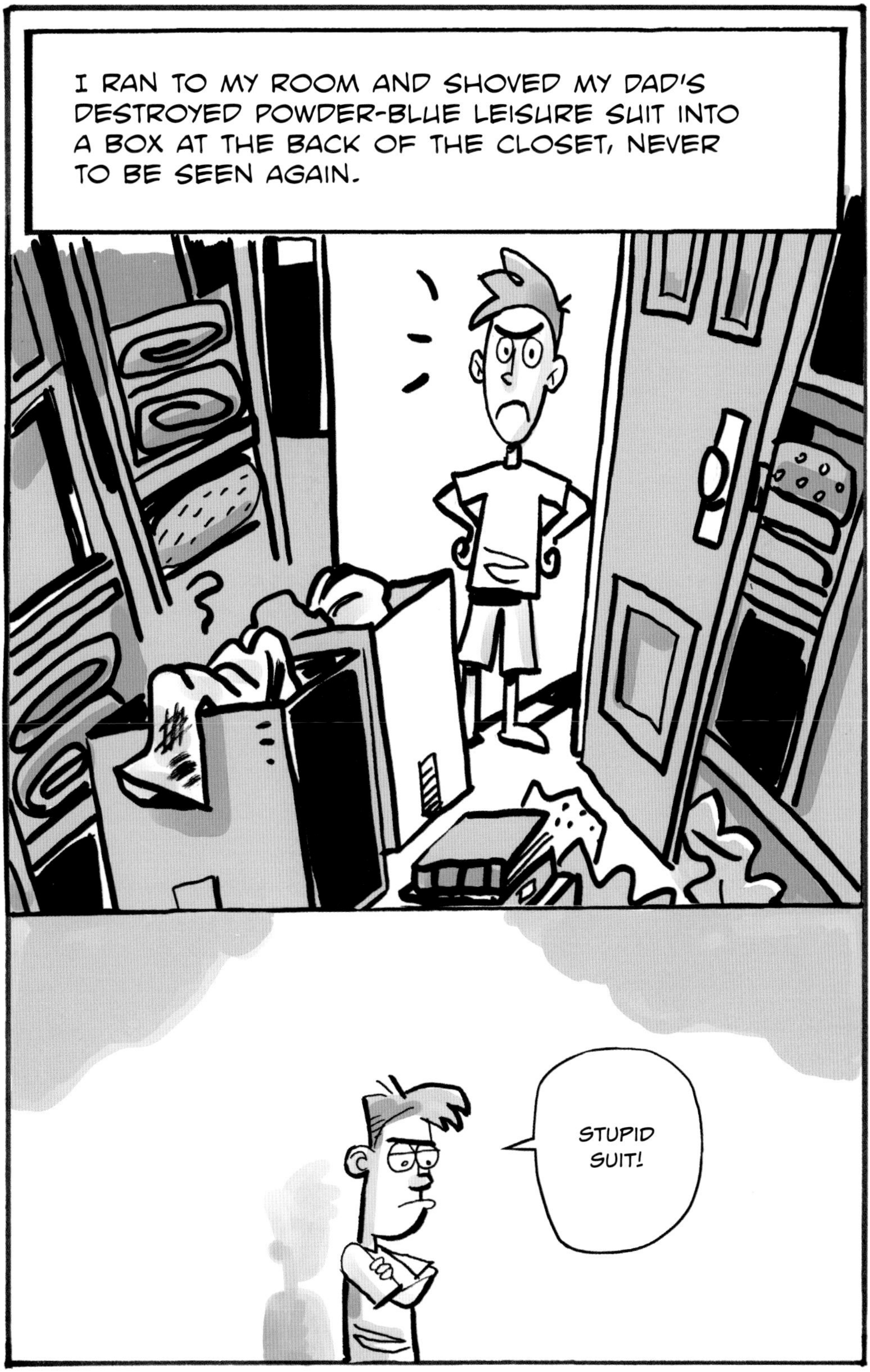
I RAN TO MY ROOM AND SHOVED MY DAD'S DESTROYED POWDER-BLUE LEISURE SUIT INTO A BOX AT THE BACK OF THE CLOSET, NEVER TO BE SEEN AGAIN.
STUPID SUIT!

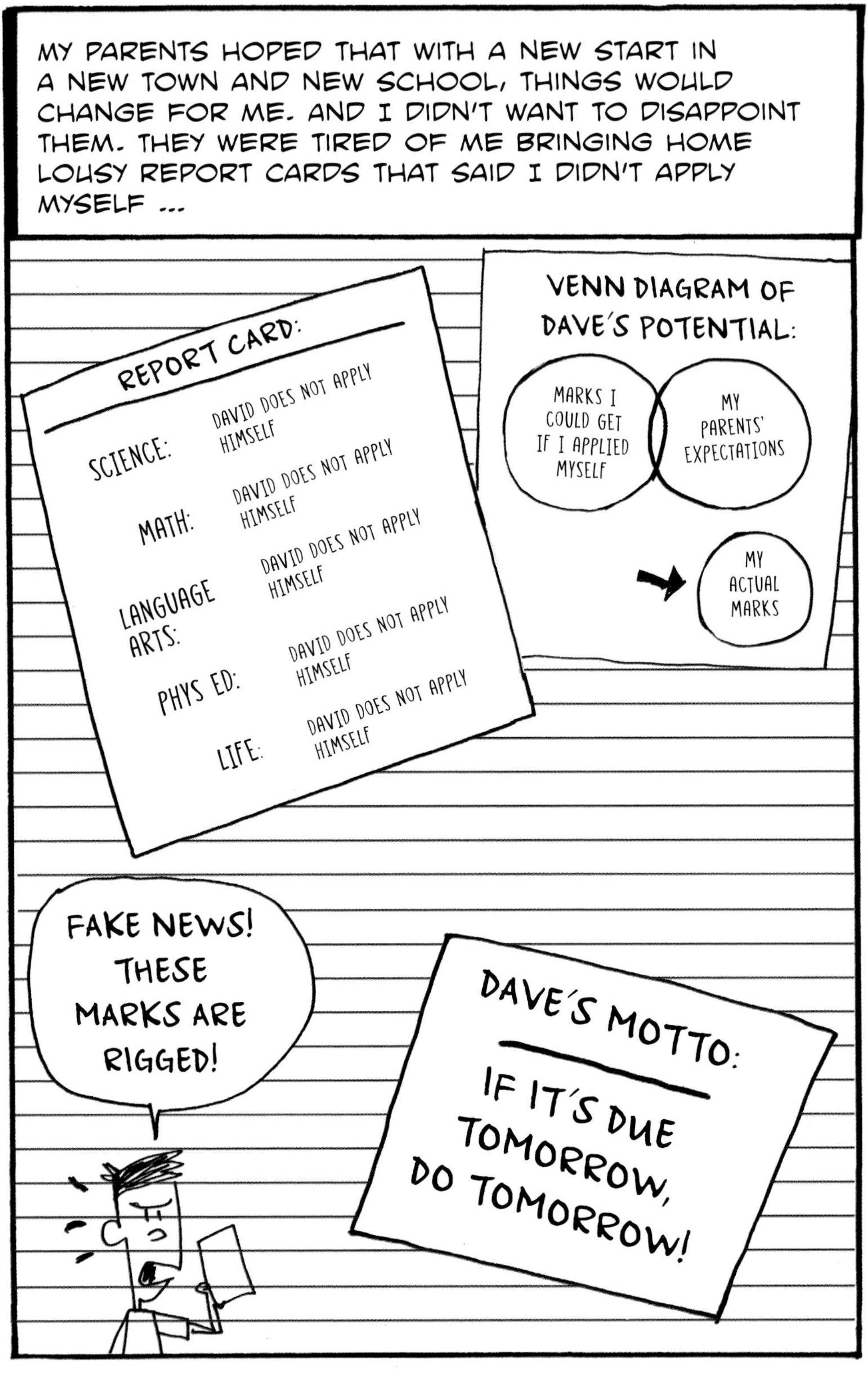
MY PARENTS HOPED THAT WITH A NEW START IN A NEW TOWN AND NEW SCHOOL, THINGS WOULD CHANGE FOR ME. AND I DIDN'T WANT TO DISAPPOINT THEM. THEY WERE TIRED OF ME BRINGING HOME LOUSY REPORT CARDS THAT SAID I DIDN'T APPLY MYSELF ...
REPORT CARD:
SCIENCE: DAVID DOES NOT APPLY HIMSELF
MATH: DAVID DOES NOT APPLY HIMSELF
LANGUAGE ARTS: DAVID DOES NOT APPLY HIMSELF
PHYS ED: DAVID DOES NOT APPLY HIMSELF
LIFE: DAVID DOES NOT APPLY HIMSELF
VENN DIAGRAM OF DAVE'S POTENTIAL:
MARKS I COULD GET IF I APPLIED MYSELF
MY PARENTS' EXPECTATIONS
MY ACTUAL MARKS
FAKE NEWS! THESE MARKS ARE RIGGED!
DAVE'S MOTTO:
IF IT'S DUE TOMORROW, DO TOMORROW!

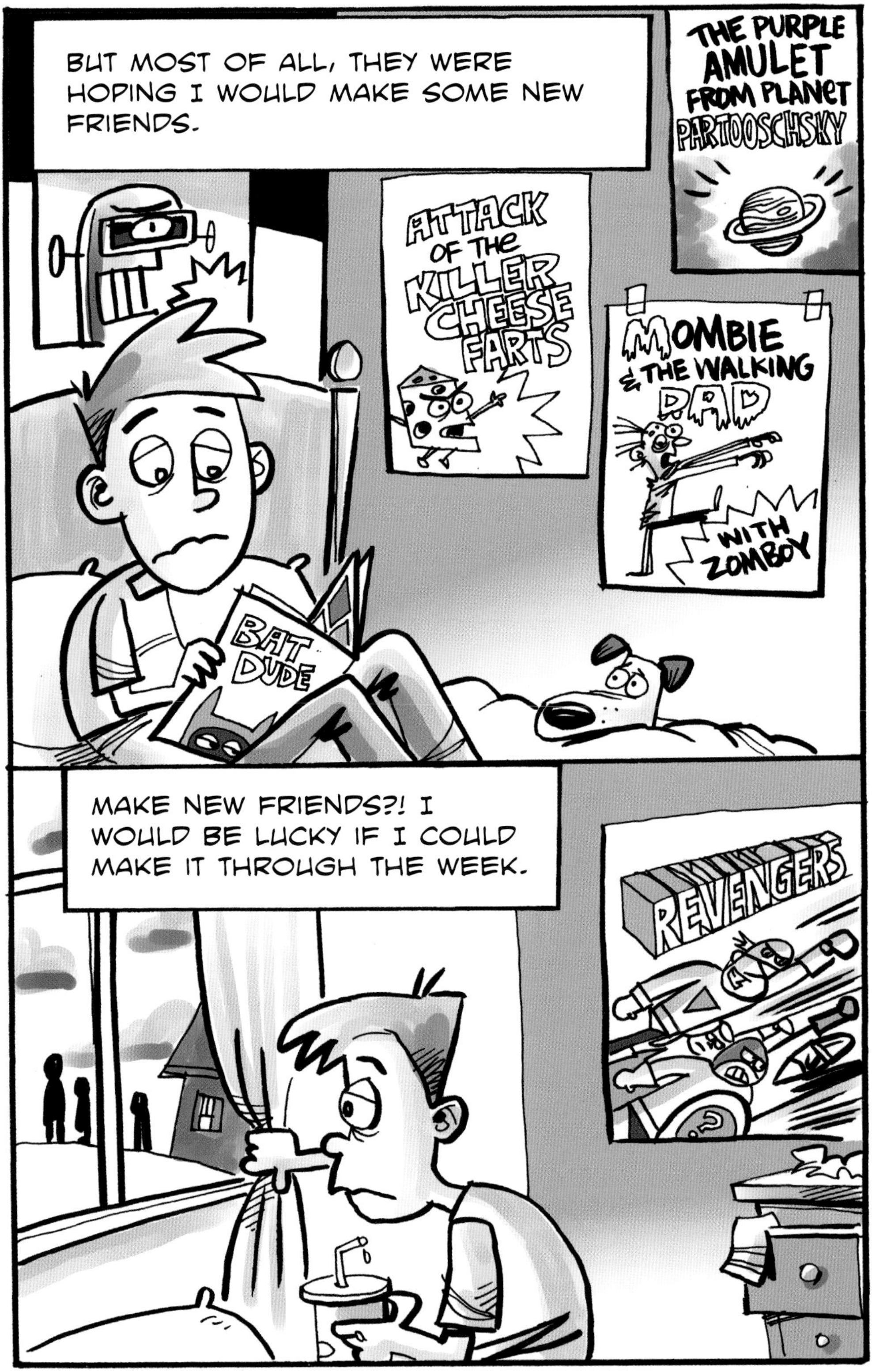
BUT MOST OF ALL, THEY WERE HOPING I WOULD MAKE SOME NEW FRIENDS.
THE PURPLE AMULET FROM PLANET PARTOOSCHSKY
ATTACK OF THE KILLER CHEESE FARTS
MOMBIE & THE WALKING DAD WITH ZOMBOY
BAT DUDE
MAKE NEW FRIENDS?! I WOULD BE LUCKY IF I COULD MAKE IT THROUGH THE WEEK.
REVENGERS

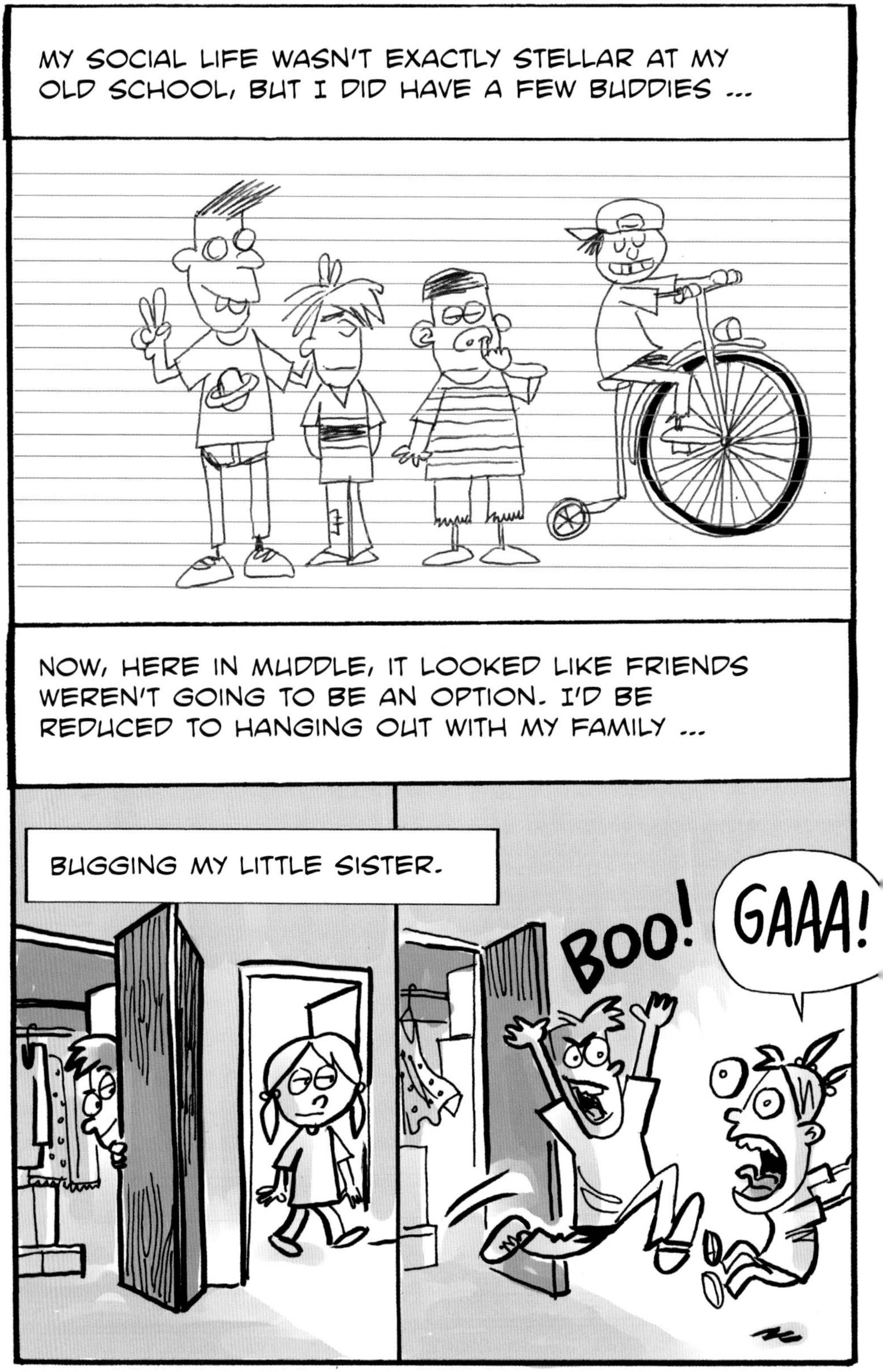
MY SOCIAL LIFE WASN'T EXACTLY STELLAR AT MY OLD SCHOOL, BUT I DID HAVE A FEW BUDDIES ...
NOW, HERE IN MUDDLE, IT LOOKED LIKE FRIENDS WEREN'T GOING TO BE AN OPTION. I'D BE REDUCED TO HANGING OUT WITH MY FAMILY ...
BUGGING MY LITTLE SISTER.
BOO!
GAAA!

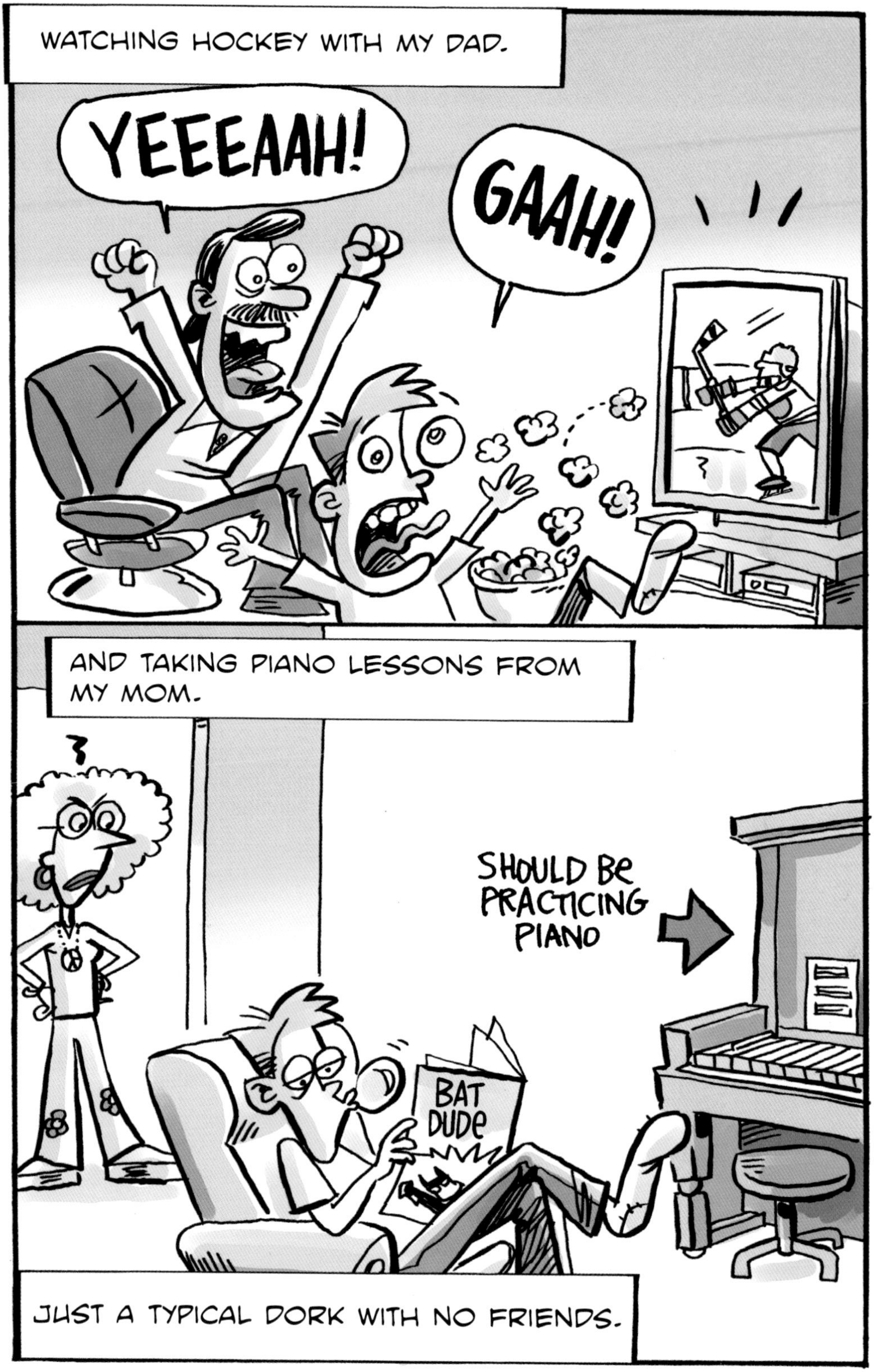
WATCHING HOCKEY WITH MY DAD.
YEEEAAH!
GAAH!
AND TAKING PIANO LESSONS FROM MY MOM.
SHOULD BE PRACTICING PIANO
BAT DUDE
JUST A TYPICAL DORK WITH NO FRIENDS.

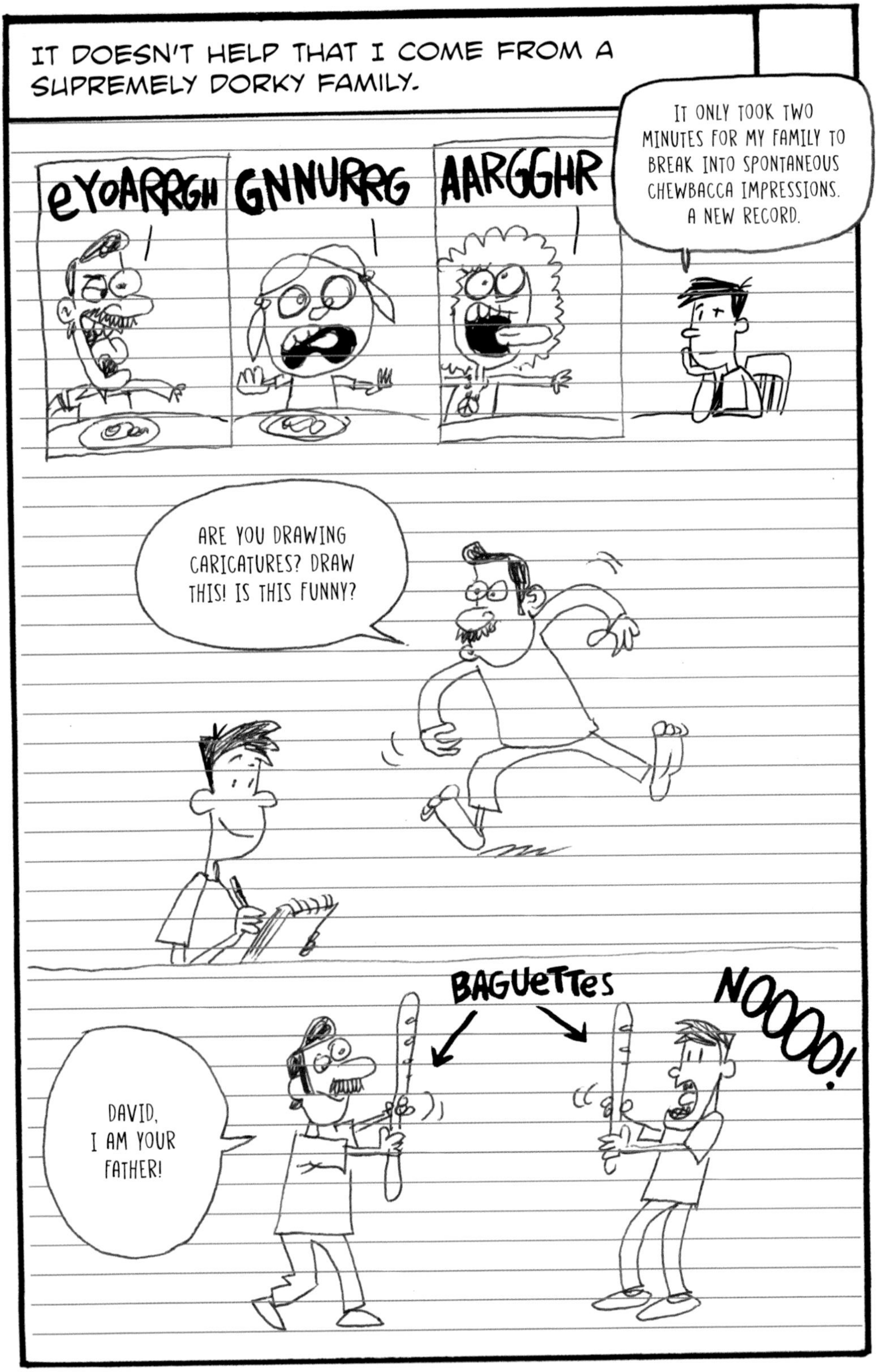
IT DOESN'T HELP THAT I COME FROM A SUPREMELY DORKY FAMILY.
eYOARRGH
GNNURRG
AARGGHR
IT ONLY TOOK TWO MINUTES FOR MY FAMILY TO BREAK INTO SPONTANEOUS CHEWBACCA IMPRESSIONS. A NEW RECORD.
ARE YOU DRAWING CARICATURES? DRAW THIS! IS THIS FUNNY?
BAGUETTES
NOOOOO!
DAVID, I AM YOUR FATHER!

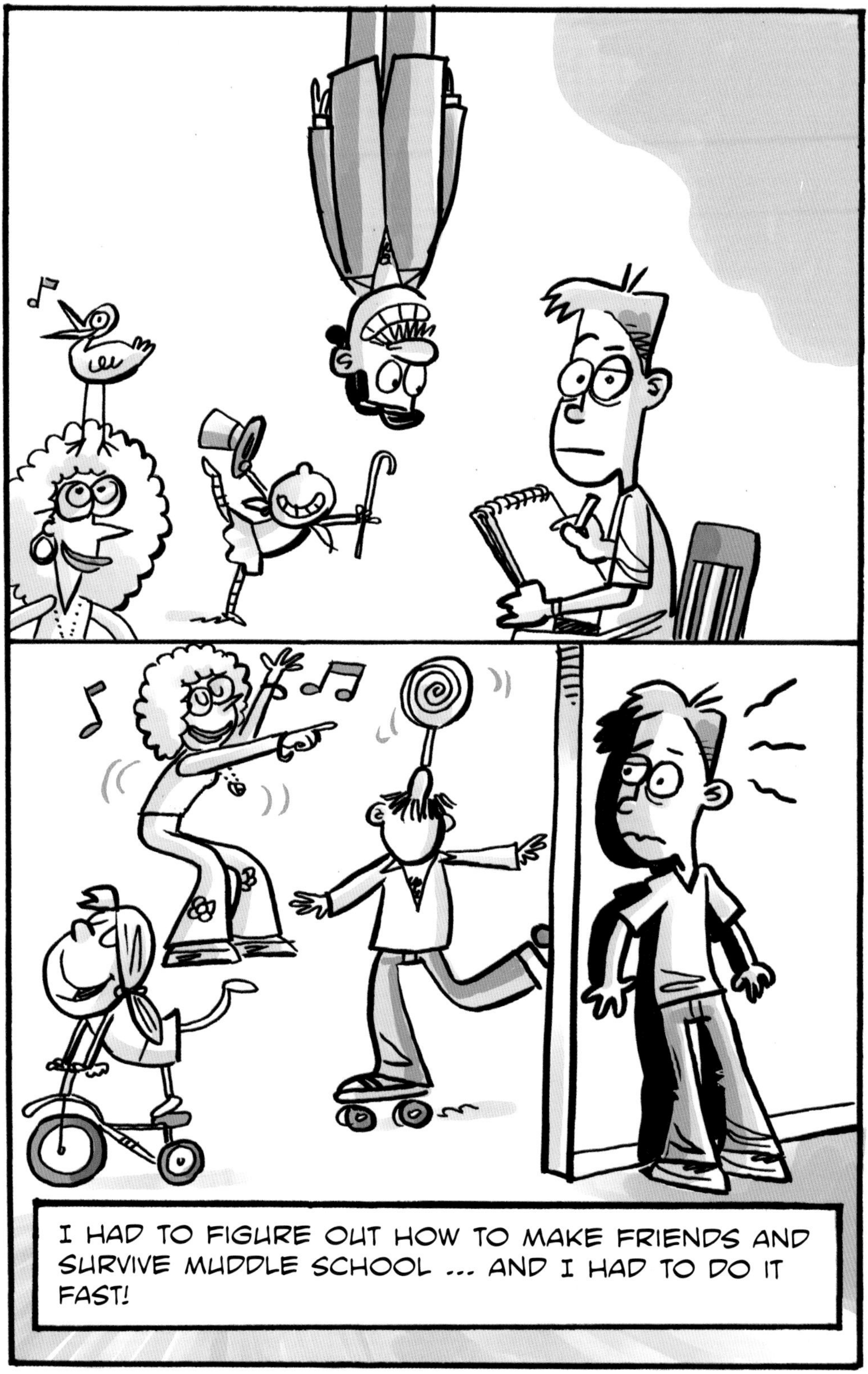
I HAD TO FIGURE OUT HOW TO MAKE FRIENDS AND SURVIVE MUDDLE SCHOOL ... AND I HAD TO DO IT FAST!

CHAPTER 2: THE NEXT DAY

THE NEXT DAY OF SCHOOL CAME WAY TOO SOON. TO DISTRACT MYSELF, I STARTED OUT THE DAY BY PLAYING A PRANK ON MY SISTER, KATE. ALL I NEEDED WAS A BAG OF COOKIES AND A TUBE OF TOOTHPASTE:

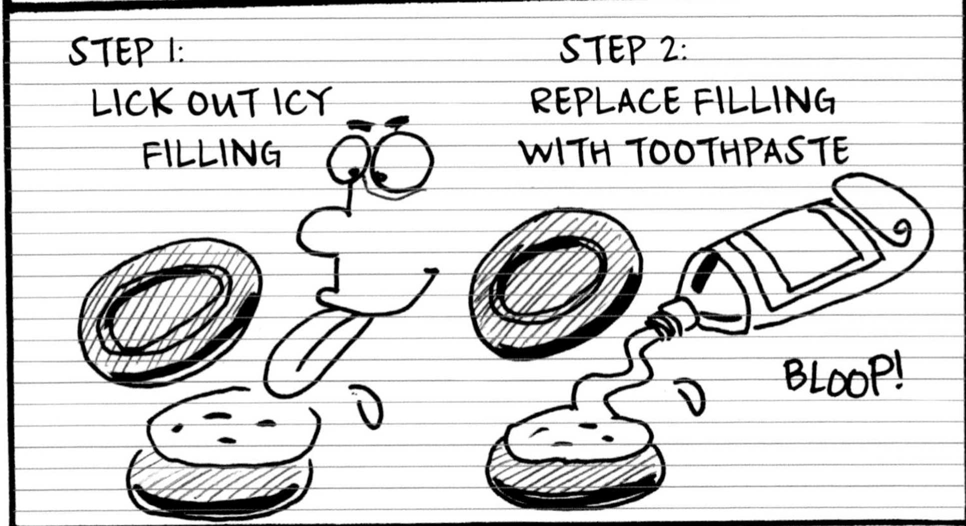
STEP 1:
LICK OUT ICY FILLING
STEP 2:
REPLACE FILLING WITH TOOTHPASTE
BLOOP!

I SOMEHOW MANAGED TO SUPRESS MY EVIL LAUGH WHEN I SAW KATE PUT THE COOKIES IN HER LUNCH.

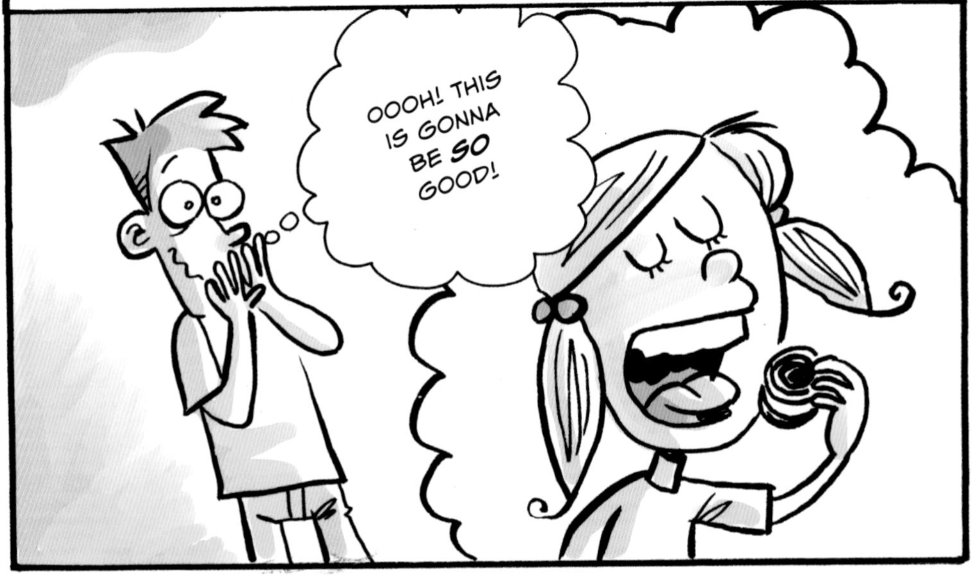
OOOH! THIS IS GONNA BE *SO* GOOD!

BUT IT WAS TIME TO GET READY. I THOUGHT IT MIGHT HELP IF I LOOKED TOUGH.

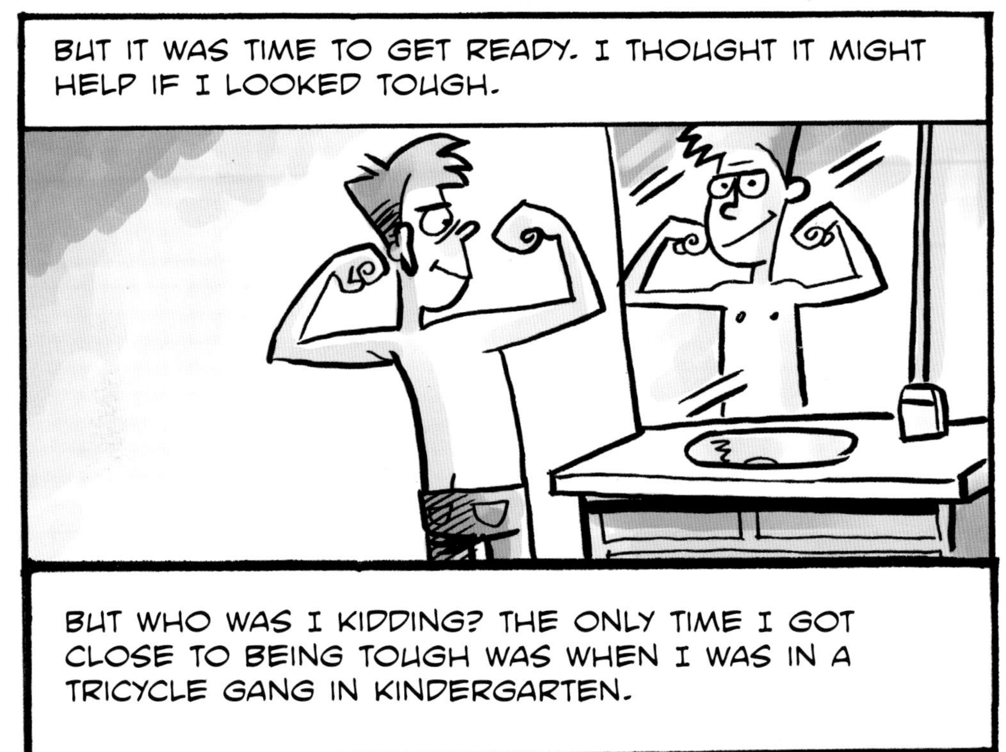

BUT WHO WAS I KIDDING? THE ONLY TIME I GOT CLOSE TO BEING TOUGH WAS WHEN I WAS IN A TRICYCLE GANG IN KINDERGARTEN.

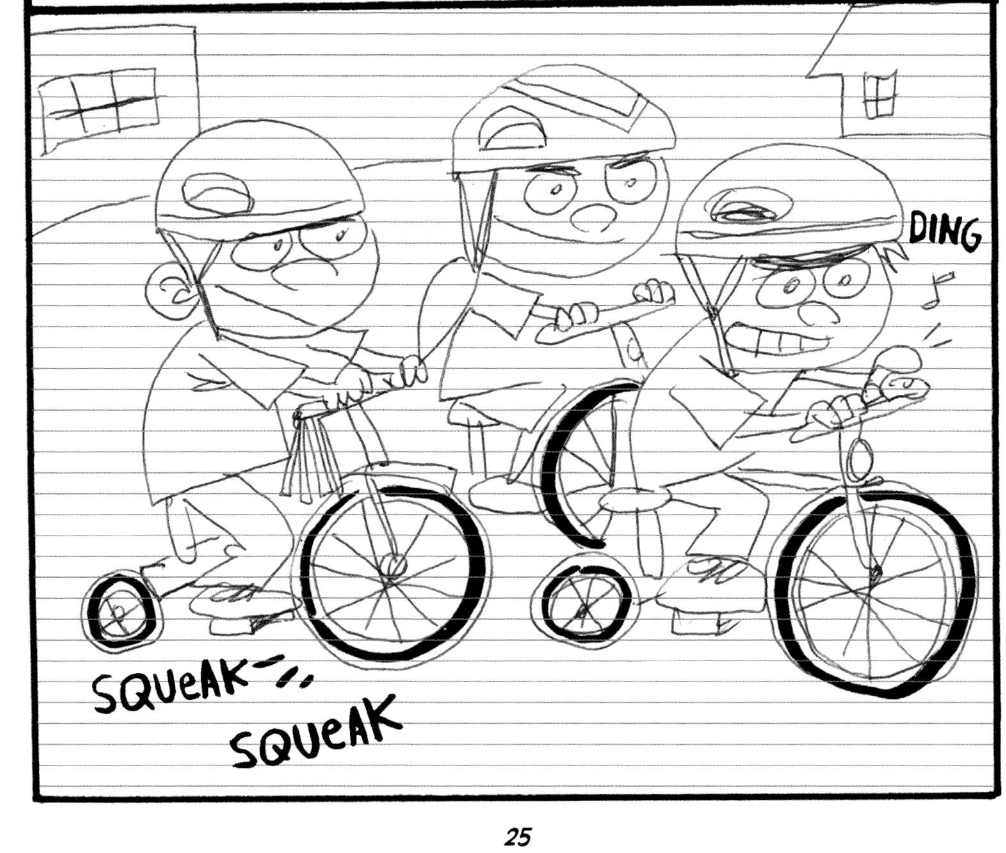
DING
SQUEAK
SQUEAK

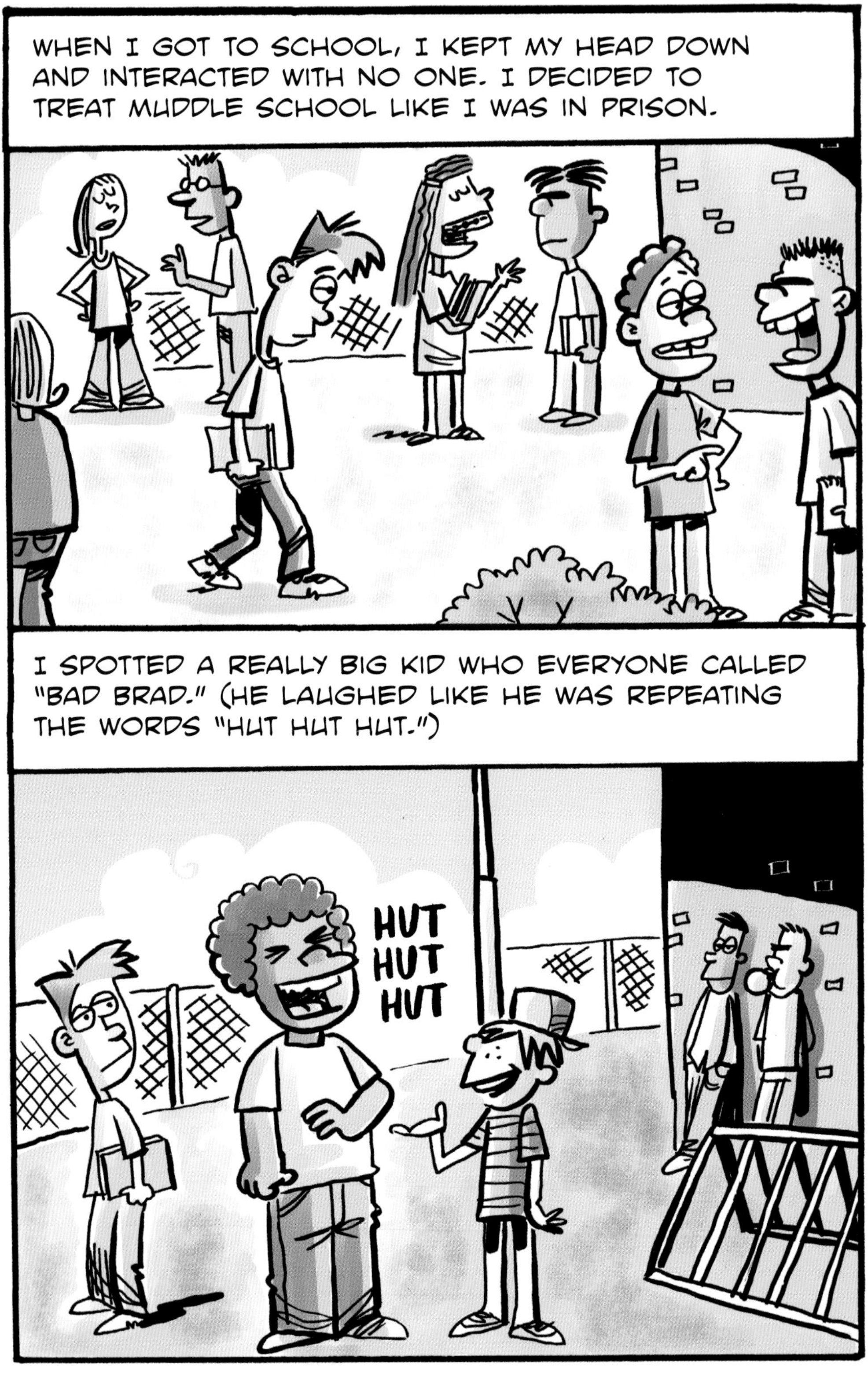
WHEN I GOT TO SCHOOL, I KEPT MY HEAD DOWN AND INTERACTED WITH NO ONE. I DECIDED TO TREAT MUDDLE SCHOOL LIKE I WAS IN PRISON.
I SPOTTED A REALLY BIG KID WHO EVERYONE CALLED "BAD BRAD." (HE LAUGHED LIKE HE WAS REPEATING THE WORDS "HUT HUT HUT.")
HUT HUT HUT

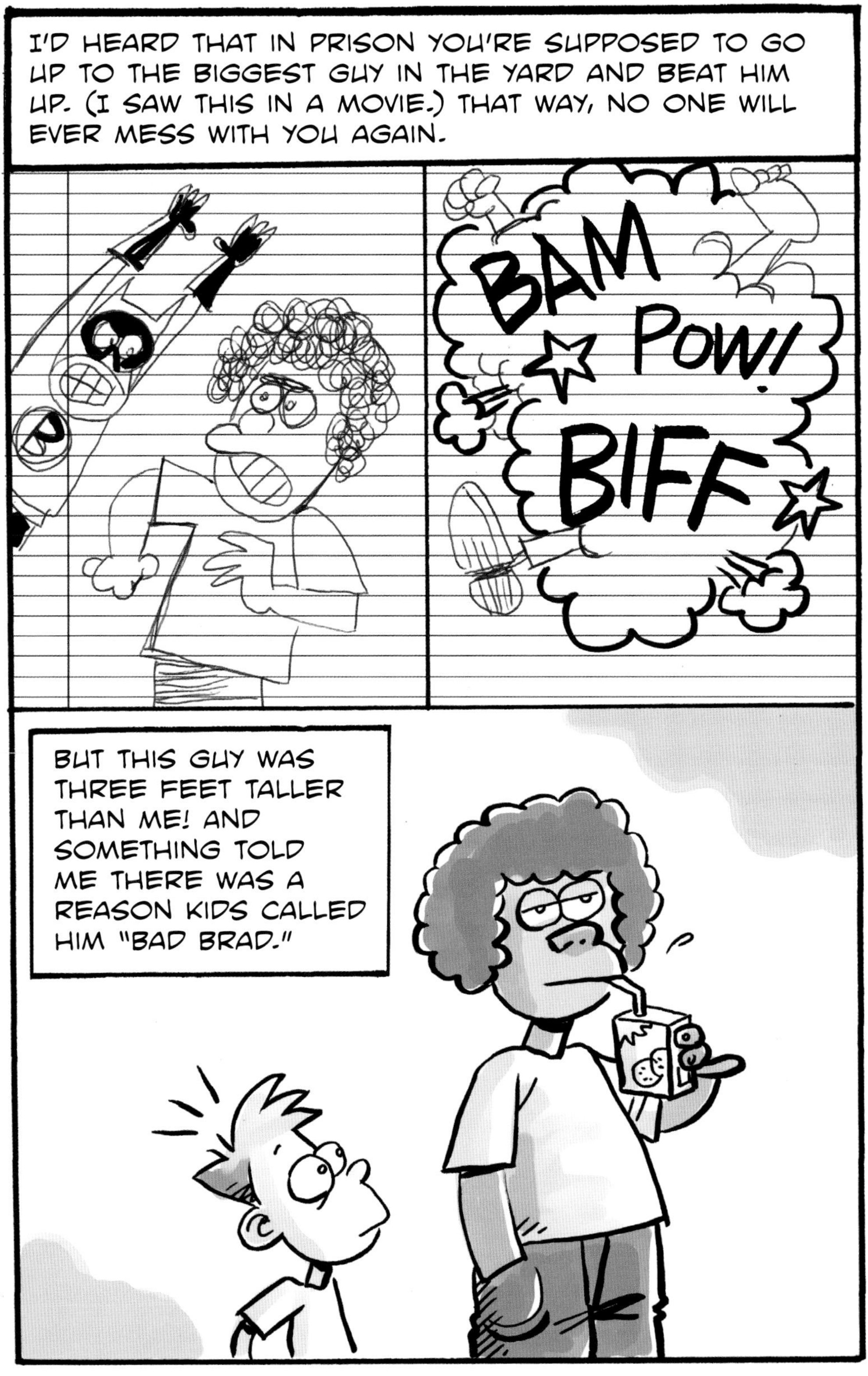
I'D HEARD THAT IN PRISON YOU'RE SUPPOSED TO GO UP TO THE BIGGEST GUY IN THE YARD AND BEAT HIM UP. (I SAW THIS IN A MOVIE.) THAT WAY, NO ONE WILL EVER MESS WITH YOU AGAIN.
BAM
POW!
BIFF
BUT THIS GUY WAS THREE FEET TALLER THAN ME! AND SOMETHING TOLD ME THERE WAS A REASON KIDS CALLED HIM "BAD BRAD."

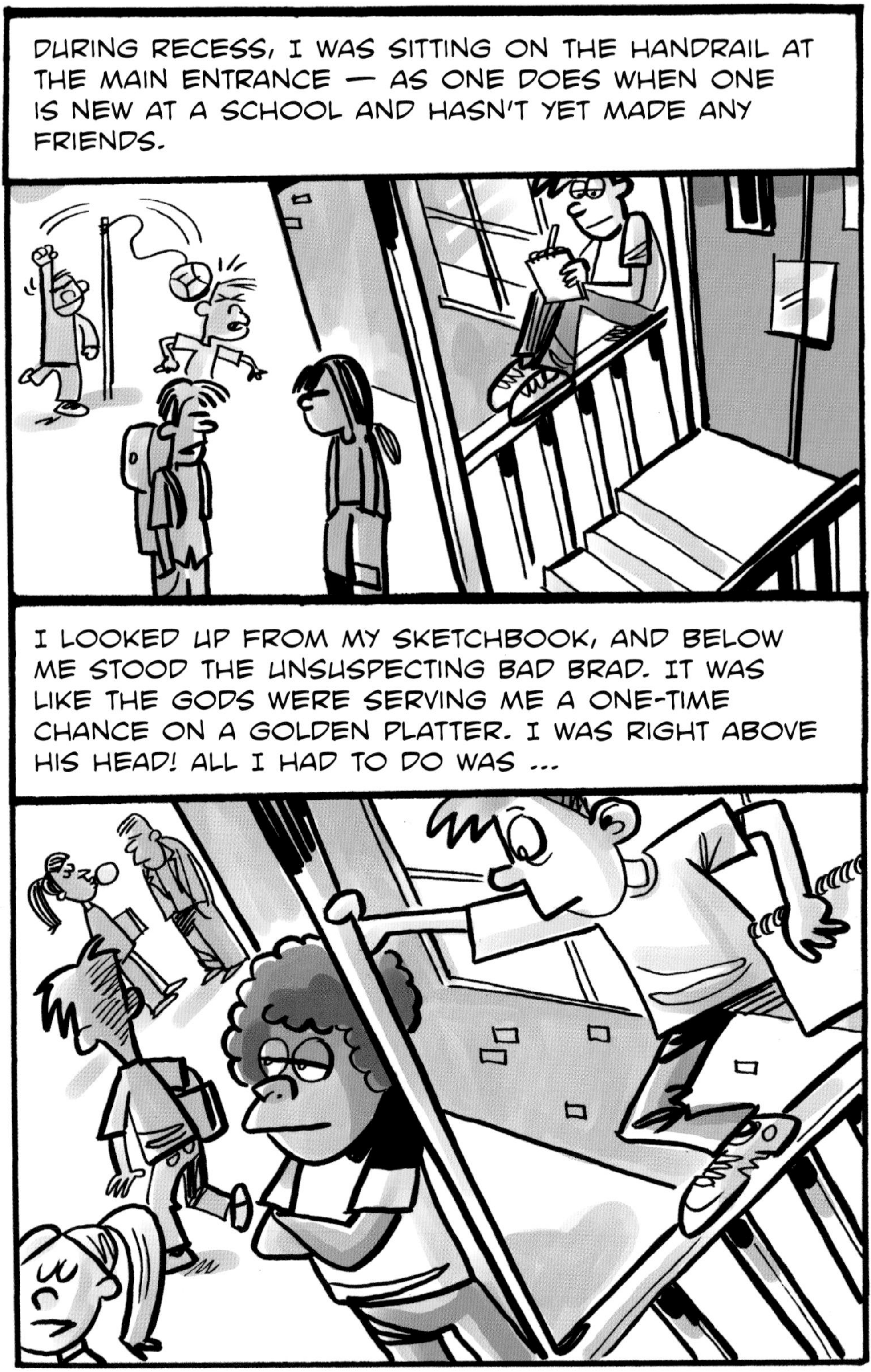
DURING RECESS, I WAS SITTING ON THE HANDRAIL AT THE MAIN ENTRANCE — AS ONE DOES WHEN ONE IS NEW AT A SCHOOL AND HASN'T YET MADE ANY FRIENDS.
I LOOKED UP FROM MY SKETCHBOOK, AND BELOW ME STOOD THE UNSUSPECTING BAD BRAD. IT WAS LIKE THE GODS WERE SERVING ME A ONE-TIME CHANCE ON A GOLDEN PLATTER. I WAS RIGHT ABOVE HIS HEAD! ALL I HAD TO DO WAS ...

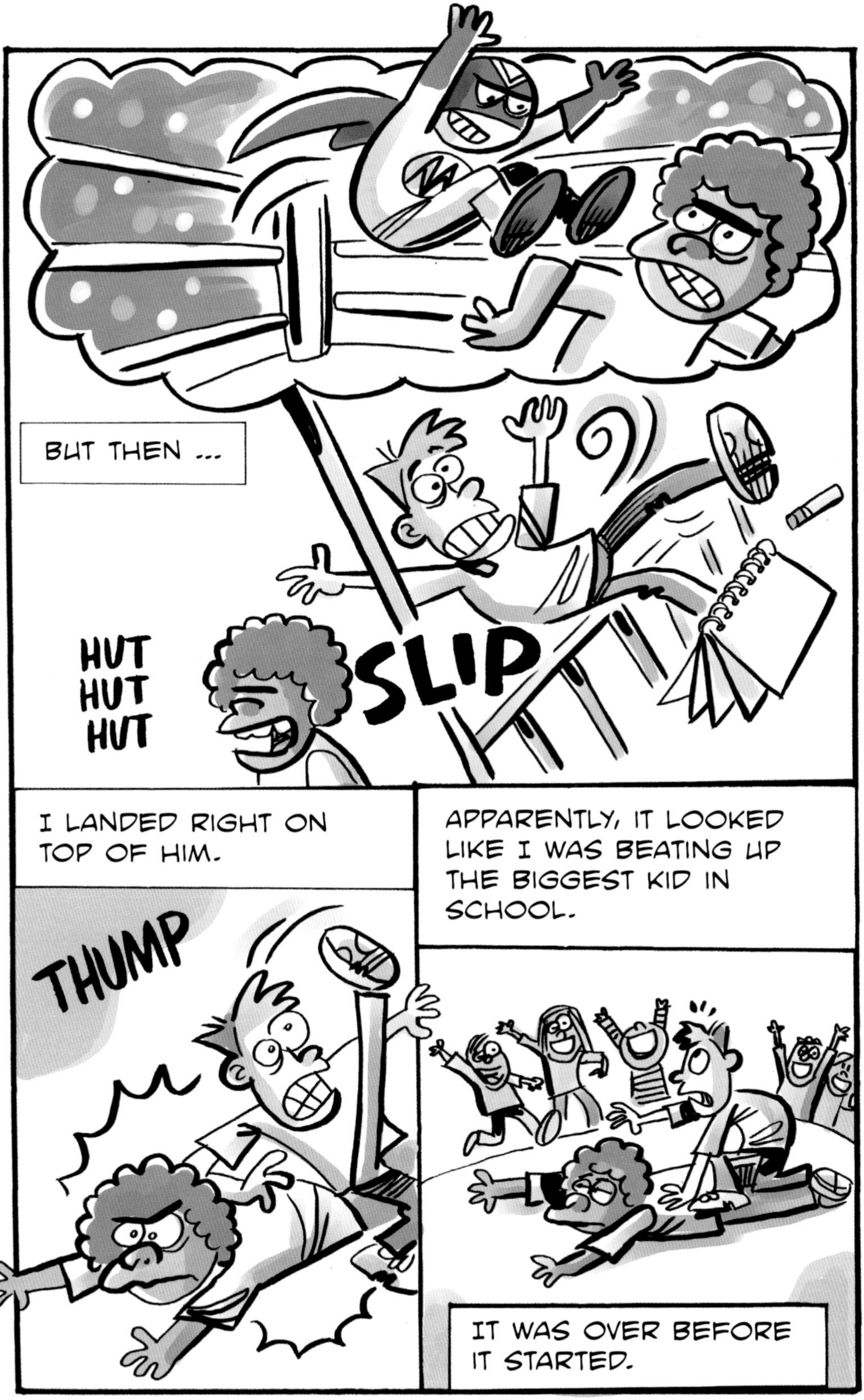
BUT THEN ...
HUT
HUT
HUT
SLIP
I LANDED RIGHT ON TOP OF HIM.
THUMP
APPARENTLY, IT LOOKED LIKE I WAS BEATING UP THE BIGGEST KID IN SCHOOL.
IT WAS OVER BEFORE IT STARTED.

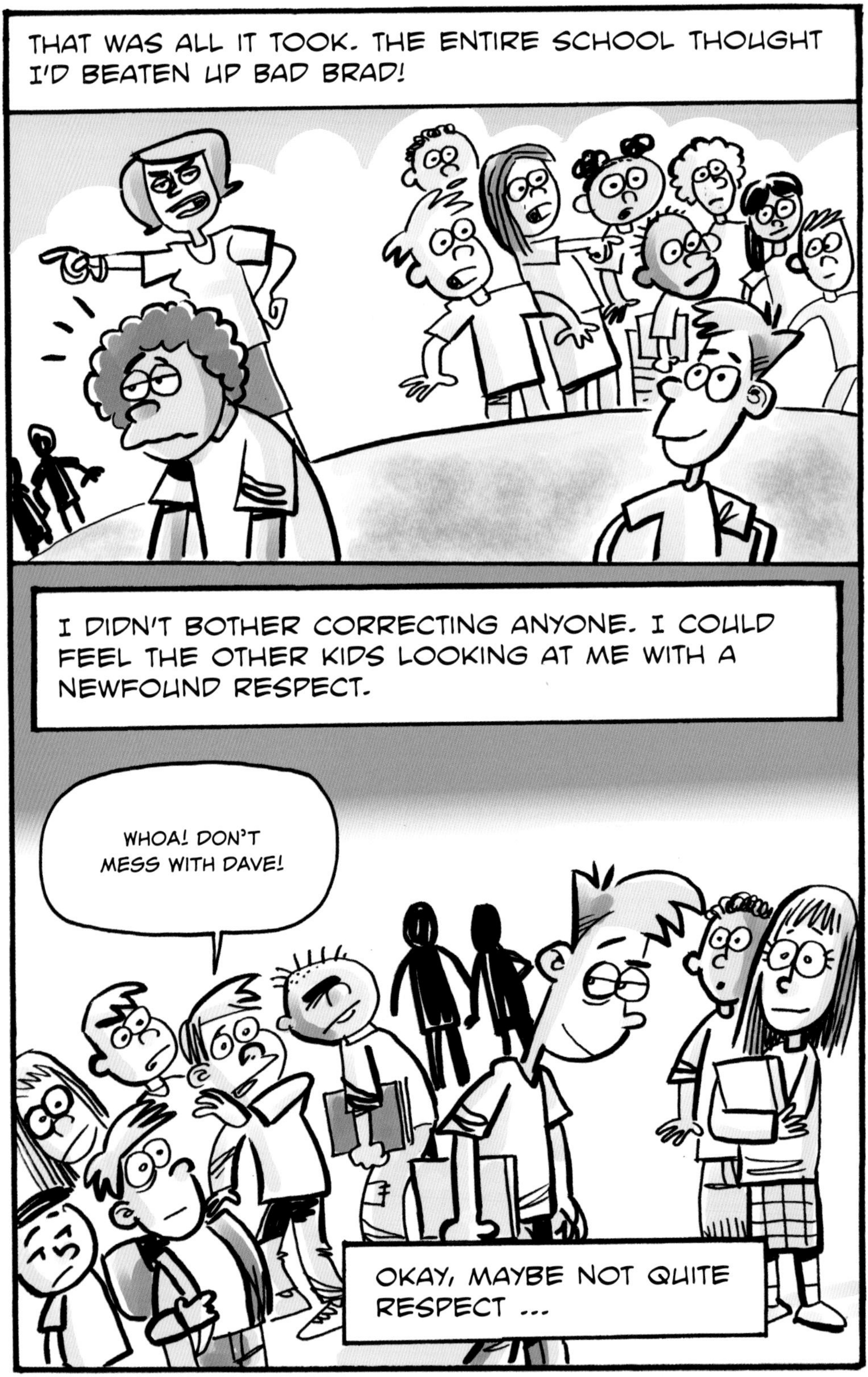
THAT WAS ALL IT TOOK. THE ENTIRE SCHOOL THOUGHT I'D BEATEN UP BAD BRAD!
I DIDN'T BOTHER CORRECTING ANYONE. I COULD FEEL THE OTHER KIDS LOOKING AT ME WITH A NEWFOUND RESPECT.
WHOA! DON'T MESS WITH DAVE!
OKAY, MAYBE NOT QUITE RESPECT ...

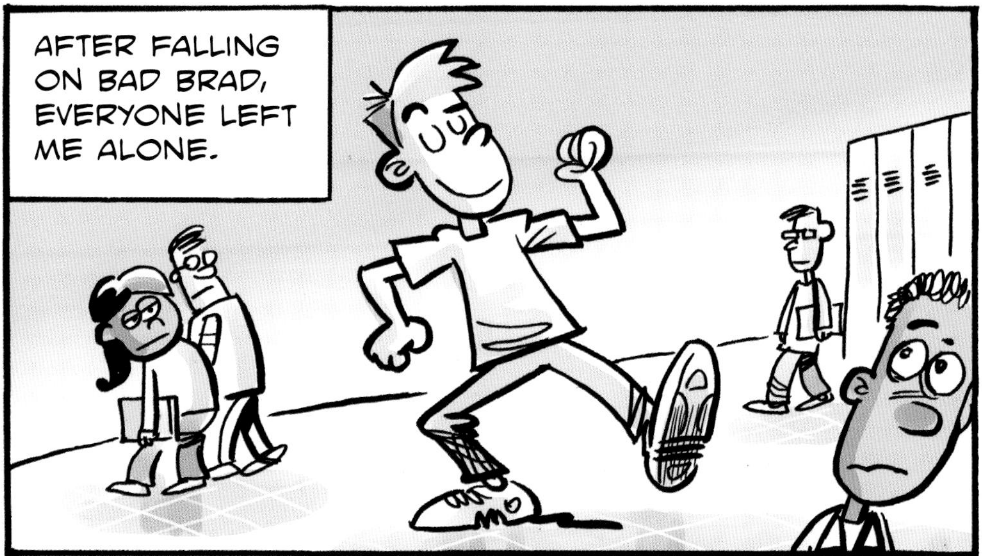
AFTER FALLING ON BAD BRAD, EVERYONE LEFT ME ALONE.

BUT THEN BAD BRAD GOT BEATEN UP AGAIN. THIS TIME BY SUSAN DEGROOT, A WIRY AND SUPERSMART GIRL WHO WAS SURPRISINGLY FIERCE. THERE WAS A RUMOR GOING AROUND THAT SHE KNEW SOME KIND OF COOL MARTIAL ART THAT NO ONE HAD EVER HEARD OF ...

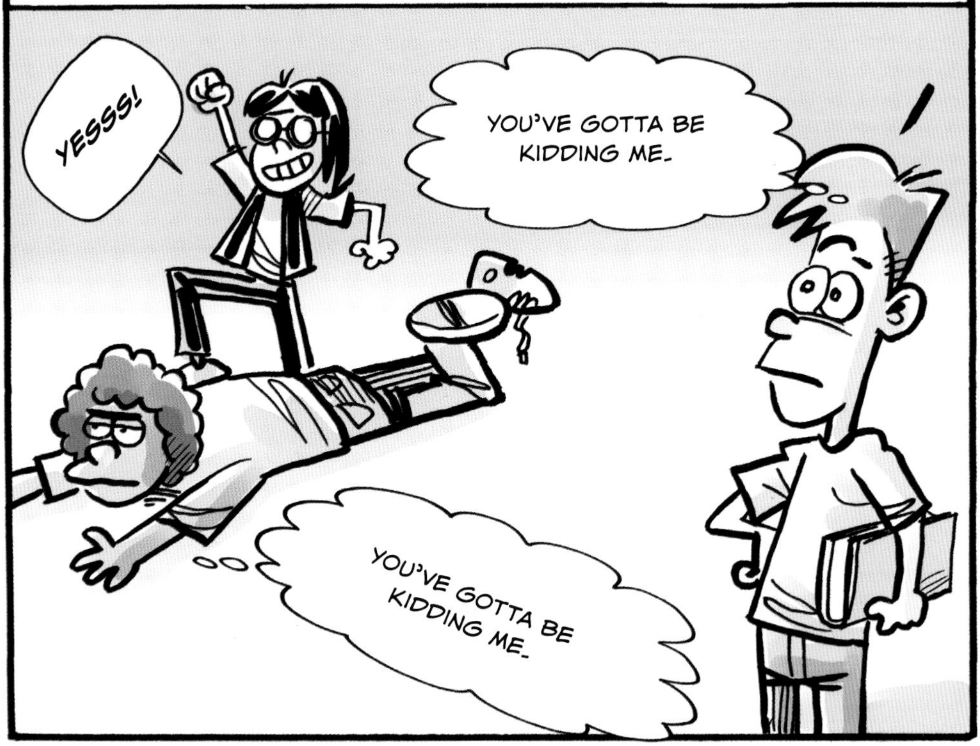
YESSS!
YOU'VE GOTTA BE KIDDING ME.
YOU'VE GOTTA BE KIDDING ME.

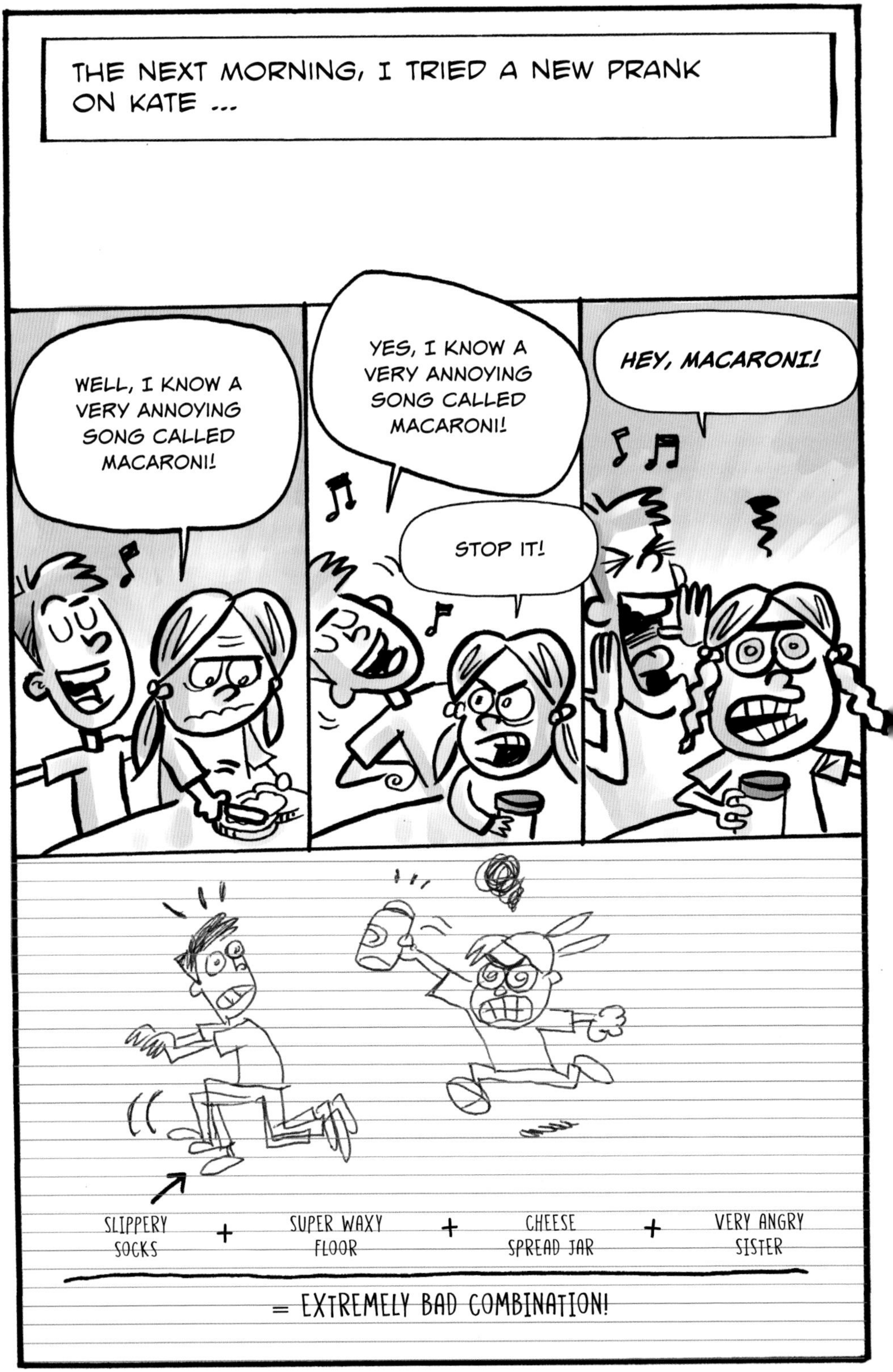
THE NEXT MORNING, I TRIED A NEW PRANK ON KATE ...
WELL, I KNOW A VERY ANNOYING SONG CALLED MACARONI!
YES, I KNOW A VERY ANNOYING SONG CALLED MACARONI!
STOP IT!
HEY, MACARONI!
SLIPPERY SOCKS
+
SUPER WAXY FLOOR
+
CHEESE SPREAD JAR
+
VERY ANGRY SISTER
= EXTREMELY BAD COMBINATION!

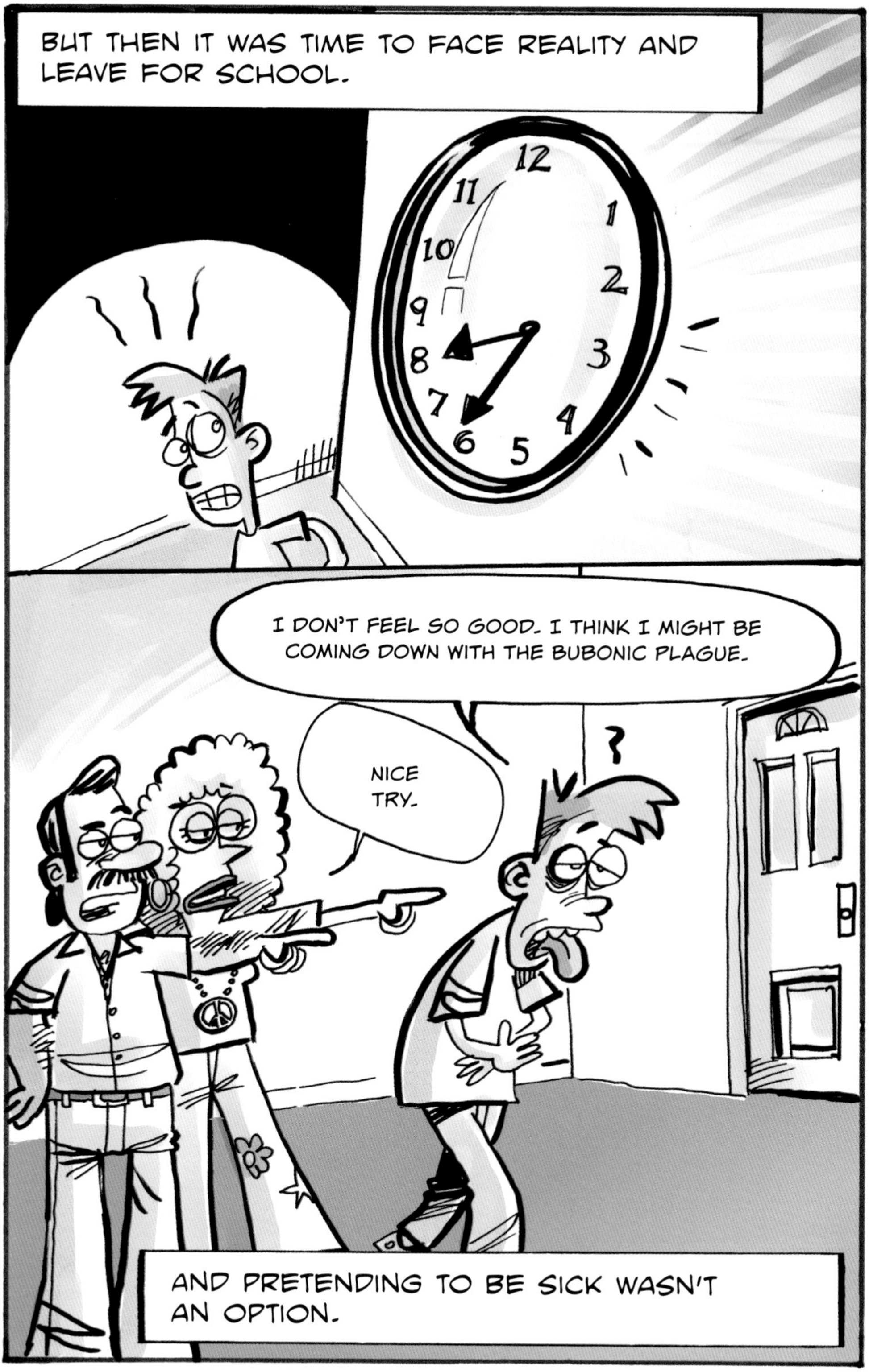
BUT THEN IT WAS TIME TO FACE REALITY AND LEAVE FOR SCHOOL.
I DON'T FEEL SO GOOD. I THINK I MIGHT BE COMING DOWN WITH THE BUBONIC PLAGUE.
NICE TRY.
AND PRETENDING TO BE SICK WASN'T AN OPTION.

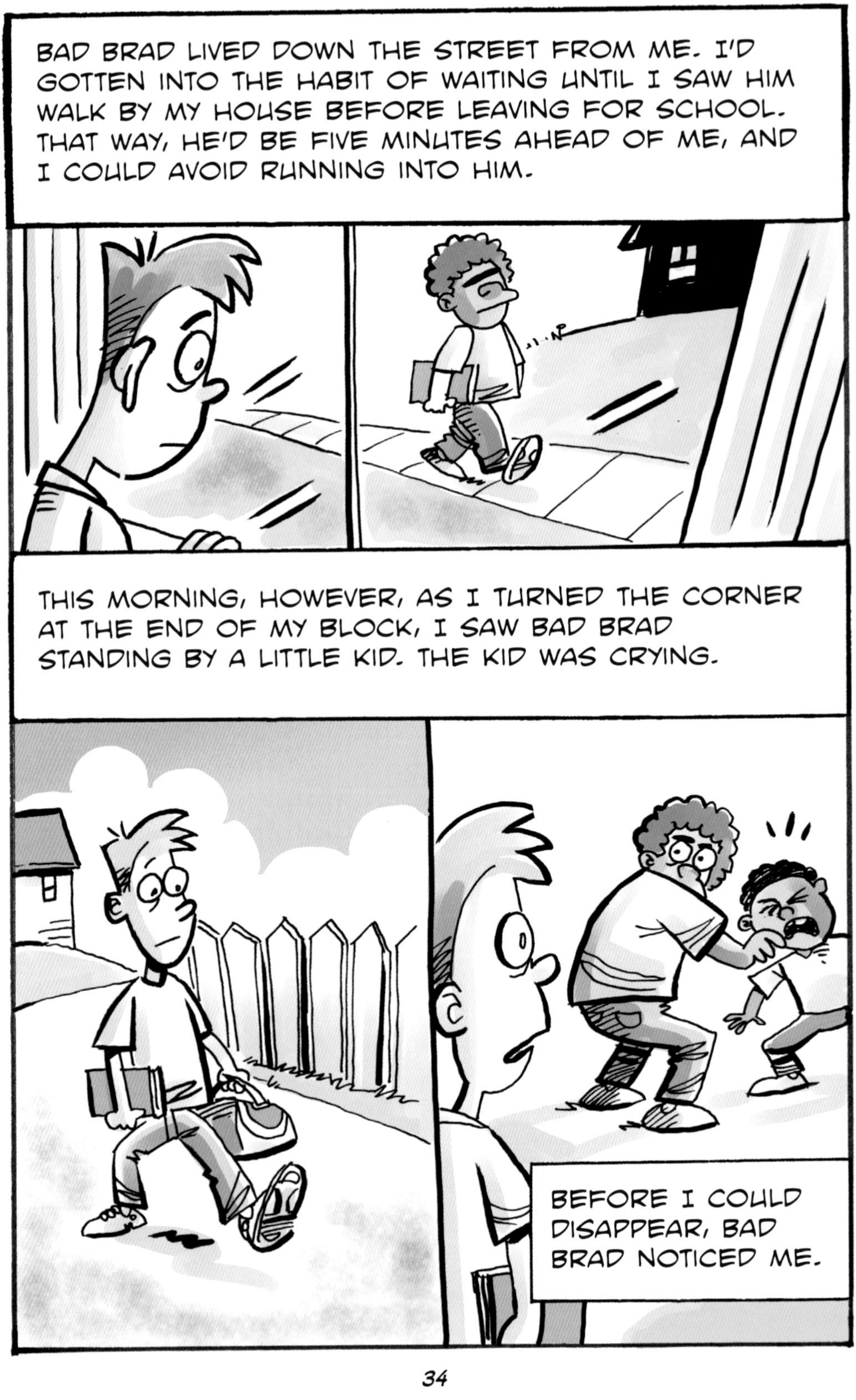
BAD BRAD LIVED DOWN THE STREET FROM ME. I'D GOTTEN INTO THE HABIT OF WAITING UNTIL I SAW HIM WALK BY MY HOUSE BEFORE LEAVING FOR SCHOOL. THAT WAY, HE'D BE FIVE MINUTES AHEAD OF ME, AND I COULD AVOID RUNNING INTO HIM.
THIS MORNING, HOWEVER, AS I TURNED THE CORNER AT THE END OF MY BLOCK, I SAW BAD BRAD STANDING BY A LITTLE KID. THE KID WAS CRYING.
BEFORE I COULD DISAPPEAR, BAD BRAD NOTICED ME.

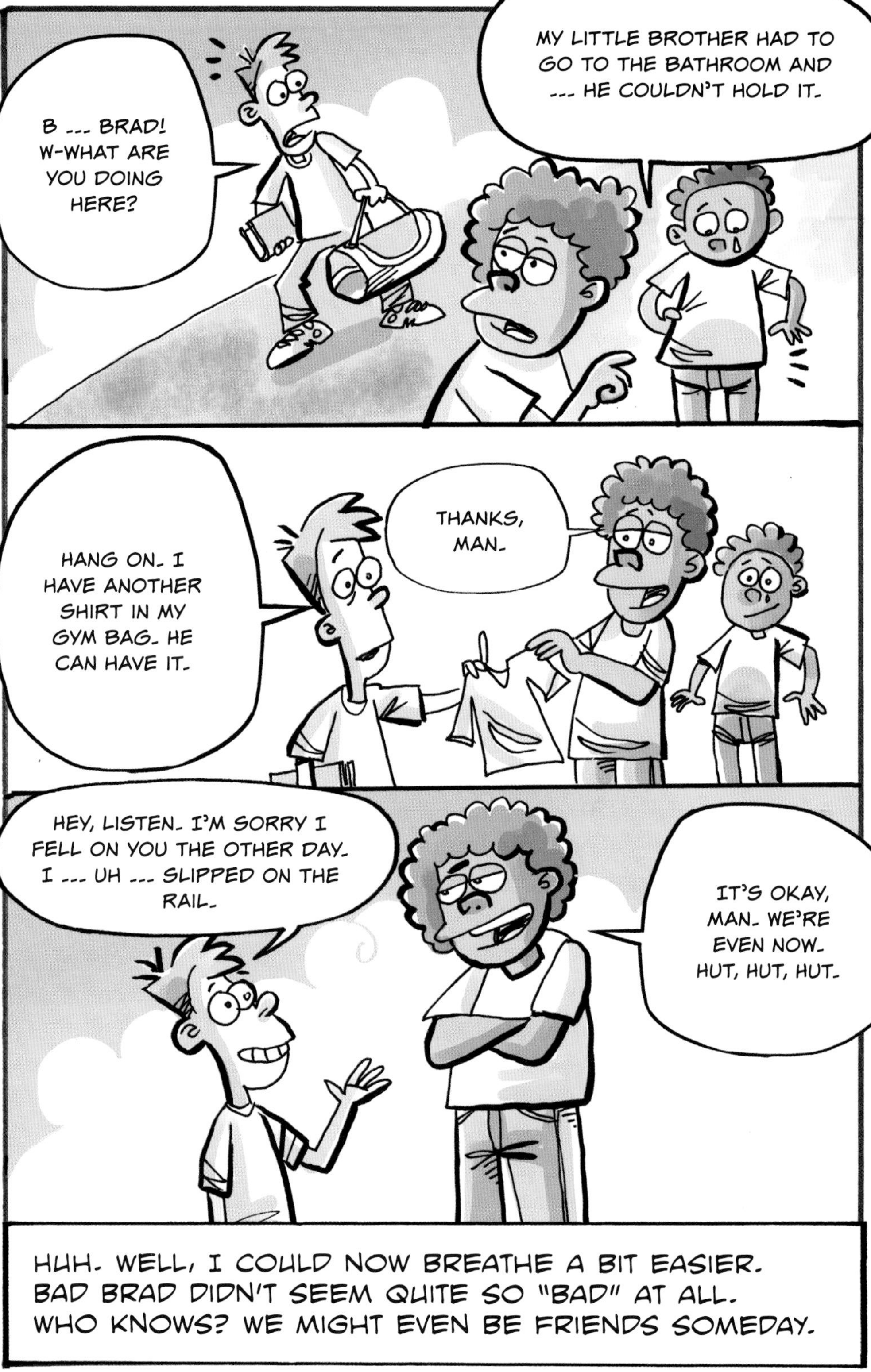
B --- BRAD! W-WHAT ARE YOU DOING HERE?
MY LITTLE BROTHER HAD TO GO TO THE BATHROOM AND --- HE COULDN'T HOLD IT.
HANG ON. I HAVE ANOTHER SHIRT IN MY GYM BAG. HE CAN HAVE IT.
THANKS, MAN.
HEY, LISTEN. I'M SORRY I FELL ON YOU THE OTHER DAY. I --- UH --- SLIPPED ON THE RAIL.
IT'S OKAY, MAN. WE'RE EVEN NOW. HUT, HUT, HUT.
HUH. WELL, I COULD NOW BREATHE A BIT EASIER. BAD BRAD DIDN'T SEEM QUITE SO "BAD" AT ALL. WHO KNOWS? WE MIGHT EVEN BE FRIENDS SOMEDAY.

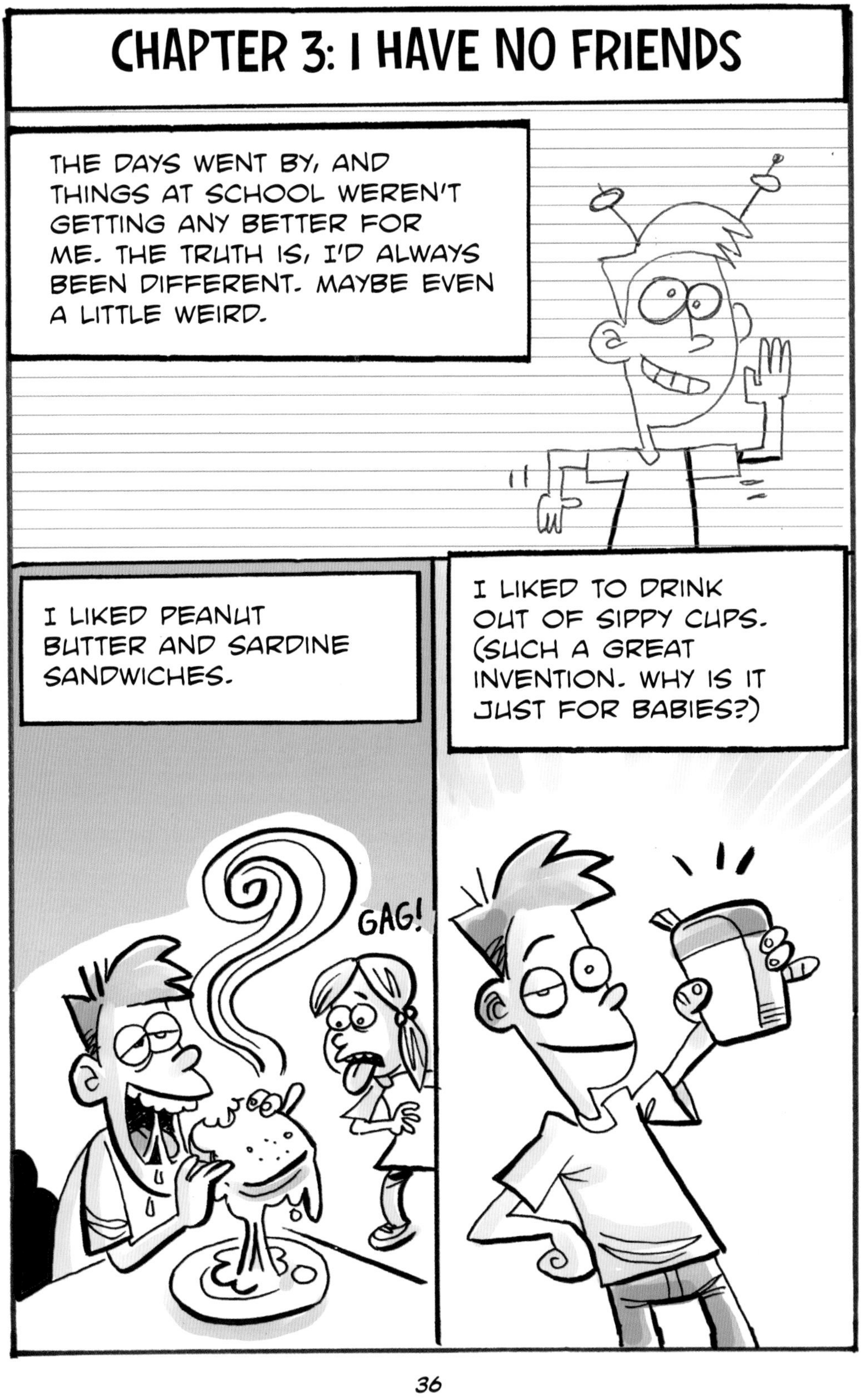
CHAPTER 3: I HAVE NO FRIENDS
THE DAYS WENT BY, AND THINGS AT SCHOOL WEREN'T GETTING ANY BETTER FOR ME. THE TRUTH IS, I'D ALWAYS BEEN DIFFERENT. MAYBE EVEN A LITTLE WEIRD.
I LIKED PEANUT BUTTER AND SARDINE SANDWICHES.
GAG!
I LIKED TO DRINK OUT OF SIPPY CUPS. (SUCH A GREAT INVENTION. WHY IS IT JUST FOR BABIES?)

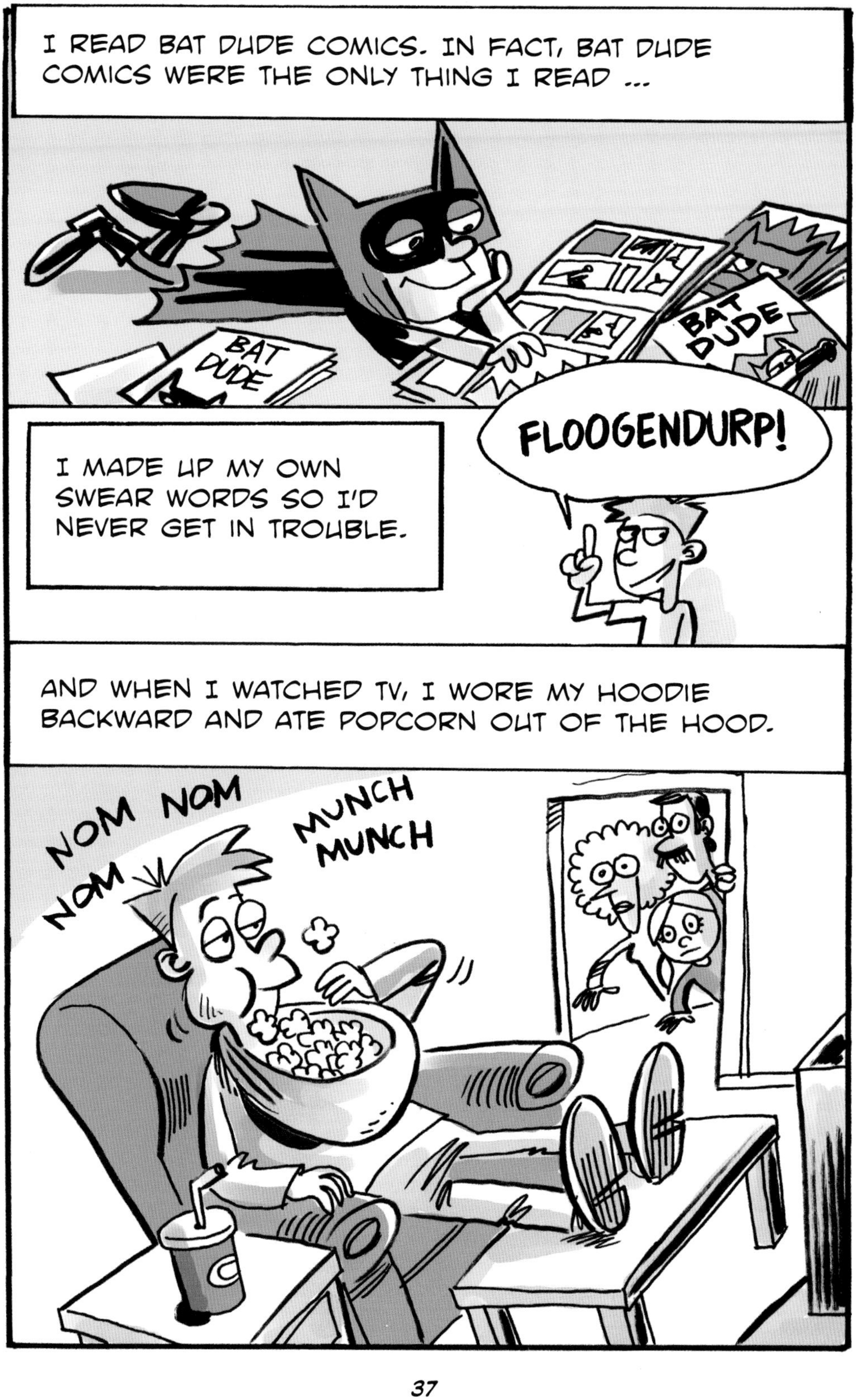
I READ BAT DUDE COMICS. IN FACT, BAT DUDE COMICS WERE THE ONLY THING I READ ...
BAT DUDE
BAT DUDE
I MADE UP MY OWN SWEAR WORDS SO I'D NEVER GET IN TROUBLE.
FLOOGENDURP!
AND WHEN I WATCHED TV, I WORE MY HOODIE BACKWARD AND ATE POPCORN OUT OF THE HOOD.
NOM NOM NOM
MUNCH MUNCH

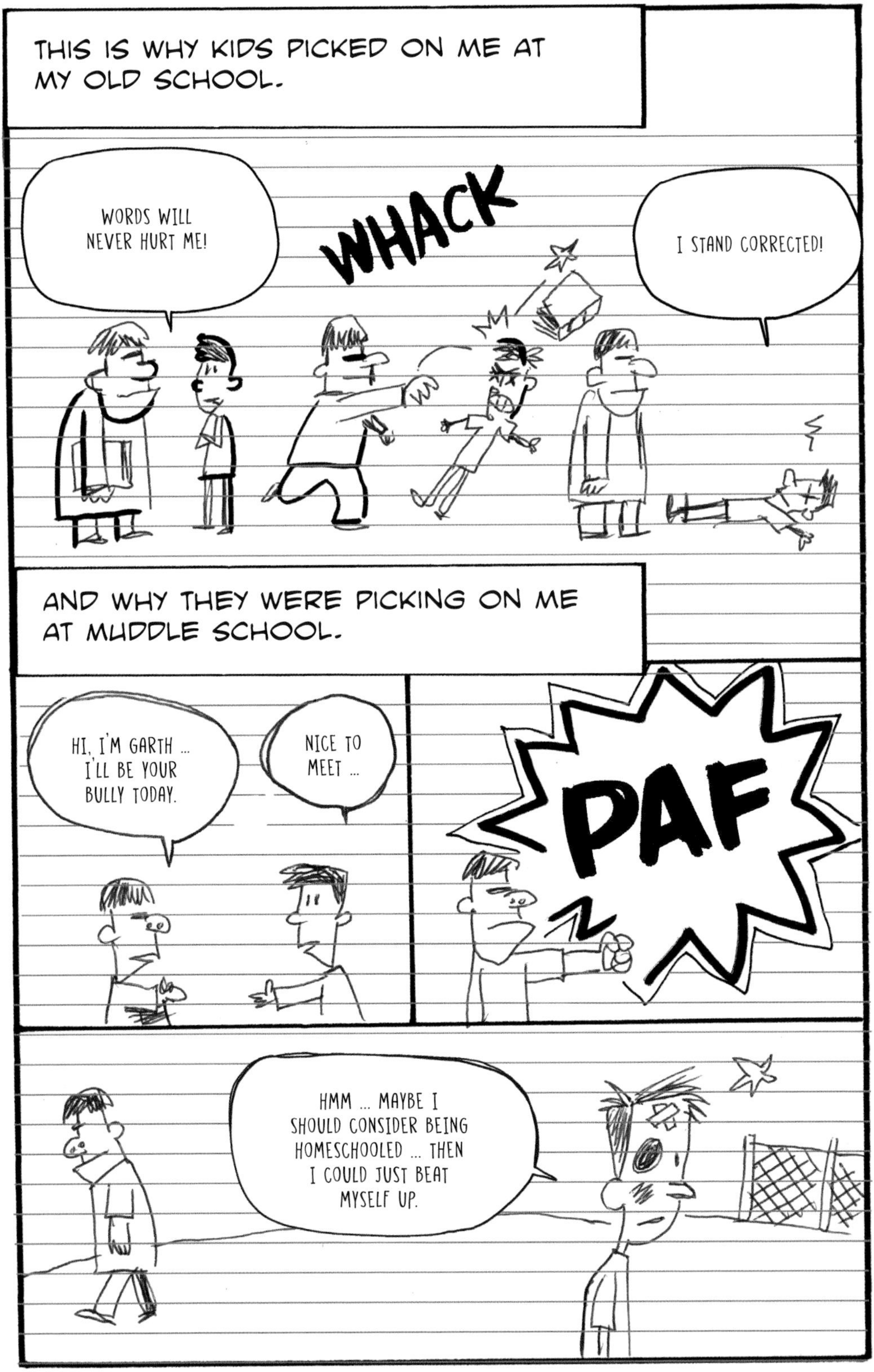
THIS IS WHY KIDS PICKED ON ME AT MY OLD SCHOOL.
WORDS WILL NEVER HURT ME!
WHACK
I STAND CORRECTED!
AND WHY THEY WERE PICKING ON ME AT MUDDLE SCHOOL.
HI, I'M GARTH ... I'LL BE YOUR BULLY TODAY.
NICE TO MEET ...
PAF
HMM ... MAYBE I SHOULD CONSIDER BEING HOMESCHOOLED ... THEN I COULD JUST BEAT MYSELF UP.

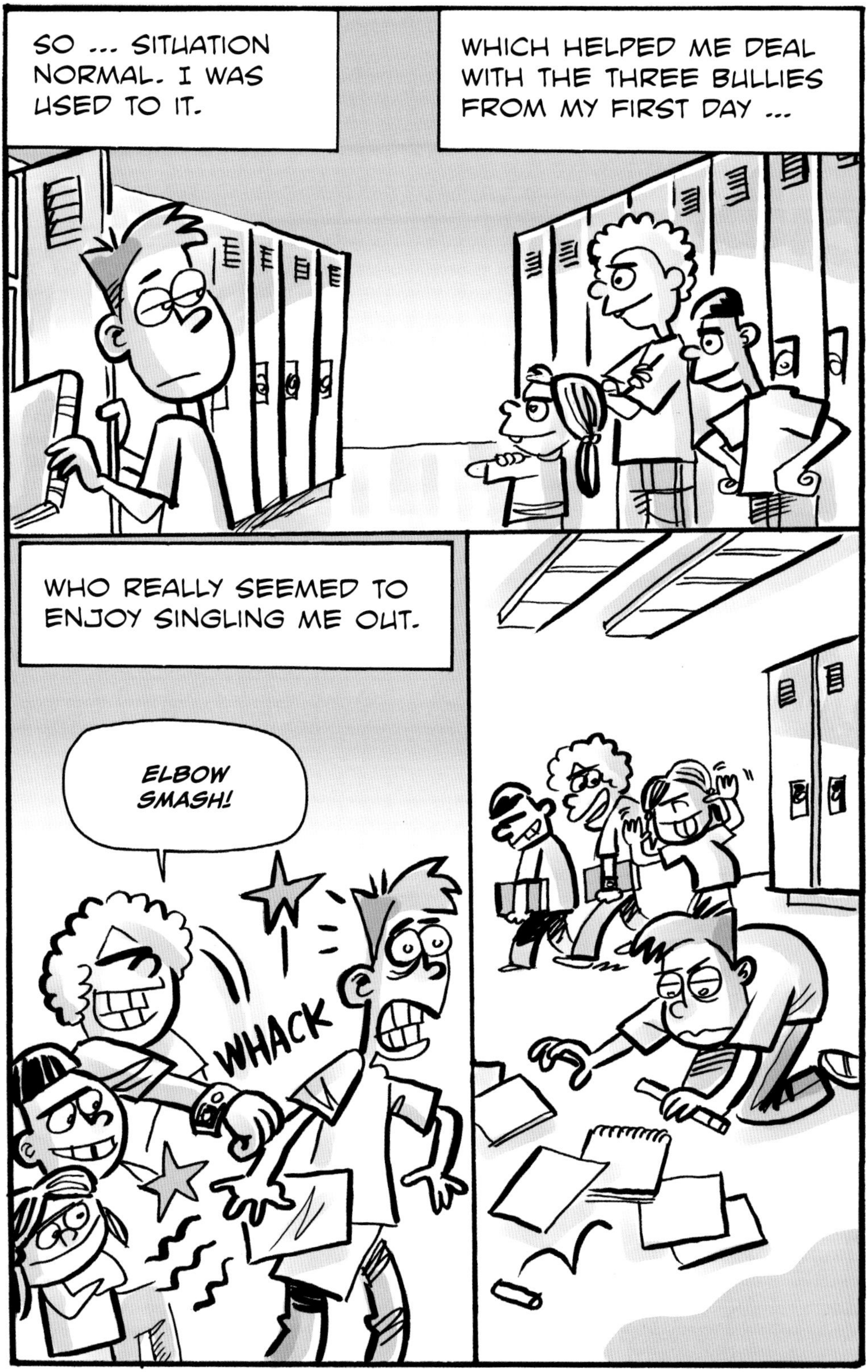
SO ... SITUATION NORMAL. I WAS USED TO IT.
WHICH HELPED ME DEAL WITH THE THREE BULLIES FROM MY FIRST DAY ...
WHO REALLY SEEMED TO ENJOY SINGLING ME OUT.
ELBOW SMASH!
WHACK

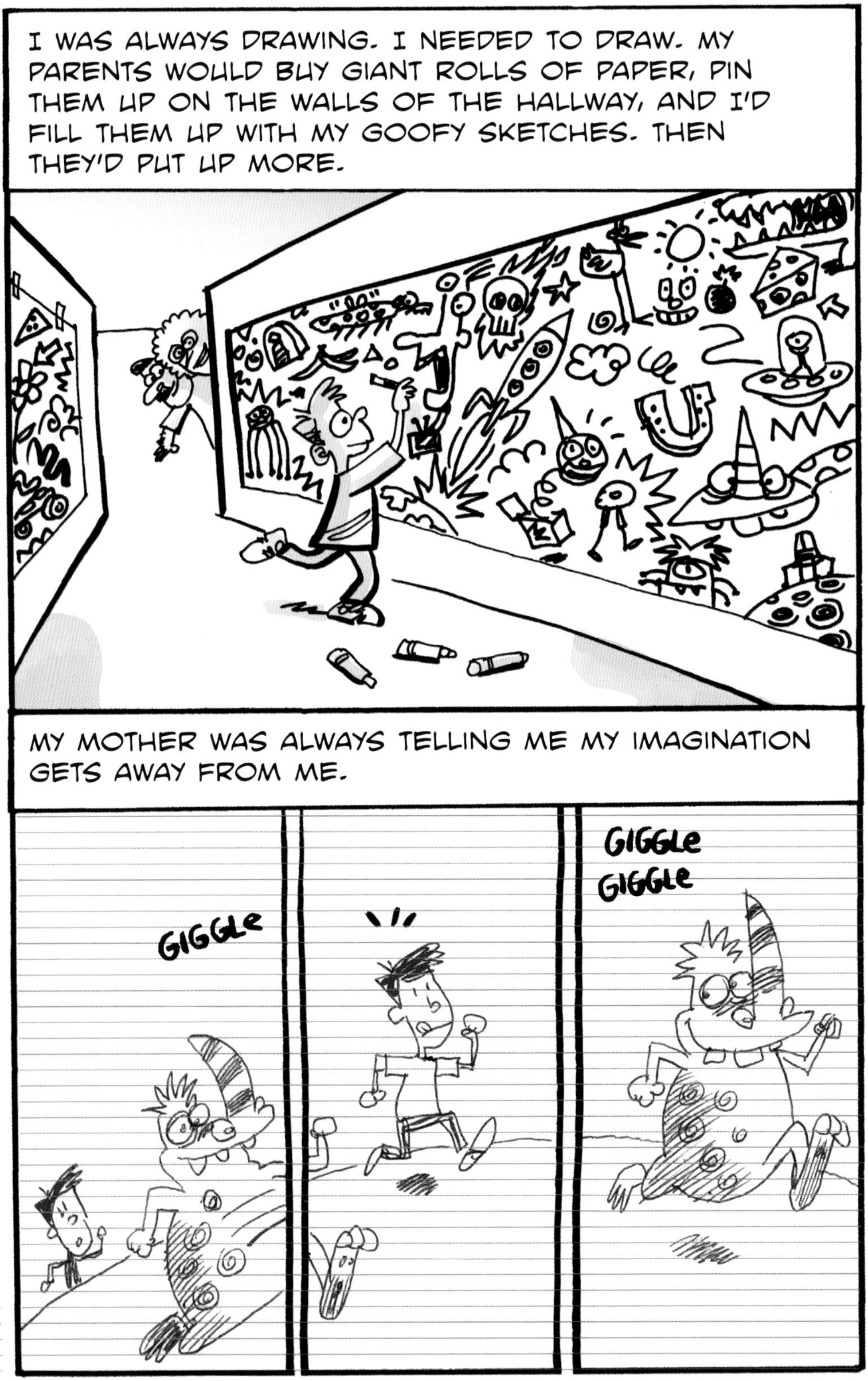
I WAS ALWAYS DRAWING. I NEEDED TO DRAW. MY PARENTS WOULD BUY GIANT ROLLS OF PAPER, PIN THEM UP ON THE WALLS OF THE HALLWAY, AND I'D FILL THEM UP WITH MY GOOFY SKETCHES. THEN THEY'D PUT UP MORE.
MY MOTHER WAS ALWAYS TELLING ME MY IMAGINATION GETS AWAY FROM ME.
GIGGLE
GIGGLE
GIGGLE

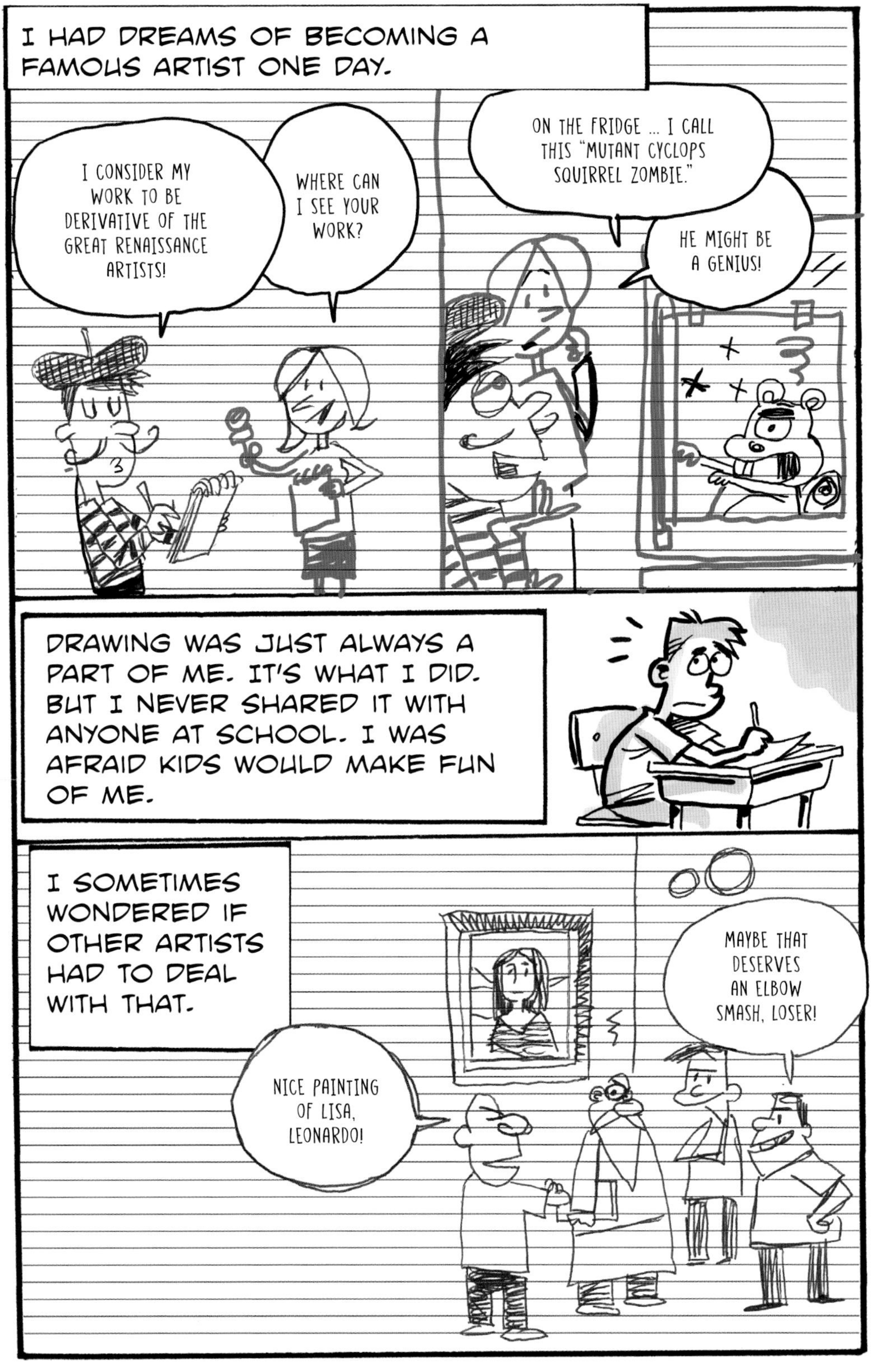
I HAD DREAMS OF BECOMING A FAMOUS ARTIST ONE DAY.
I CONSIDER MY WORK TO BE DERIVATIVE OF THE GREAT RENAISSANCE ARTISTS!
WHERE CAN I SEE YOUR WORK?
ON THE FRIDGE ... I CALL THIS "MUTANT CYCLOPS SQUIRREL ZOMBIE."
HE MIGHT BE A GENIUS!
DRAWING WAS JUST ALWAYS A PART OF ME. IT'S WHAT I DID. BUT I NEVER SHARED IT WITH ANYONE AT SCHOOL. I WAS AFRAID KIDS WOULD MAKE FUN OF ME.
I SOMETIMES WONDERED IF OTHER ARTISTS HAD TO DEAL WITH THAT.
NICE PAINTING OF LISA, LEONARDO!
MAYBE THAT DESERVES AN ELBOW SMASH, LOSER!

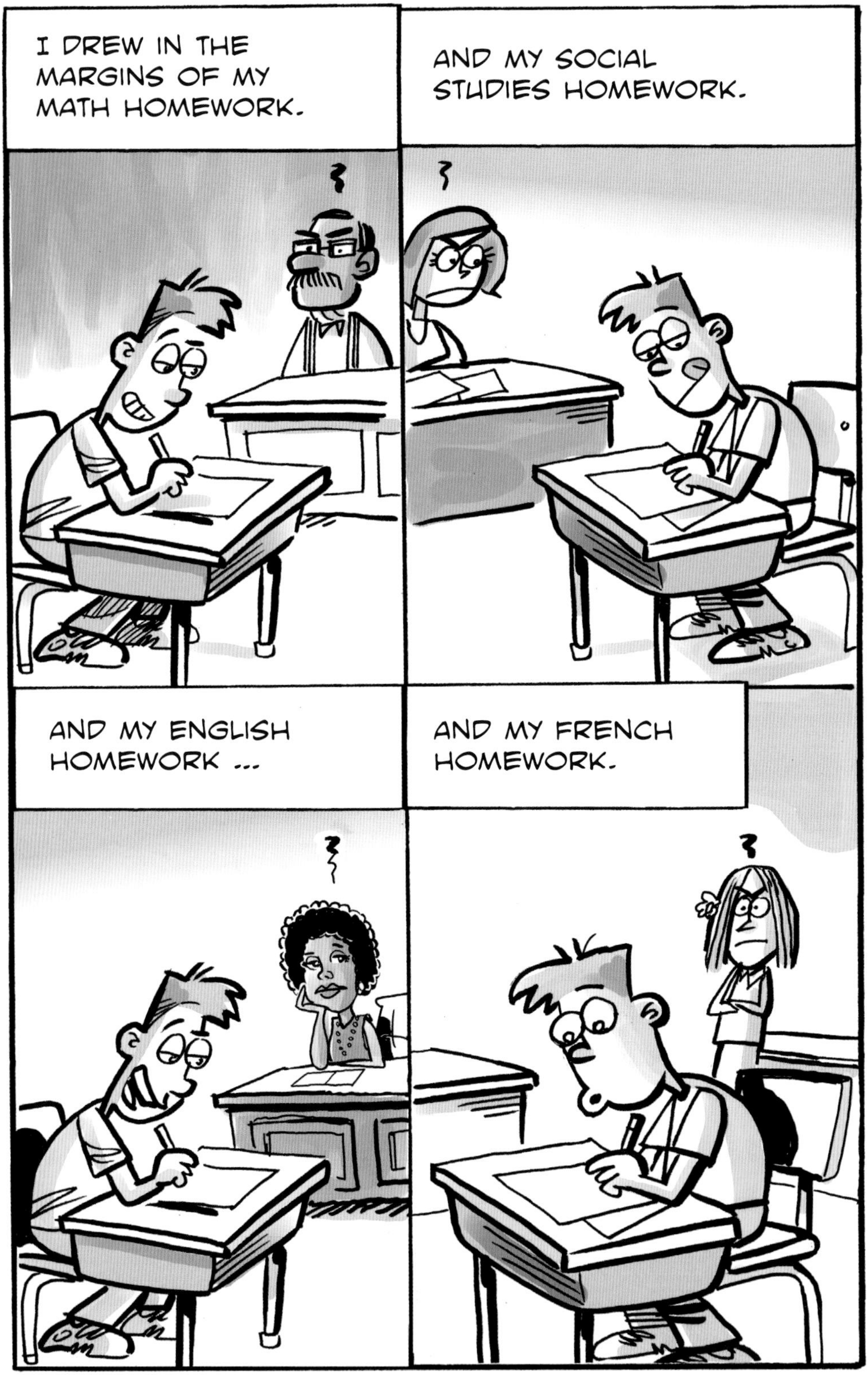
I DREW IN THE MARGINS OF MY MATH HOMEWORK.
AND MY SOCIAL STUDIES HOMEWORK.
AND MY ENGLISH HOMEWORK ...
AND MY FRENCH HOMEWORK.

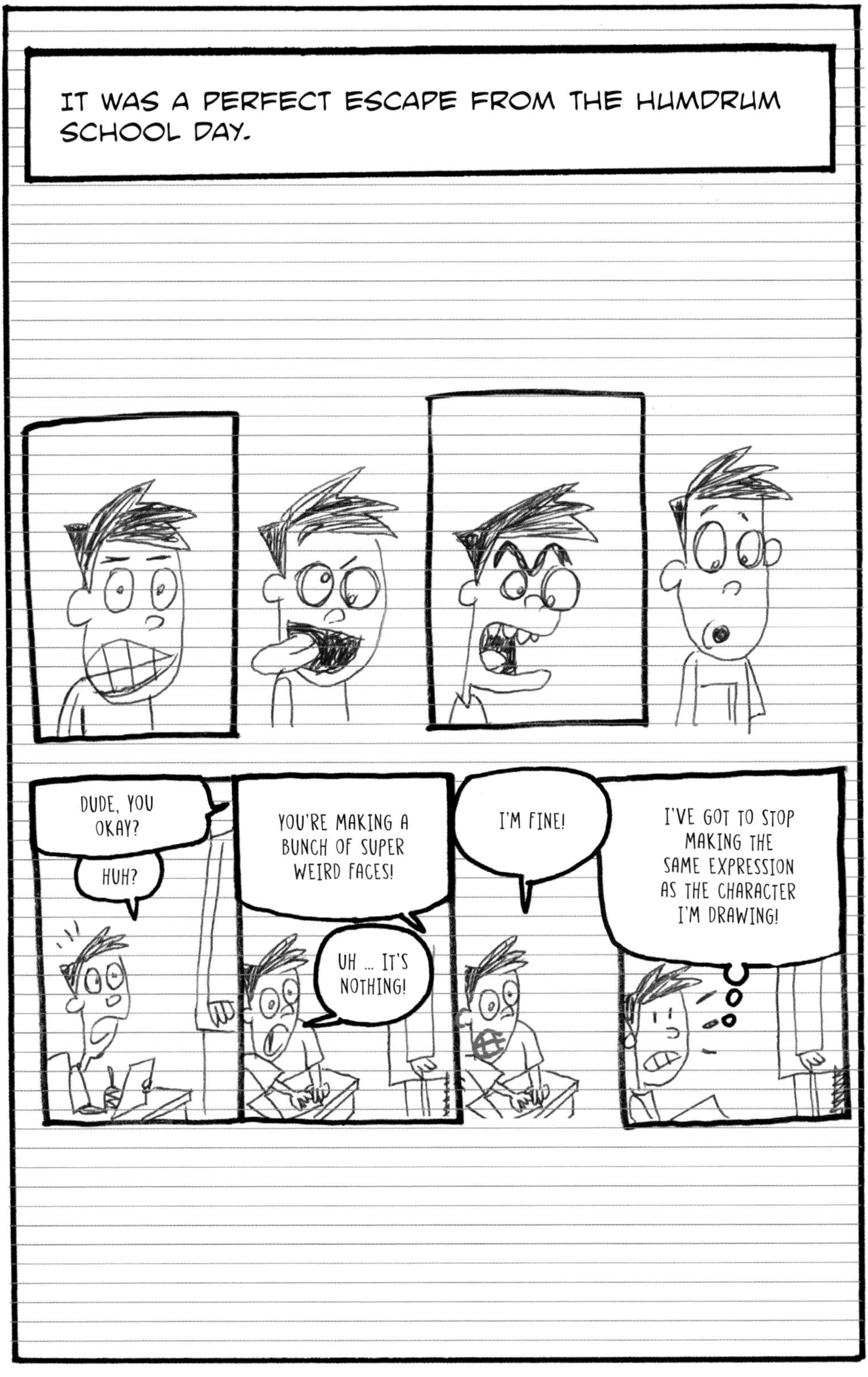
IT WAS A PERFECT ESCAPE FROM THE HUMDRUM SCHOOL DAY.
DUDE, YOU OKAY?
HUH?
YOU'RE MAKING A BUNCH OF SUPER WEIRD FACES!
UH ... IT'S NOTHING!
I'M FINE!
I'VE GOT TO STOP MAKING THE SAME EXPRESSION AS THE CHARACTER I'M DRAWING!

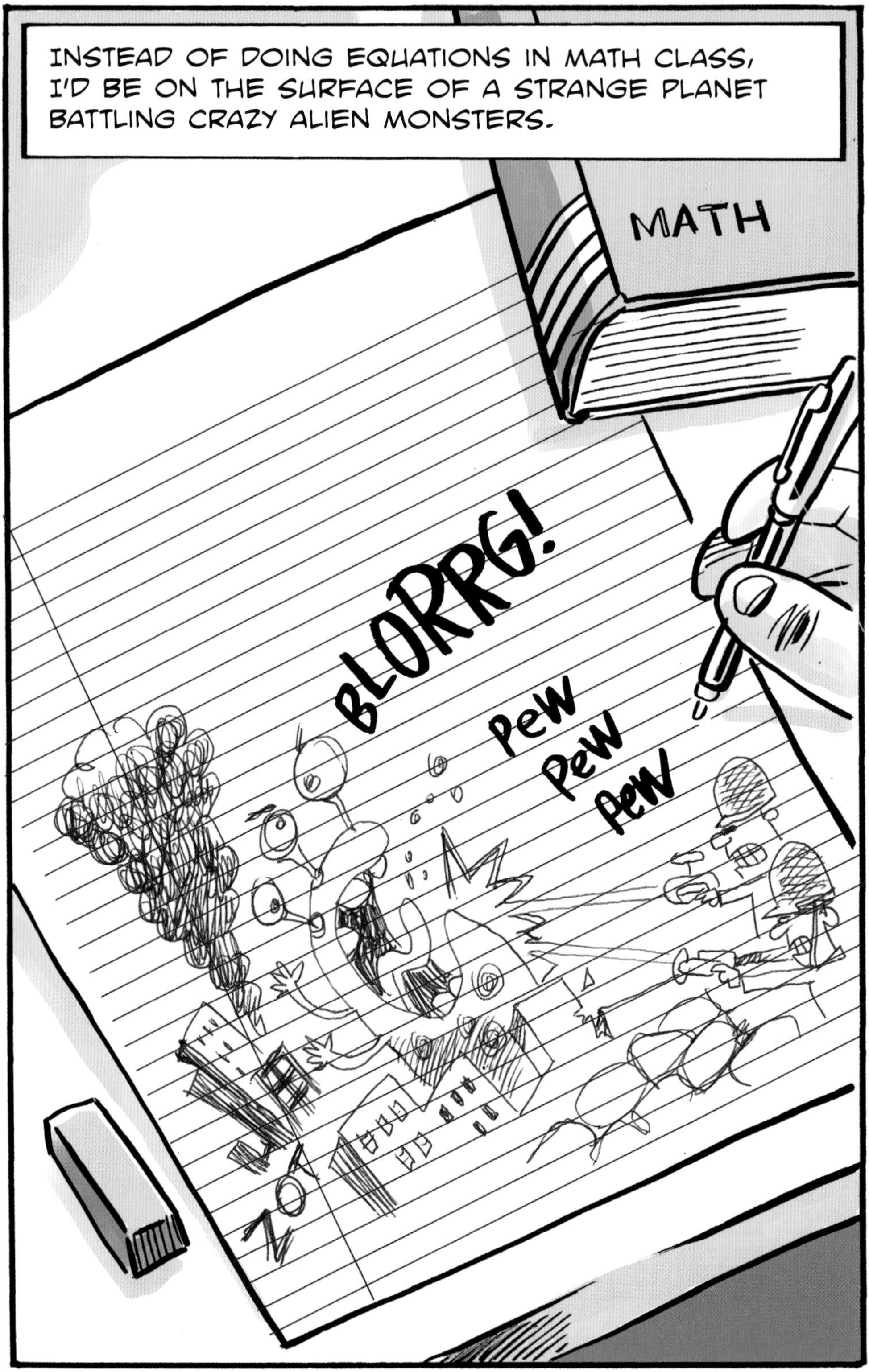
INSTEAD OF DOING EQUATIONS IN MATH CLASS, I'D BE ON THE SURFACE OF A STRANGE PLANET BATTLING CRAZY ALIEN MONSTERS.
MATH
BLORRG!
PEW
PEW
PEW

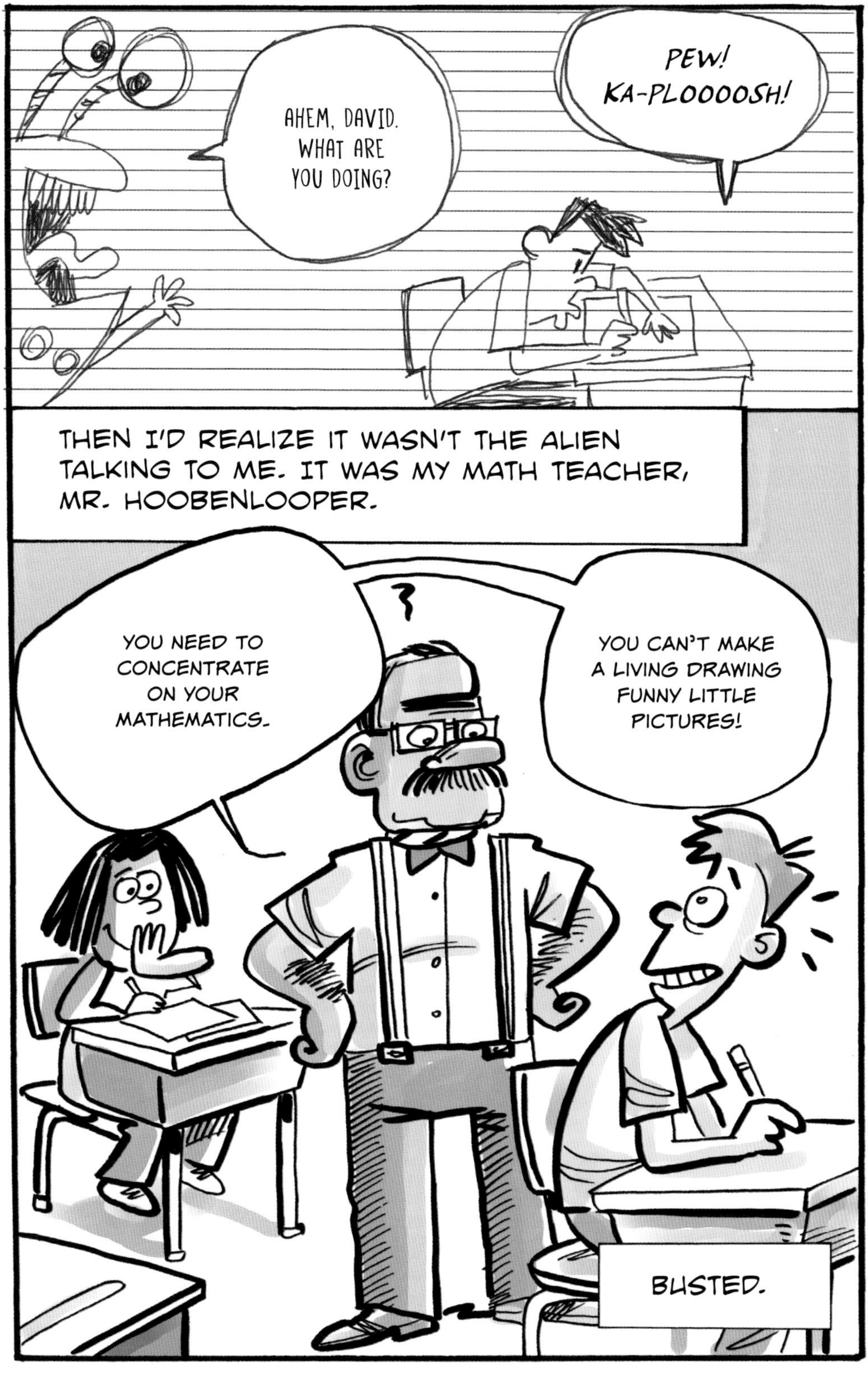
AHEM, DAVID. WHAT ARE YOU DOING?
PEW! KA-PLOOOOSH!
THEN I'D REALIZE IT WASN'T THE ALIEN TALKING TO ME. IT WAS MY MATH TEACHER, MR. HOOBENLOOPER.
YOU NEED TO CONCENTRATE ON YOUR MATHEMATICS.
?
YOU CAN'T MAKE A LIVING DRAWING FUNNY LITTLE PICTURES!
BUSTED.

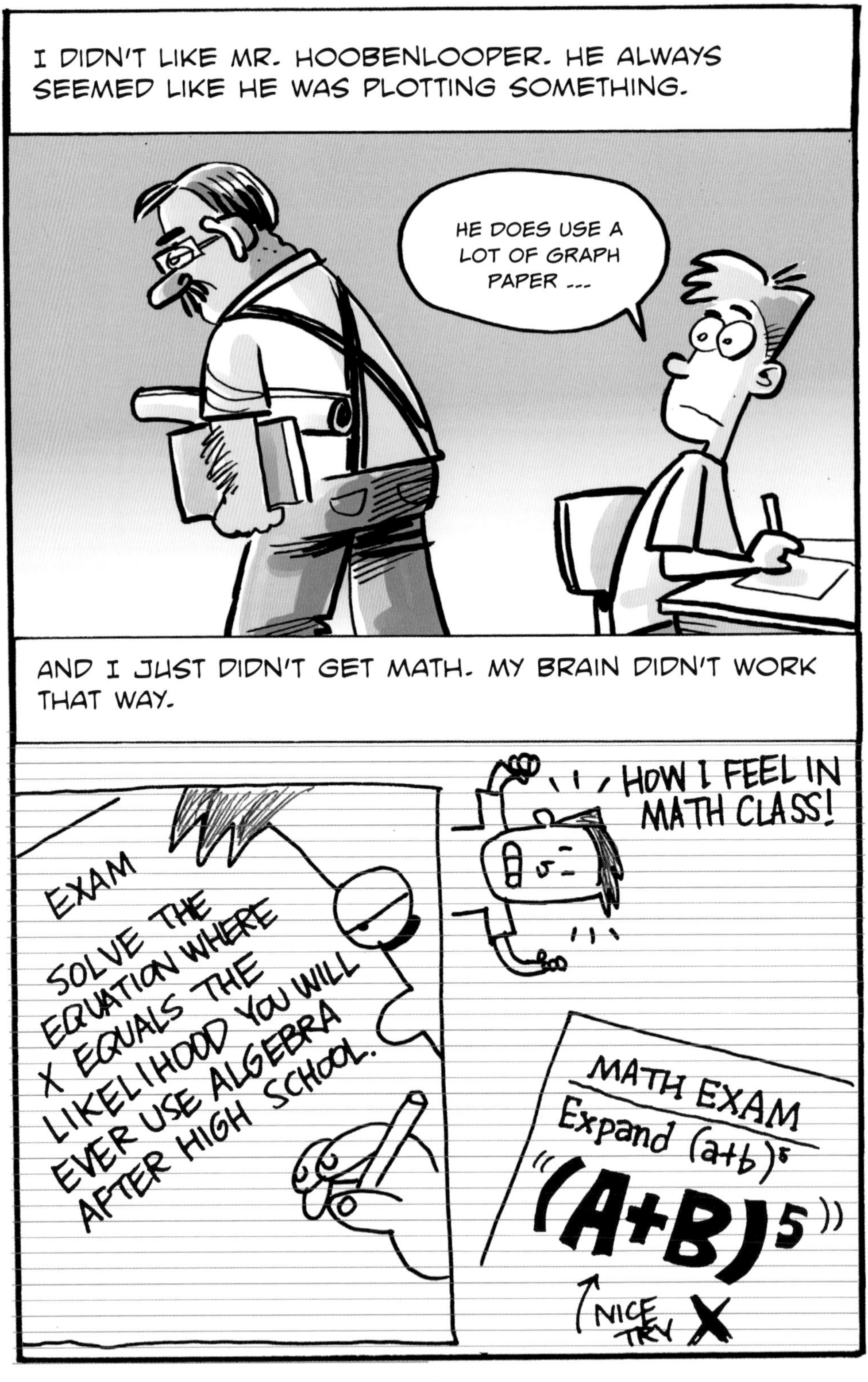
I DIDN'T LIKE MR. HOOBENLOOPER. HE ALWAYS SEEMED LIKE HE WAS PLOTTING SOMETHING.
HE DOES USE A LOT OF GRAPH PAPER ...
AND I JUST DIDN'T GET MATH. MY BRAIN DIDN'T WORK THAT WAY.
EXAM
SOLVE THE EQUATION WHERE X EQUALS THE LIKELIHOOD YOU WILL EVER USE ALGEBRA AFTER HIGH SCHOOL.
HOW I FEEL IN MATH CLASS!
MATH EXAM
Expand (a+b)5
"(A+B)5"
NICE TRY

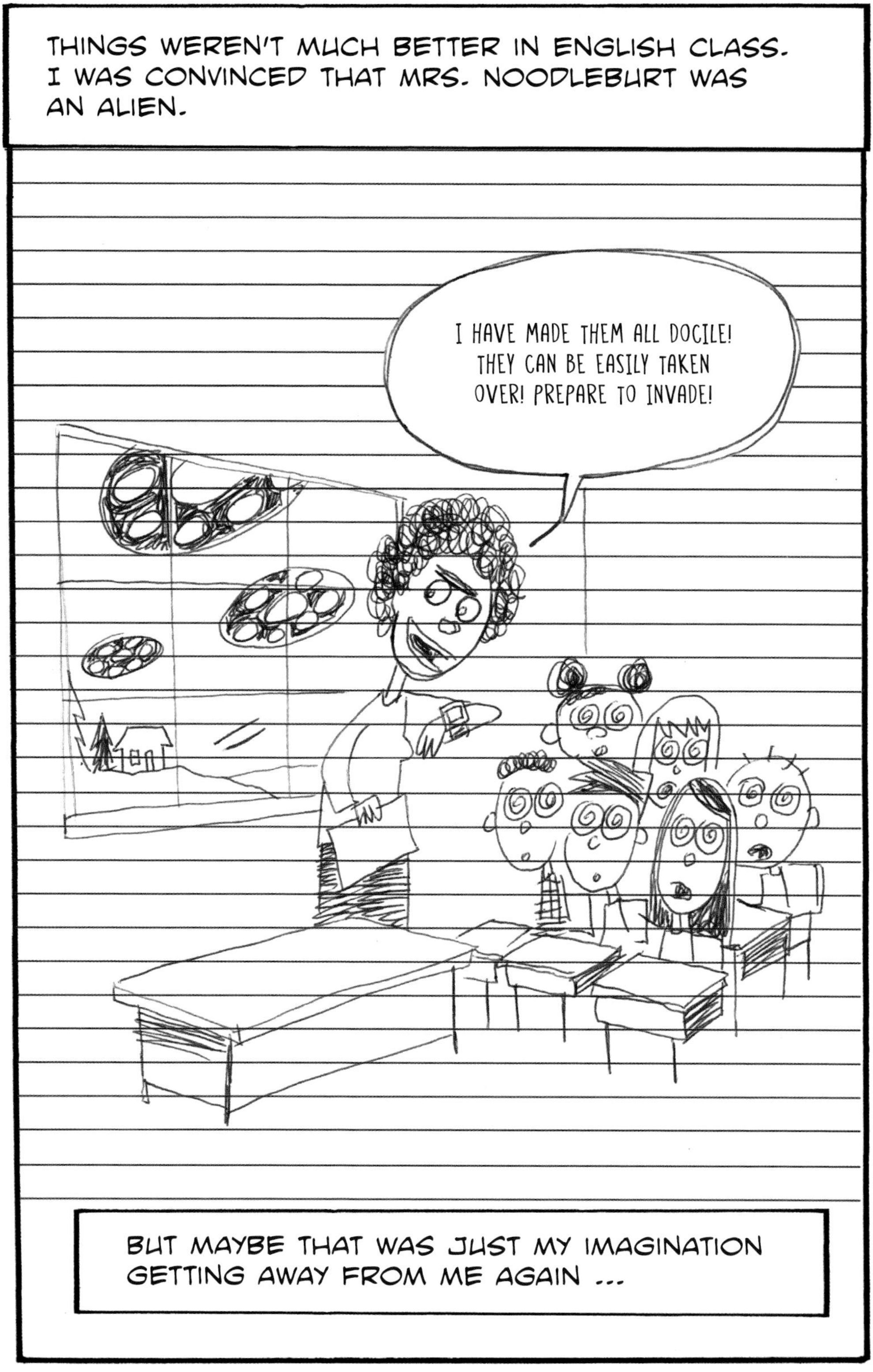
THINGS WEREN'T MUCH BETTER IN ENGLISH CLASS. I WAS CONVINCED THAT MRS. NOODLEBURT WAS AN ALIEN.
I HAVE MADE THEM ALL DOCILE! THEY CAN BE EASILY TAKEN OVER! PREPARE TO INVADE!
BUT MAYBE THAT WAS JUST MY IMAGINATION GETTING AWAY FROM ME AGAIN ...

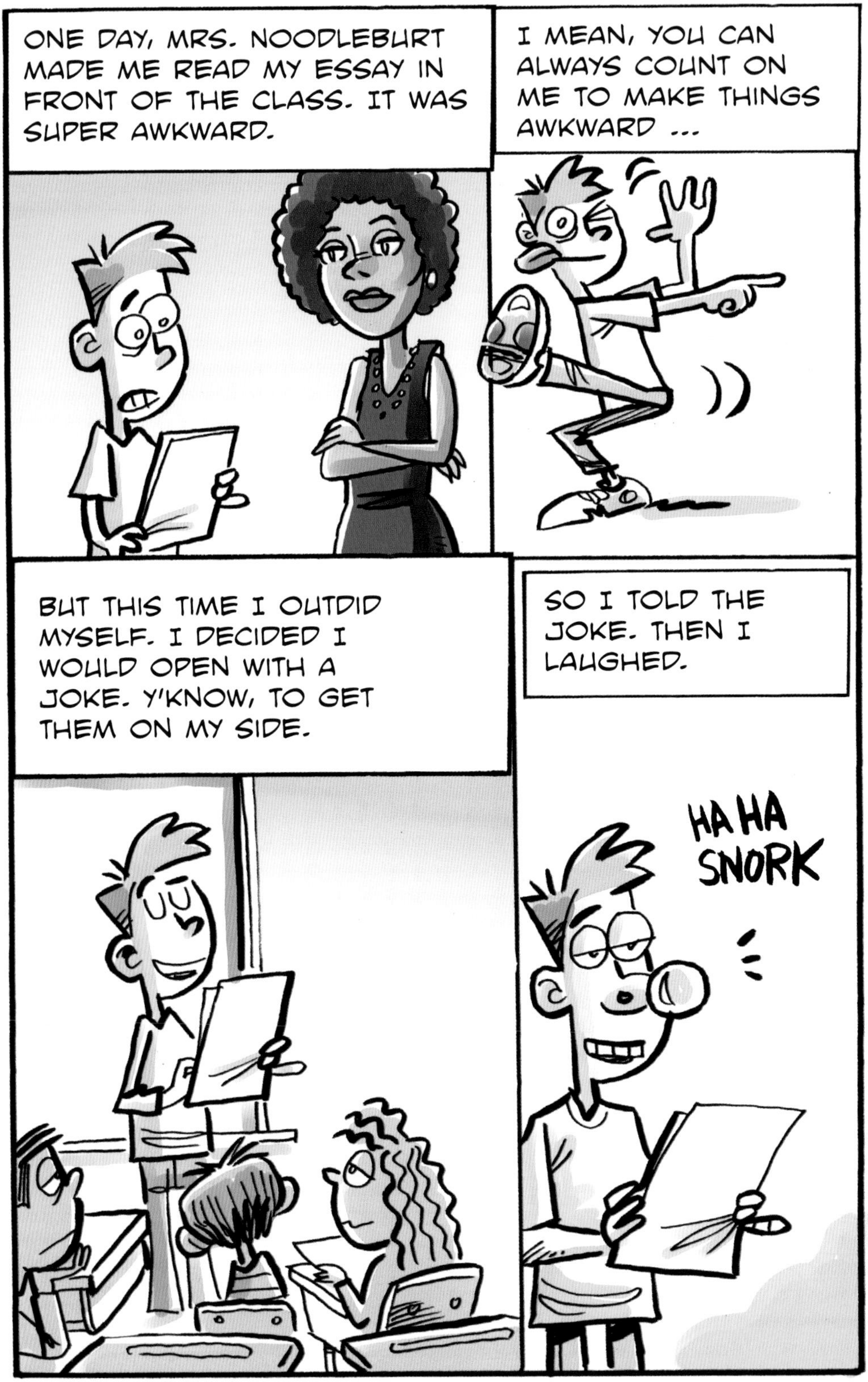
ONE DAY, MRS. NOODLEBURT MADE ME READ MY ESSAY IN FRONT OF THE CLASS. IT WAS SUPER AWKWARD.
I MEAN, YOU CAN ALWAYS COUNT ON ME TO MAKE THINGS AWKWARD ...
BUT THIS TIME I OUTDID MYSELF. I DECIDED I WOULD OPEN WITH A JOKE. Y'KNOW, TO GET THEM ON MY SIDE.
SO I TOLD THE JOKE. THEN I LAUGHED.
HA HA SNORK

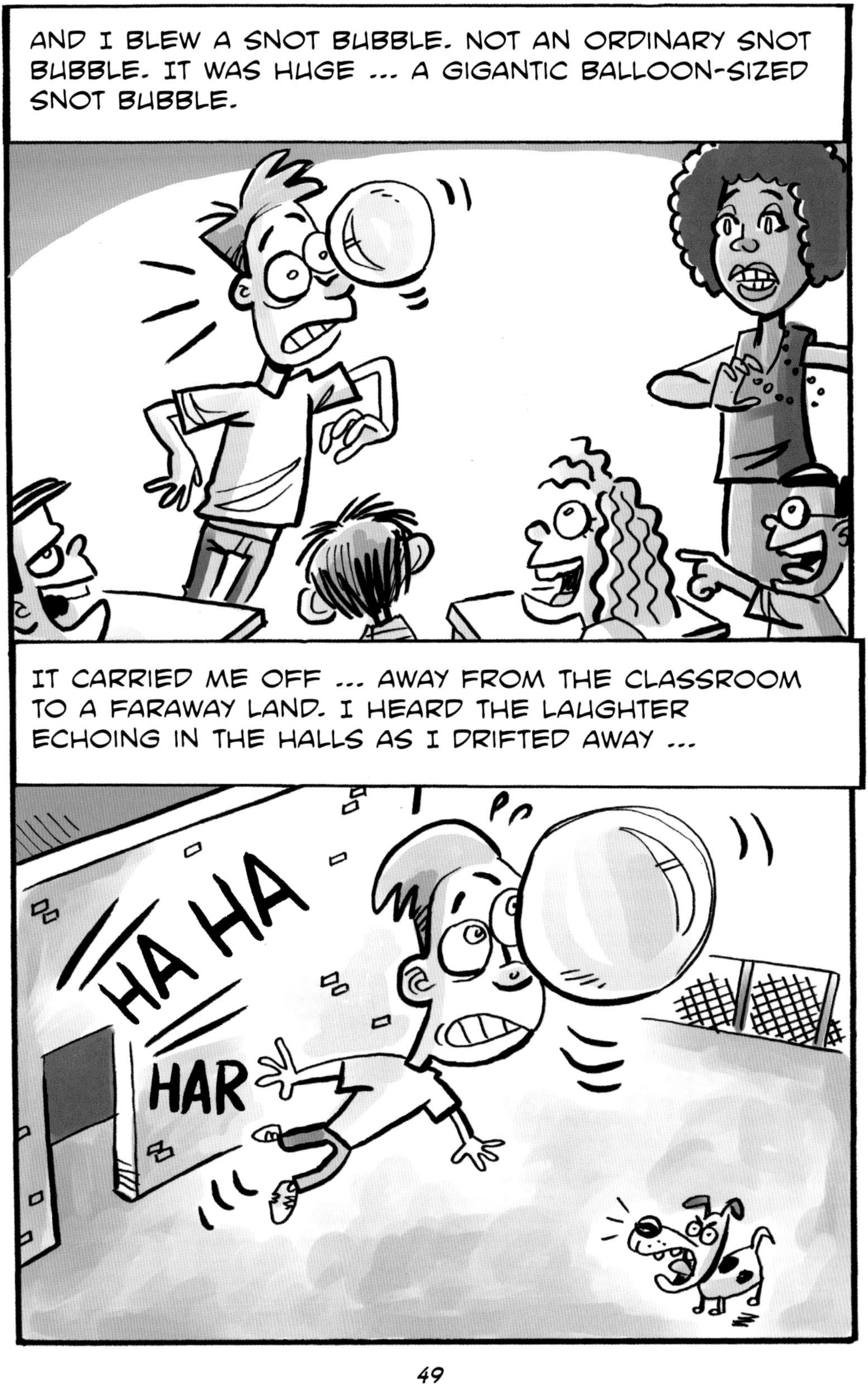
AND I BLEW A SNOT BUBBLE. NOT AN ORDINARY SNOT BUBBLE. IT WAS HUGE ... A GIGANTIC BALLOON-SIZED SNOT BUBBLE.
IT CARRIED ME OFF ... AWAY FROM THE CLASSROOM TO A FARAWAY LAND. I HEARD THE LAUGHTER ECHOING IN THE HALLS AS I DRIFTED AWAY ...
HA HA
HAR

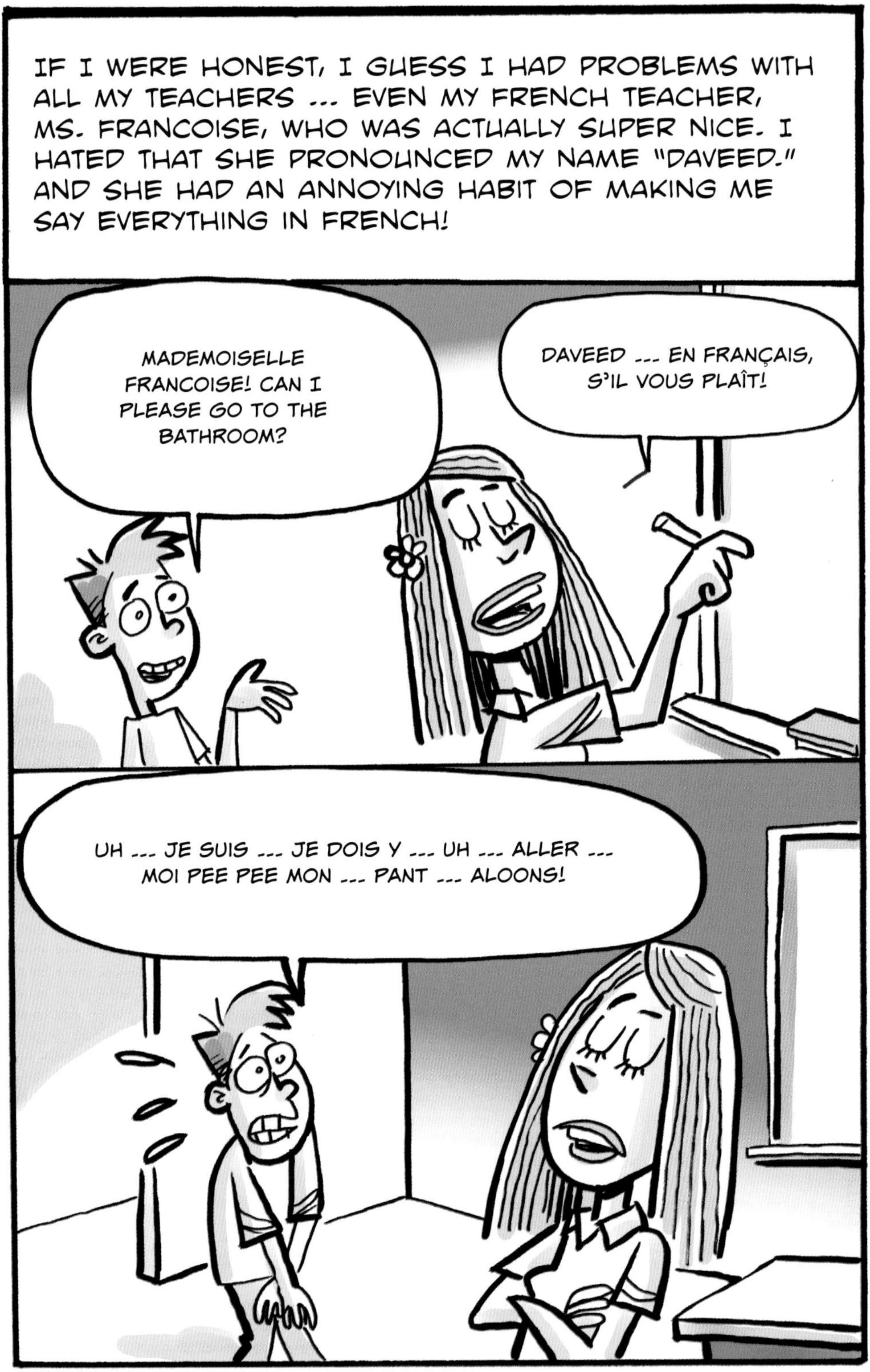
IF I WERE HONEST, I GUESS I HAD PROBLEMS WITH ALL MY TEACHERS ... EVEN MY FRENCH TEACHER, MS. FRANCOISE, WHO WAS ACTUALLY SUPER NICE. I HATED THAT SHE PRONOUNCED MY NAME "DAVEED." AND SHE HAD AN ANNOYING HABIT OF MAKING ME SAY EVERYTHING IN FRENCH!
MADEMOISELLE FRANCOISE! CAN I PLEASE GO TO THE BATHROOM?
DAVEED ... EN FRANÇAIS, S'IL VOUS PLAÎT!
UH ... JE SUIS ... JE DOIS Y ... UH ... ALLER ... MOI PEE PEE MON ... PANT ... ALOONS!

I HOPED THERE WOULD NEVER BE AN ACTUAL EMERGENCY. LIKE, SAY, A ZOMBIE APOCALYPSE ...

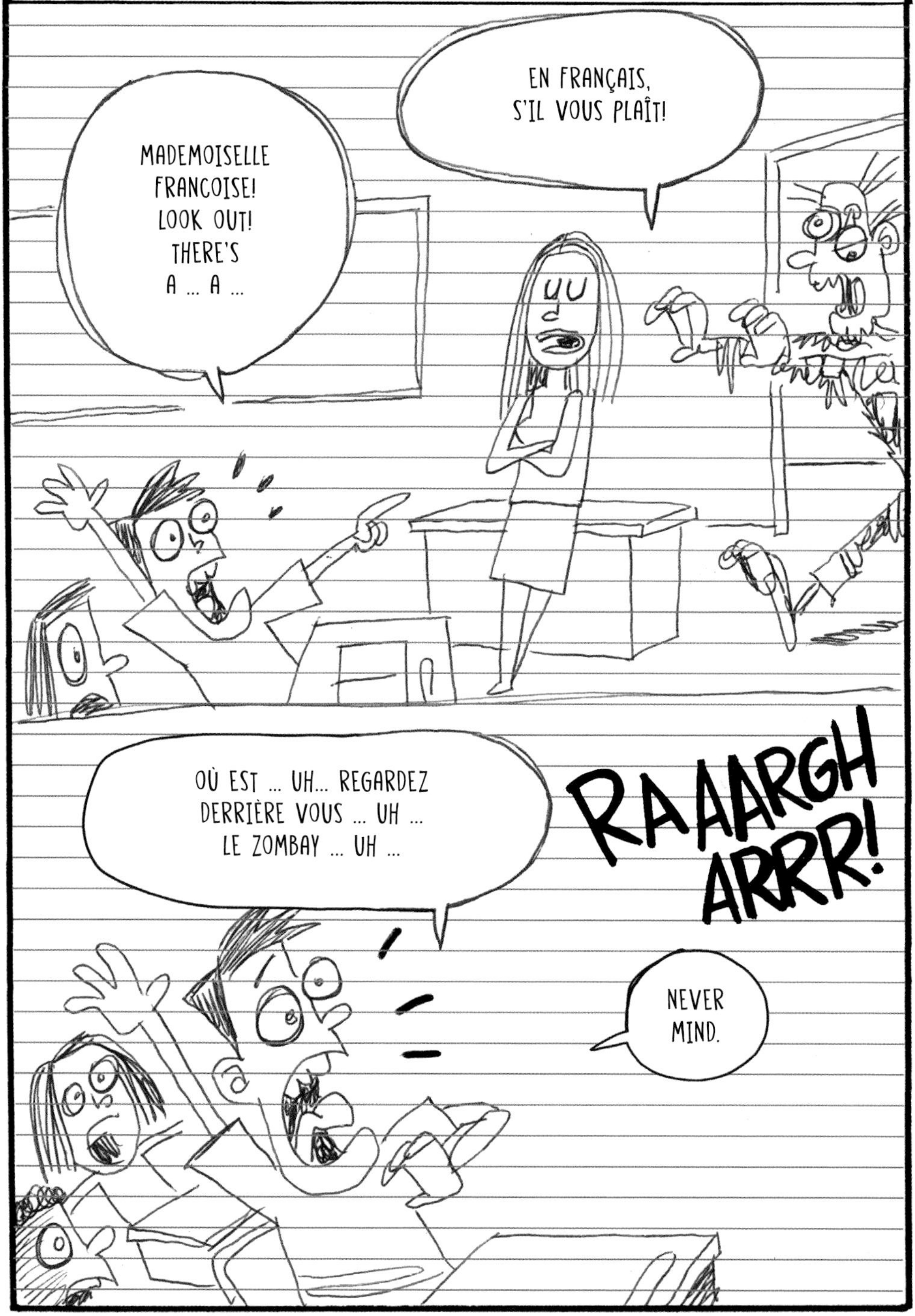

MADEMOISELLE FRANCOISE! LOOK OUT! THERE'S A ... A ...
EN FRANÇAIS, S'IL VOUS PLAÎT!
OÙ EST ... UH... REGARDEZ DERRIÈRE VOUS ... UH ... LE ZOMBAY ... UH ...
RAAARGH ARRR!
NEVER MIND.

CHAPTER 4: NOT ALL BAD

DESPITE MY TROUBLES, THERE ACTUALLY WAS A GOOD SIDE TO MUDDLE. I DID HAVE A REASON TO GET OUT OF BED EVERY MORNING, OTHER THAN THE DAILY PRANK I PLAYED ON MY SISTER ...

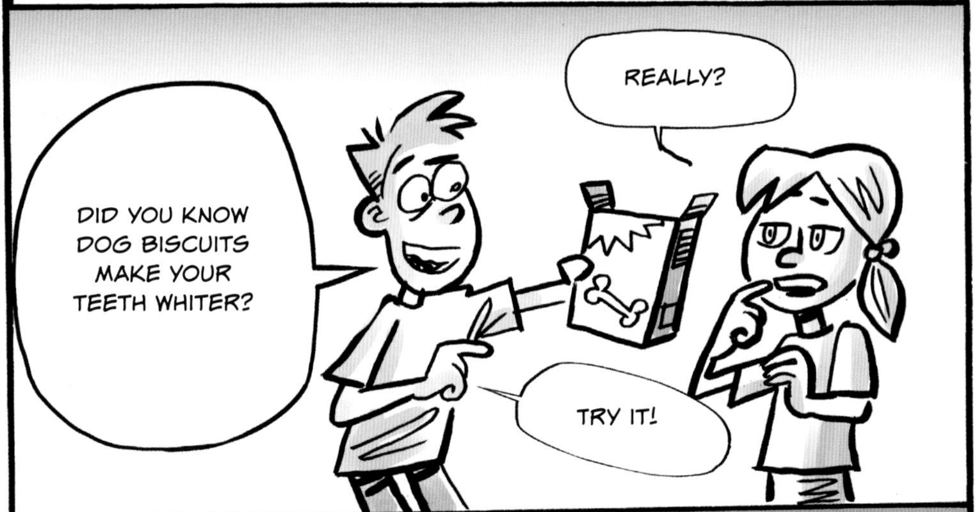
DID YOU KNOW DOG BISCUITS MAKE YOUR TEETH WHITER?
REALLY?
TRY IT!

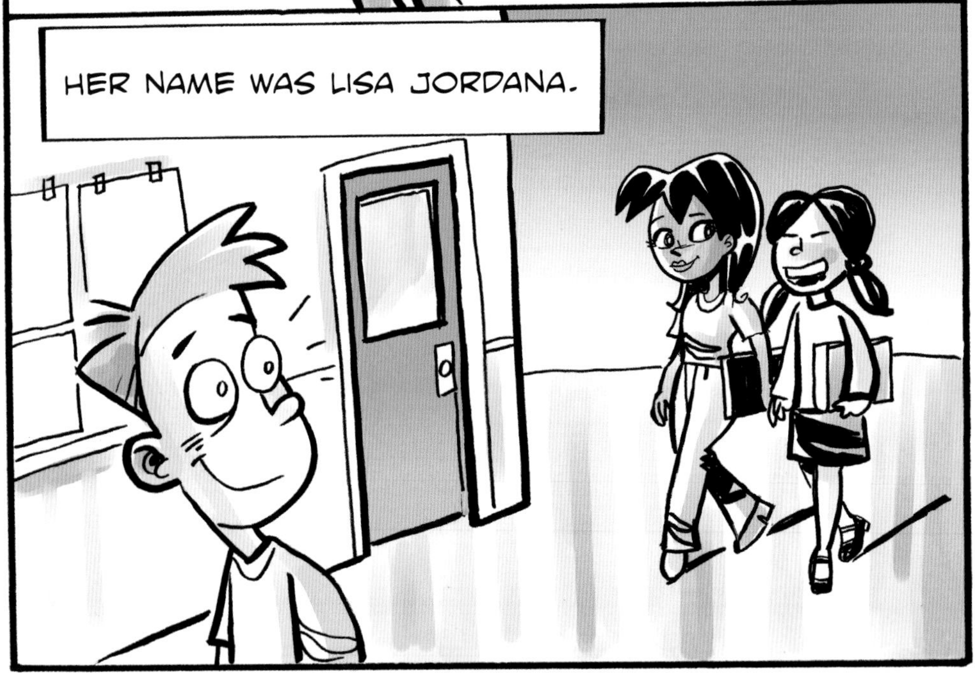
HER NAME WAS LISA JORDANA.

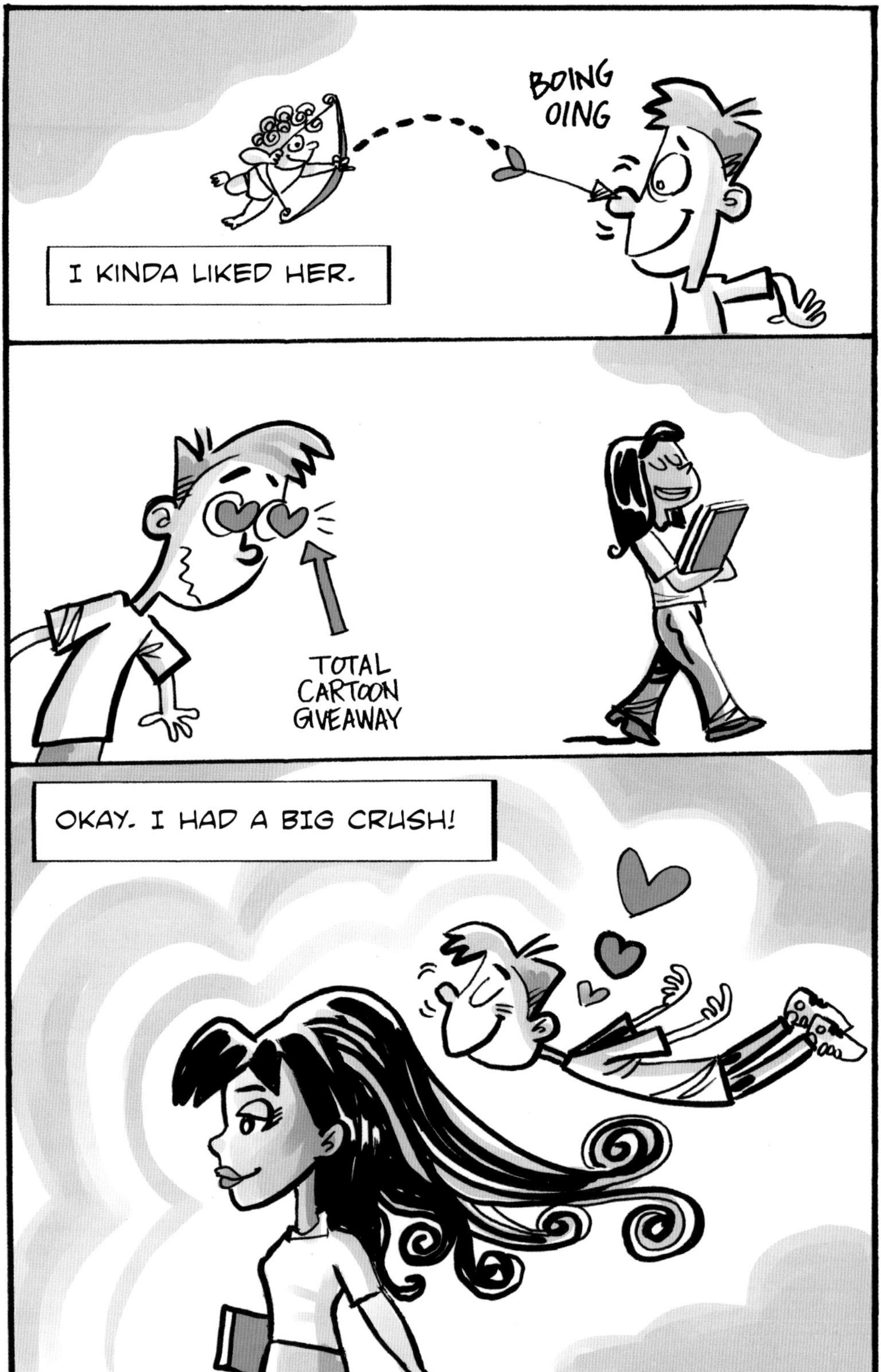
BOING
OING
I KINDA LIKED HER.
TOTAL CARTOON GIVEAWAY
OKAY. I HAD A BIG CRUSH!

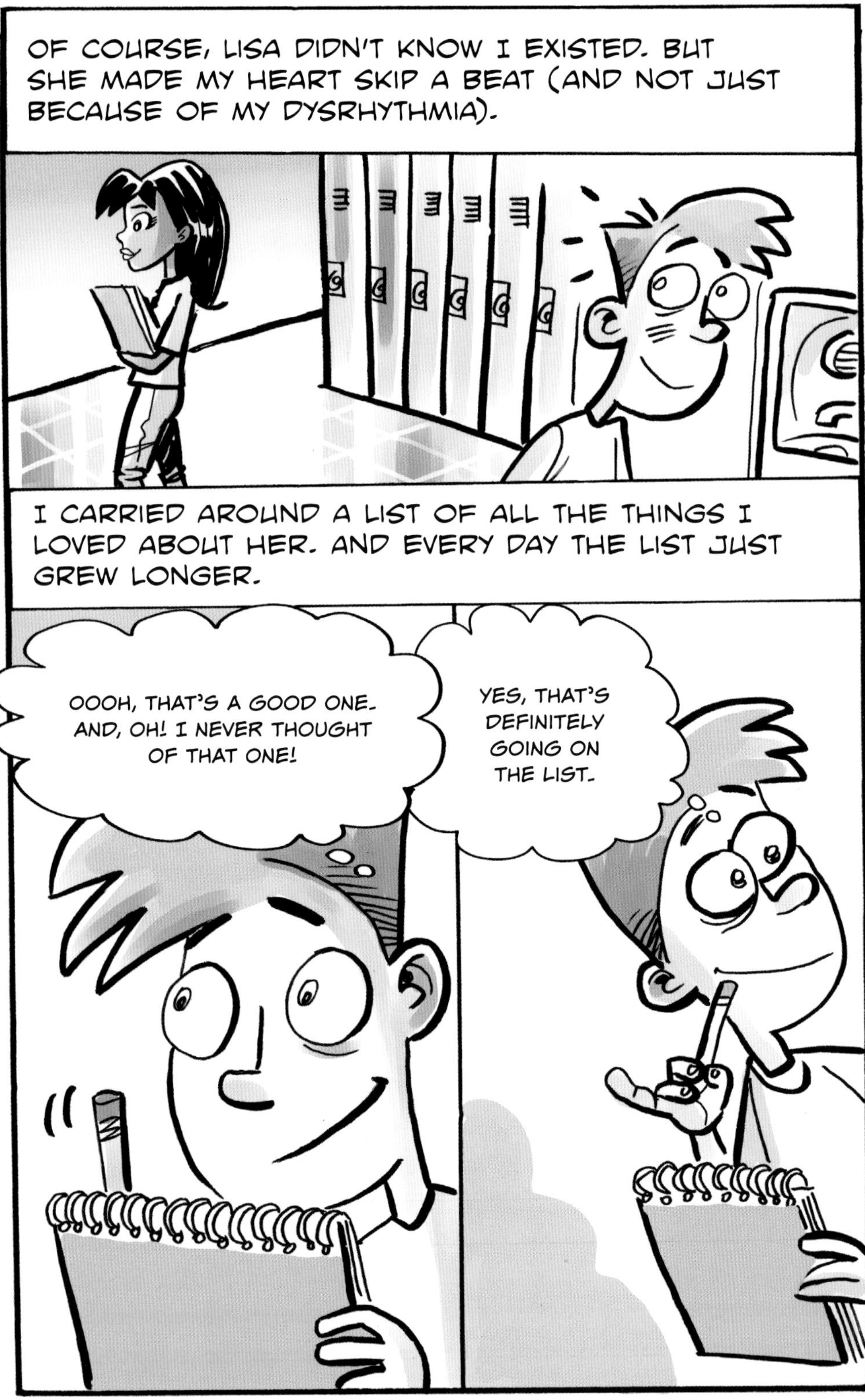
OF COURSE, LISA DIDN'T KNOW I EXISTED. BUT SHE MADE MY HEART SKIP A BEAT (AND NOT JUST BECAUSE OF MY DYSRHYTHMIA).
I CARRIED AROUND A LIST OF ALL THE THINGS I LOVED ABOUT HER. AND EVERY DAY THE LIST JUST GREW LONGER.
OOOH, THAT'S A GOOD ONE. AND, OH! I NEVER THOUGHT OF THAT ONE!
YES, THAT'S DEFINITELY GOING ON THE LIST.

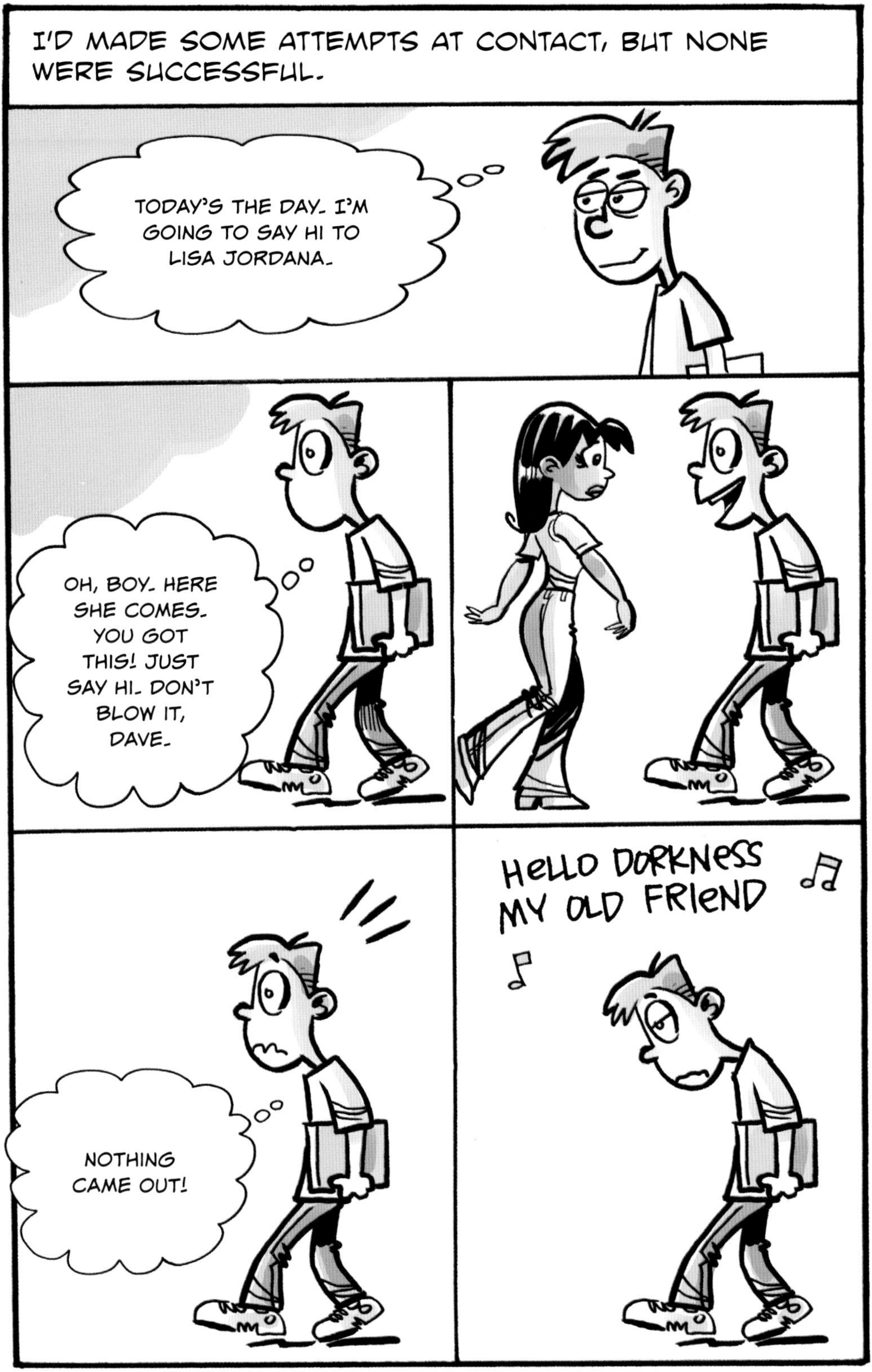
I'D MADE SOME ATTEMPTS AT CONTACT, BUT NONE WERE SUCCESSFUL.
TODAY'S THE DAY. I'M GOING TO SAY HI TO LISA JORDANA.
OH, BOY. HERE SHE COMES. YOU GOT THIS! JUST SAY HI. DON'T BLOW IT, DAVE.
NOTHING CAME OUT!
HELLO DORKNESS MY OLD FRIEND

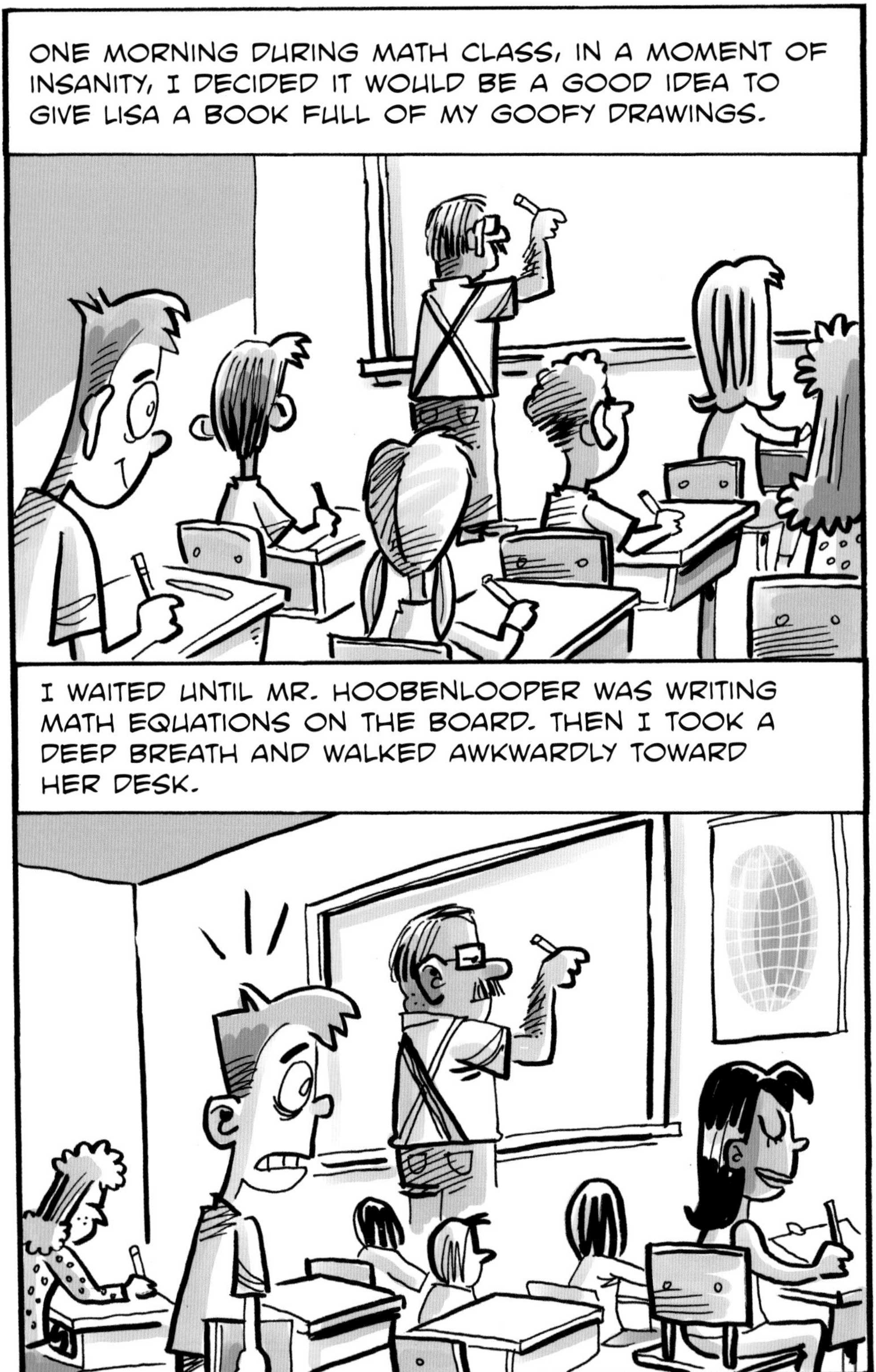
ONE MORNING DURING MATH CLASS, IN A MOMENT OF INSANITY, I DECIDED IT WOULD BE A GOOD IDEA TO GIVE LISA A BOOK FULL OF MY GOOFY DRAWINGS.
I WAITED UNTIL MR. HOOBENLOOPER WAS WRITING MATH EQUATIONS ON THE BOARD. THEN I TOOK A DEEP BREATH AND WALKED AWKWARDLY TOWARD HER DESK.

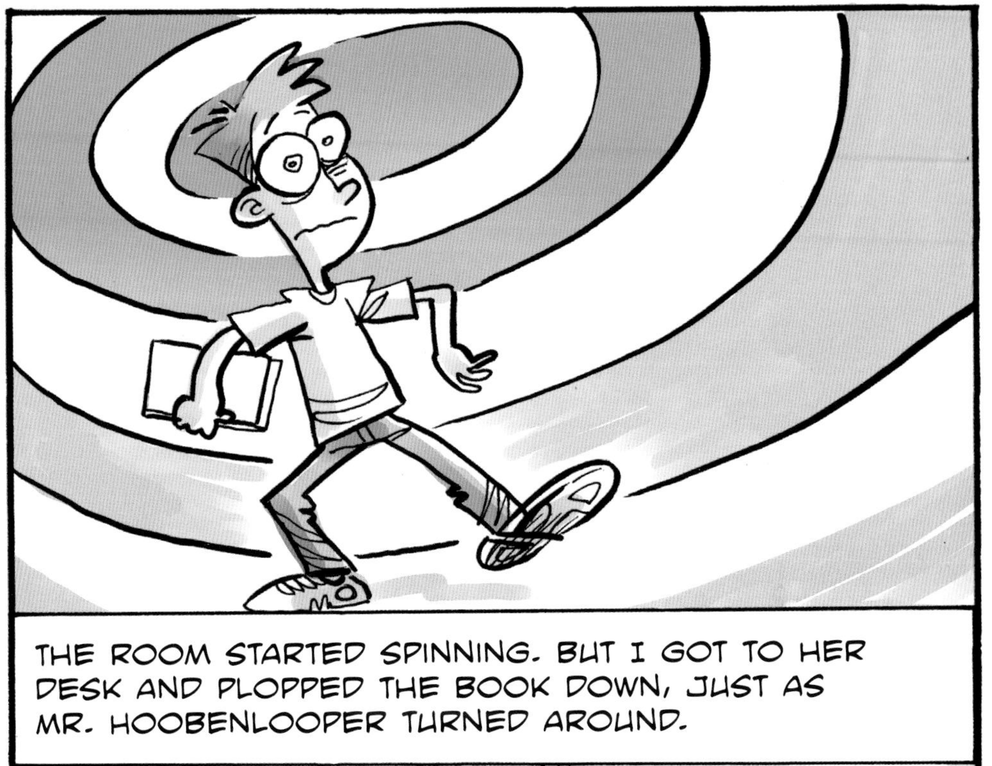

THE ROOM STARTED SPINNING. BUT I GOT TO HER DESK AND PLOPPED THE BOOK DOWN, JUST AS MR. HOOBENLOOPER TURNED AROUND.

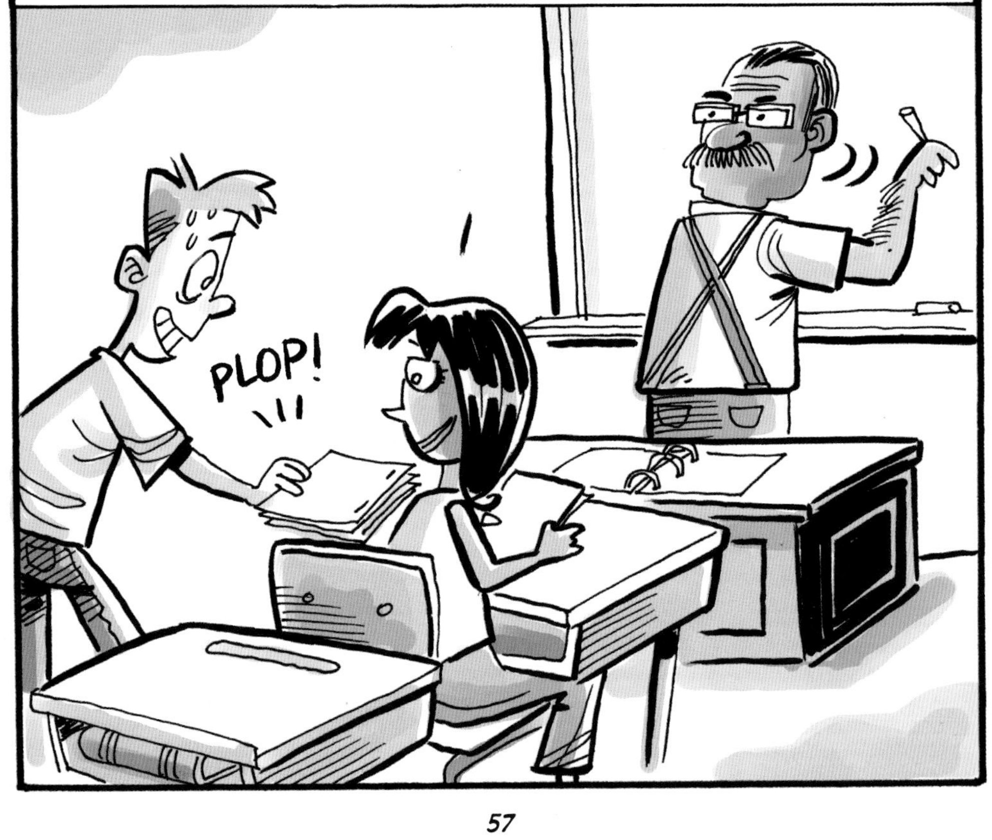
PLOP!

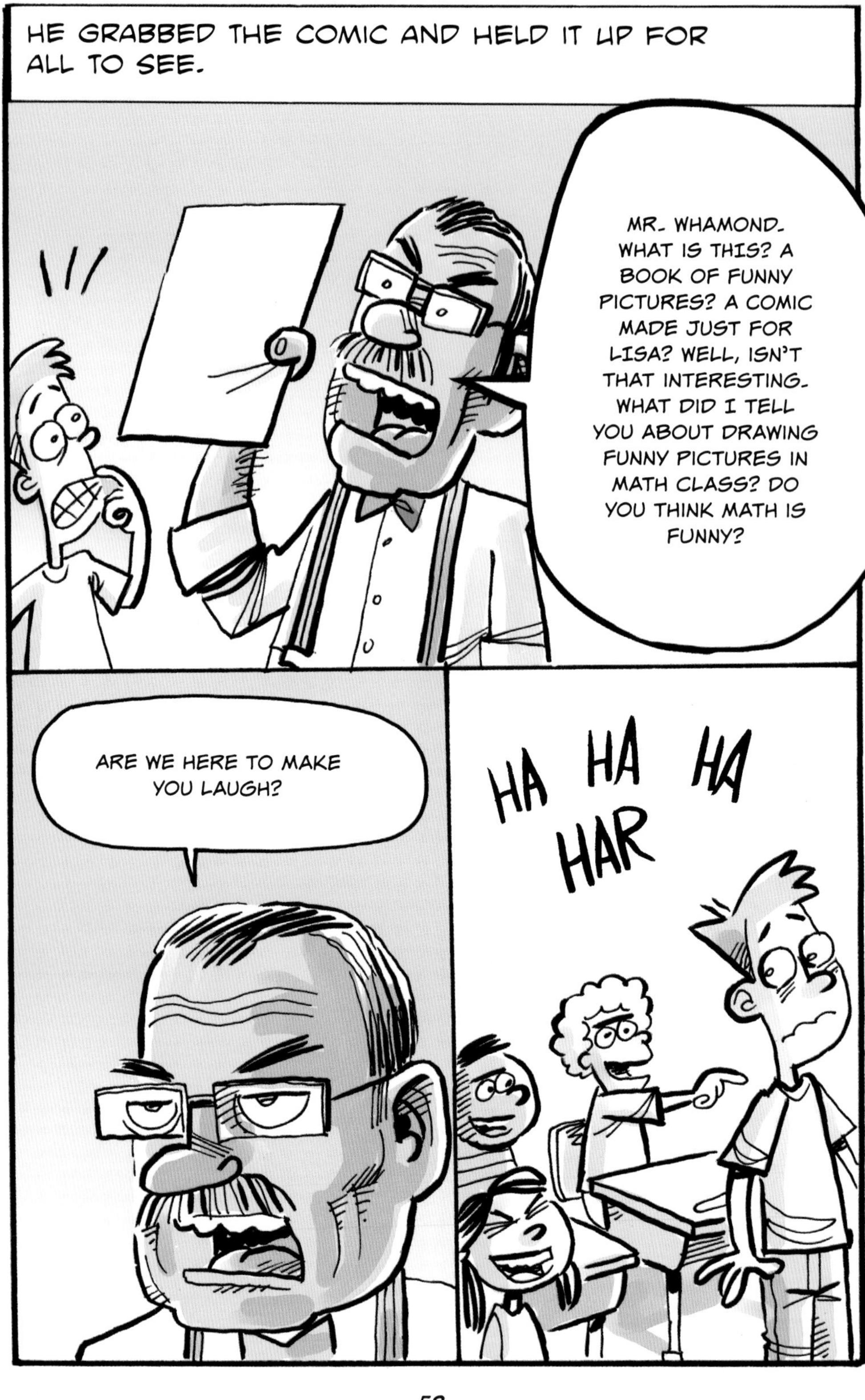
HE GRABBED THE COMIC AND HELD IT UP FOR ALL TO SEE.
MR. WHAMOND. WHAT IS THIS? A BOOK OF FUNNY PICTURES? A COMIC MADE JUST FOR LISA? WELL, ISN'T THAT INTERESTING. WHAT DID I TELL YOU ABOUT DRAWING FUNNY PICTURES IN MATH CLASS? DO YOU THINK MATH IS FUNNY?
ARE WE HERE TO MAKE YOU LAUGH?
HA HA HA
HAR

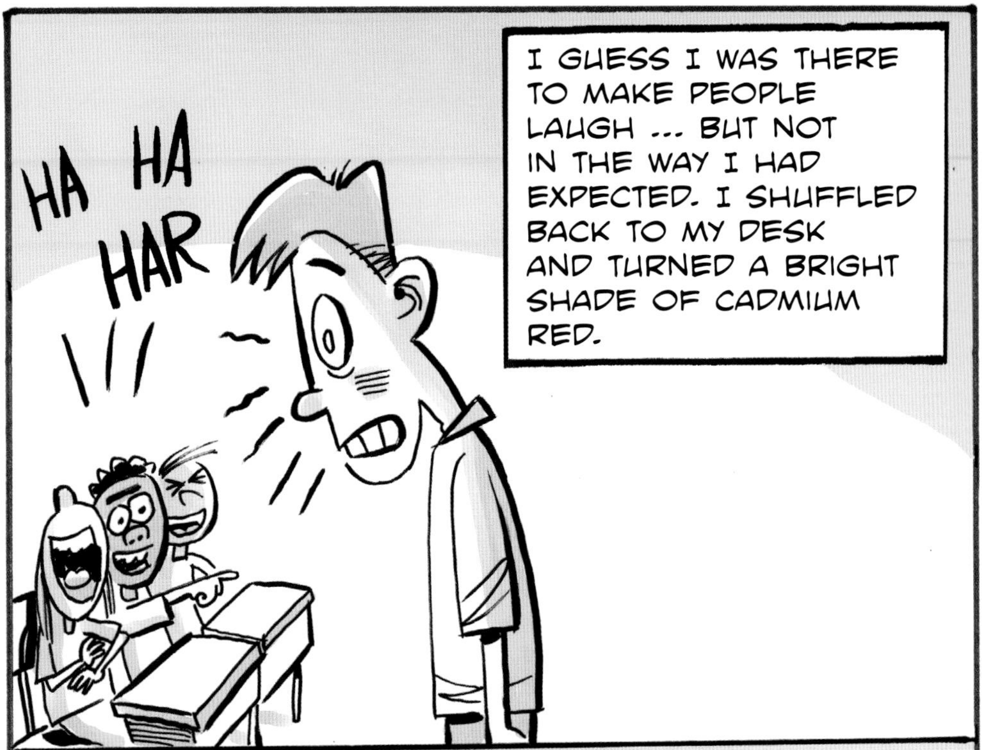
HA HA
HAR
I GUESS I WAS THERE TO MAKE PEOPLE LAUGH ... BUT NOT IN THE WAY I HAD EXPECTED. I SHUFFLED BACK TO MY DESK AND TURNED A BRIGHT SHADE OF CADMIUM RED.

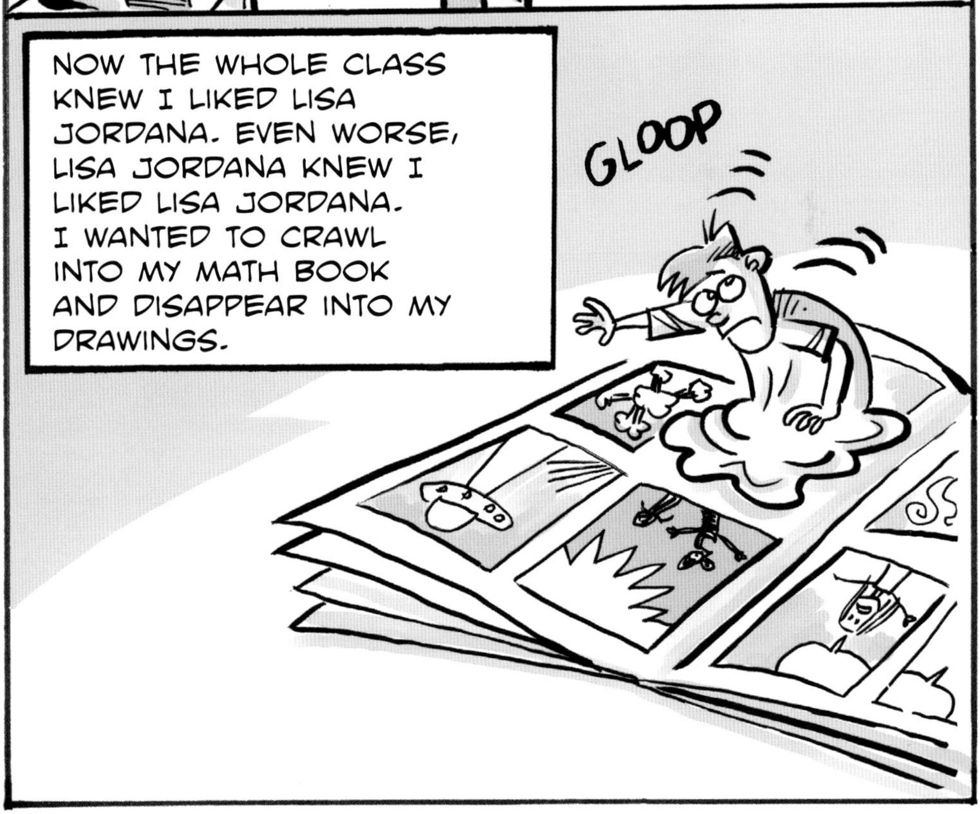
NOW THE WHOLE CLASS KNEW I LIKED LISA JORDANA. EVEN WORSE, LISA JORDANA KNEW I LIKED LISA JORDANA. I WANTED TO CRAWL INTO MY MATH BOOK AND DISAPPEAR INTO MY DRAWINGS.
GLOOP

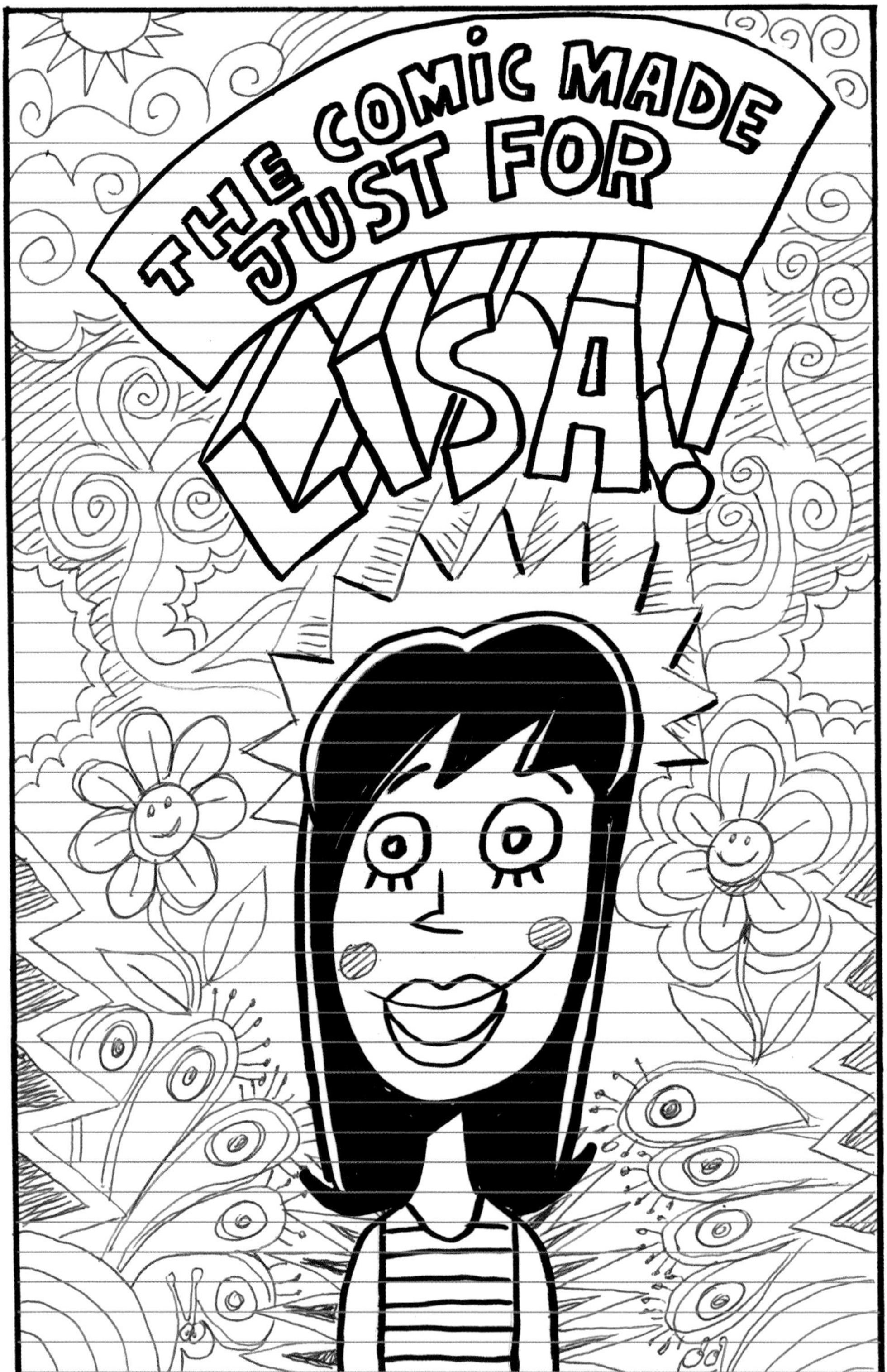
THE COMIC MADE JUST FOR
LISA!

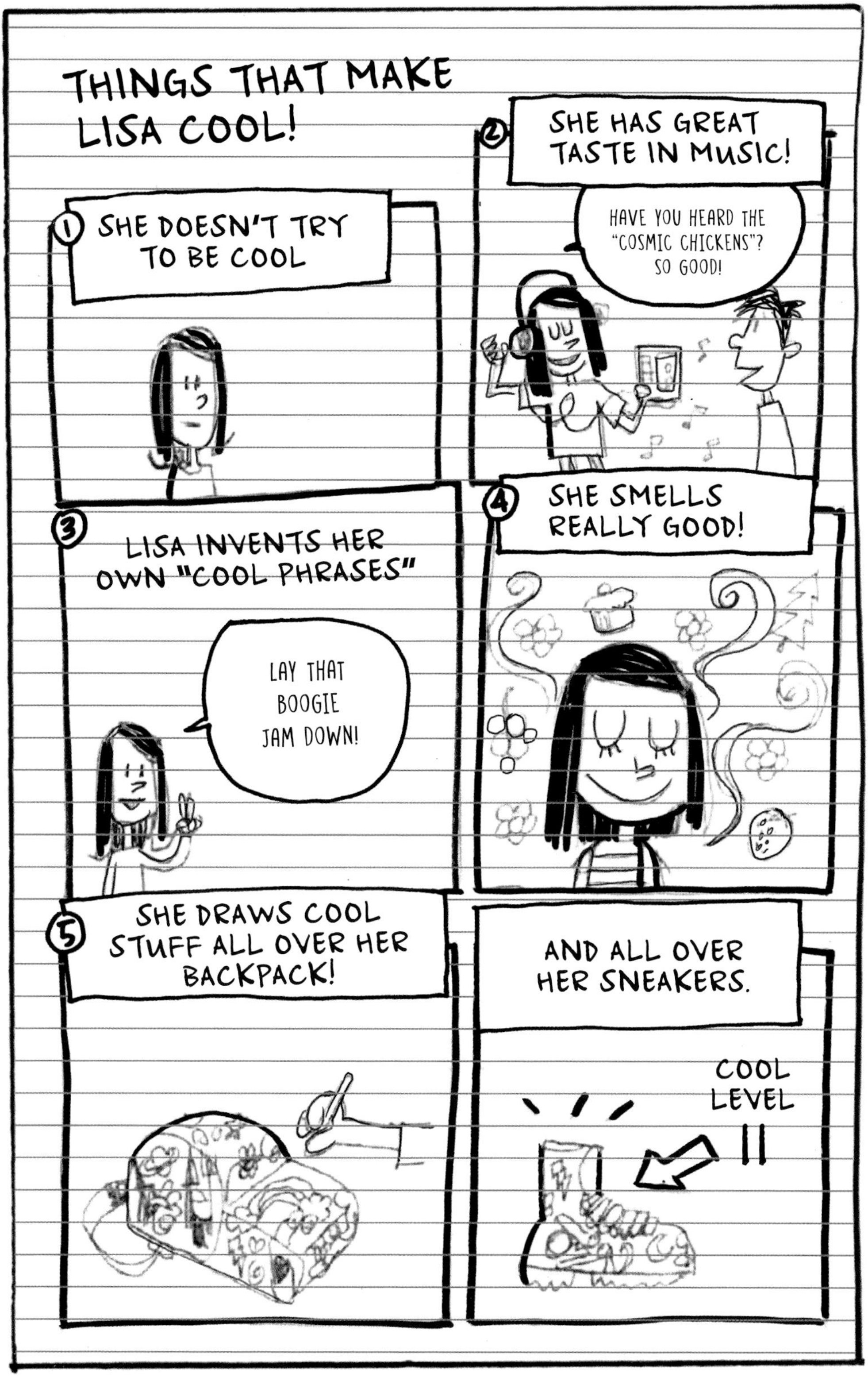
THINGS THAT MAKE LISA COOL!
1 SHE DOESN'T TRY TO BE COOL
2 SHE HAS GREAT TASTE IN MUSIC!
HAVE YOU HEARD THE "COSMIC CHICKENS"? SO GOOD!
3 LISA INVENTS HER OWN "COOL PHRASES"
LAY THAT BOOGIE JAM DOWN!
4 SHE SMELLS REALLY GOOD!
5 SHE DRAWS COOL STUFF ALL OVER HER BACKPACK!
AND ALL OVER HER SNEAKERS.
COOL LEVEL

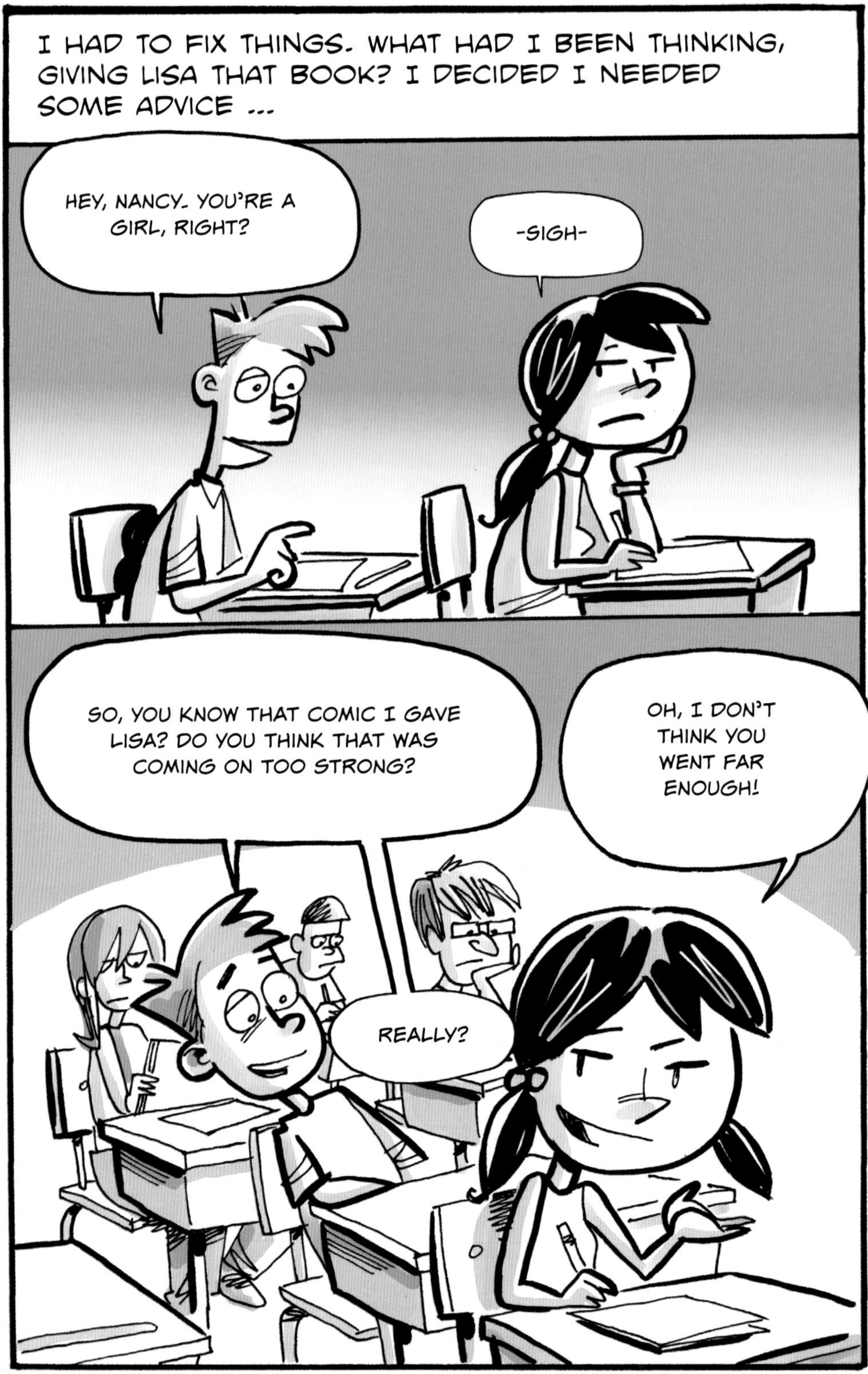
I HAD TO FIX THINGS. WHAT HAD I BEEN THINKING, GIVING LISA THAT BOOK? I DECIDED I NEEDED SOME ADVICE ...
HEY, NANCY. YOU'RE A GIRL, RIGHT?
-SIGH-
SO, YOU KNOW THAT COMIC I GAVE LISA? DO YOU THINK THAT WAS COMING ON TOO STRONG?
OH, I DON'T THINK YOU WENT FAR ENOUGH!
REALLY?

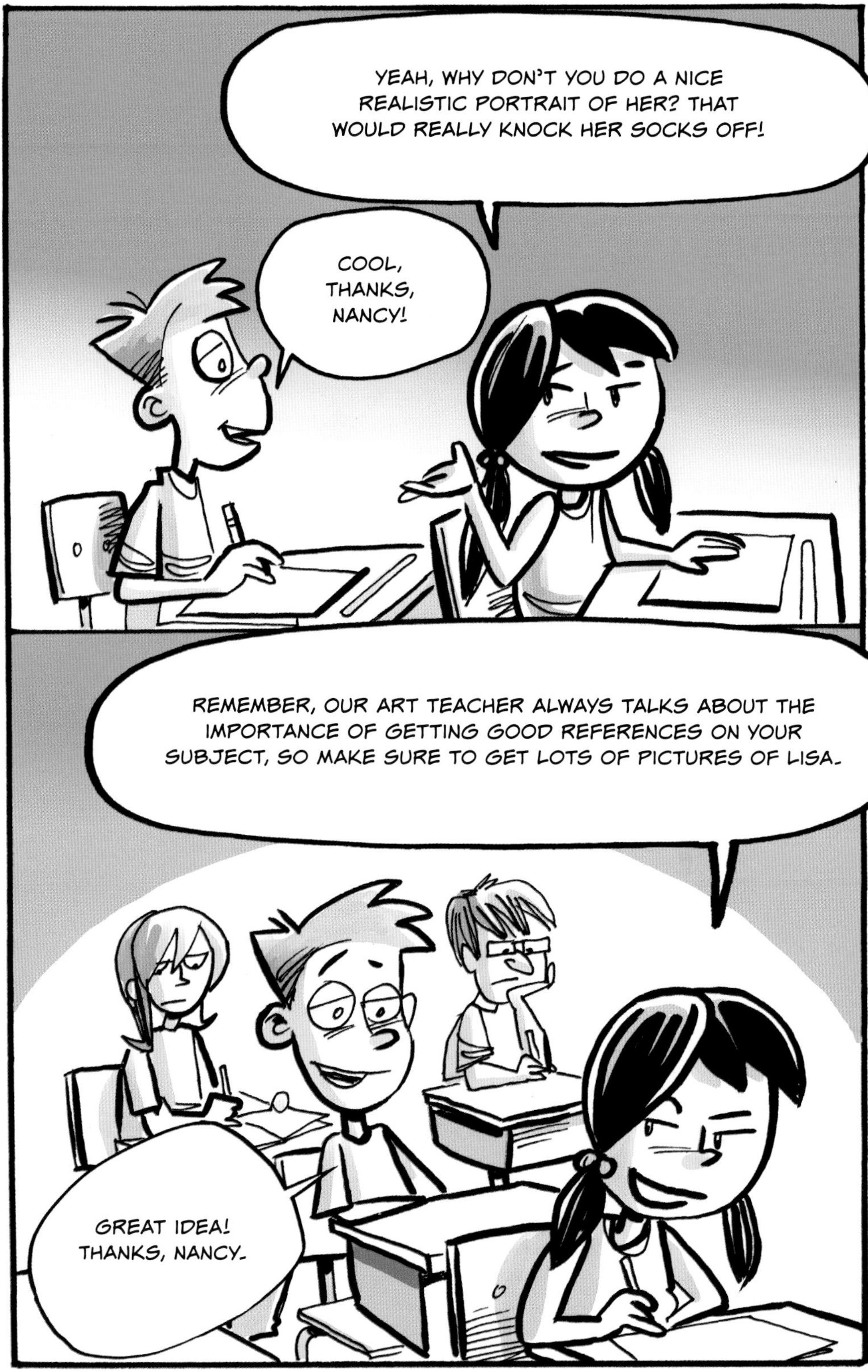
YEAH, WHY DON'T YOU DO A NICE REALISTIC PORTRAIT OF HER? THAT WOULD REALLY KNOCK HER SOCKS OFF!
COOL, THANKS, NANCY!
REMEMBER, OUR ART TEACHER ALWAYS TALKS ABOUT THE IMPORTANCE OF GETTING GOOD REFERENCES ON YOUR SUBJECT, SO MAKE SURE TO GET LOTS OF PICTURES OF LISA.
GREAT IDEA! THANKS, NANCY.

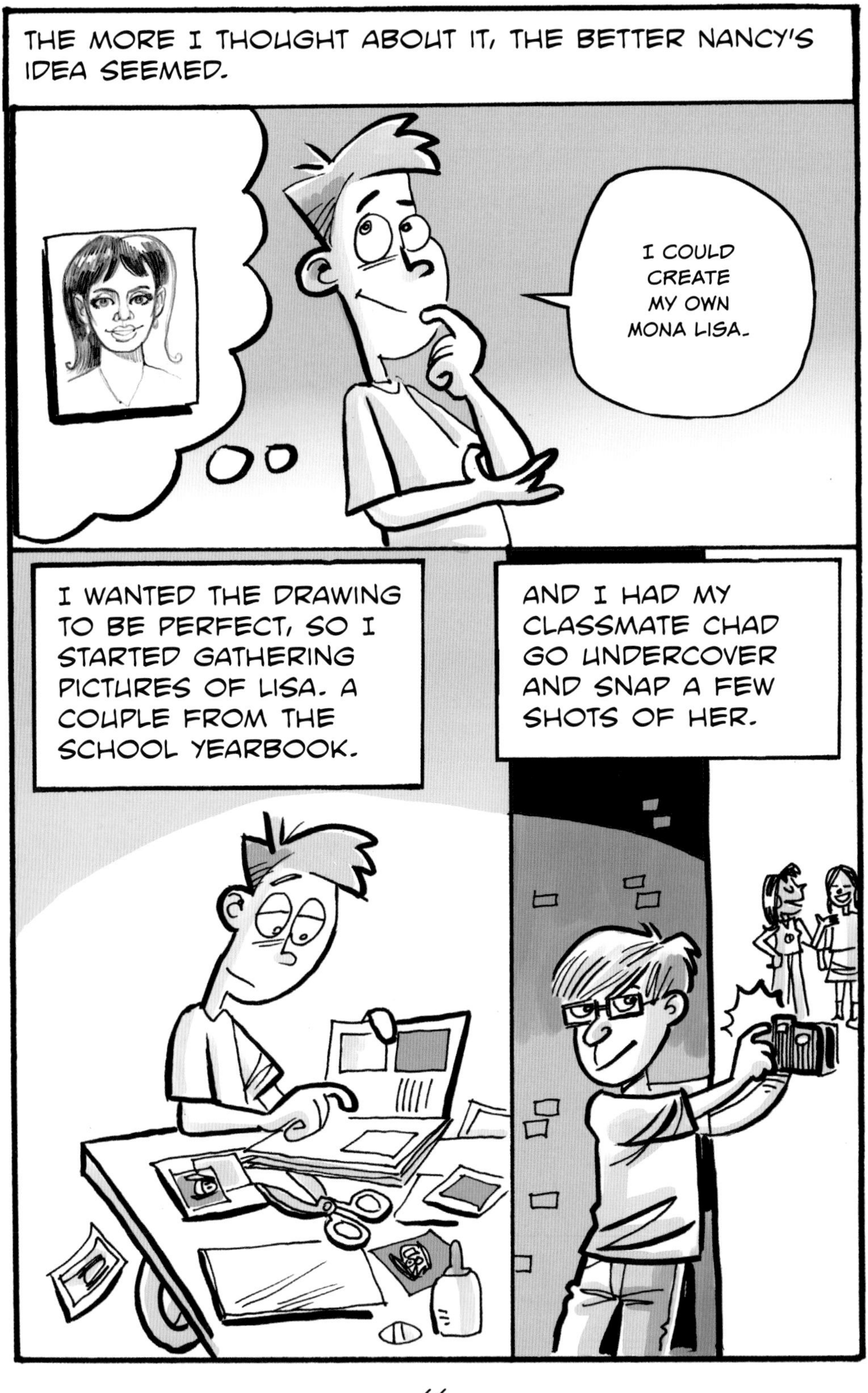
THE MORE I THOUGHT ABOUT IT, THE BETTER NANCY'S IDEA SEEMED.
I COULD CREATE MY OWN MONA LISA.
I WANTED THE DRAWING TO BE PERFECT, SO I STARTED GATHERING PICTURES OF LISA. A COUPLE FROM THE SCHOOL YEARBOOK.
AND I HAD MY CLASSMATE CHAD GO UNDERCOVER AND SNAP A FEW SHOTS OF HER.

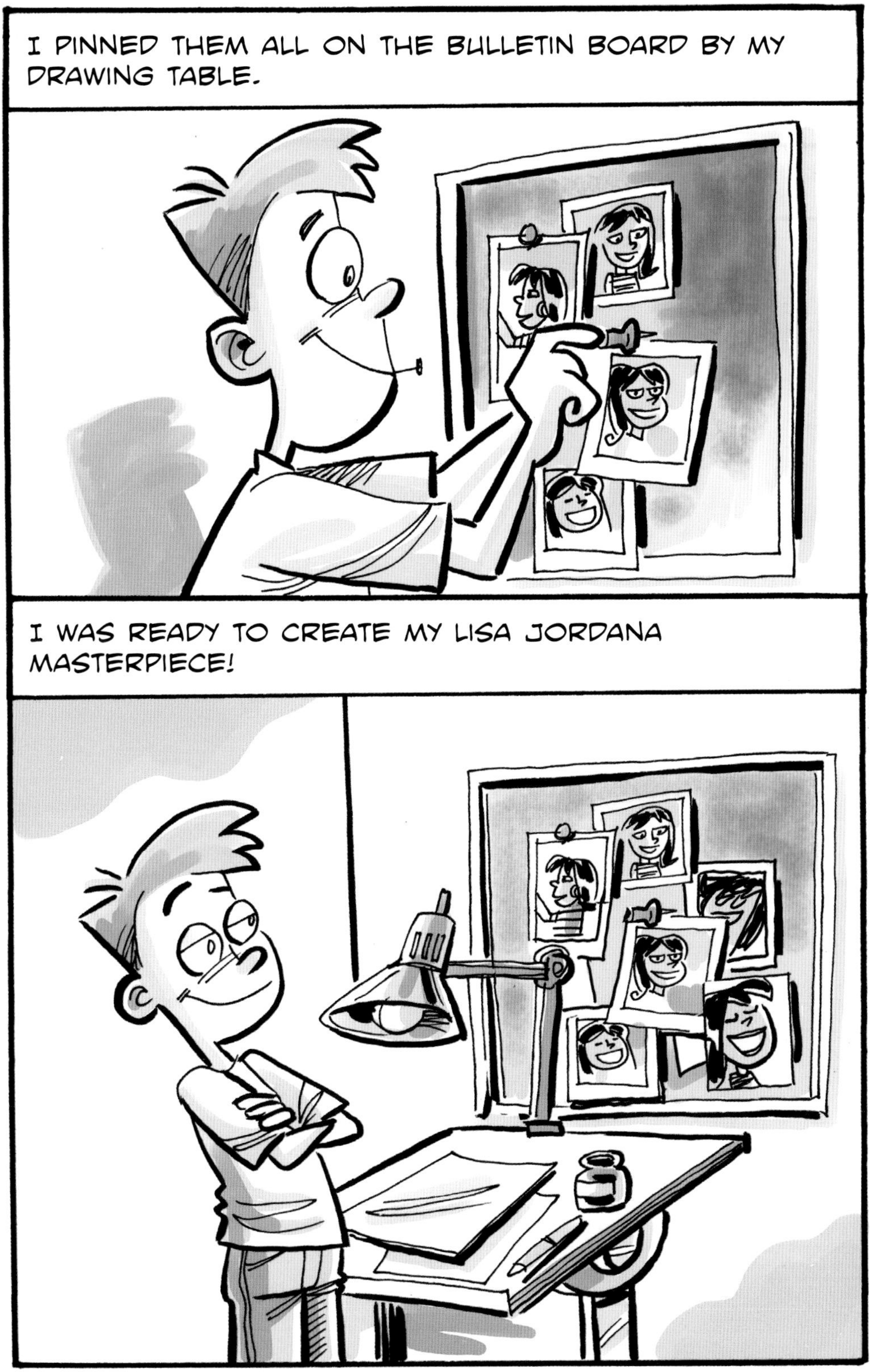
I PINNED THEM ALL ON THE BULLETIN BOARD BY MY DRAWING TABLE.
I WAS READY TO CREATE MY LISA JORDANA MASTERPIECE!

CHAPTER 5: GET OUTTA TOWN

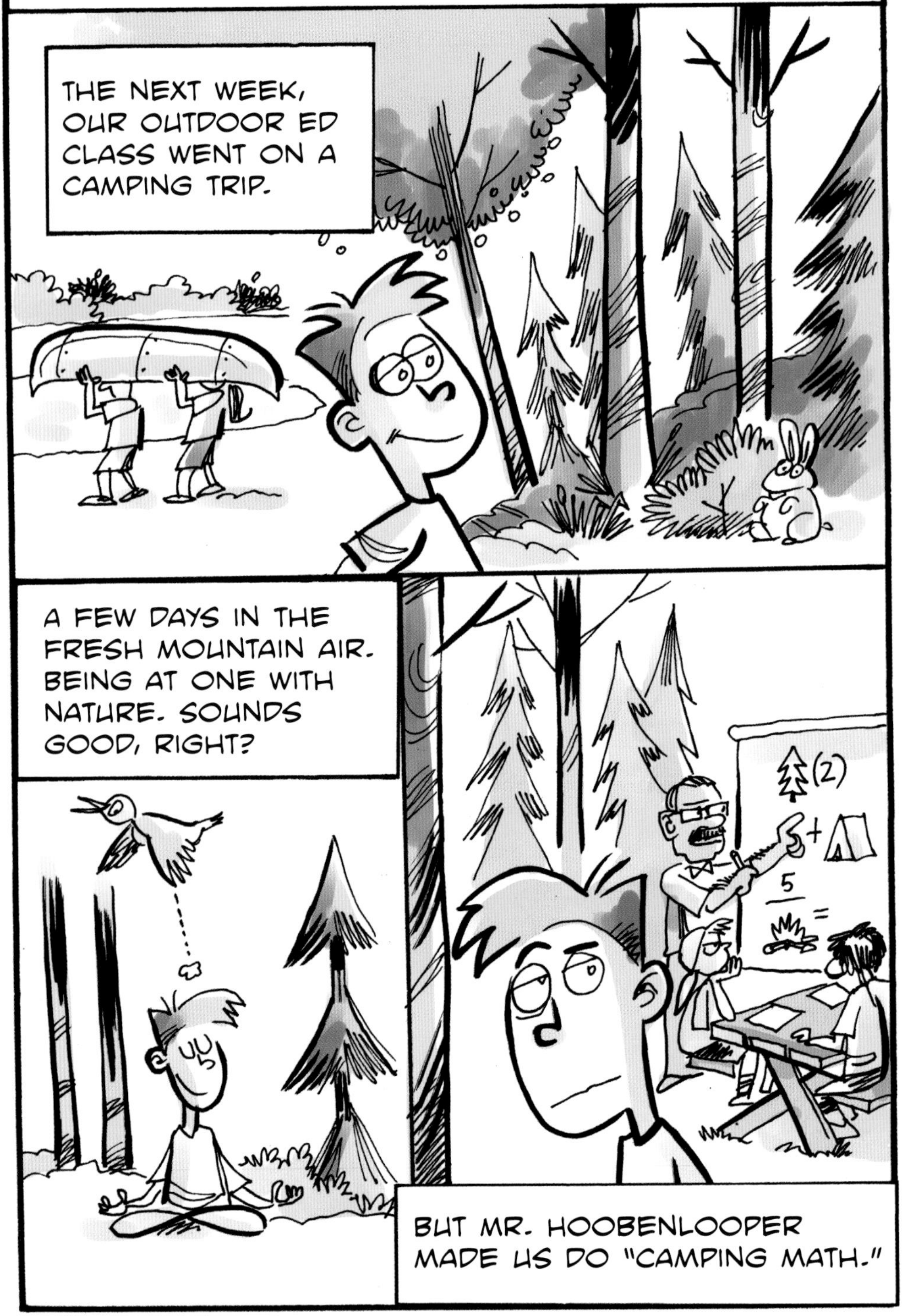
THE NEXT WEEK, OUR OUTDOOR ED CLASS WENT ON A CAMPING TRIP.
A FEW DAYS IN THE FRESH MOUNTAIN AIR. BEING AT ONE WITH NATURE. SOUNDS GOOD, RIGHT?
BUT MR. HOOBENLOOPER MADE US DO "CAMPING MATH."

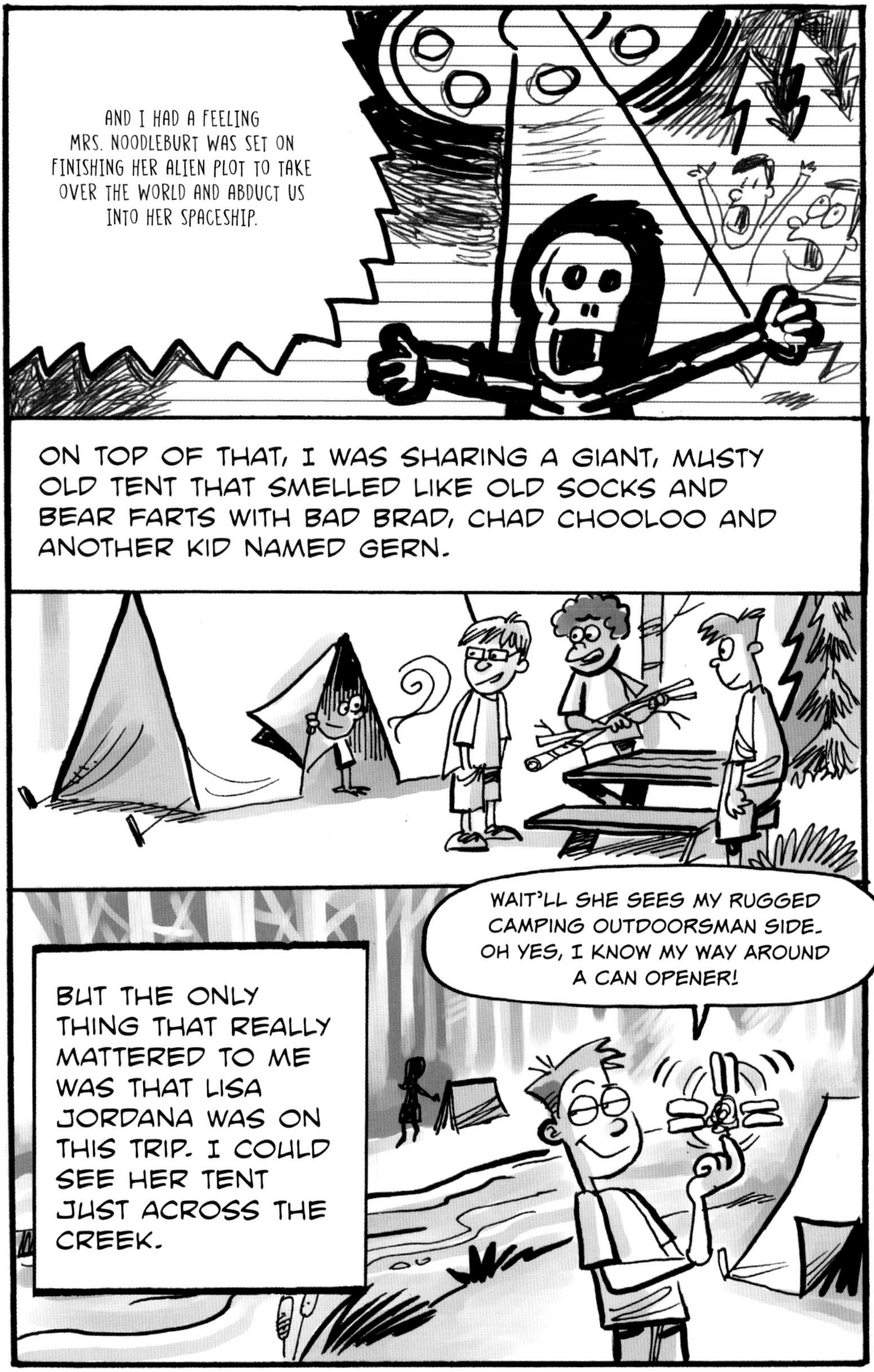
AND I HAD A FEELING MRS. NOODLEBURT WAS SET ON FINISHING HER ALIEN PLOT TO TAKE OVER THE WORLD AND ABDUCT US INTO HER SPACESHIP.
ON TOP OF THAT, I WAS SHARING A GIANT, MUSTY OLD TENT THAT SMELLED LIKE OLD SOCKS AND BEAR FARTS WITH BAD BRAD, CHAD CHOOLOO AND ANOTHER KID NAMED GERN.
BUT THE ONLY THING THAT REALLY MATTERED TO ME WAS THAT LISA JORDANA WAS ON THIS TRIP. I COULD SEE HER TENT JUST ACROSS THE CREEK.
WAIT'LL SHE SEES MY RUGGED CAMPING OUTDOORSMAN SIDE. OH YES, I KNOW MY WAY AROUND A CAN OPENER!

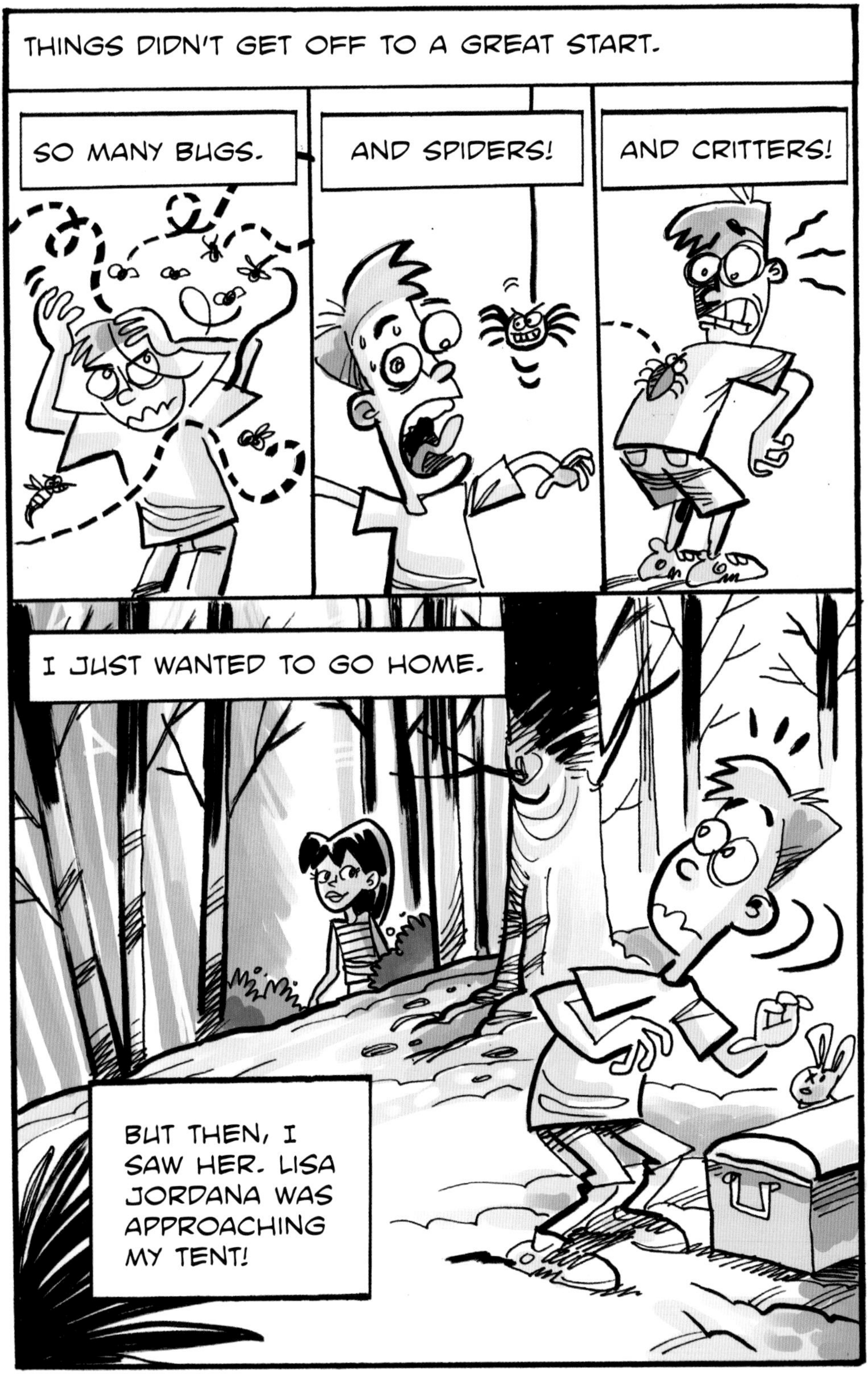
THINGS DIDN'T GET OFF TO A GREAT START.
SO MANY BUGS.
AND SPIDERS!
AND CRITTERS!
I JUST WANTED TO GO HOME.
BUT THEN, I SAW HER. LISA JORDANA WAS APPROACHING MY TENT!

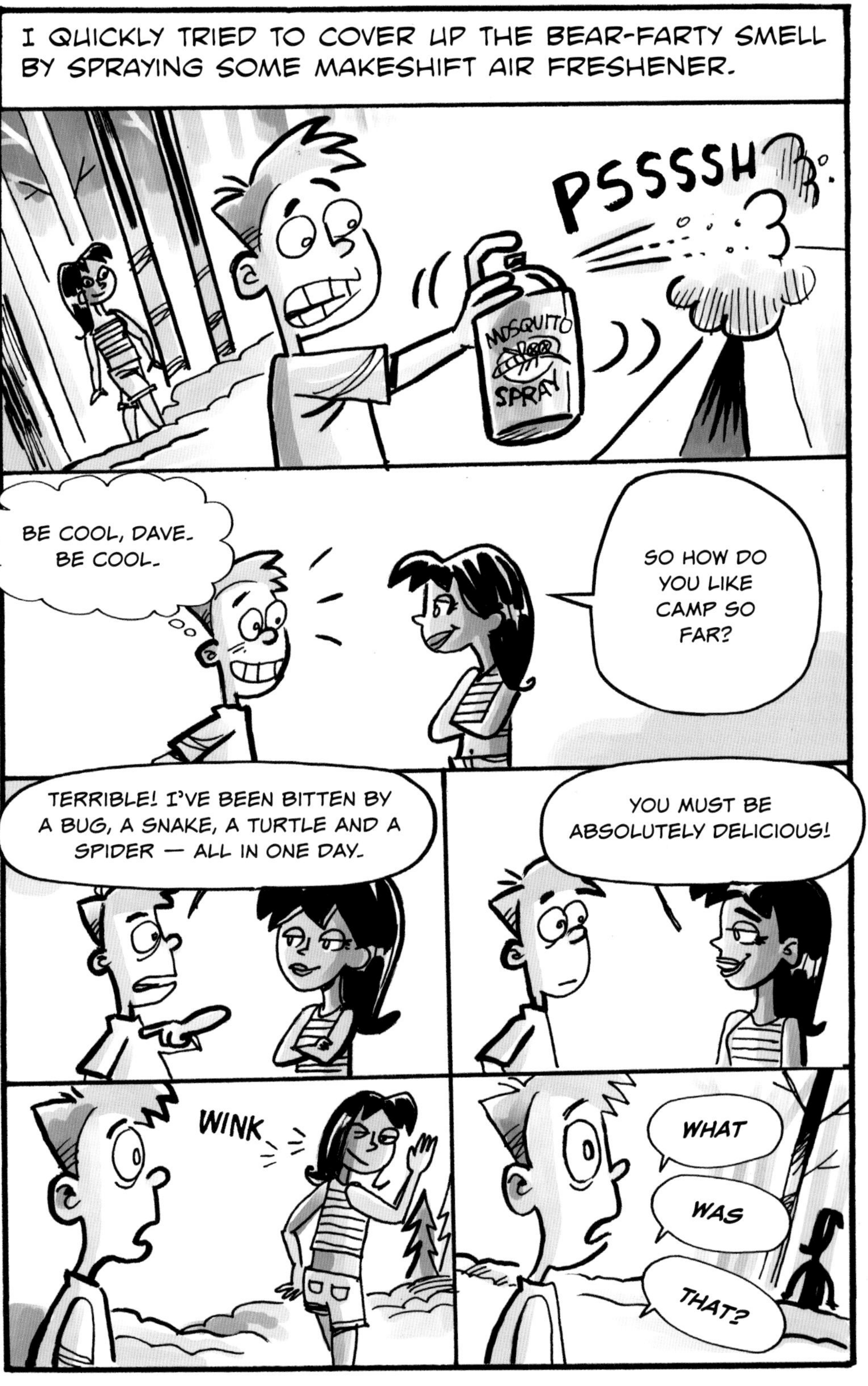
I QUICKLY TRIED TO COVER UP THE BEAR-FARTY SMELL BY SPRAYING SOME MAKESHIFT AIR FRESHENER.
PSSSSH
MOSQUITO SPRAY
BE COOL, DAVE. BE COOL.
SO HOW DO YOU LIKE CAMP SO FAR?
TERRIBLE! I'VE BEEN BITTEN BY A BUG, A SNAKE, A TURTLE AND A SPIDER — ALL IN ONE DAY.
YOU MUST BE ABSOLUTELY DELICIOUS!
WINK
WHAT
WAS
THAT?

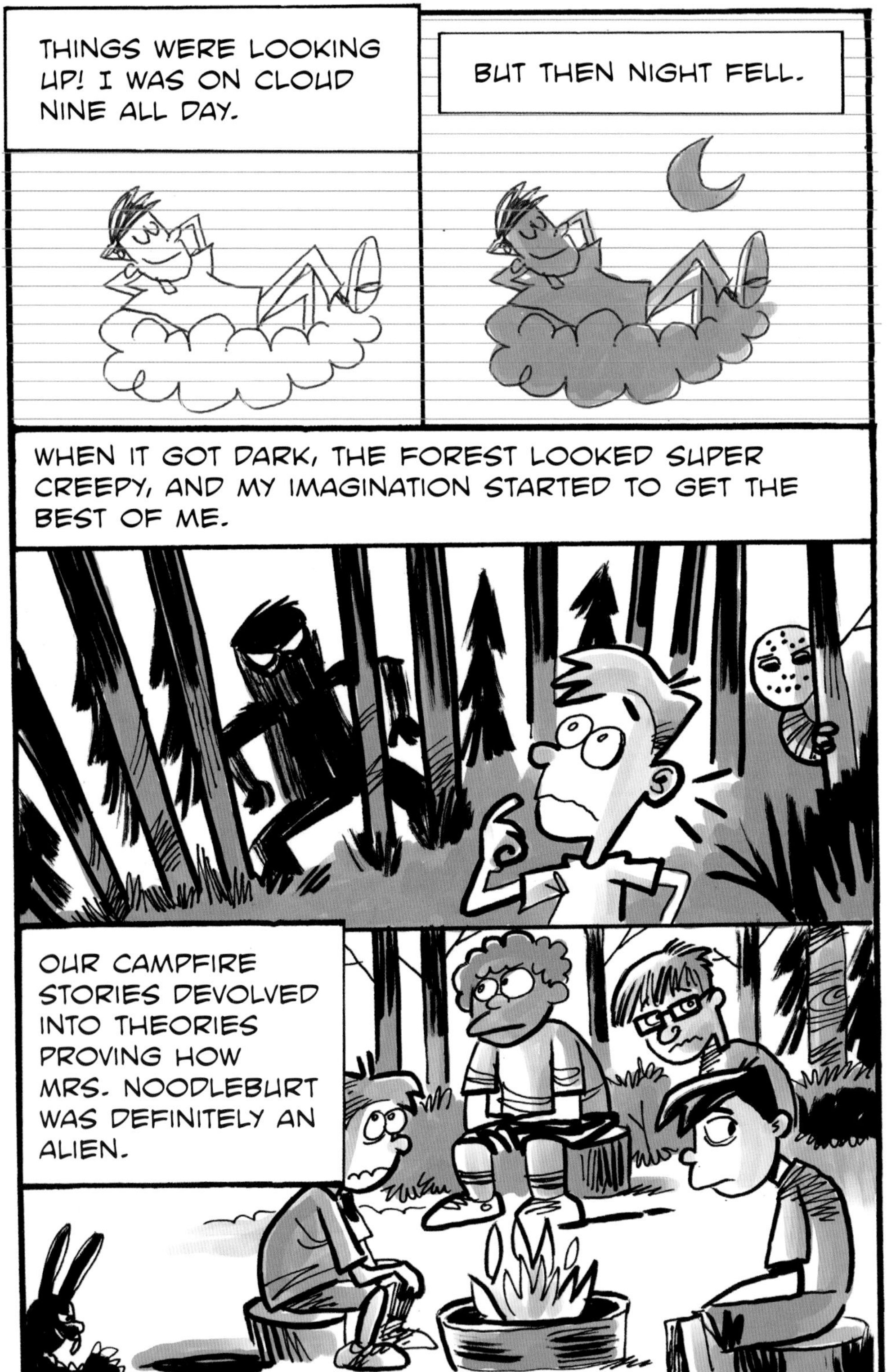
THINGS WERE LOOKING UP! I WAS ON CLOUD NINE ALL DAY.
BUT THEN NIGHT FELL.
WHEN IT GOT DARK, THE FOREST LOOKED SUPER CREEPY, AND MY IMAGINATION STARTED TO GET THE BEST OF ME.
OUR CAMPFIRE STORIES DEVOLVED INTO THEORIES PROVING HOW MRS. NOODLEBURT WAS DEFINITELY AN ALIEN.

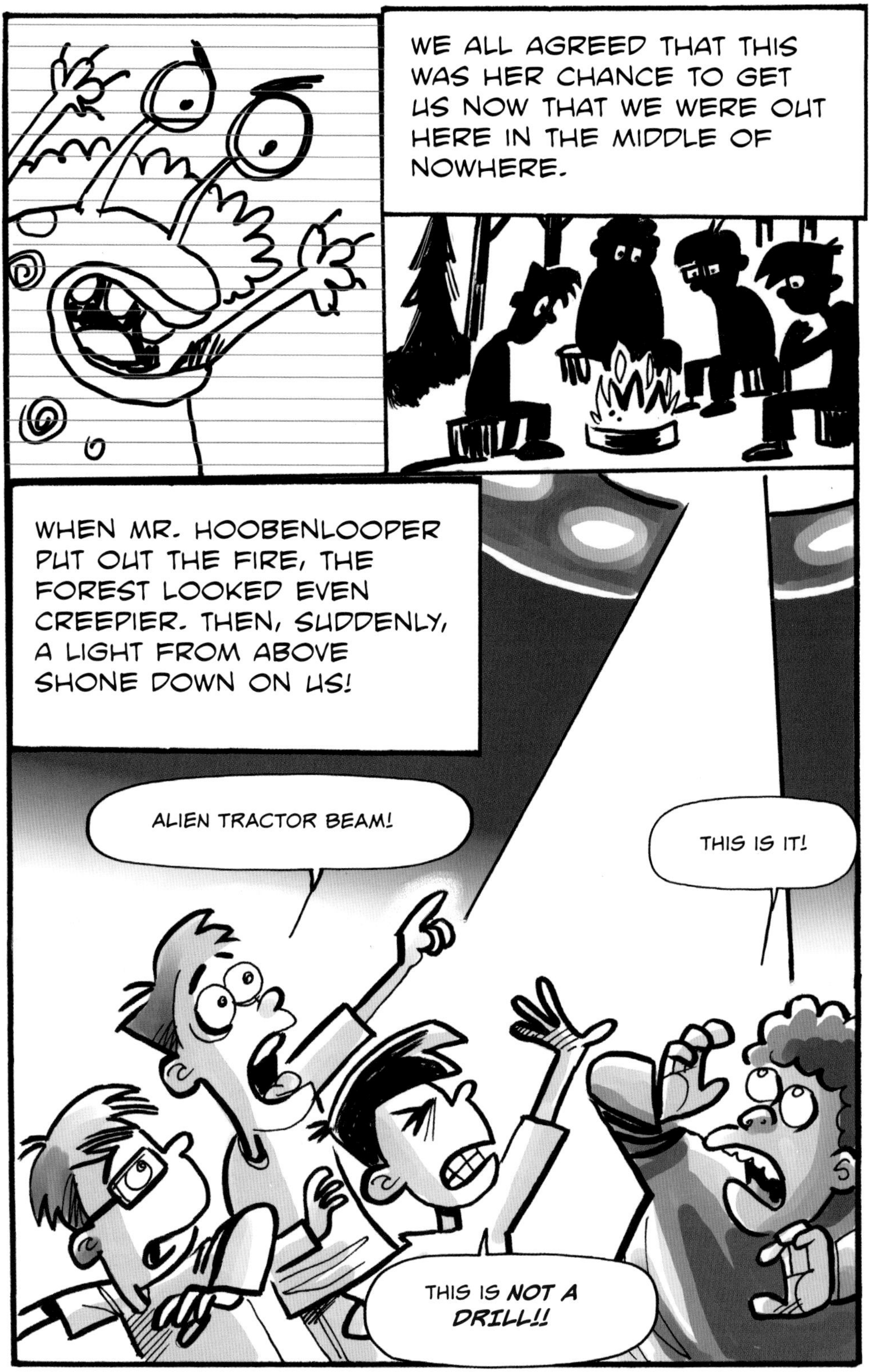

WE ALL AGREED THAT THIS WAS HER CHANCE TO GET US NOW THAT WE WERE OUT HERE IN THE MIDDLE OF NOWHERE.
WHEN MR. HOOBENLOOPER PUT OUT THE FIRE, THE FOREST LOOKED EVEN CREEPIER. THEN, SUDDENLY, A LIGHT FROM ABOVE SHONE DOWN ON US!
ALIEN TRACTOR BEAM!
THIS IS IT!
THIS IS *NOT A DRILL!!*

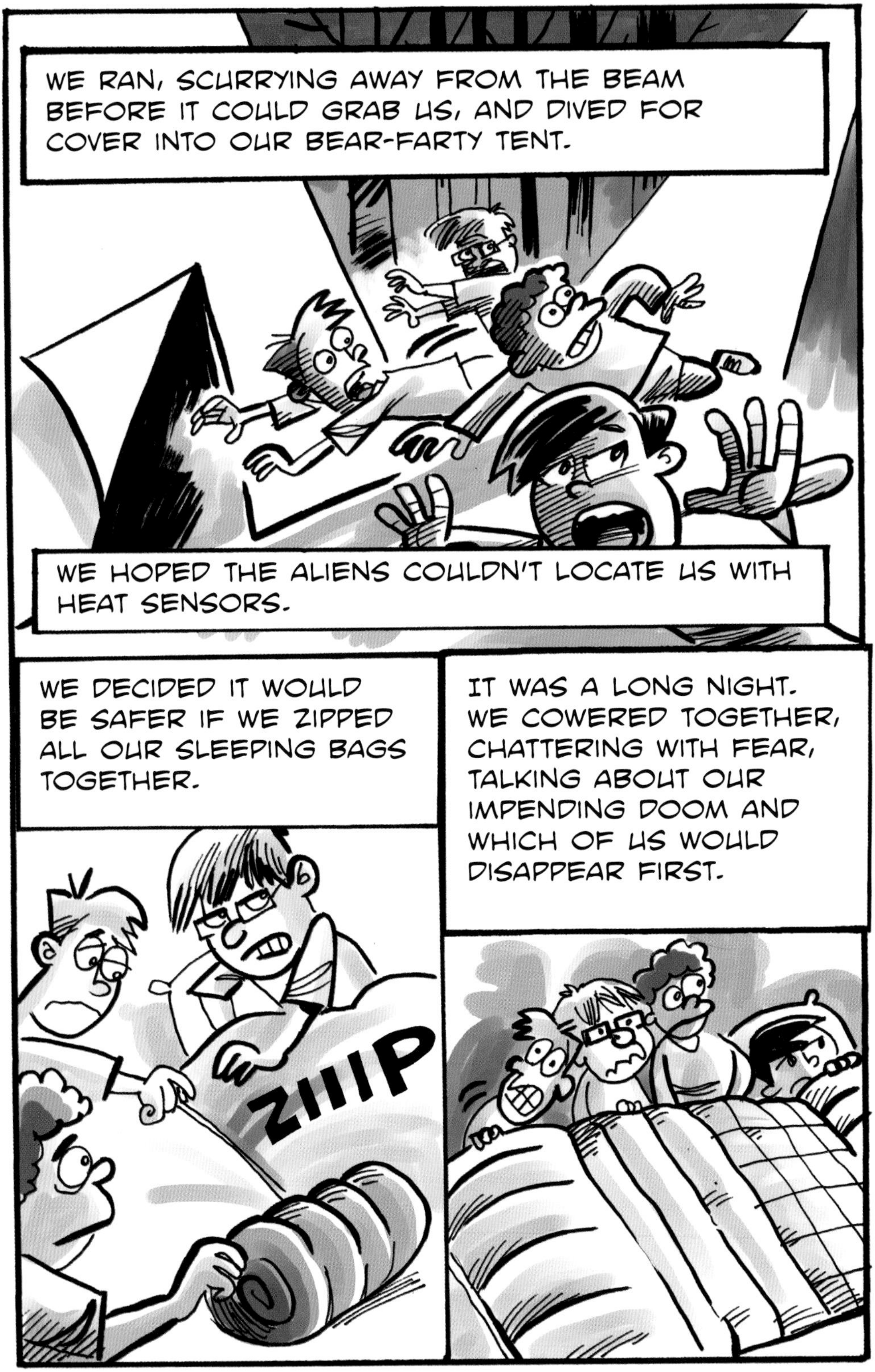
WE RAN, SCURRYING AWAY FROM THE BEAM BEFORE IT COULD GRAB US, AND DIVED FOR COVER INTO OUR BEAR-FARTY TENT.
WE HOPED THE ALIENS COULDN'T LOCATE US WITH HEAT SENSORS.
WE DECIDED IT WOULD BE SAFER IF WE ZIPPED ALL OUR SLEEPING BAGS TOGETHER.
ZIIIP
IT WAS A LONG NIGHT. WE COWERED TOGETHER, CHATTERING WITH FEAR, TALKING ABOUT OUR IMPENDING DOOM AND WHICH OF US WOULD DISAPPEAR FIRST.

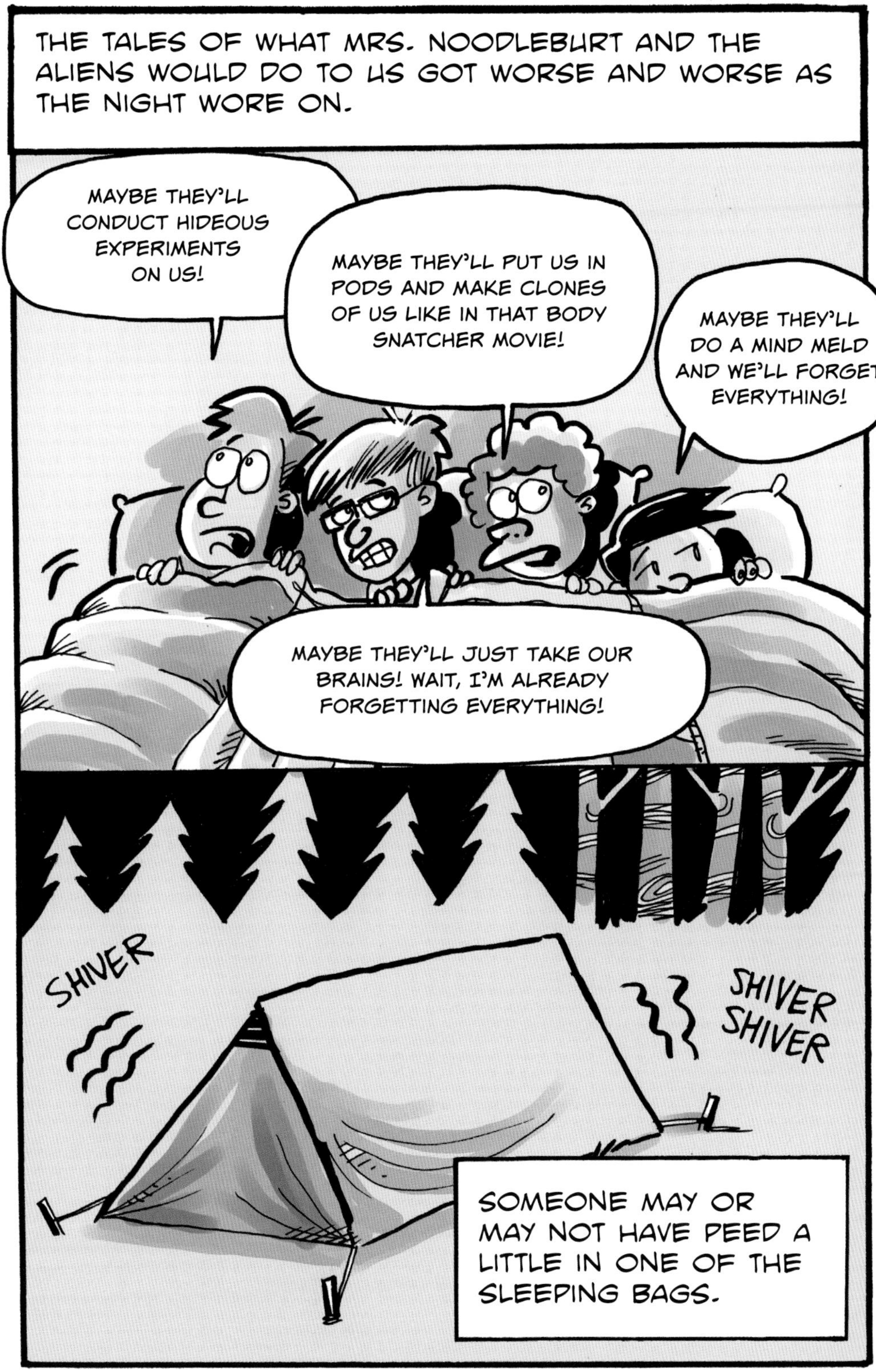
THE TALES OF WHAT MRS. NOODLEBURT AND THE ALIENS WOULD DO TO US GOT WORSE AND WORSE AS THE NIGHT WORE ON.
MAYBE THEY'LL CONDUCT HIDEOUS EXPERIMENTS ON US!
MAYBE THEY'LL PUT US IN PODS AND MAKE CLONES OF US LIKE IN THAT BODY SNATCHER MOVIE!
MAYBE THEY'LL DO A MIND MELD AND WE'LL FORGET EVERYTHING!
MAYBE THEY'LL JUST TAKE OUR BRAINS! WAIT, I'M ALREADY FORGETTING EVERYTHING!
SHIVER
SHIVER SHIVER
SOMEONE MAY OR MAY NOT HAVE PEED A LITTLE IN ONE OF THE SLEEPING BAGS.

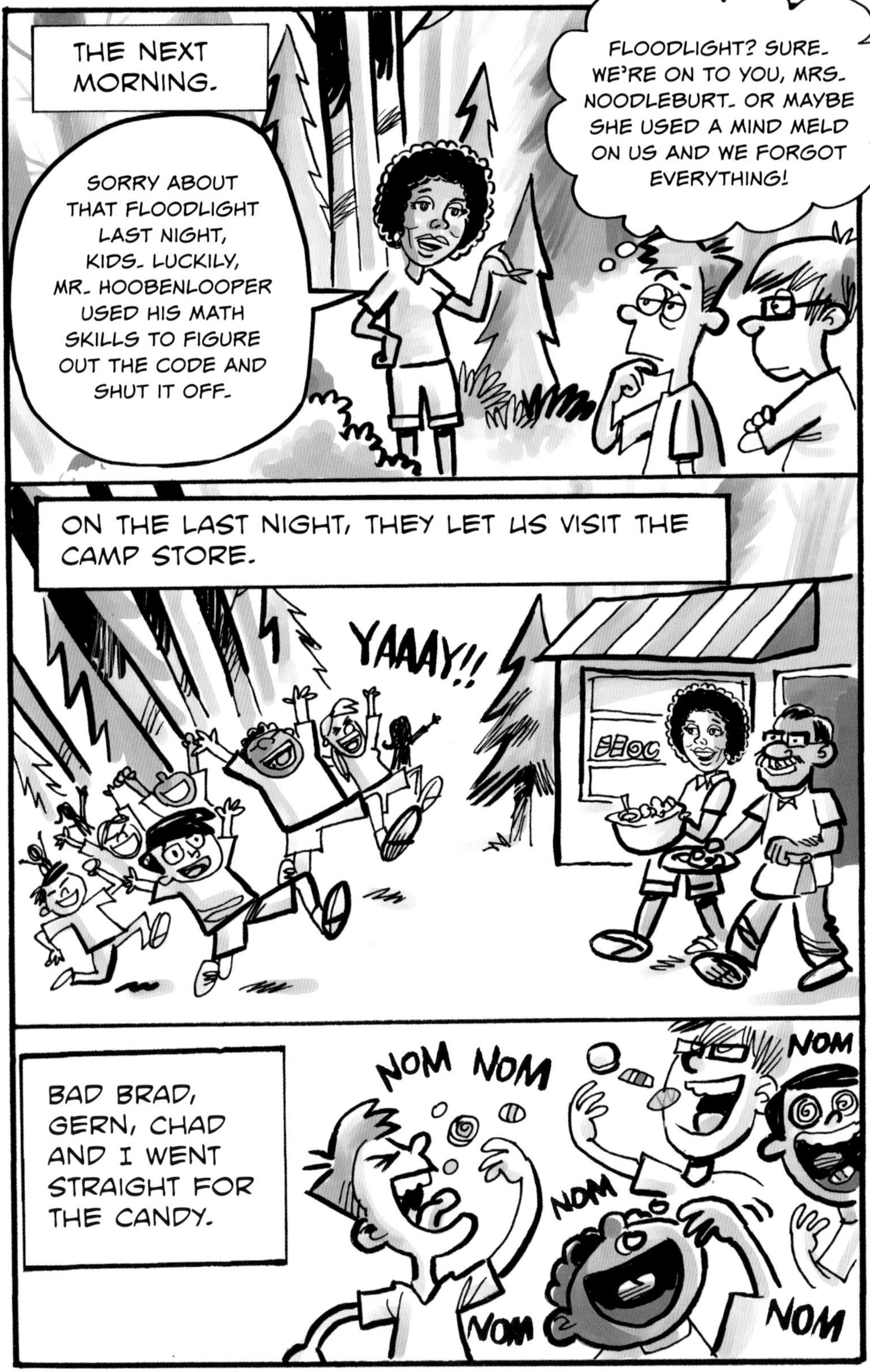
THE NEXT MORNING.
SORRY ABOUT THAT FLOODLIGHT LAST NIGHT, KIDS. LUCKILY, MR. HOOBENLOOPER USED HIS MATH SKILLS TO FIGURE OUT THE CODE AND SHUT IT OFF.
FLOODLIGHT? SURE. WE'RE ON TO YOU, MRS. NOODLEBURT. OR MAYBE SHE USED A MIND MELD ON US AND WE FORGOT EVERYTHING!
ON THE LAST NIGHT, THEY LET US VISIT THE CAMP STORE.
YAAAY!!
BAD BRAD, GERN, CHAD AND I WENT STRAIGHT FOR THE CANDY.
NOM NOM
NOM
NOM
NOM
NOM
NOM

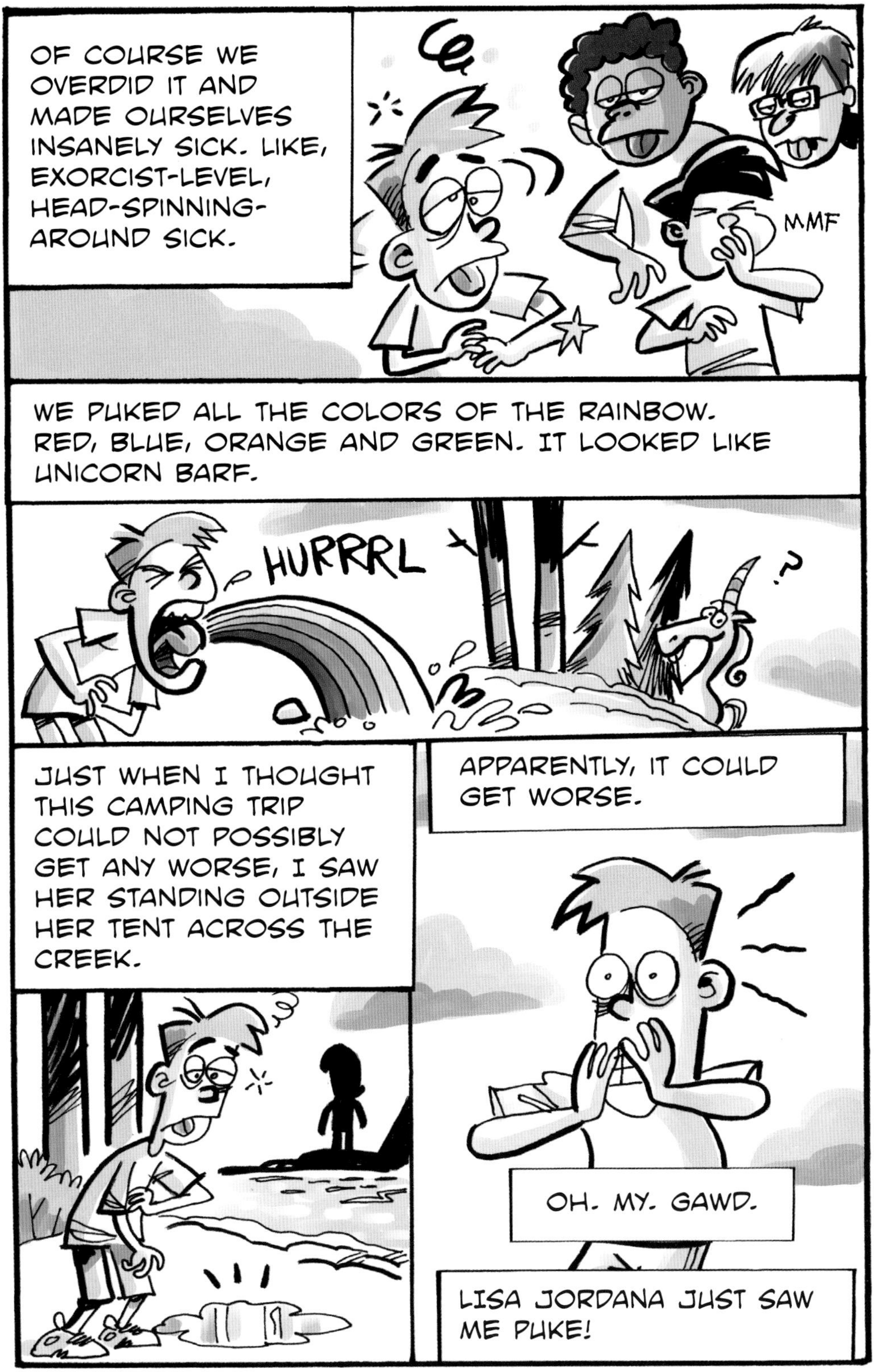

OF COURSE WE OVERDID IT AND MADE OURSELVES INSANELY SICK. LIKE, EXORCIST-LEVEL, HEAD-SPINNING-AROUND SICK.
MMF
WE PUKED ALL THE COLORS OF THE RAINBOW. RED, BLUE, ORANGE AND GREEN. IT LOOKED LIKE UNICORN BARF.
HURRRL
?
JUST WHEN I THOUGHT THIS CAMPING TRIP COULD NOT POSSIBLY GET ANY WORSE, I SAW HER STANDING OUTSIDE HER TENT ACROSS THE CREEK.
APPARENTLY, IT COULD GET WORSE.
OH. MY. GAWD.
LISA JORDANA JUST SAW ME PUKE!

CHAPTER 6: ACTUALLY GLAD TO BE BACK IN MUDDLE!

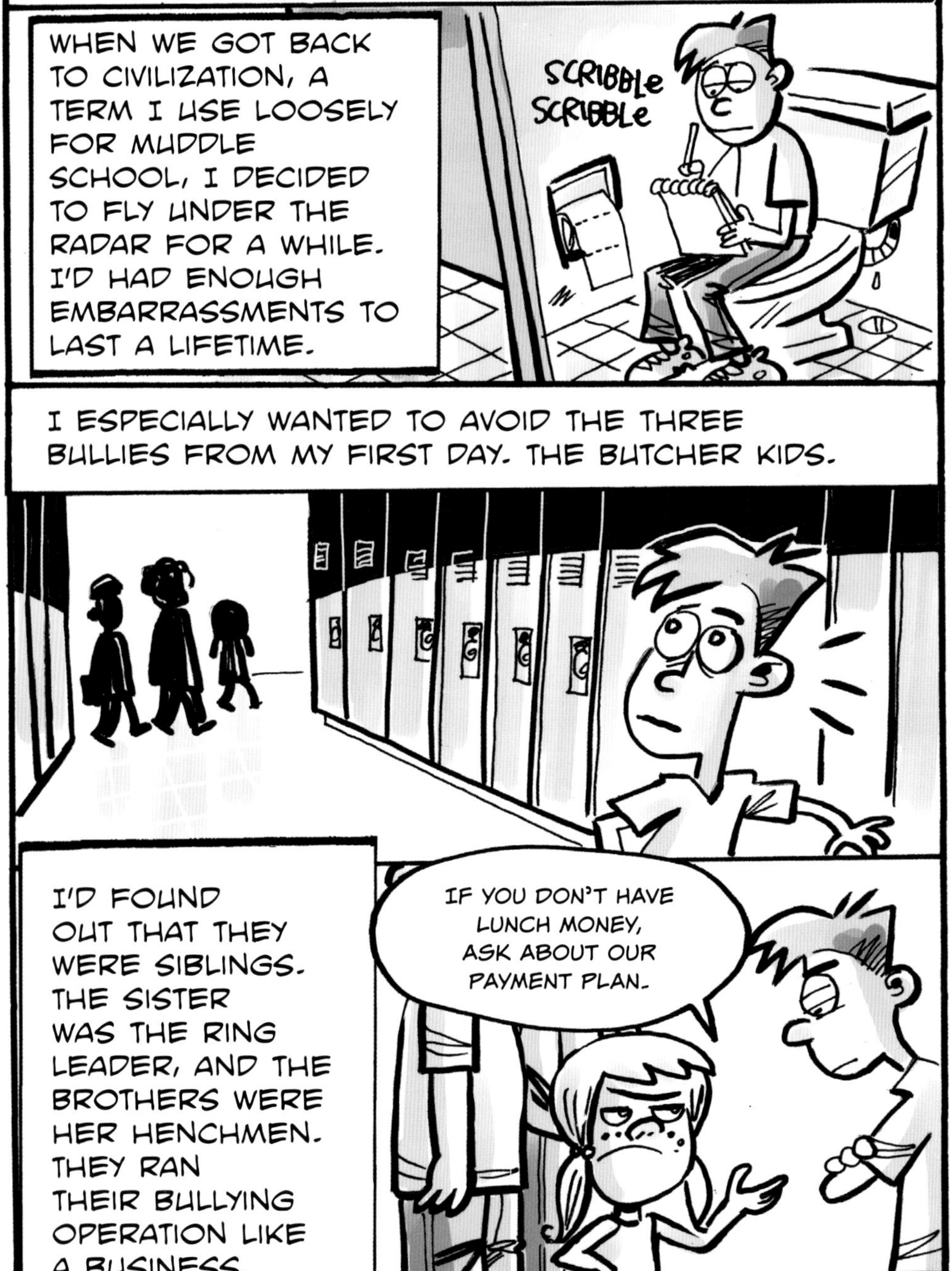

WHEN WE GOT BACK TO CIVILIZATION, A TERM I USE LOOSELY FOR MUDDLE SCHOOL, I DECIDED TO FLY UNDER THE RADAR FOR A WHILE. I'D HAD ENOUGH EMBARRASSMENTS TO LAST A LIFETIME.
SCRIBBLE SCRIBBLE
I ESPECIALLY WANTED TO AVOID THE THREE BULLIES FROM MY FIRST DAY. THE BUTCHER KIDS.
I'D FOUND OUT THAT THEY WERE SIBLINGS. THE SISTER WAS THE RING LEADER, AND THE BROTHERS WERE HER HENCHMEN. THEY RAN THEIR BULLYING OPERATION LIKE A BUSINESS.
IF YOU DON'T HAVE LUNCH MONEY, ASK ABOUT OUR PAYMENT PLAN.

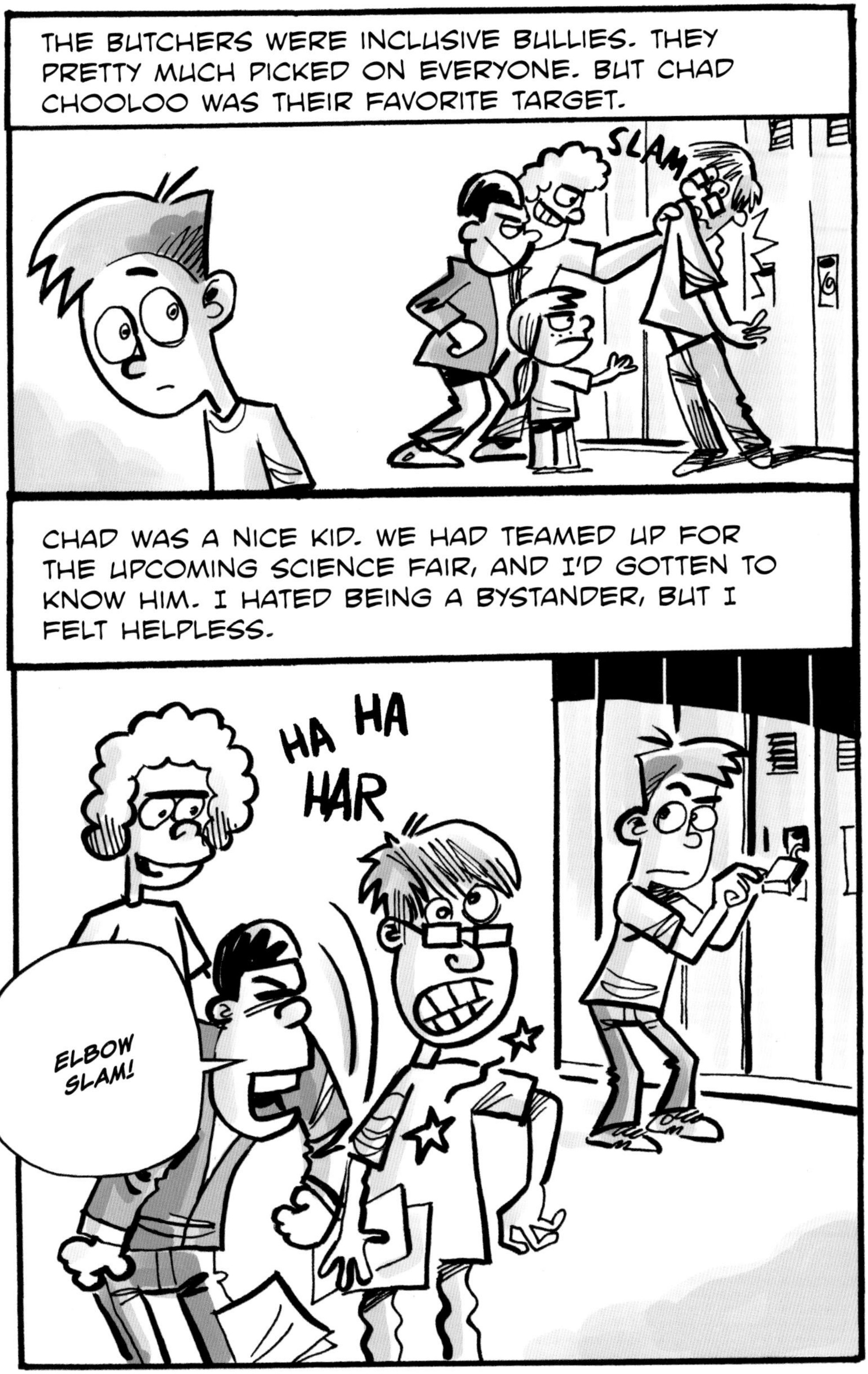
THE BUTCHERS WERE INCLUSIVE BULLIES. THEY PRETTY MUCH PICKED ON EVERYONE. BUT CHAD CHOOLOO WAS THEIR FAVORITE TARGET.
SLAM
CHAD WAS A NICE KID. WE HAD TEAMED UP FOR THE UPCOMING SCIENCE FAIR, AND I'D GOTTEN TO KNOW HIM. I HATED BEING A BYSTANDER, BUT I FELT HELPLESS.
HA HA
HAR
ELBOW SLAM!

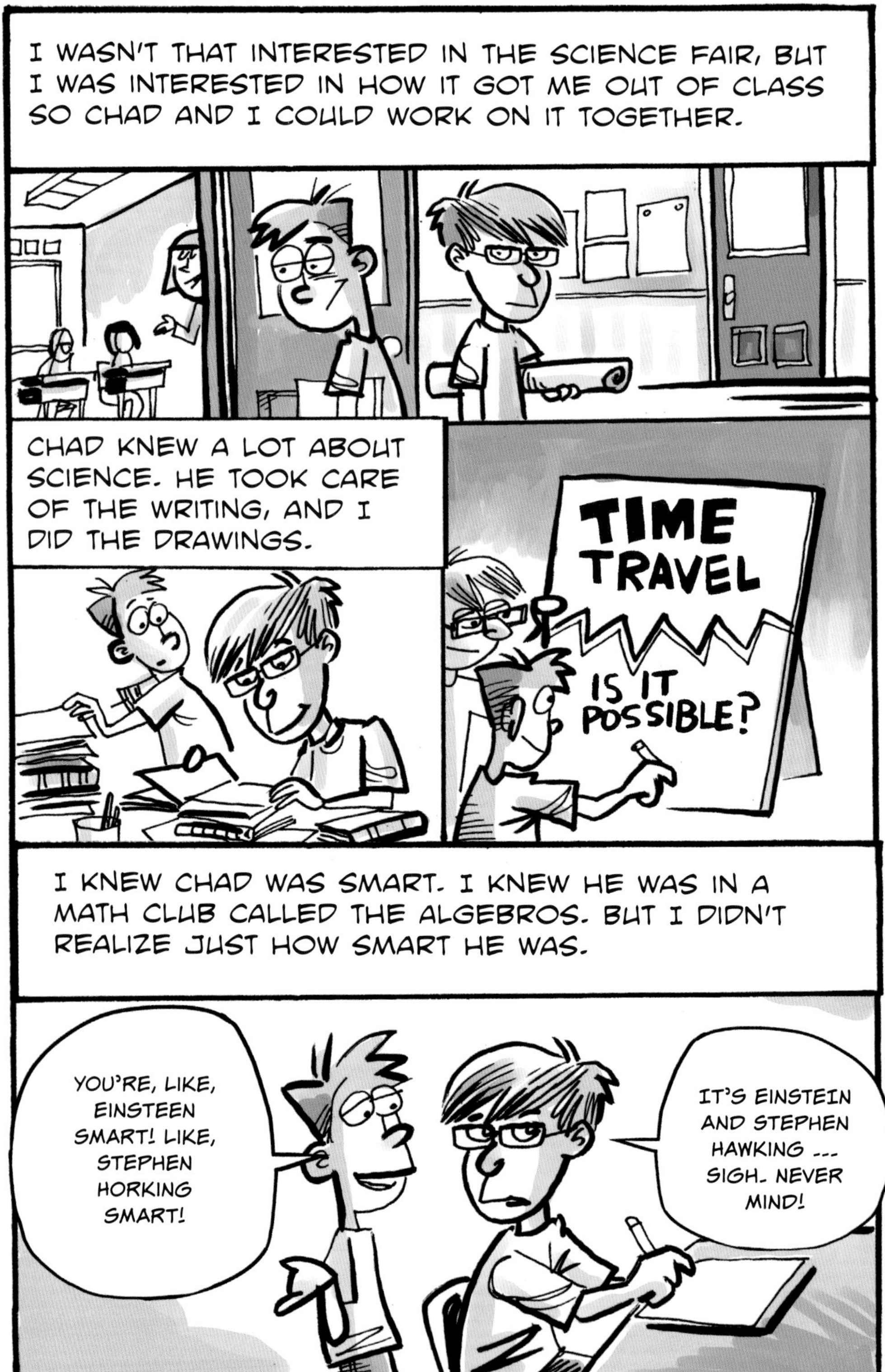
I WASN'T THAT INTERESTED IN THE SCIENCE FAIR, BUT I WAS INTERESTED IN HOW IT GOT ME OUT OF CLASS SO CHAD AND I COULD WORK ON IT TOGETHER.
CHAD KNEW A LOT ABOUT SCIENCE. HE TOOK CARE OF THE WRITING, AND I DID THE DRAWINGS.
TIME TRAVEL
IS IT POSSIBLE?
I KNEW CHAD WAS SMART. I KNEW HE WAS IN A MATH CLUB CALLED THE ALGEBROS. BUT I DIDN'T REALIZE JUST HOW SMART HE WAS.
YOU'RE, LIKE, EINSTEEN SMART! LIKE, STEPHEN HORKING SMART!
IT'S EINSTEIN AND STEPHEN HAWKING ... SIGH. NEVER MIND!

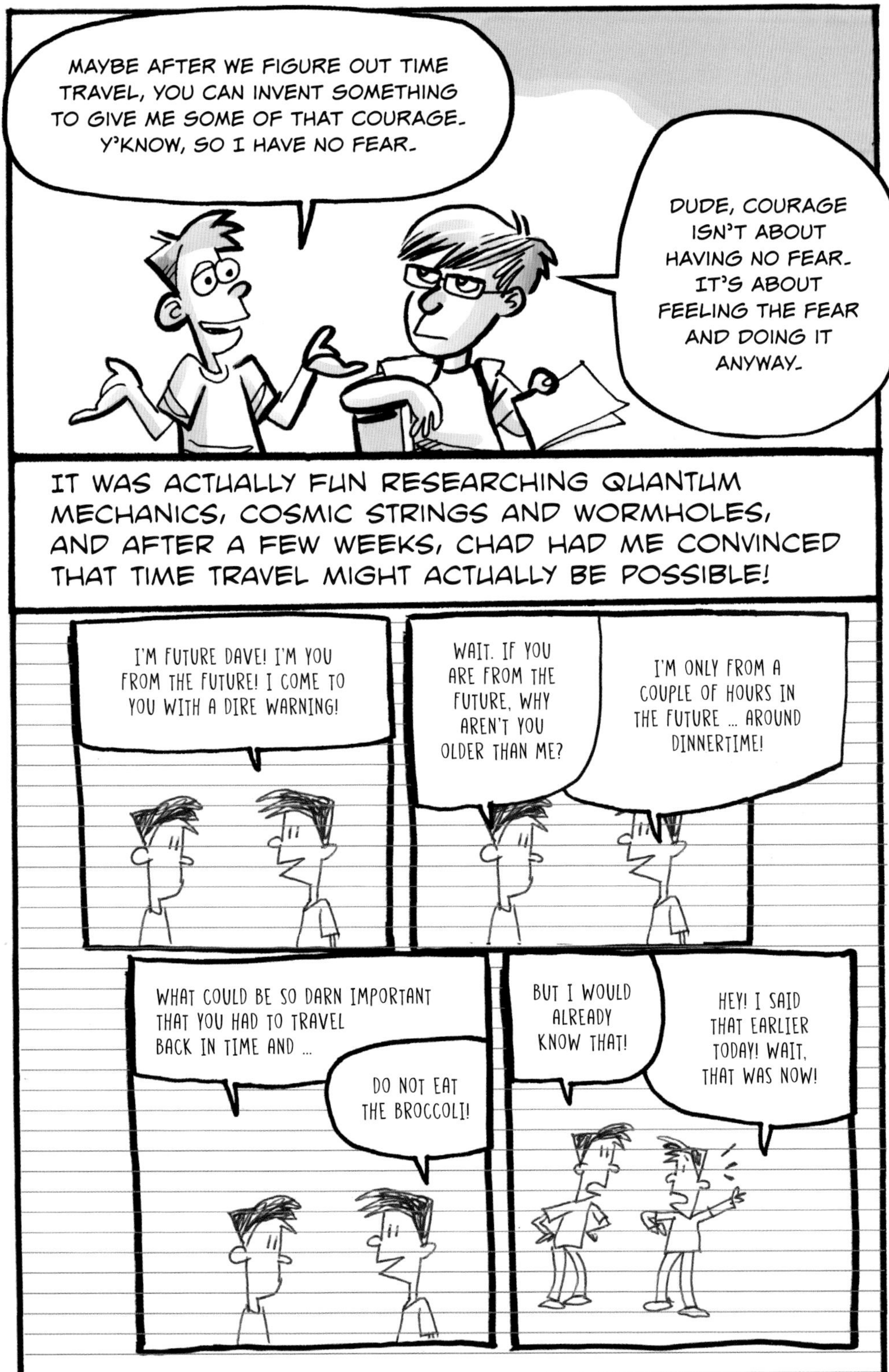
MAYBE AFTER WE FIGURE OUT TIME TRAVEL, YOU CAN INVENT SOMETHING TO GIVE ME SOME OF THAT COURAGE. Y'KNOW, SO I HAVE NO FEAR.
DUDE, COURAGE ISN'T ABOUT HAVING NO FEAR. IT'S ABOUT FEELING THE FEAR AND DOING IT ANYWAY.
IT WAS ACTUALLY FUN RESEARCHING QUANTUM MECHANICS, COSMIC STRINGS AND WORMHOLES, AND AFTER A FEW WEEKS, CHAD HAD ME CONVINCED THAT TIME TRAVEL MIGHT ACTUALLY BE POSSIBLE!
I'M FUTURE DAVE! I'M YOU FROM THE FUTURE! I COME TO YOU WITH A DIRE WARNING!
WAIT. IF YOU ARE FROM THE FUTURE, WHY AREN'T YOU OLDER THAN ME?
I'M ONLY FROM A COUPLE OF HOURS IN THE FUTURE ... AROUND DINNERTIME!
WHAT COULD BE SO DARN IMPORTANT THAT YOU HAD TO TRAVEL BACK IN TIME AND ...
DO NOT EAT THE BROCCOLI!
BUT I WOULD ALREADY KNOW THAT!
HEY! I SAID THAT EARLIER TODAY! WAIT, THAT WAS NOW!

CHAPTER 7: HAPPY BIRTHDAY TO ME

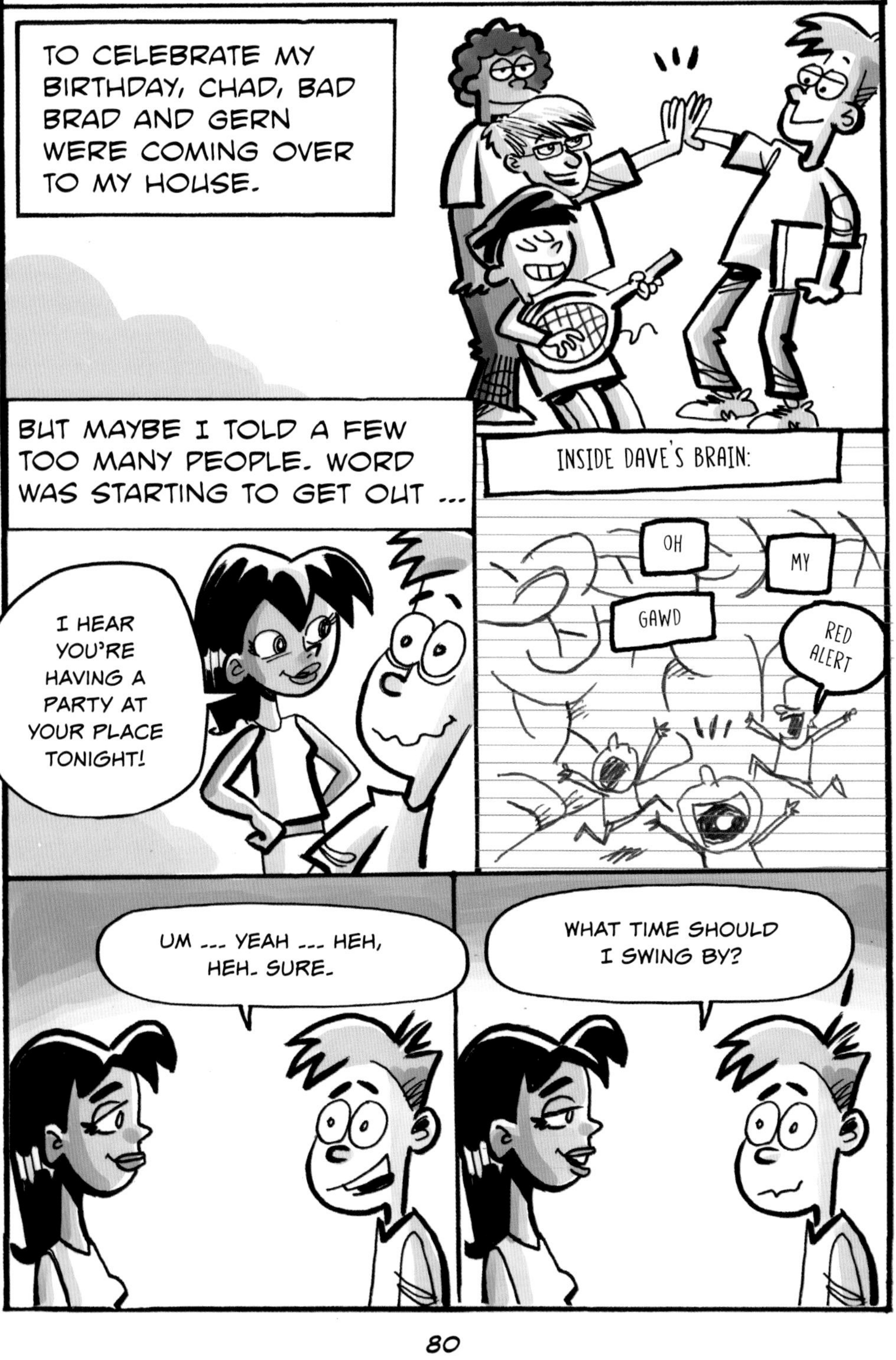
TO CELEBRATE MY BIRTHDAY, CHAD, BAD BRAD AND GERN WERE COMING OVER TO MY HOUSE.
BUT MAYBE I TOLD A FEW TOO MANY PEOPLE. WORD WAS STARTING TO GET OUT ...
I HEAR YOU'RE HAVING A PARTY AT YOUR PLACE TONIGHT!
INSIDE DAVE'S BRAIN:
OH
MY
GAWD
RED ALERT
UM ... YEAH ... HEH, HEH. SURE.
WHAT TIME SHOULD I SWING BY?

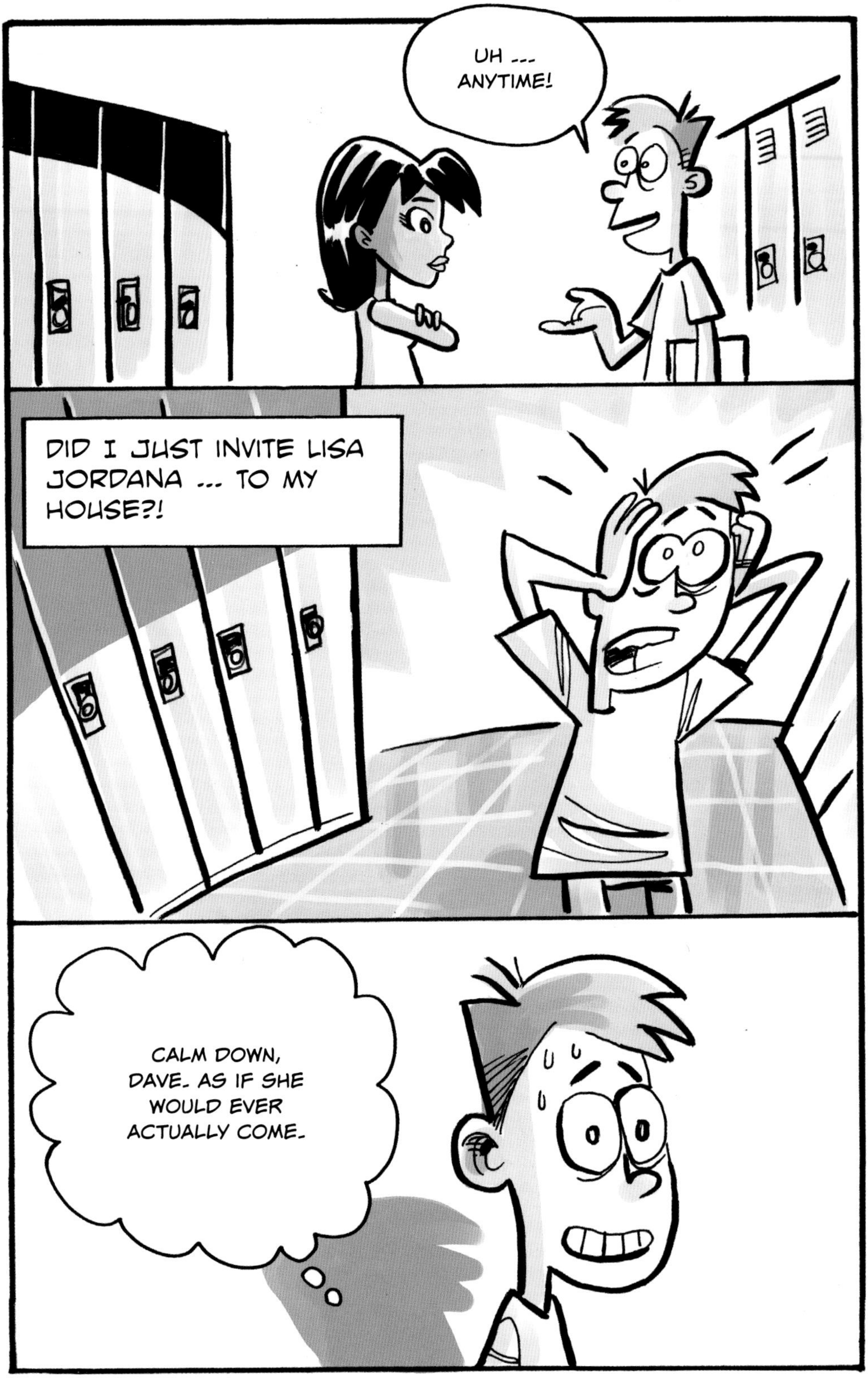
UH ---
ANYTIME!
DID I JUST INVITE LISA JORDANA --- TO MY HOUSE?!
CALM DOWN, DAVE. AS IF SHE WOULD EVER ACTUALLY COME.

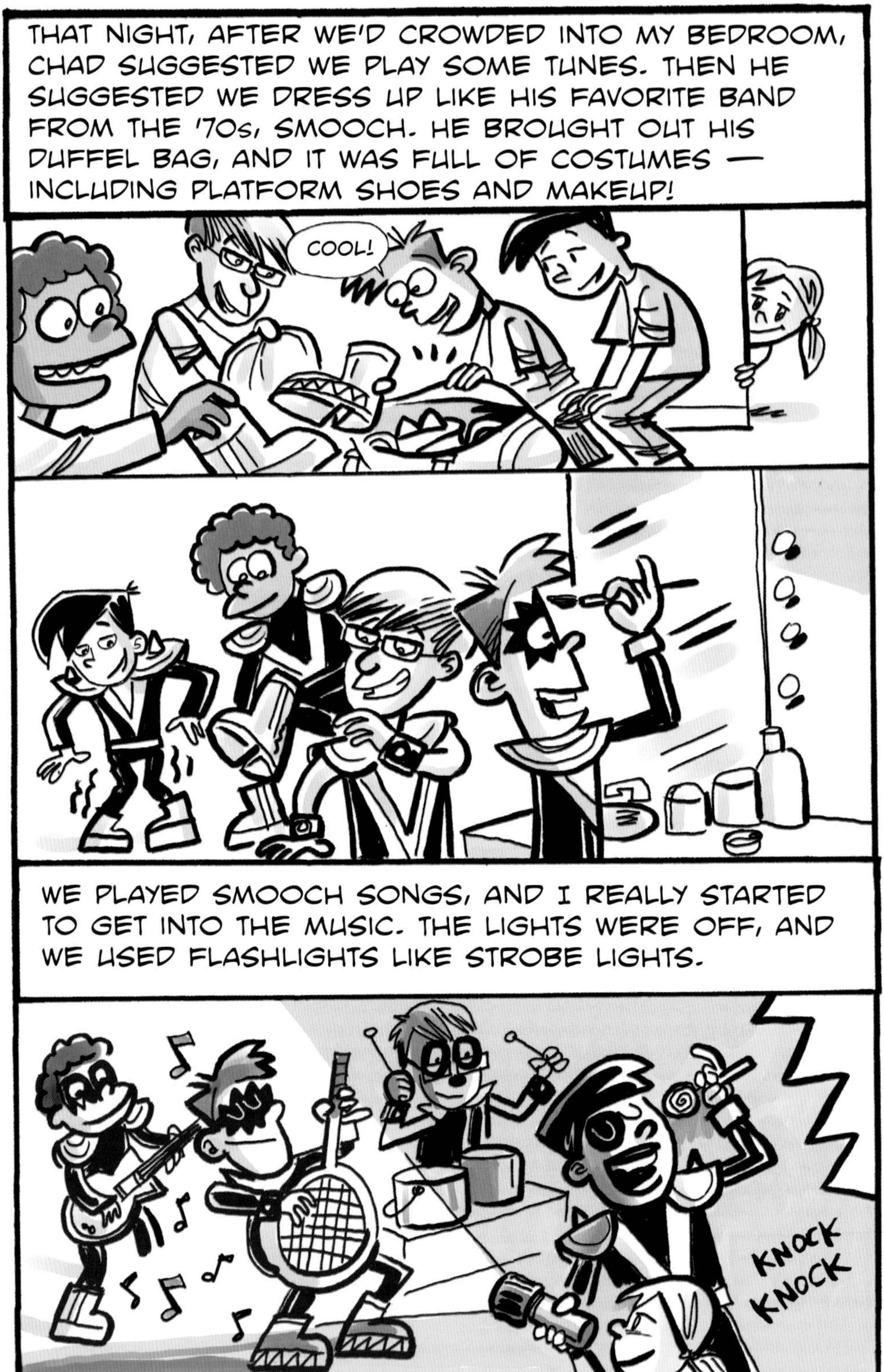
THAT NIGHT, AFTER WE'D CROWDED INTO MY BEDROOM, CHAD SUGGESTED WE PLAY SOME TUNES. THEN HE SUGGESTED WE DRESS UP LIKE HIS FAVORITE BAND FROM THE '70s, SMOOCH. HE BROUGHT OUT HIS DUFFEL BAG, AND IT WAS FULL OF COSTUMES — INCLUDING PLATFORM SHOES AND MAKEUP!
COOL!
WE PLAYED SMOOCH SONGS, AND I REALLY STARTED TO GET INTO THE MUSIC. THE LIGHTS WERE OFF, AND WE USED FLASHLIGHTS LIKE STROBE LIGHTS.
KNOCK KNOCK

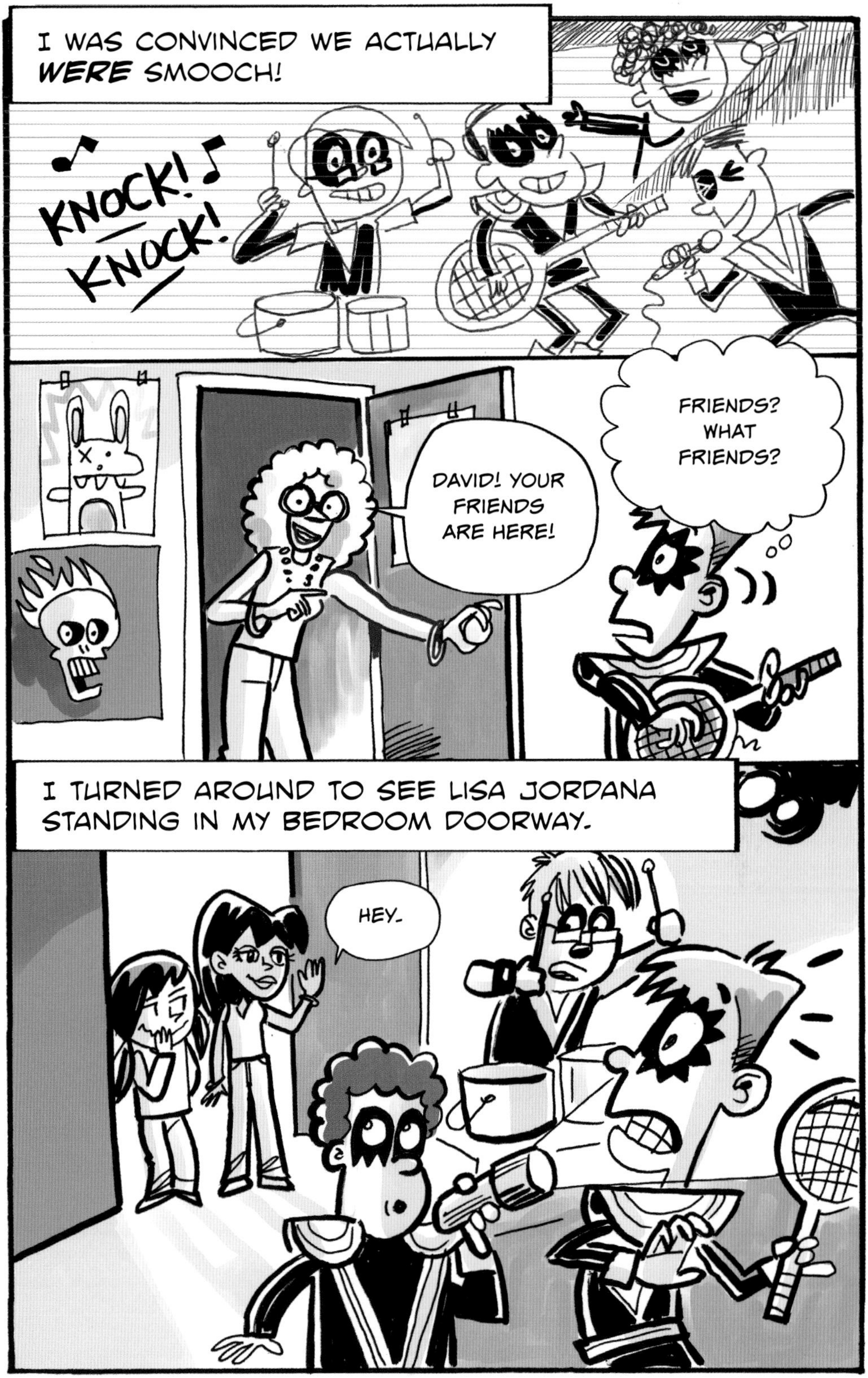
I WAS CONVINCED WE ACTUALLY ***WERE*** SMOOCH!
KNOCK! KNOCK!
DAVID! YOUR FRIENDS ARE HERE!
FRIENDS? WHAT FRIENDS?
I TURNED AROUND TO SEE LISA JORDANA STANDING IN MY BEDROOM DOORWAY.
HEY.

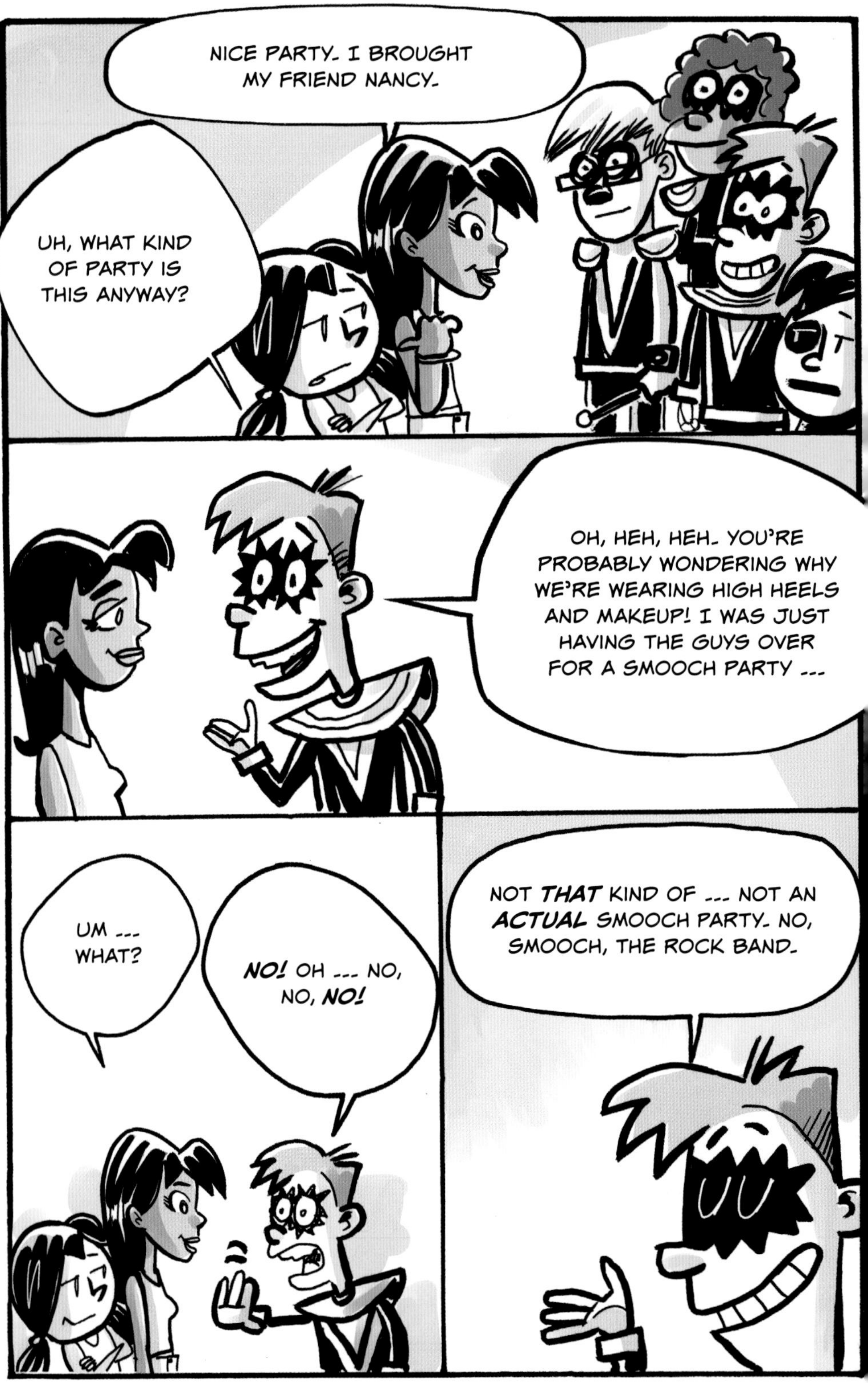
NICE PARTY. I BROUGHT MY FRIEND NANCY.
UH, WHAT KIND OF PARTY IS THIS ANYWAY?
OH, HEH, HEH. YOU'RE PROBABLY WONDERING WHY WE'RE WEARING HIGH HEELS AND MAKEUP! I WAS JUST HAVING THE GUYS OVER FOR A SMOOCH PARTY ...
UM ... WHAT?
NO! OH ... NO, NO, NO!
NOT THAT KIND OF ... NOT AN ACTUAL SMOOCH PARTY. NO, SMOOCH, THE ROCK BAND.

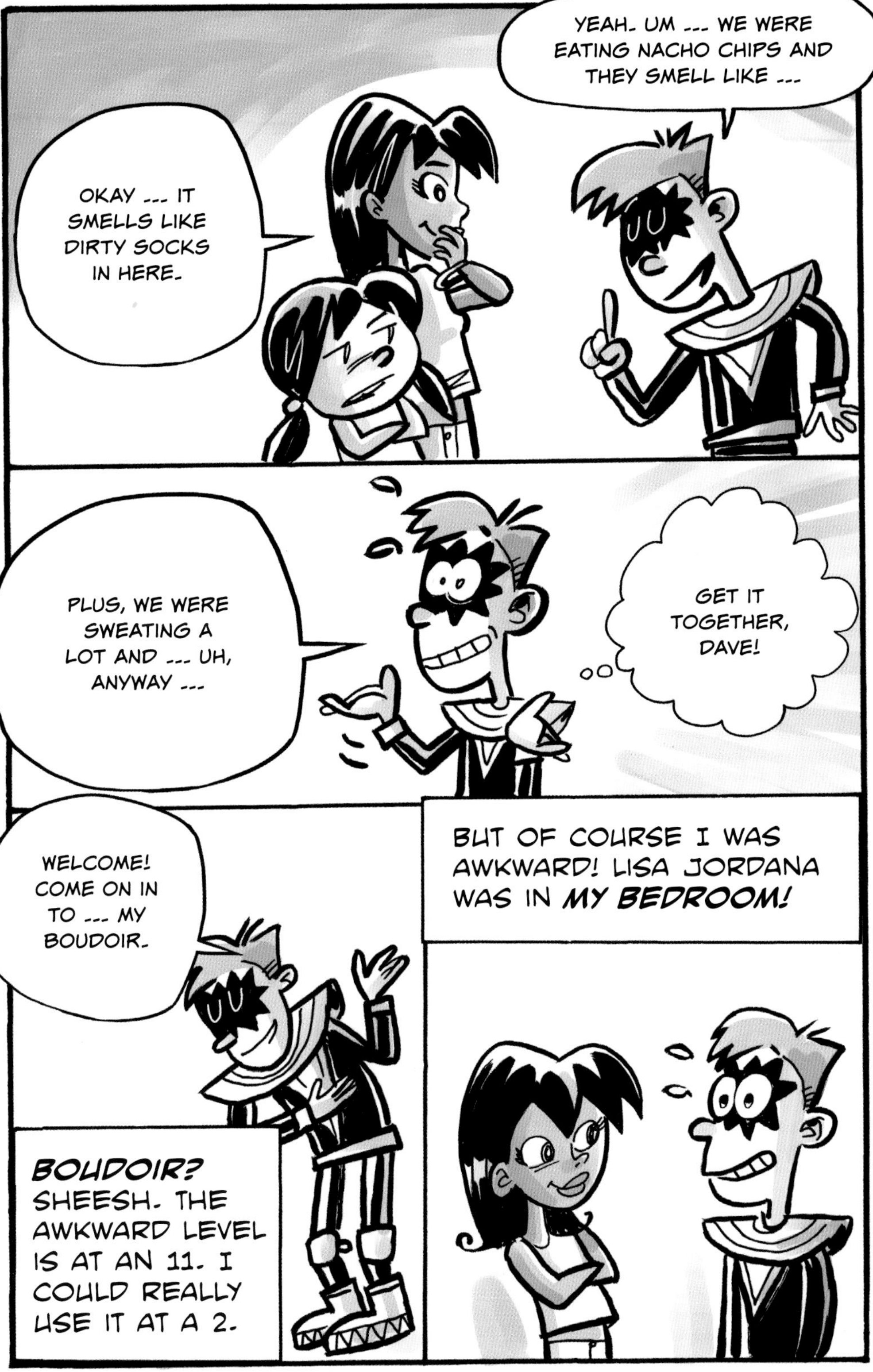
YEAH. UM ... WE WERE EATING NACHO CHIPS AND THEY SMELL LIKE ...
OKAY ... IT SMELLS LIKE DIRTY SOCKS IN HERE.
PLUS, WE WERE SWEATING A LOT AND ... UH, ANYWAY ...
GET IT TOGETHER, DAVE!
WELCOME! COME ON IN TO ... MY BOUDOIR.
BOUDOIR? SHEESH. THE AWKWARD LEVEL IS AT AN 11. I COULD REALLY USE IT AT A 2.
BUT OF COURSE I WAS AWKWARD! LISA JORDANA WAS IN MY BEDROOM!

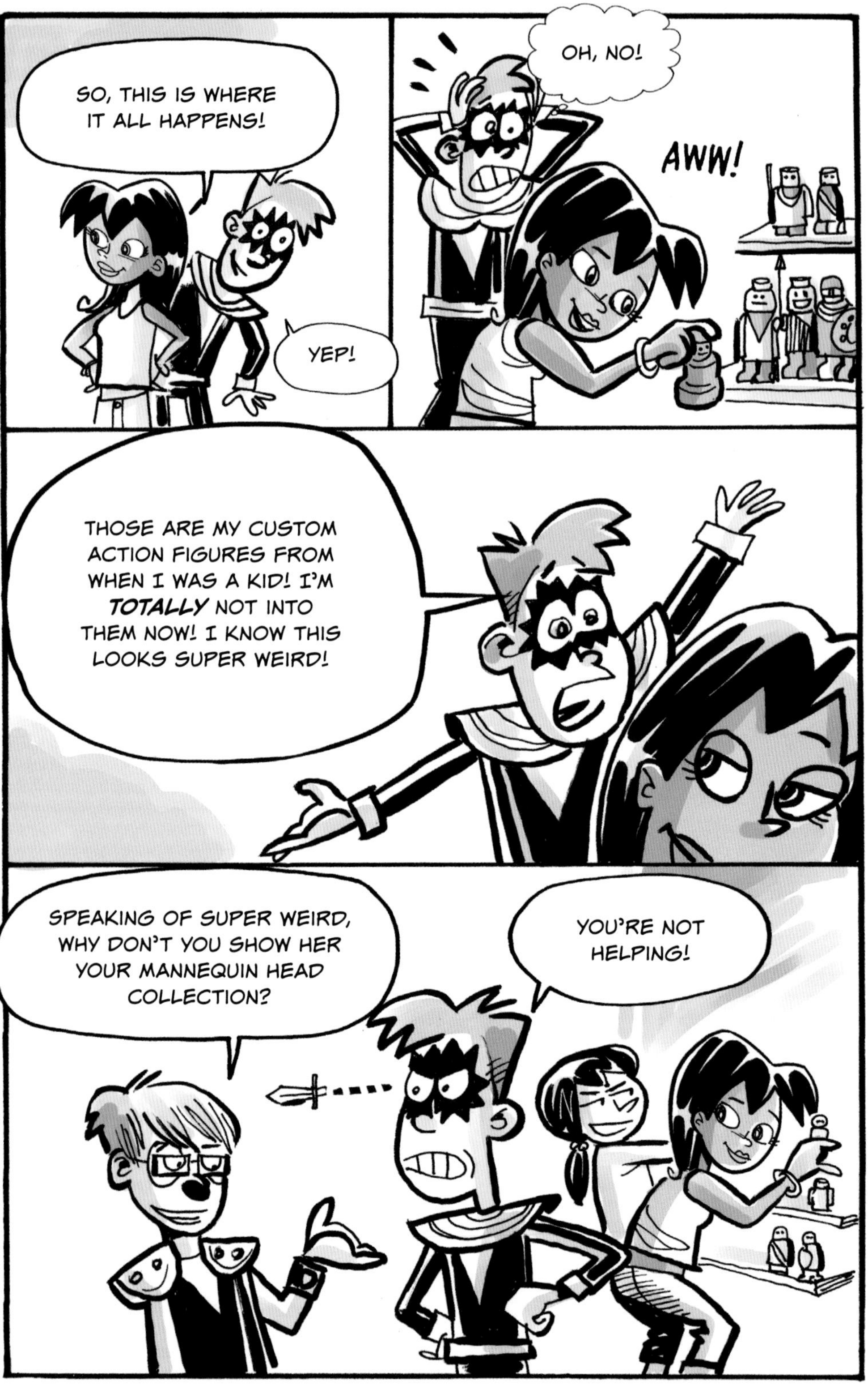
SO, THIS IS WHERE IT ALL HAPPENS!
YEP!
OH, NO!
AWW!
THOSE ARE MY CUSTOM ACTION FIGURES FROM WHEN I WAS A KID! I'M *TOTALLY* NOT INTO THEM NOW! I KNOW THIS LOOKS SUPER WEIRD!
SPEAKING OF SUPER WEIRD, WHY DON'T YOU SHOW HER YOUR MANNEQUIN HEAD COLLECTION?
YOU'RE NOT HELPING!

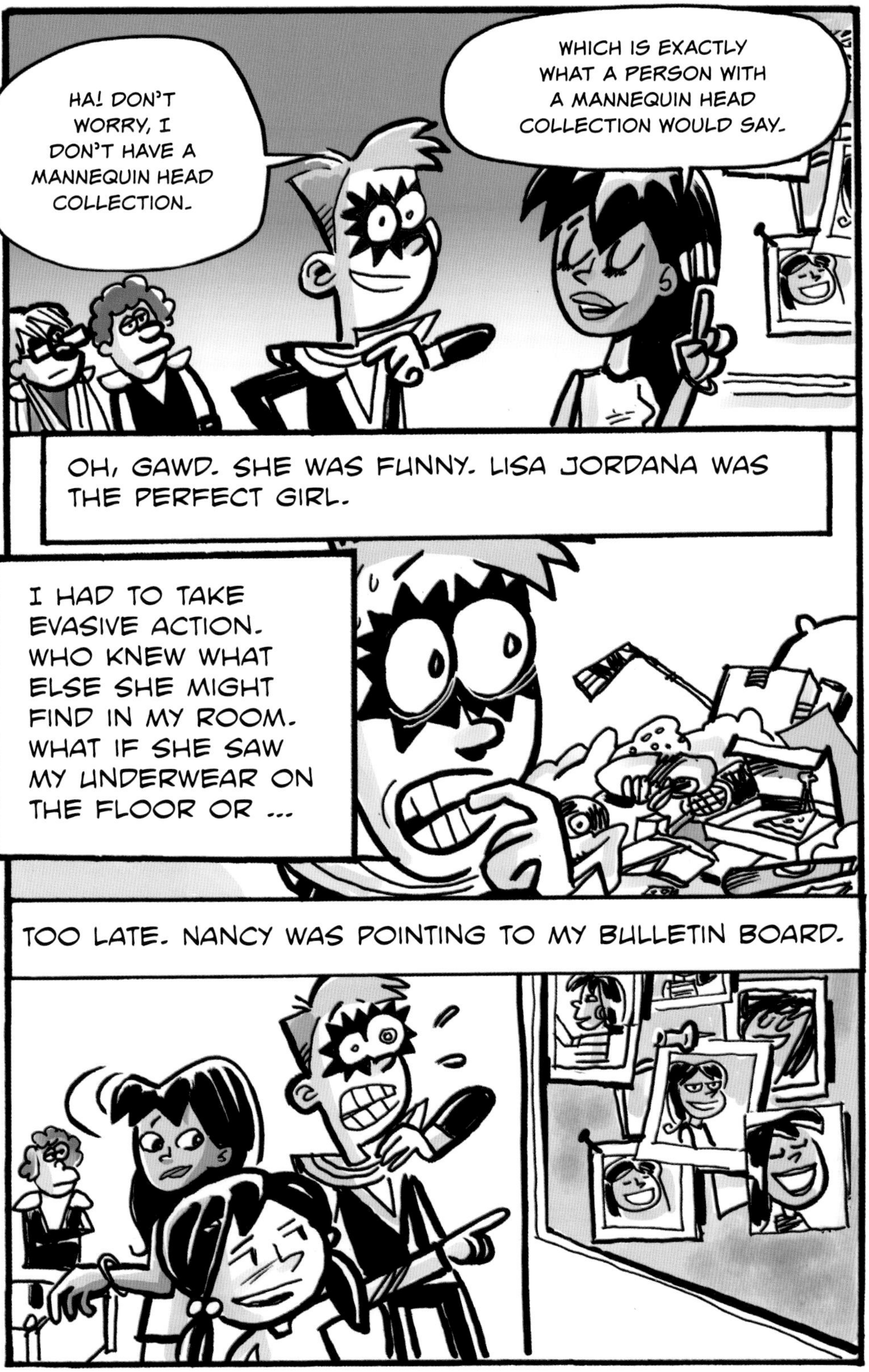

HA! DON'T WORRY, I DON'T HAVE A MANNEQUIN HEAD COLLECTION.
WHICH IS EXACTLY WHAT A PERSON WITH A MANNEQUIN HEAD COLLECTION WOULD SAY.
OH, GAWD. SHE WAS FUNNY. LISA JORDANA WAS THE PERFECT GIRL.
I HAD TO TAKE EVASIVE ACTION. WHO KNEW WHAT ELSE SHE MIGHT FIND IN MY ROOM. WHAT IF SHE SAW MY UNDERWEAR ON THE FLOOR OR ...
TOO LATE. NANCY WAS POINTING TO MY BULLETIN BOARD.

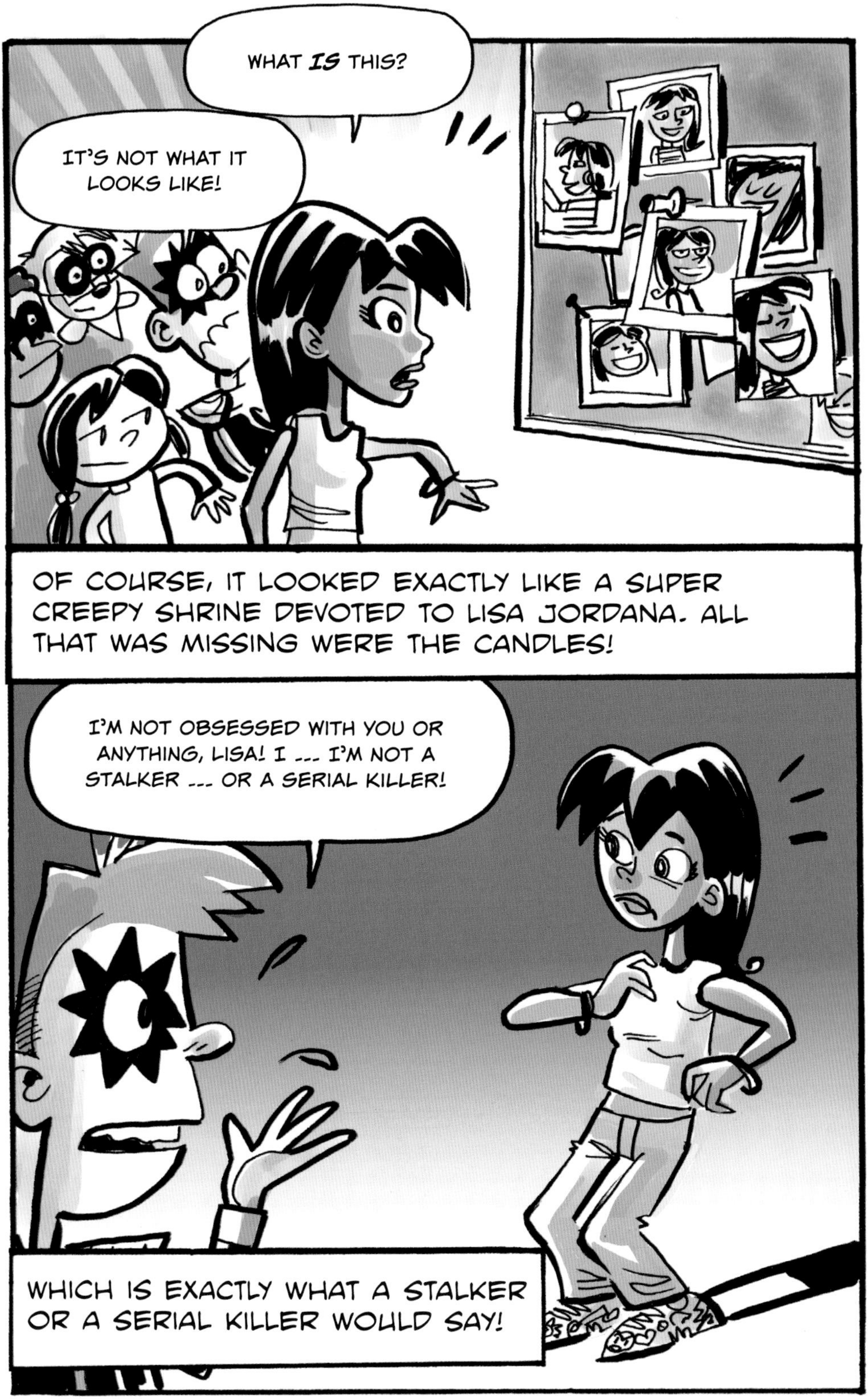

WHAT IS THIS?
IT'S NOT WHAT IT LOOKS LIKE!
OF COURSE, IT LOOKED EXACTLY LIKE A SUPER CREEPY SHRINE DEVOTED TO LISA JORDANA. ALL THAT WAS MISSING WERE THE CANDLES!
I'M NOT OBSESSED WITH YOU OR ANYTHING, LISA! I --- I'M NOT A STALKER --- OR A SERIAL KILLER!
WHICH IS EXACTLY WHAT A STALKER OR A SERIAL KILLER WOULD SAY!

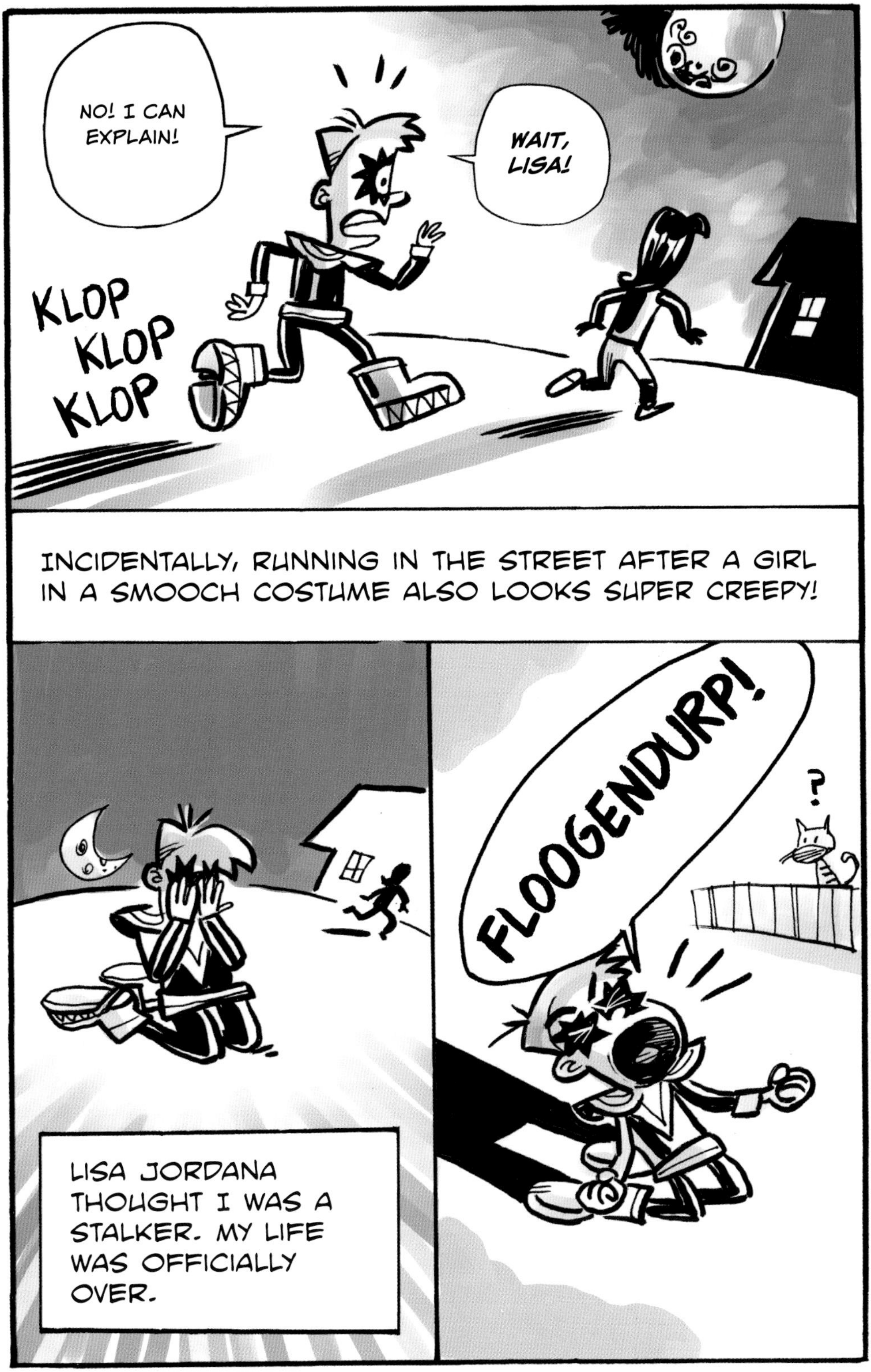
NO! I CAN EXPLAIN!
WAIT, LISA!
KLOP KLOP KLOP
INCIDENTALLY, RUNNING IN THE STREET AFTER A GIRL IN A SMOOCH COSTUME ALSO LOOKS SUPER CREEPY!
LISA JORDANA THOUGHT I WAS A STALKER. MY LIFE WAS OFFICIALLY OVER.
FLOOGENDURP!
?

CHAPTER 8: IF I COULD TURN BACK TIME

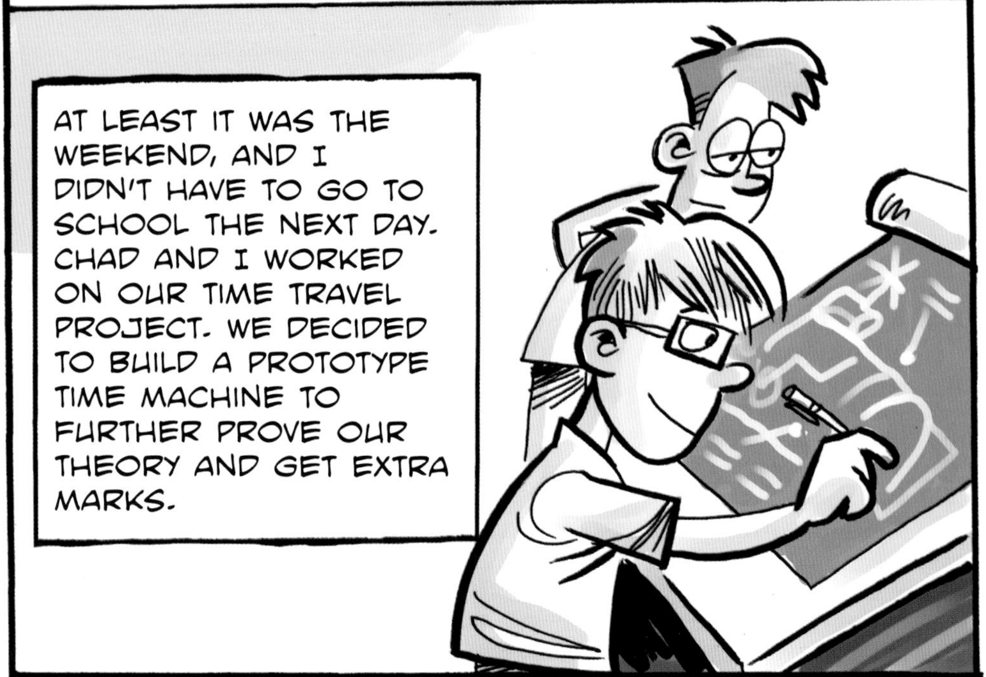
AT LEAST IT WAS THE WEEKEND, AND I DIDN'T HAVE TO GO TO SCHOOL THE NEXT DAY. CHAD AND I WORKED ON OUR TIME TRAVEL PROJECT. WE DECIDED TO BUILD A PROTOTYPE TIME MACHINE TO FURTHER PROVE OUR THEORY AND GET EXTRA MARKS.

I DESIGNED IT, BUT CHAD DID MOST OF THE WORK ON THE CONSTRUCTION. (WELL, I DID PUT THE PIPE IN THE MIDDLE.)

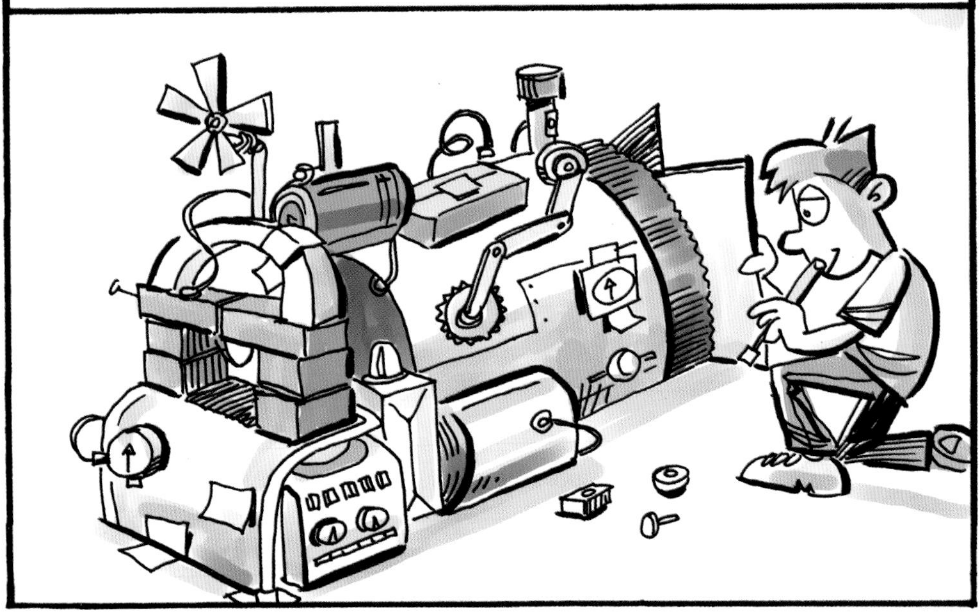

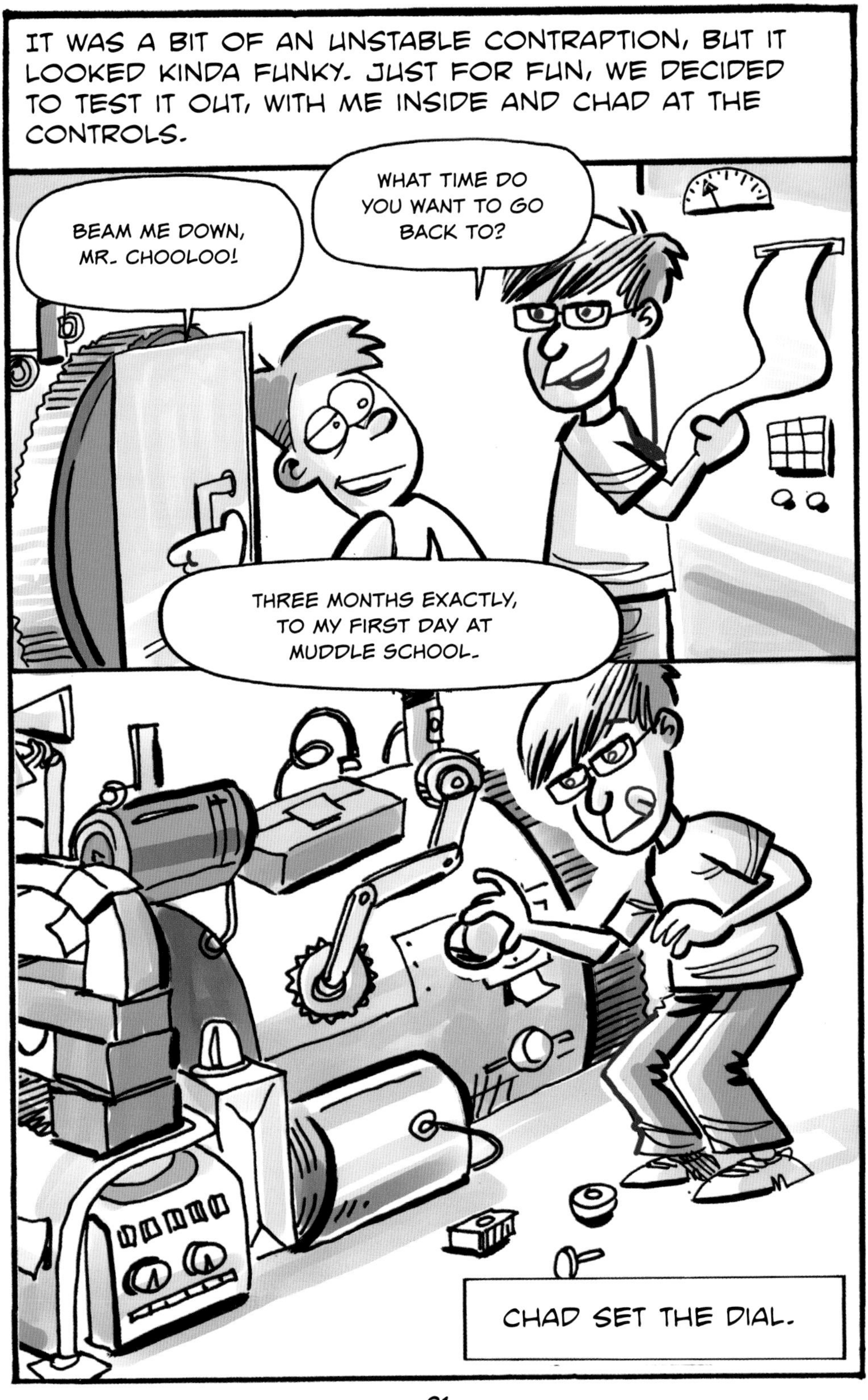
IT WAS A BIT OF AN UNSTABLE CONTRAPTION, BUT IT LOOKED KINDA FUNKY. JUST FOR FUN, WE DECIDED TO TEST IT OUT, WITH ME INSIDE AND CHAD AT THE CONTROLS.
BEAM ME DOWN, MR. CHOOLOO!
WHAT TIME DO YOU WANT TO GO BACK TO?
THREE MONTHS EXACTLY, TO MY FIRST DAY AT MUDDLE SCHOOL.
CHAD SET THE DIAL.

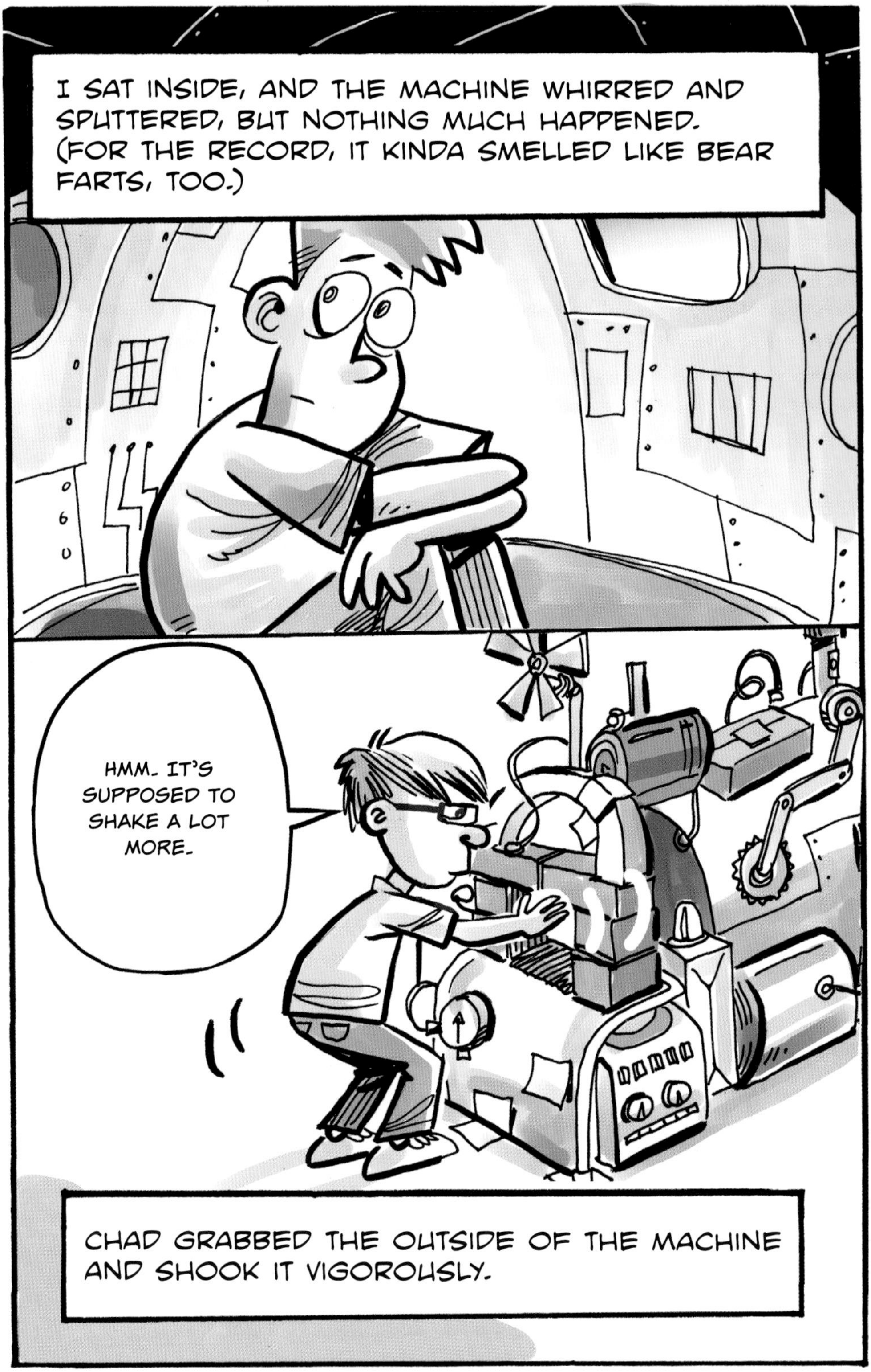
I SAT INSIDE, AND THE MACHINE WHIRRED AND SPUTTERED, BUT NOTHING MUCH HAPPENED. (FOR THE RECORD, IT KINDA SMELLED LIKE BEAR FARTS, TOO.)
HMM. IT'S SUPPOSED TO SHAKE A LOT MORE.
CHAD GRABBED THE OUTSIDE OF THE MACHINE AND SHOOK IT VIGOROUSLY.

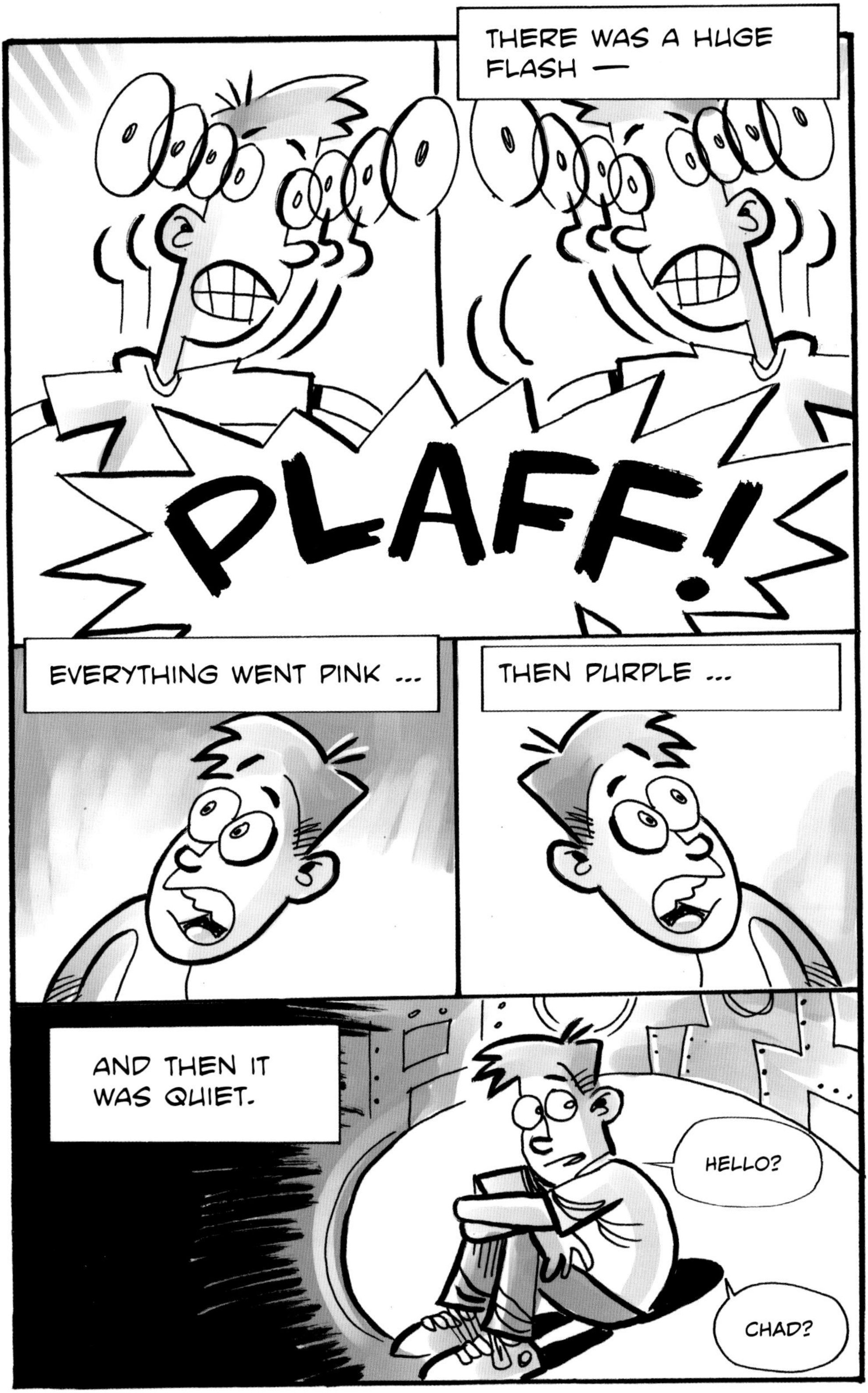
THERE WAS A HUGE FLASH —
PLAFF!
EVERYTHING WENT PINK ...
THEN PURPLE ...
AND THEN IT WAS QUIET.
HELLO?
CHAD?

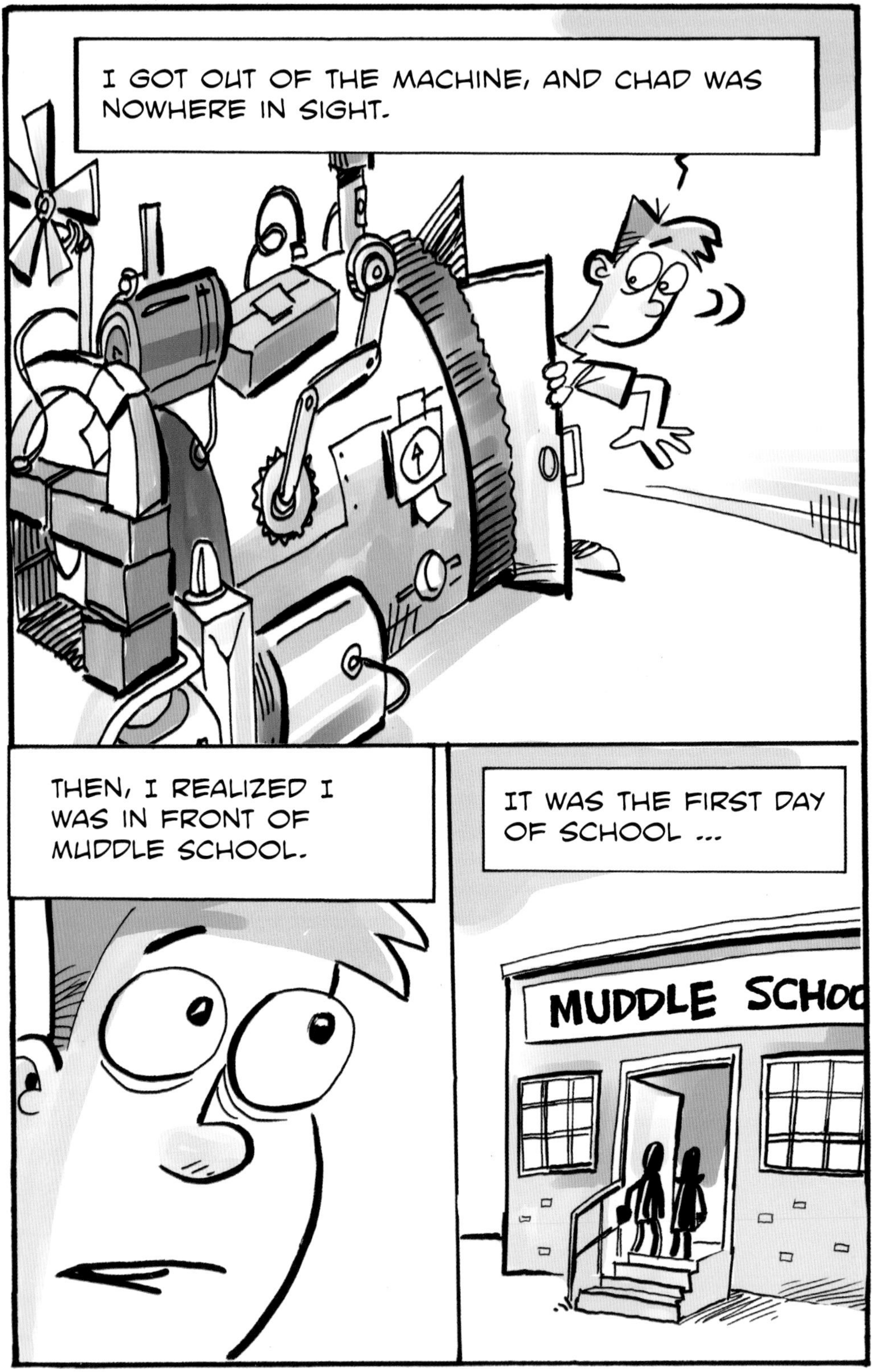
I GOT OUT OF THE MACHINE, AND CHAD WAS NOWHERE IN SIGHT.
THEN, I REALIZED I WAS IN FRONT OF MUDDLE SCHOOL.
IT WAS THE FIRST DAY OF SCHOOL ...
MUDDLE SCHO

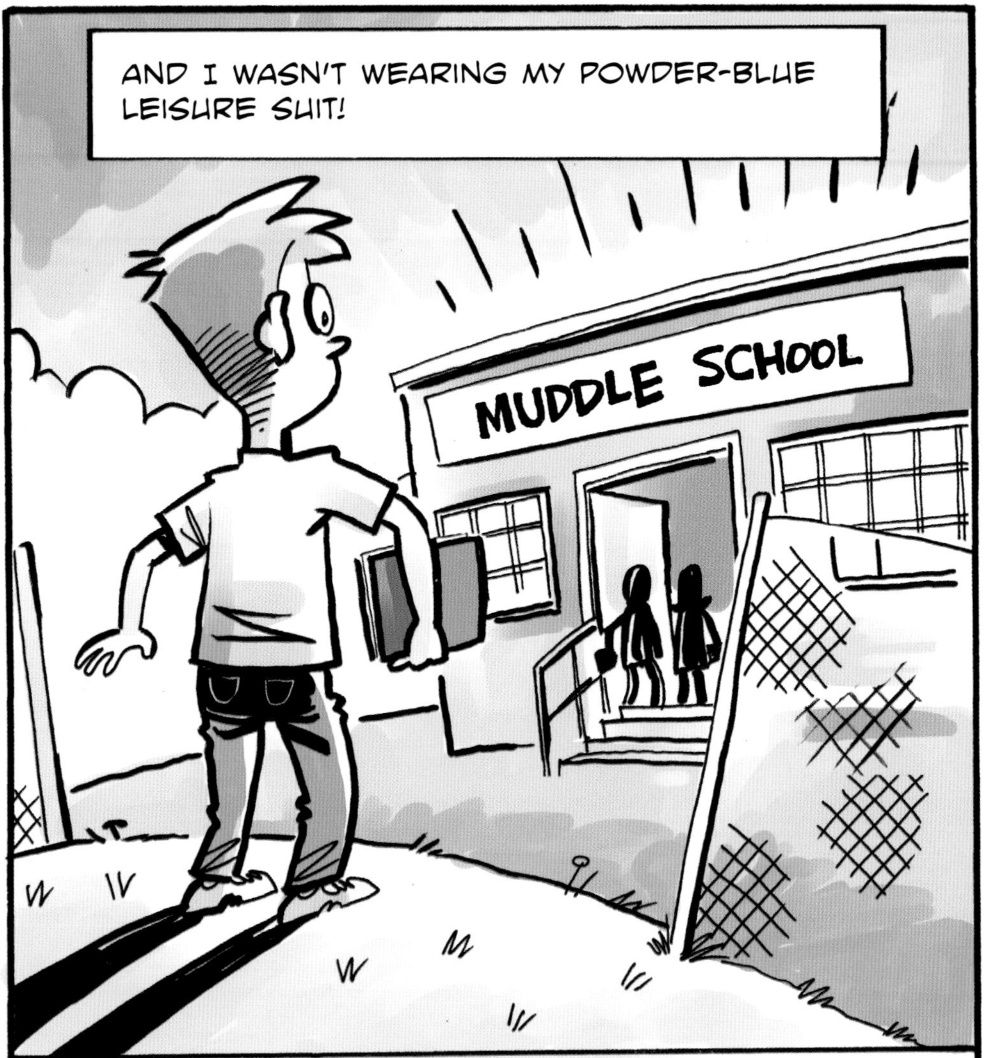
AND I WASN'T WEARING MY POWDER-BLUE LEISURE SUIT!
MUDDLE SCHOOL

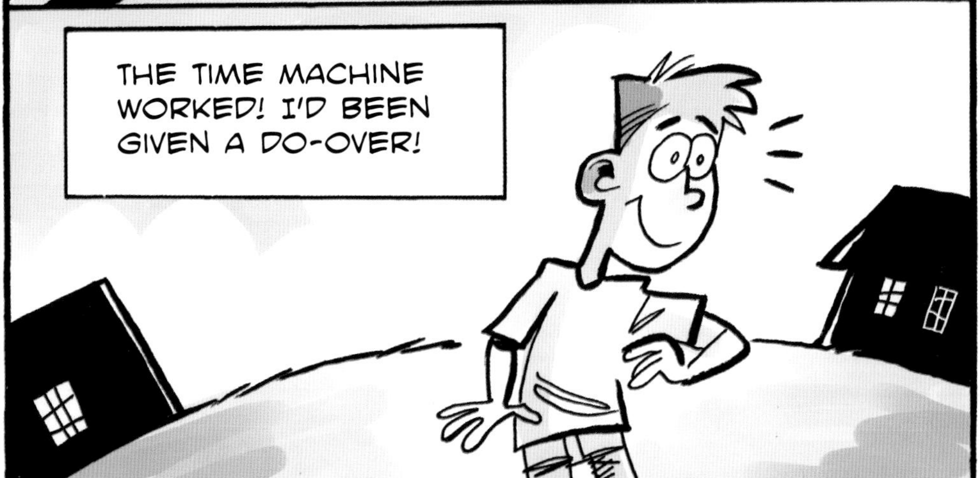
THE TIME MACHINE WORKED! I'D BEEN GIVEN A DO-OVER!

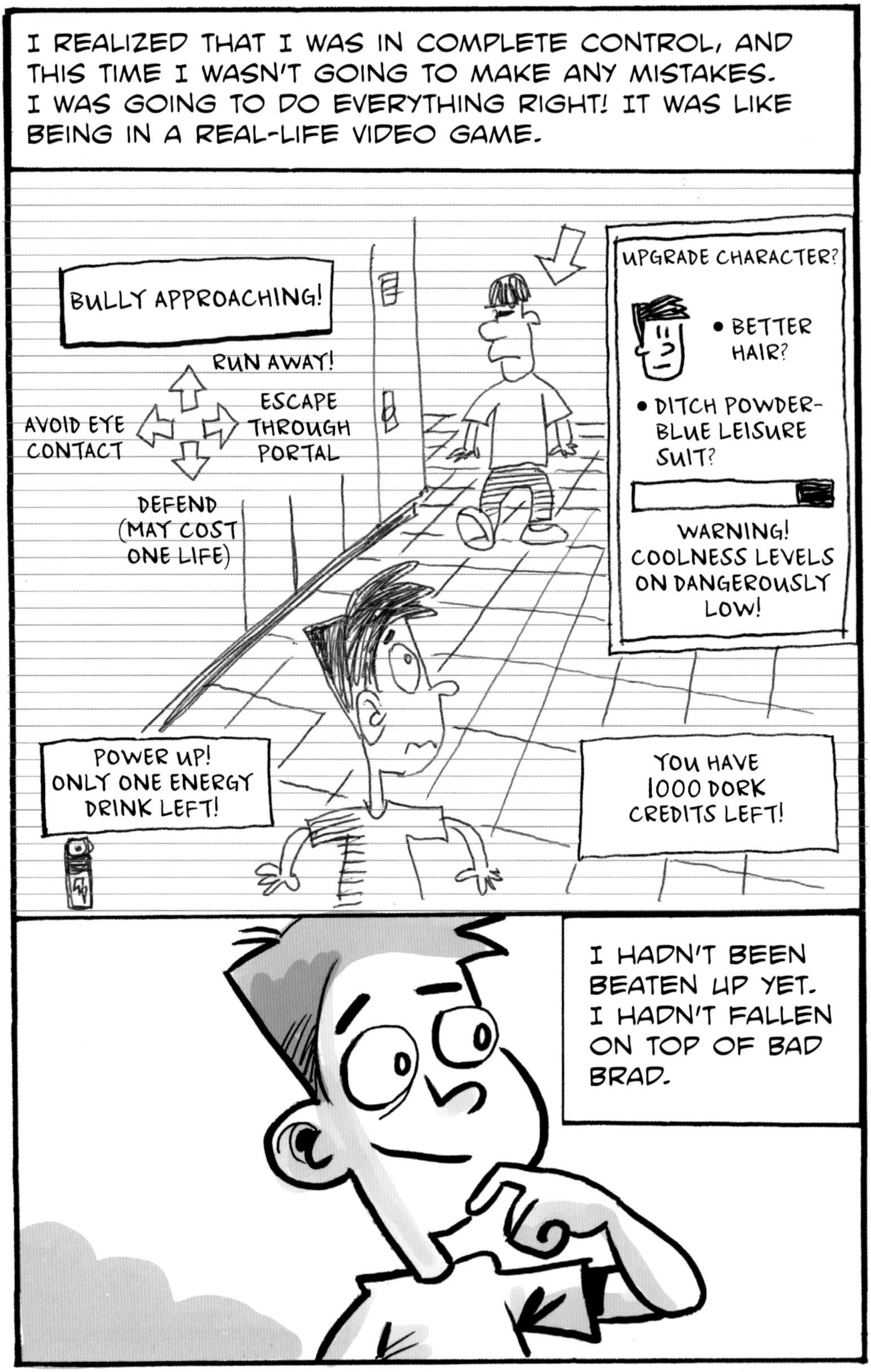
I REALIZED THAT I WAS IN COMPLETE CONTROL, AND THIS TIME I WASN'T GOING TO MAKE ANY MISTAKES. I WAS GOING TO DO EVERYTHING RIGHT! IT WAS LIKE BEING IN A REAL-LIFE VIDEO GAME.
BULLY APPROACHING!
RUN AWAY!
ESCAPE THROUGH PORTAL
AVOID EYE CONTACT
DEFEND (MAY COST ONE LIFE)
UPGRADE CHARACTER?
• BETTER HAIR?
• DITCH POWDER-BLUE LEISURE SUIT?
WARNING! COOLNESS LEVELS ON DANGEROUSLY LOW!
POWER UP! ONLY ONE ENERGY DRINK LEFT!
YOU HAVE 1000 DORK CREDITS LEFT!
I HADN'T BEEN BEATEN UP YET. I HADN'T FALLEN ON TOP OF BAD BRAD.

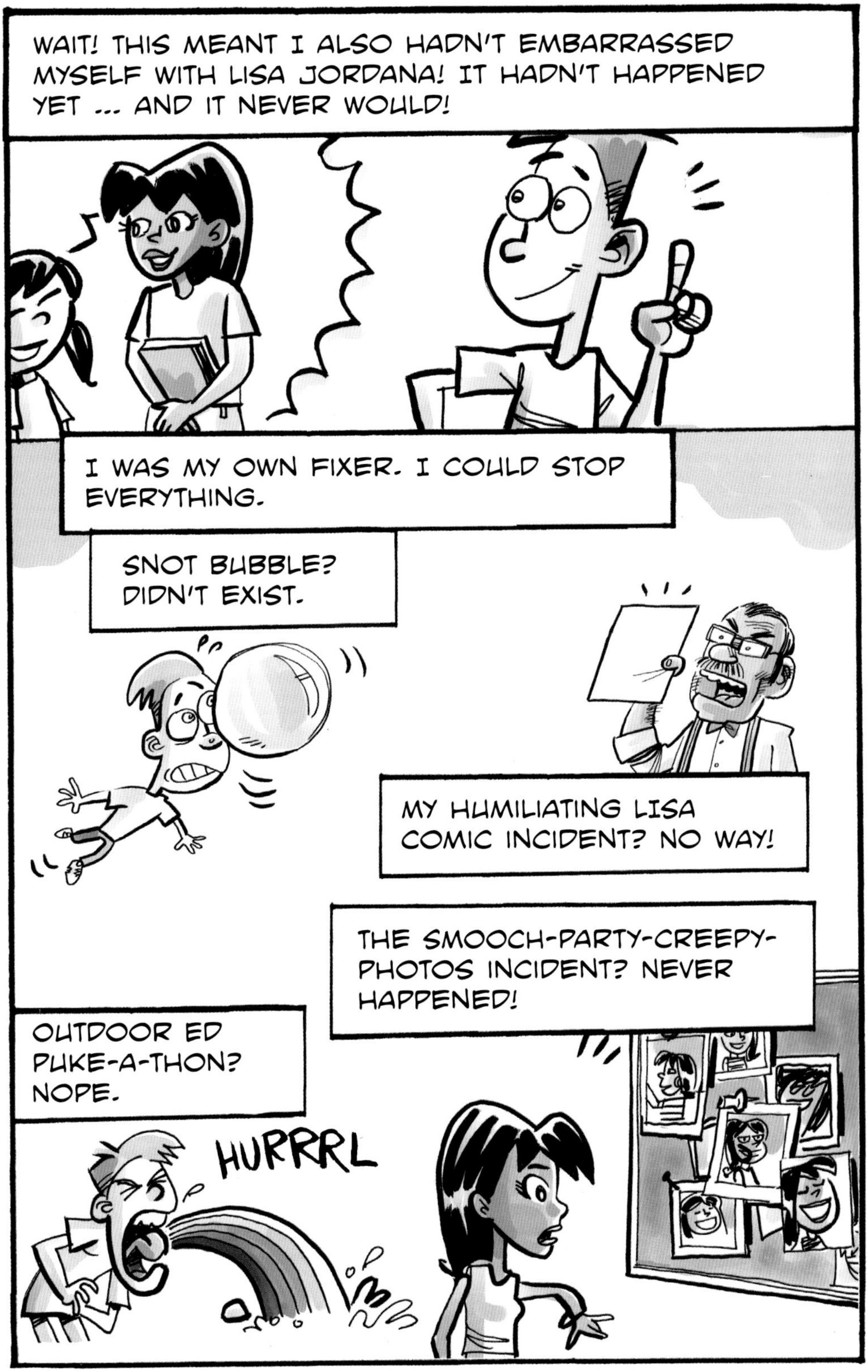
WAIT! THIS MEANT I ALSO HADN'T EMBARRASSED MYSELF WITH LISA JORDANA! IT HADN'T HAPPENED YET ... AND IT NEVER WOULD!
I WAS MY OWN FIXER. I COULD STOP EVERYTHING.
SNOT BUBBLE? DIDN'T EXIST.
MY HUMILIATING LISA COMIC INCIDENT? NO WAY!
THE SMOOCH-PARTY-CREEPY-PHOTOS INCIDENT? NEVER HAPPENED!
OUTDOOR ED PUKE-A-THON? NOPE.
HURRRL

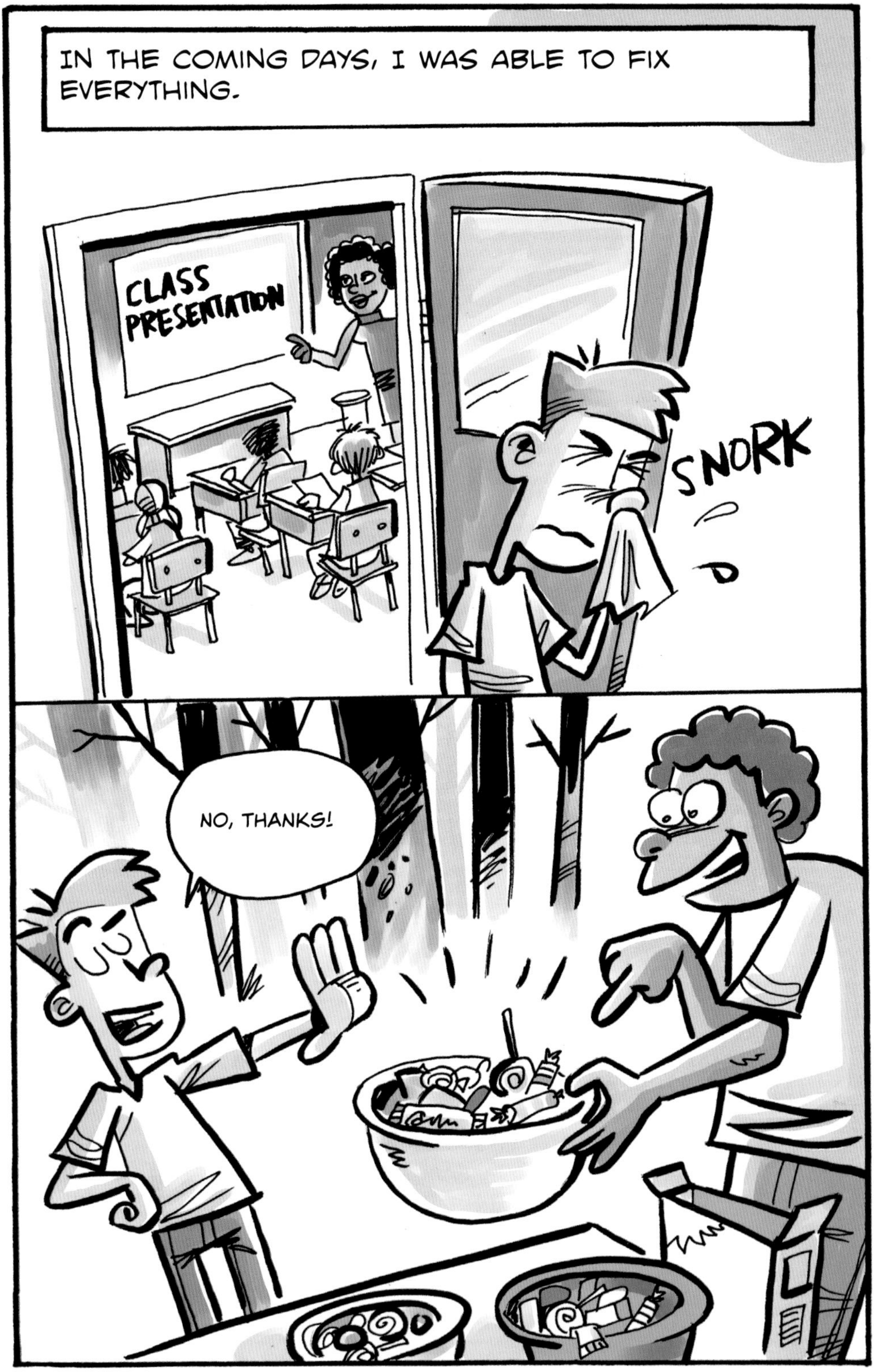
IN THE COMING DAYS, I WAS ABLE TO FIX EVERYTHING.
CLASS PRESENTATION
SNORK
NO, THANKS!

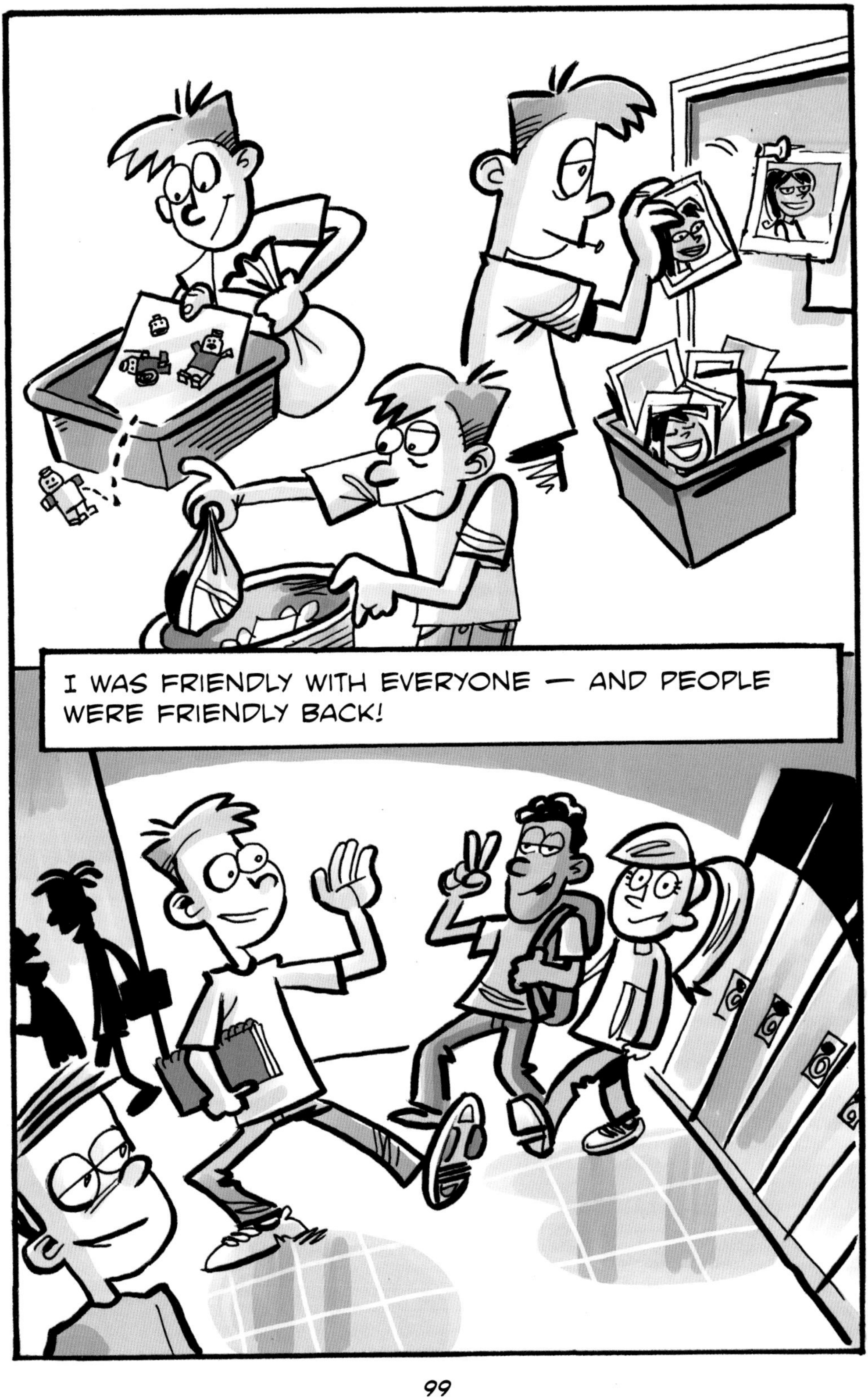
I WAS FRIENDLY WITH EVERYONE — AND PEOPLE WERE FRIENDLY BACK!

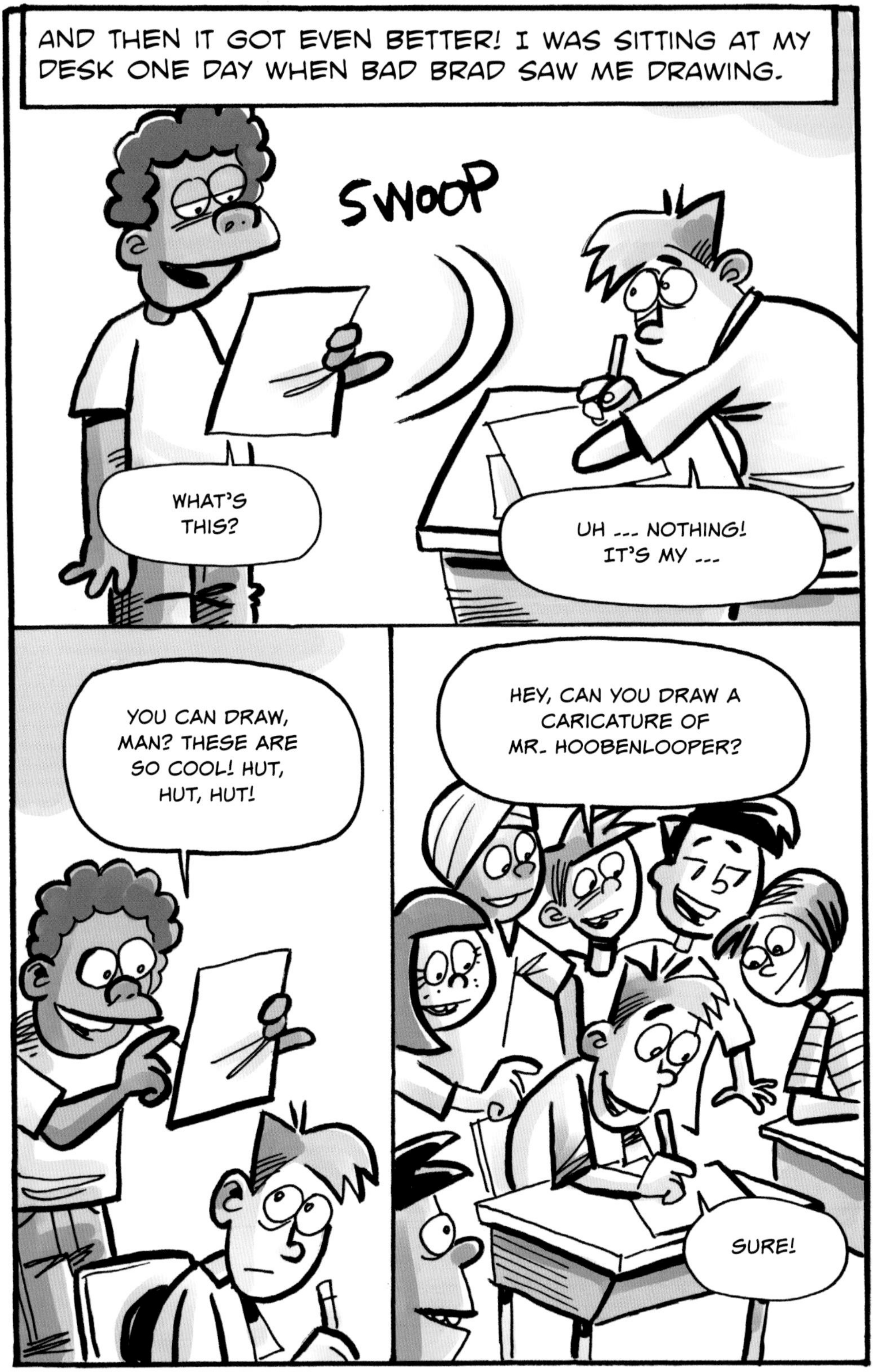
AND THEN IT GOT EVEN BETTER! I WAS SITTING AT MY DESK ONE DAY WHEN BAD BRAD SAW ME DRAWING.
SWOOP
WHAT'S THIS?
UH ... NOTHING! IT'S MY ...
YOU CAN DRAW, MAN? THESE ARE SO COOL! HUT, HUT, HUT!
HEY, CAN YOU DRAW A CARICATURE OF MR. HOOBENLOOPER?
SURE!

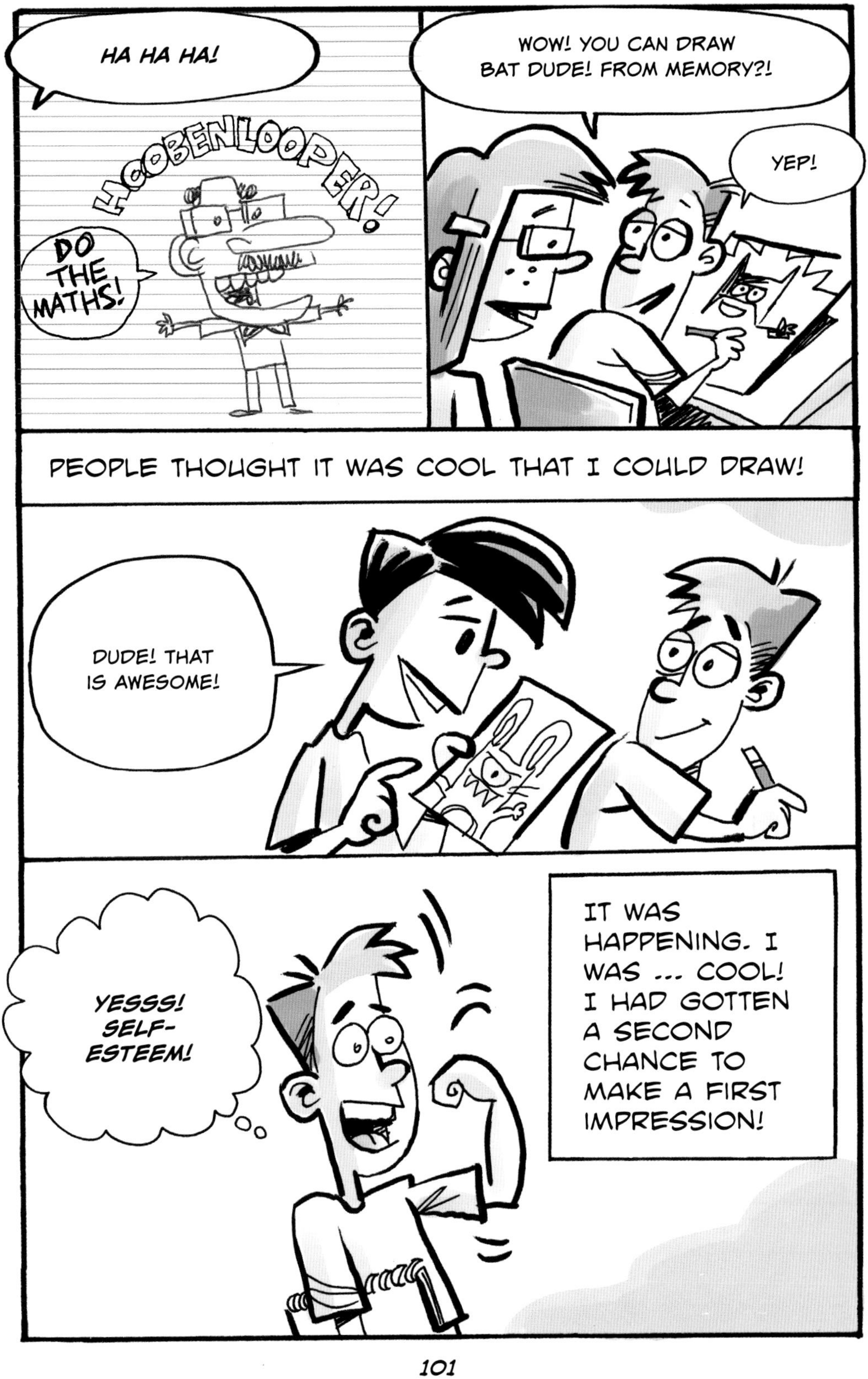
HA HA HA!
HOOBENLOOPER!
DO THE MATHS!
WOW! YOU CAN DRAW BAT DUDE! FROM MEMORY?!
YEP!
PEOPLE THOUGHT IT WAS COOL THAT I COULD DRAW!
DUDE! THAT IS AWESOME!
YESSS! SELF-ESTEEM!
IT WAS HAPPENING. I WAS ... COOL! I HAD GOTTEN A SECOND CHANCE TO MAKE A FIRST IMPRESSION!

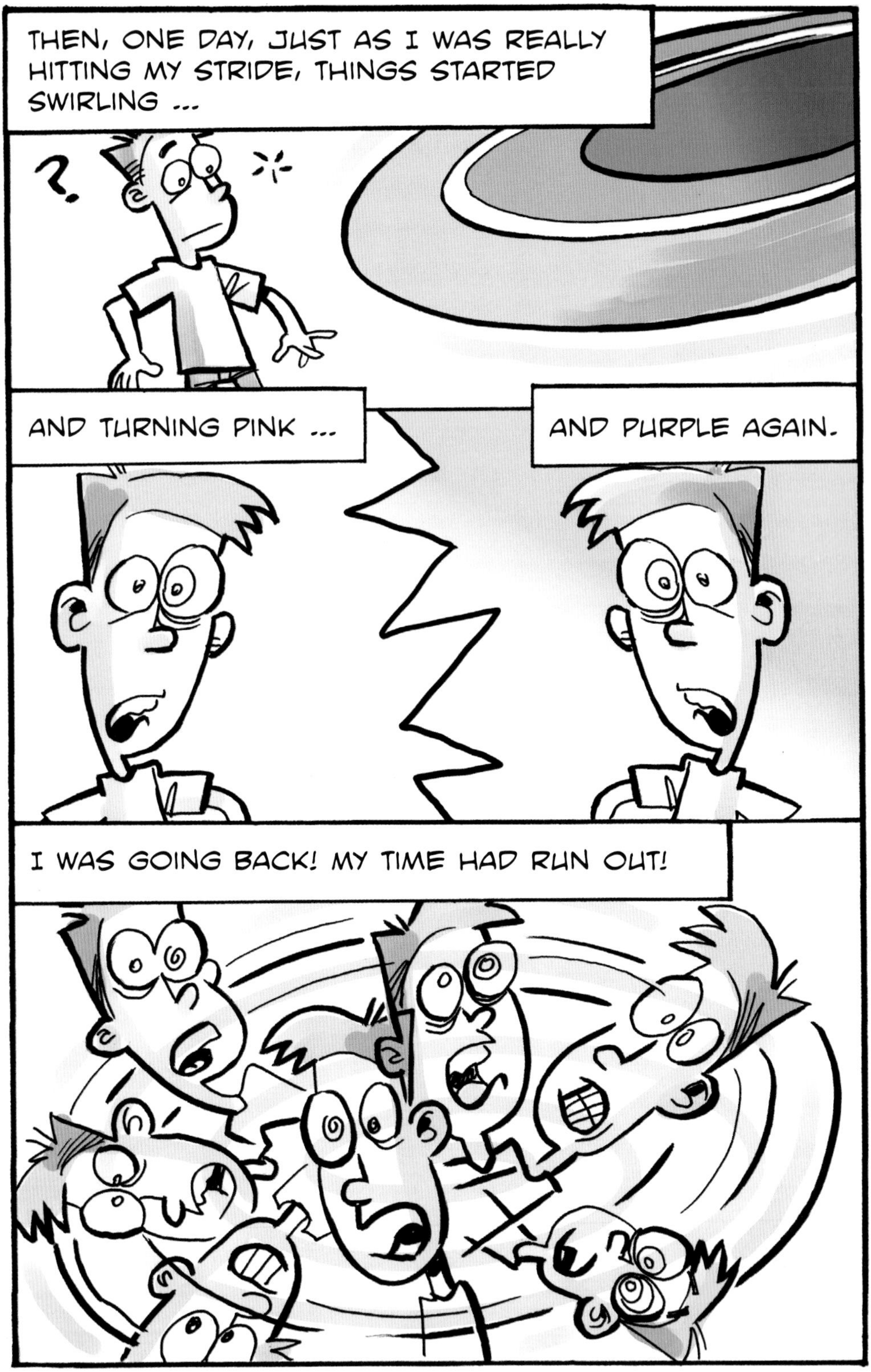
THEN, ONE DAY, JUST AS I WAS REALLY HITTING MY STRIDE, THINGS STARTED SWIRLING ...
AND TURNING PINK ...
AND PURPLE AGAIN.
I WAS GOING BACK! MY TIME HAD RUN OUT!

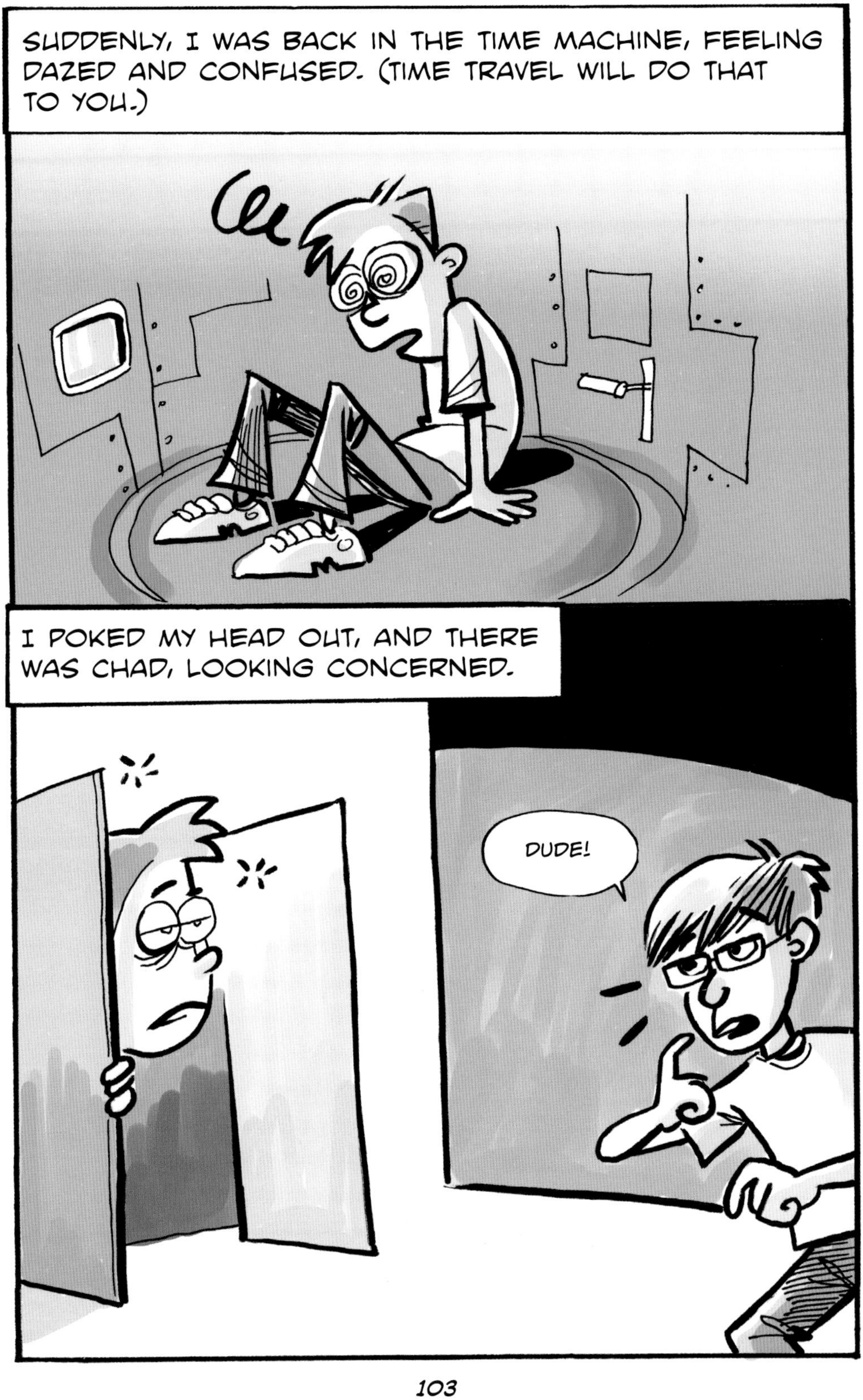
SUDDENLY, I WAS BACK IN THE TIME MACHINE, FEELING DAZED AND CONFUSED. (TIME TRAVEL WILL DO THAT TO YOU.)
I POKED MY HEAD OUT, AND THERE WAS CHAD, LOOKING CONCERNED.
DUDE!

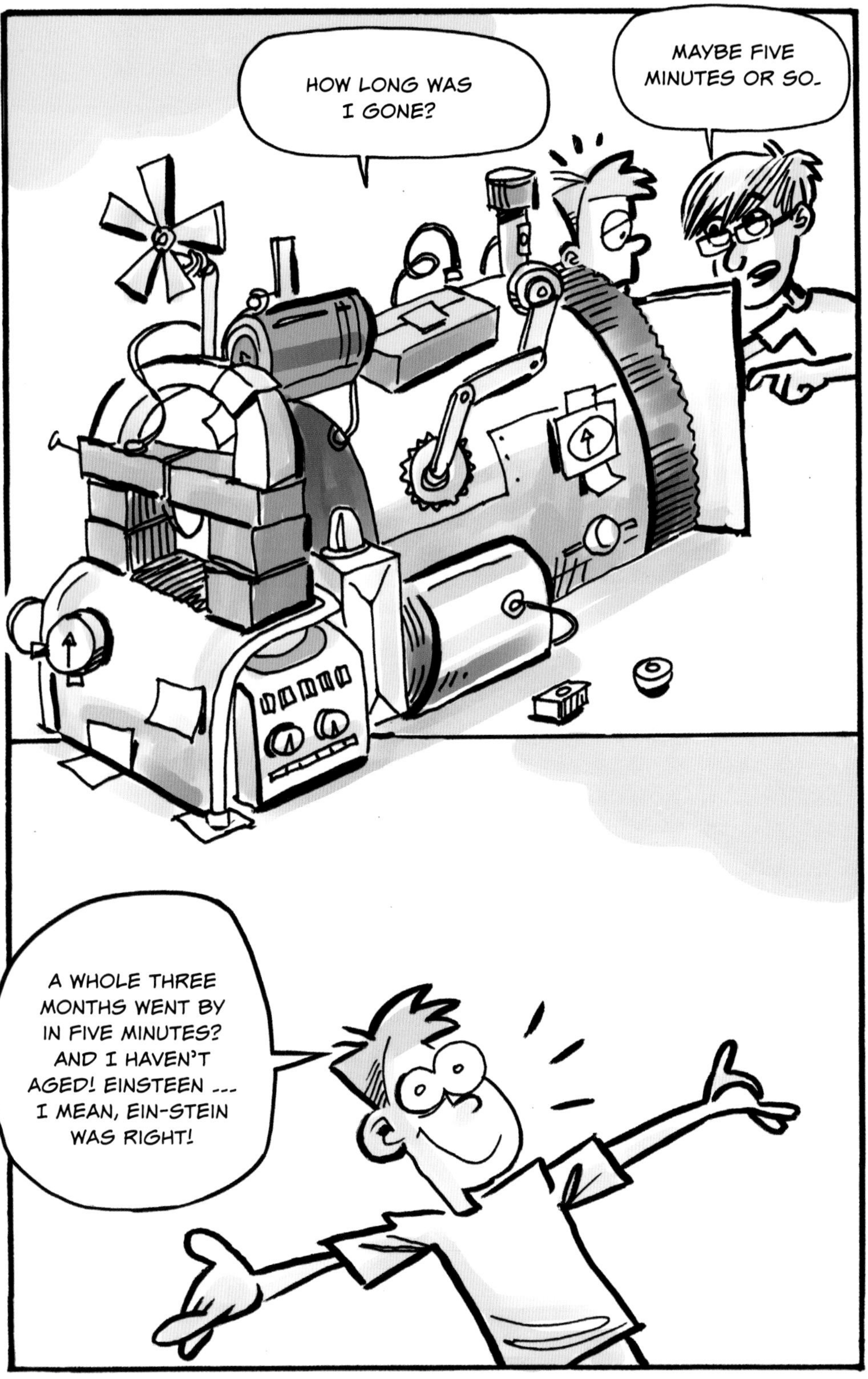
HOW LONG WAS I GONE?
MAYBE FIVE MINUTES OR SO.
A WHOLE THREE MONTHS WENT BY IN FIVE MINUTES? AND I HAVEN'T AGED! EINSTEEN ... I MEAN, EIN-STEIN WAS RIGHT!

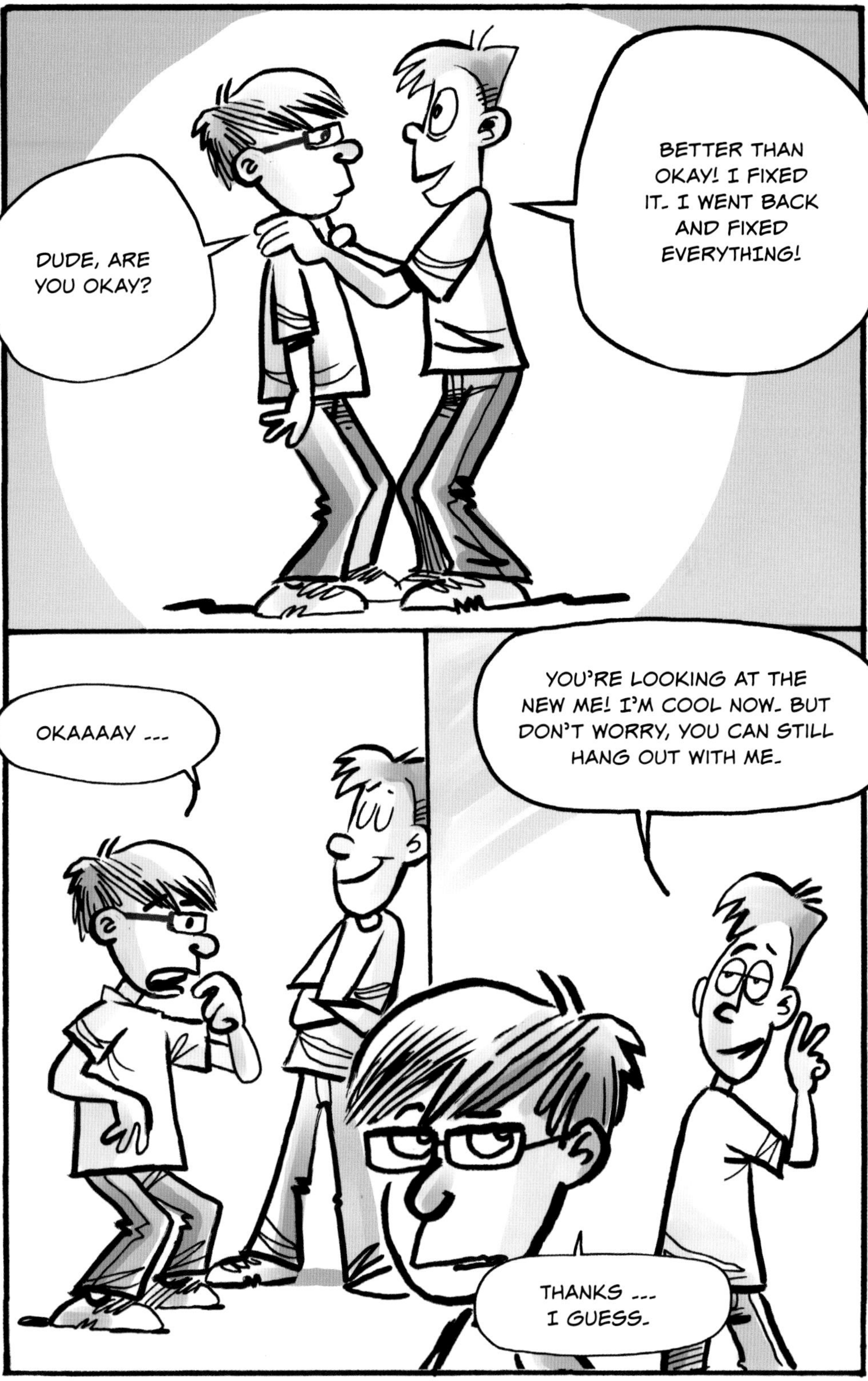
DUDE, ARE YOU OKAY?
BETTER THAN OKAY! I FIXED IT. I WENT BACK AND FIXED EVERYTHING!
OKAAAAY ...
YOU'RE LOOKING AT THE NEW ME! I'M COOL NOW. BUT DON'T WORRY, YOU CAN STILL HANG OUT WITH ME.
THANKS ... I GUESS.

CHAPTER 9: IT'S COOL TO BE COOL!

AS I WALKED DOWN THE MUDDLE SCHOOL HALLS, EVERYTHING SEEMED DIFFERENT AND ALIVE NOW THAT I WAS COOL. AND NO ONE HAD ANY IDEA THAT I HAD CHANGED TIME AND SPACE. NO ONE KNEW ABOUT ALL OF THE STUPID THINGS I'D DONE. IT HAD ALL BEEN ERASED.

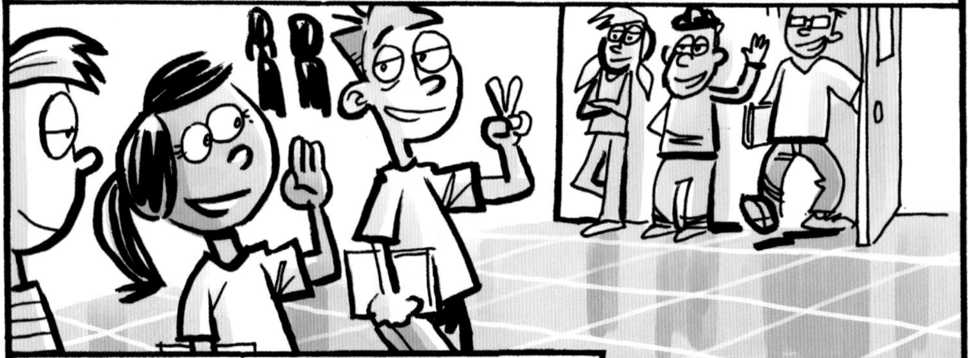

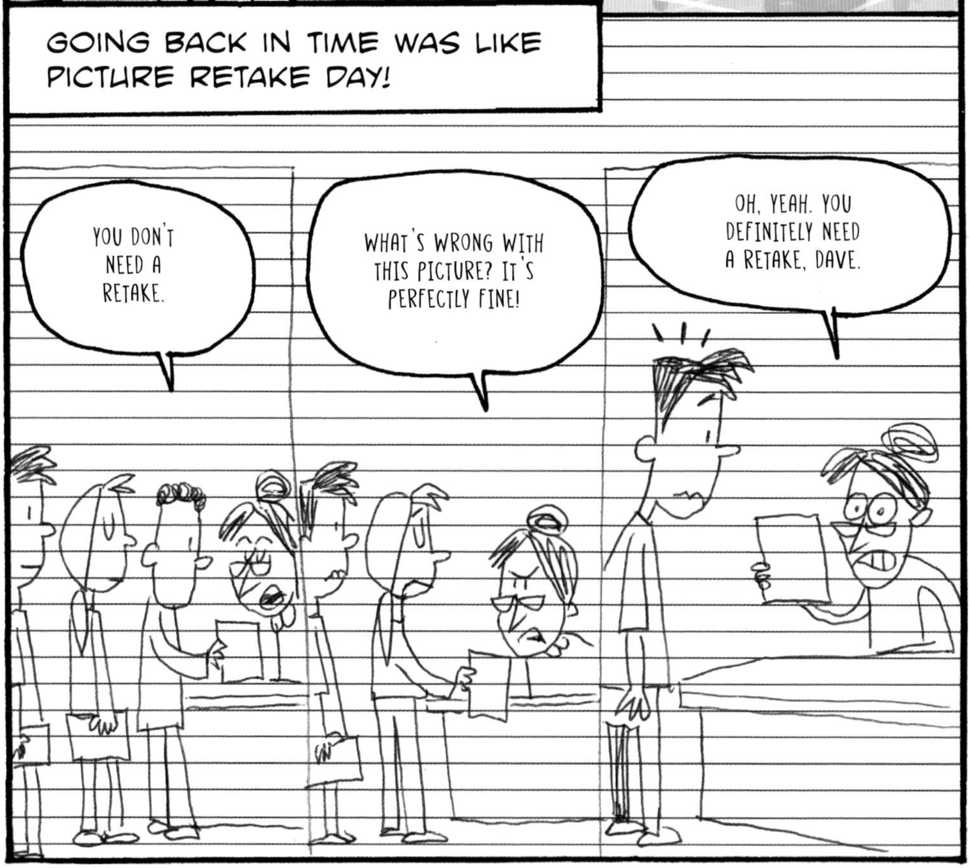
GOING BACK IN TIME WAS LIKE PICTURE RETAKE DAY!
YOU DON'T NEED A RETAKE.
WHAT'S WRONG WITH THIS PICTURE? IT'S PERFECTLY FINE!
OH, YEAH. YOU DEFINITELY NEED A RETAKE, DAVE.

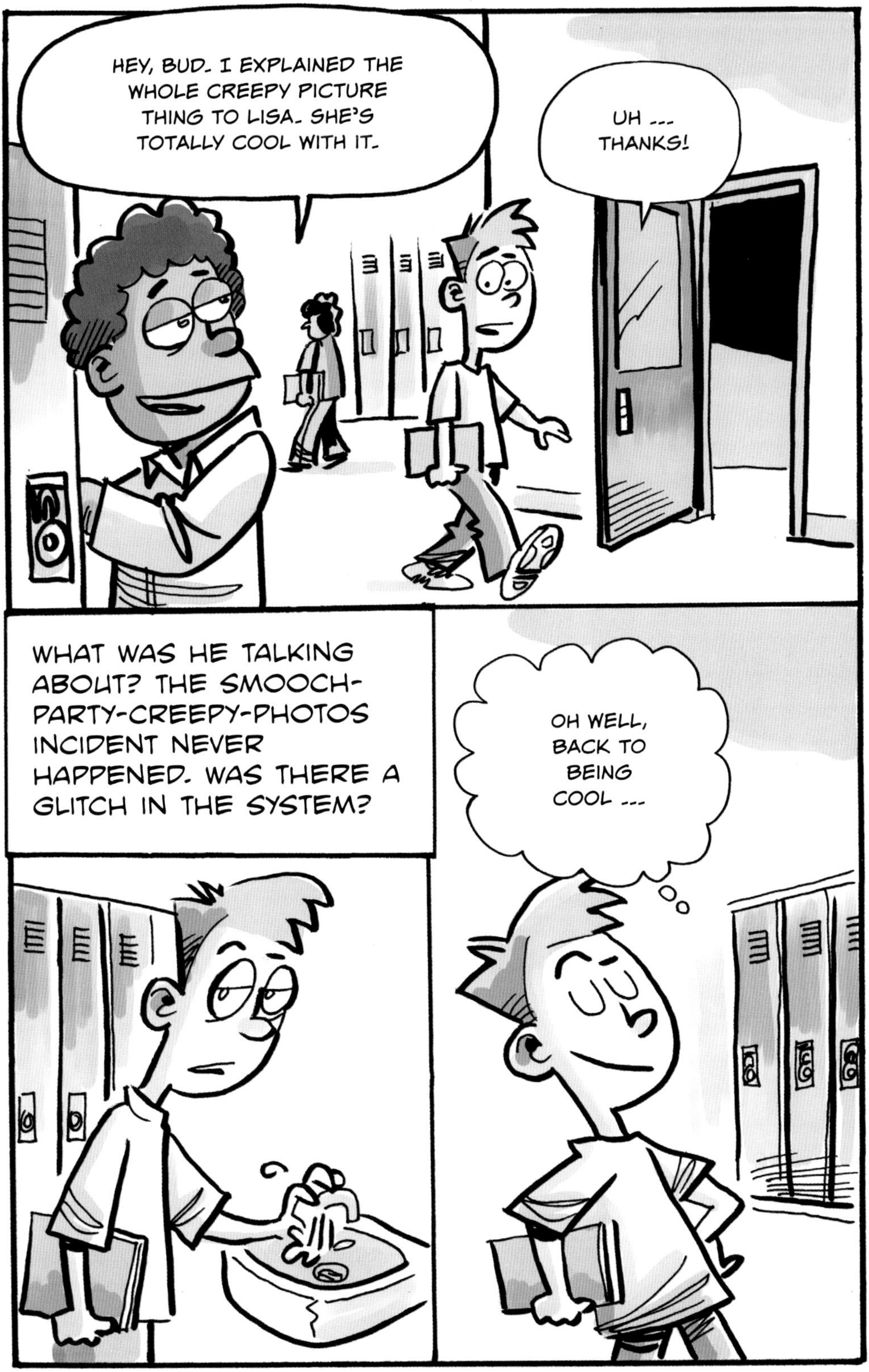
HEY, BUD. I EXPLAINED THE WHOLE CREEPY PICTURE THING TO LISA. SHE'S TOTALLY COOL WITH IT.
UH ... THANKS!
WHAT WAS HE TALKING ABOUT? THE SMOOCH-PARTY-CREEPY-PHOTOS INCIDENT NEVER HAPPENED. WAS THERE A GLITCH IN THE SYSTEM?
OH WELL, BACK TO BEING COOL ...

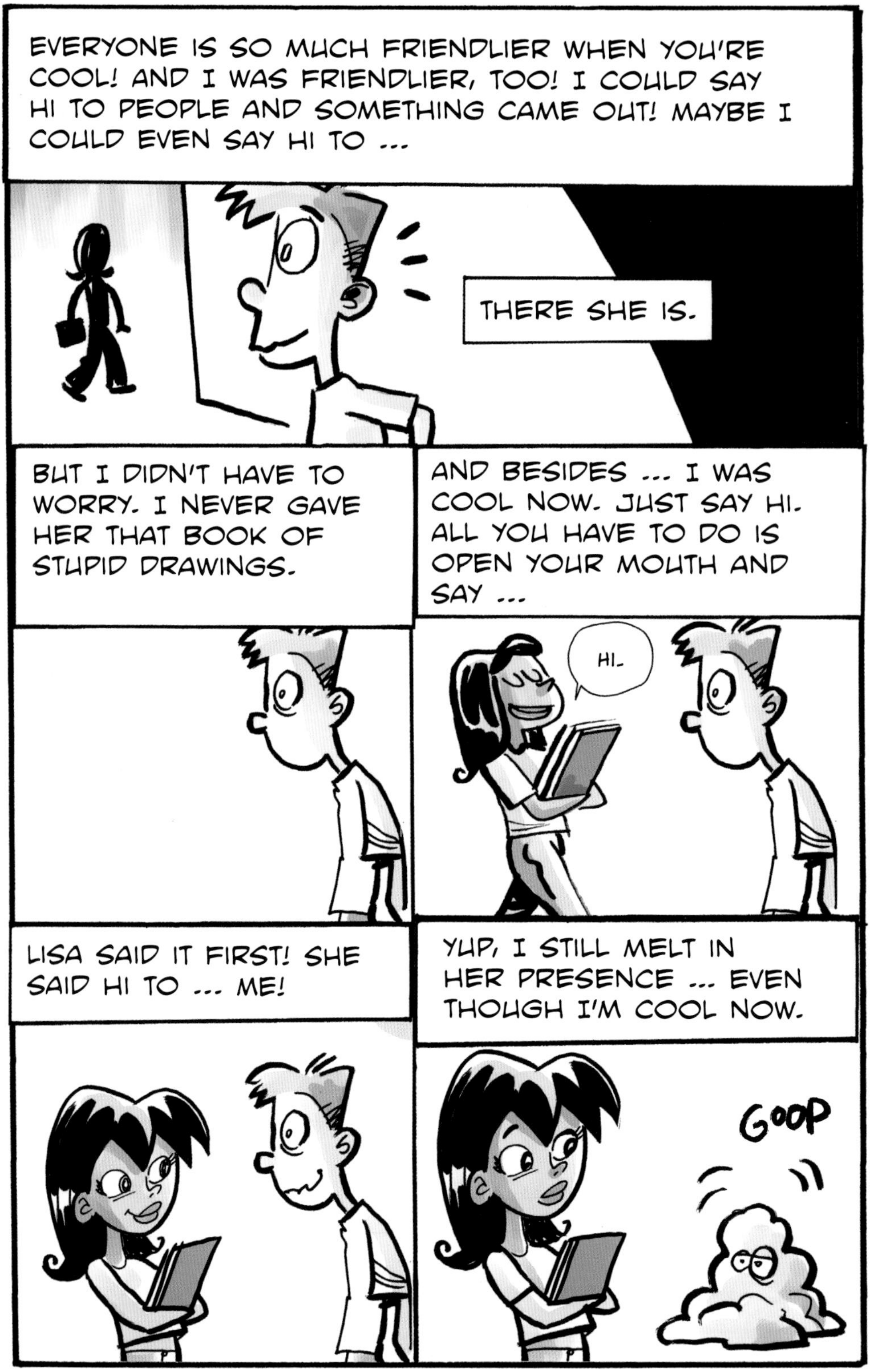
EVERYONE IS SO MUCH FRIENDLIER WHEN YOU'RE COOL! AND I WAS FRIENDLIER, TOO! I COULD SAY HI TO PEOPLE AND SOMETHING CAME OUT! MAYBE I COULD EVEN SAY HI TO ...
THERE SHE IS.
BUT I DIDN'T HAVE TO WORRY. I NEVER GAVE HER THAT BOOK OF STUPID DRAWINGS.
AND BESIDES ... I WAS COOL NOW. JUST SAY HI. ALL YOU HAVE TO DO IS OPEN YOUR MOUTH AND SAY ...
HI.
LISA SAID IT FIRST! SHE SAID HI TO ... ME!
YUP, I STILL MELT IN HER PRESENCE ... EVEN THOUGH I'M COOL NOW.
GOOP

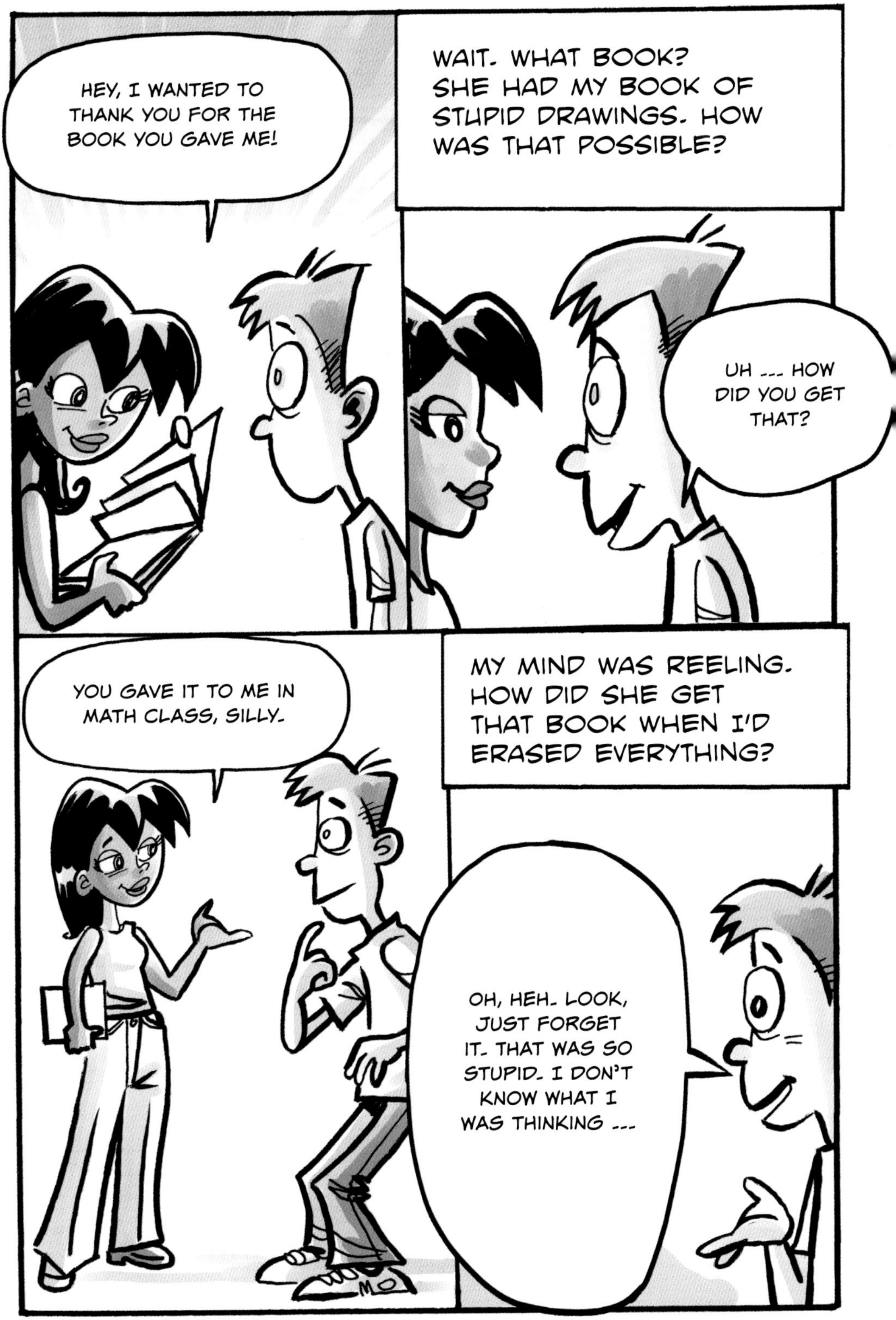
HEY, I WANTED TO THANK YOU FOR THE BOOK YOU GAVE ME!
WAIT. WHAT BOOK? SHE HAD MY BOOK OF STUPID DRAWINGS. HOW WAS THAT POSSIBLE?
UH ... HOW DID YOU GET THAT?
YOU GAVE IT TO ME IN MATH CLASS, SILLY.
MY MIND WAS REELING. HOW DID SHE GET THAT BOOK WHEN I'D ERASED EVERYTHING?
OH, HEH. LOOK, JUST FORGET IT. THAT WAS SO STUPID. I DON'T KNOW WHAT I WAS THINKING ...

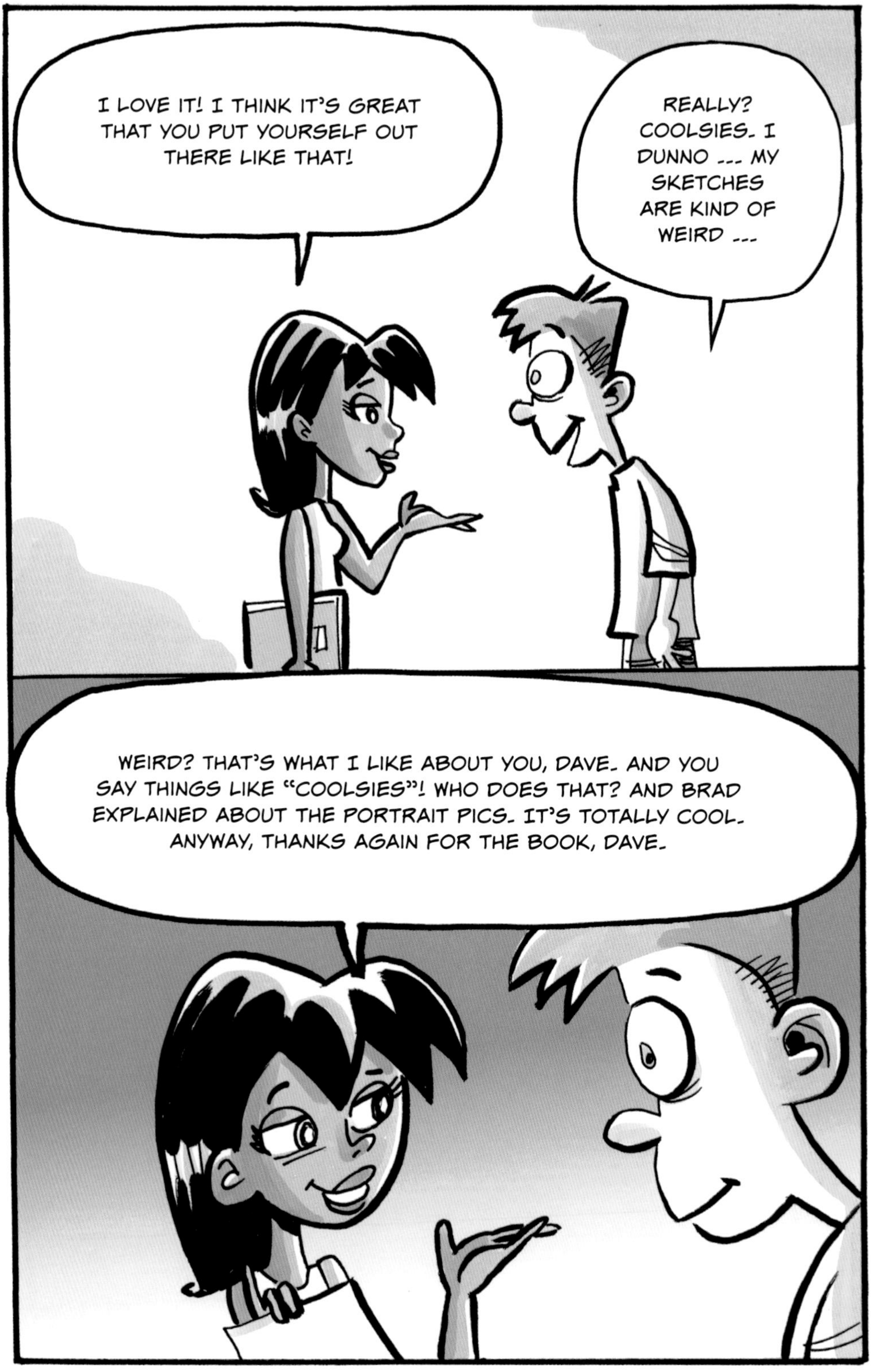
I LOVE IT! I THINK IT'S GREAT THAT YOU PUT YOURSELF OUT THERE LIKE THAT!
REALLY? COOLSIES. I DUNNO ... MY SKETCHES ARE KIND OF WEIRD ...
WEIRD? THAT'S WHAT I LIKE ABOUT YOU, DAVE. AND YOU SAY THINGS LIKE "COOLSIES"! WHO DOES THAT? AND BRAD EXPLAINED ABOUT THE PORTRAIT PICS. IT'S TOTALLY COOL. ANYWAY, THANKS AGAIN FOR THE BOOK, DAVE.

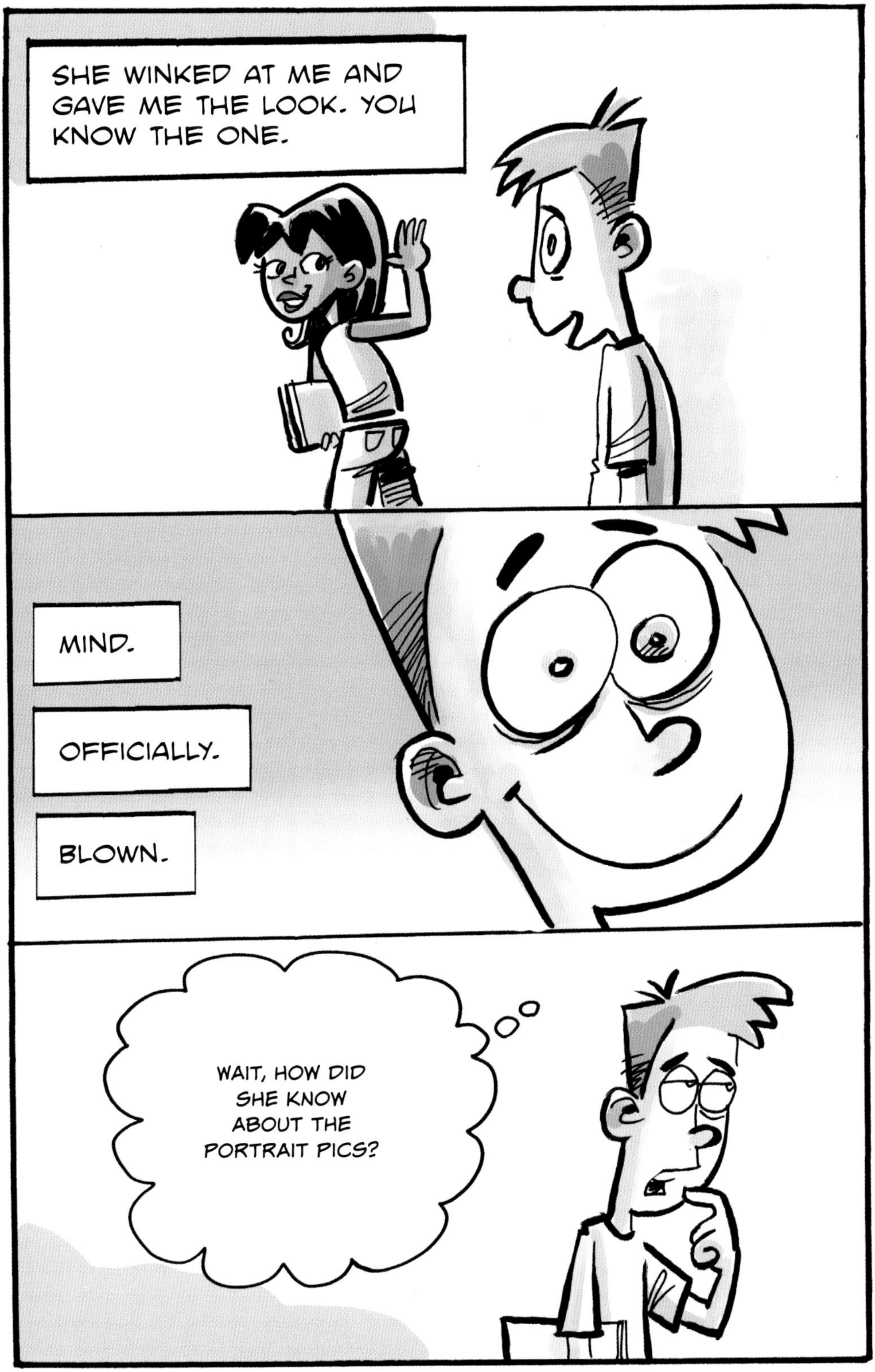
SHE WINKED AT ME AND GAVE ME THE LOOK. YOU KNOW THE ONE.
MIND.
OFFICIALLY.
BLOWN.
WAIT, HOW DID SHE KNOW ABOUT THE PORTRAIT PICS?

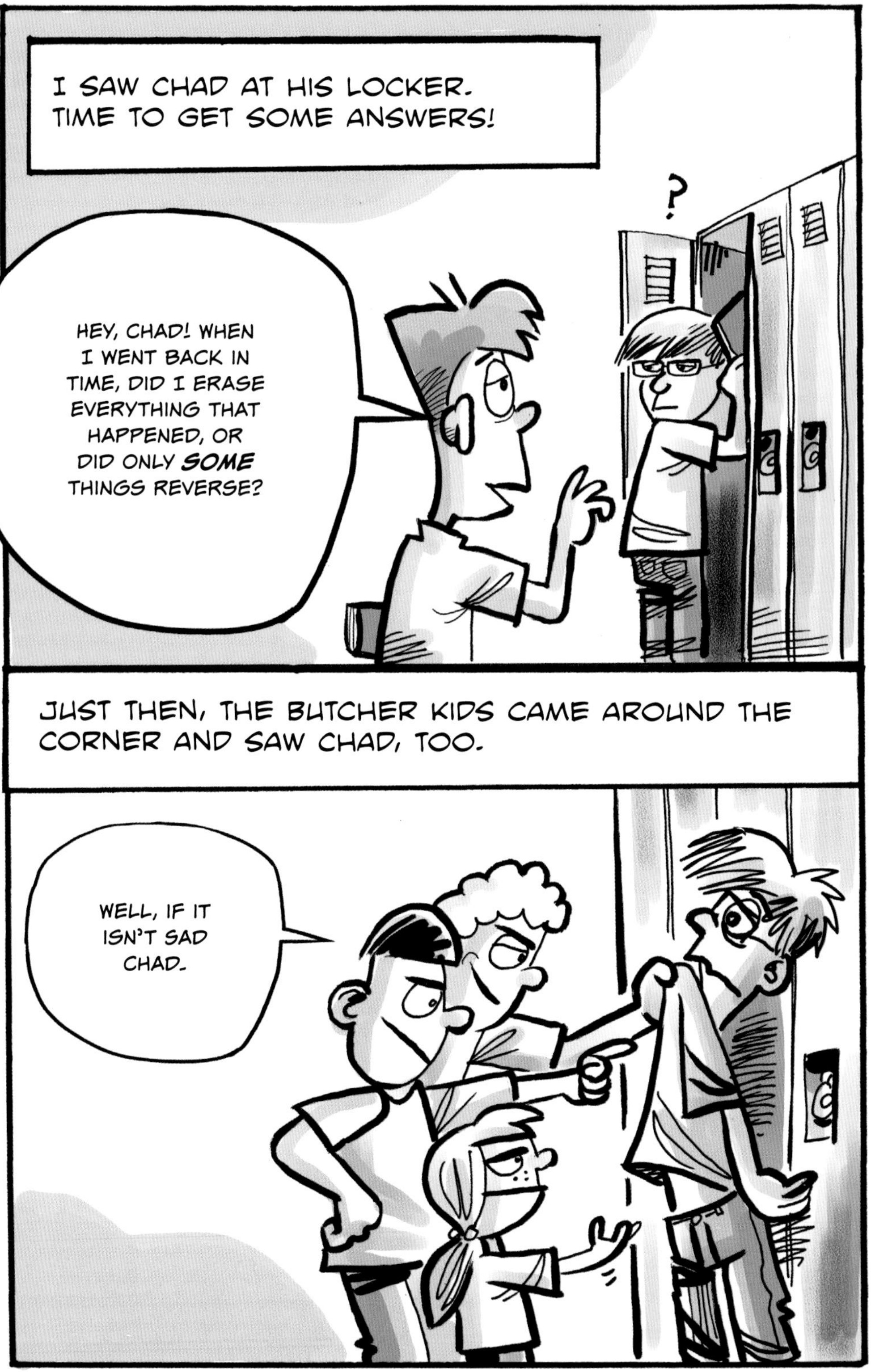
I SAW CHAD AT HIS LOCKER. TIME TO GET SOME ANSWERS!
?
HEY, CHAD! WHEN I WENT BACK IN TIME, DID I ERASE EVERYTHING THAT HAPPENED, OR DID ONLY ***SOME*** THINGS REVERSE?
JUST THEN, THE BUTCHER KIDS CAME AROUND THE CORNER AND SAW CHAD, TOO.
WELL, IF IT ISN'T SAD CHAD.

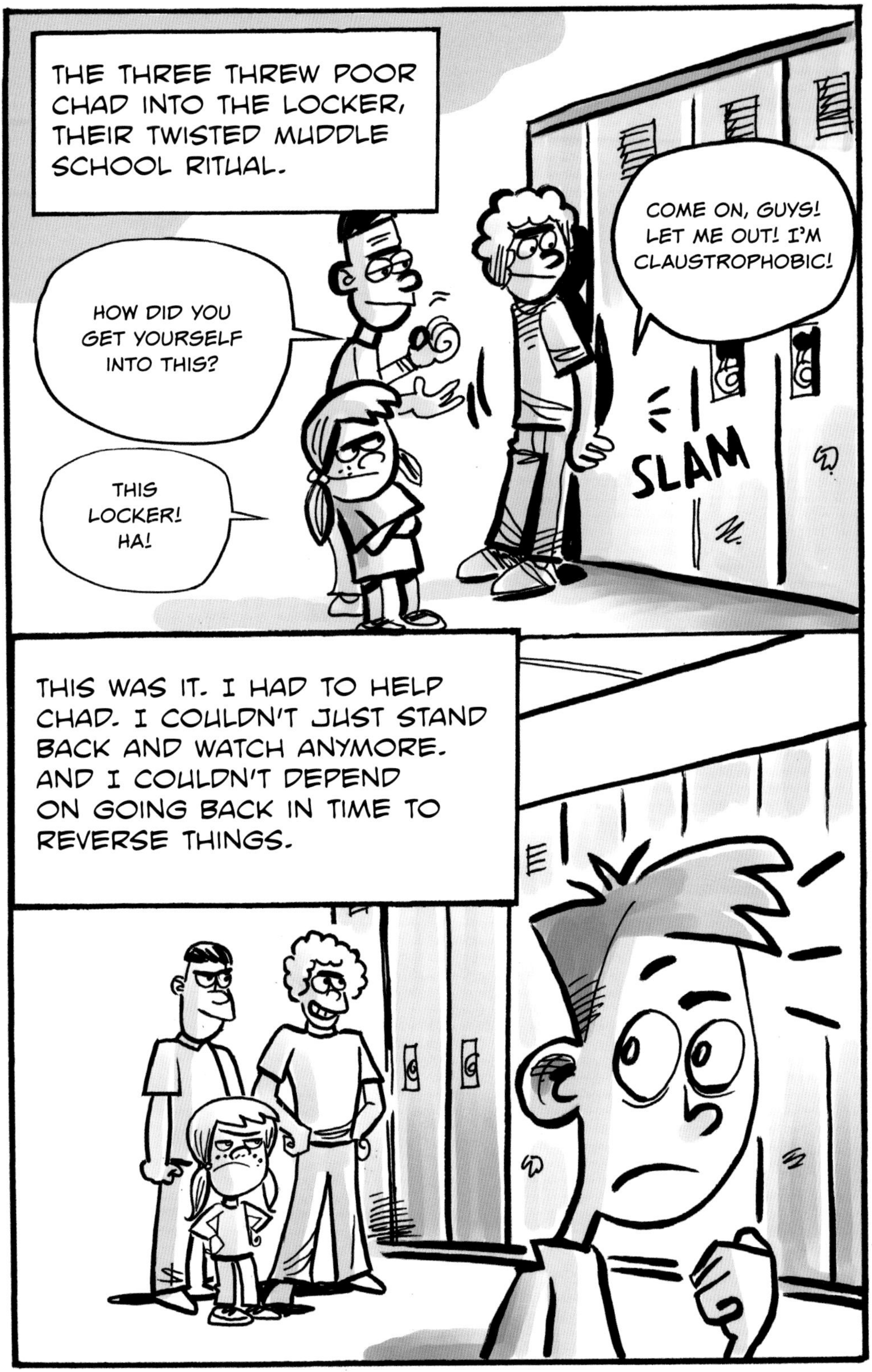
THE THREE THREW POOR CHAD INTO THE LOCKER, THEIR TWISTED MUDDLE SCHOOL RITUAL.
HOW DID YOU GET YOURSELF INTO THIS?
COME ON, GUYS! LET ME OUT! I'M CLAUSTROPHOBIC!
SLAM
THIS LOCKER! HA!
THIS WAS IT. I HAD TO HELP CHAD. I COULDN'T JUST STAND BACK AND WATCH ANYMORE. AND I COULDN'T DEPEND ON GOING BACK IN TIME TO REVERSE THINGS.

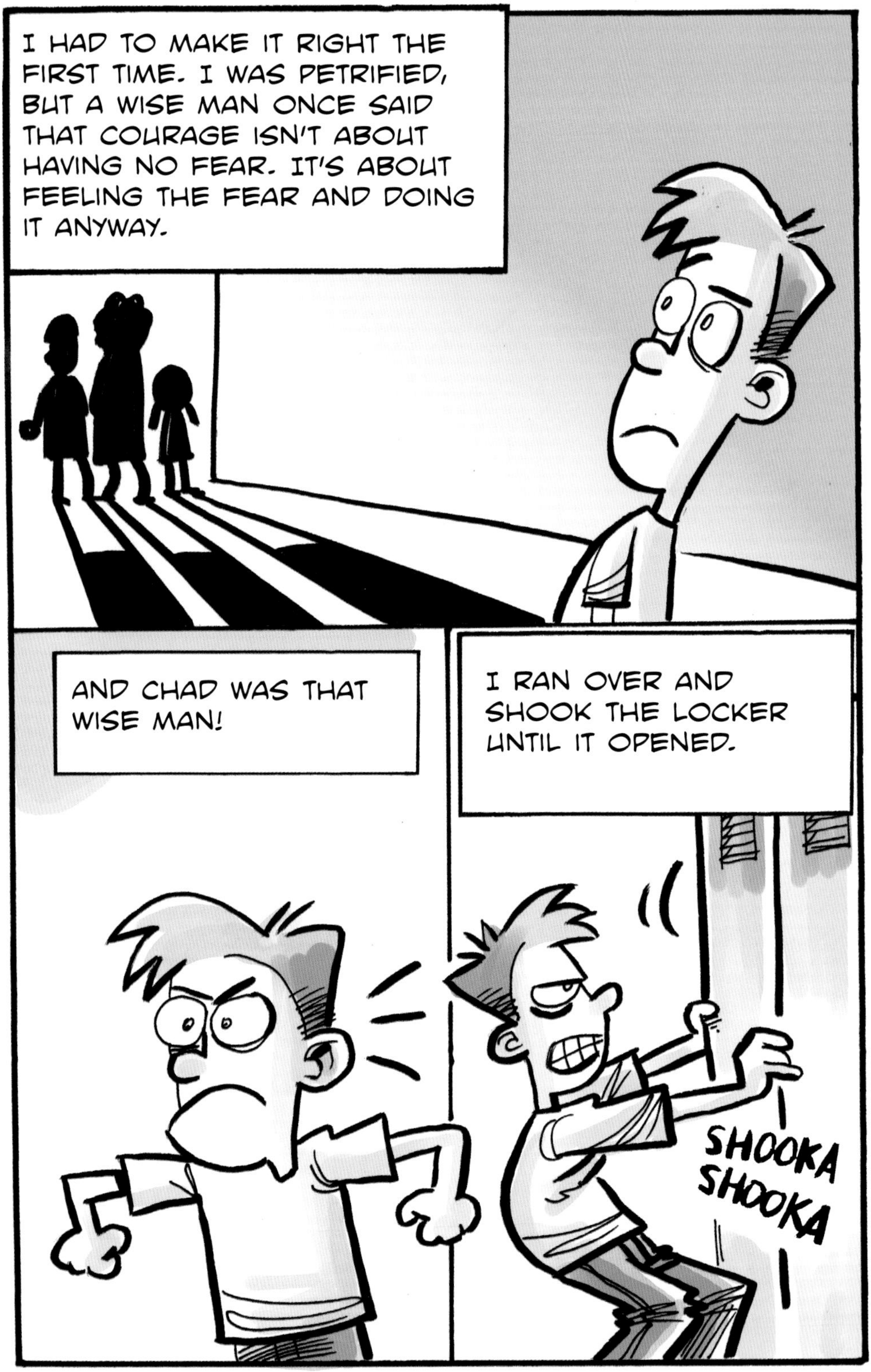
I HAD TO MAKE IT RIGHT THE FIRST TIME. I WAS PETRIFIED, BUT A WISE MAN ONCE SAID THAT COURAGE ISN'T ABOUT HAVING NO FEAR. IT'S ABOUT FEELING THE FEAR AND DOING IT ANYWAY.
AND CHAD WAS THAT WISE MAN!
I RAN OVER AND SHOOK THE LOCKER UNTIL IT OPENED.
SHOOKA SHOOKA

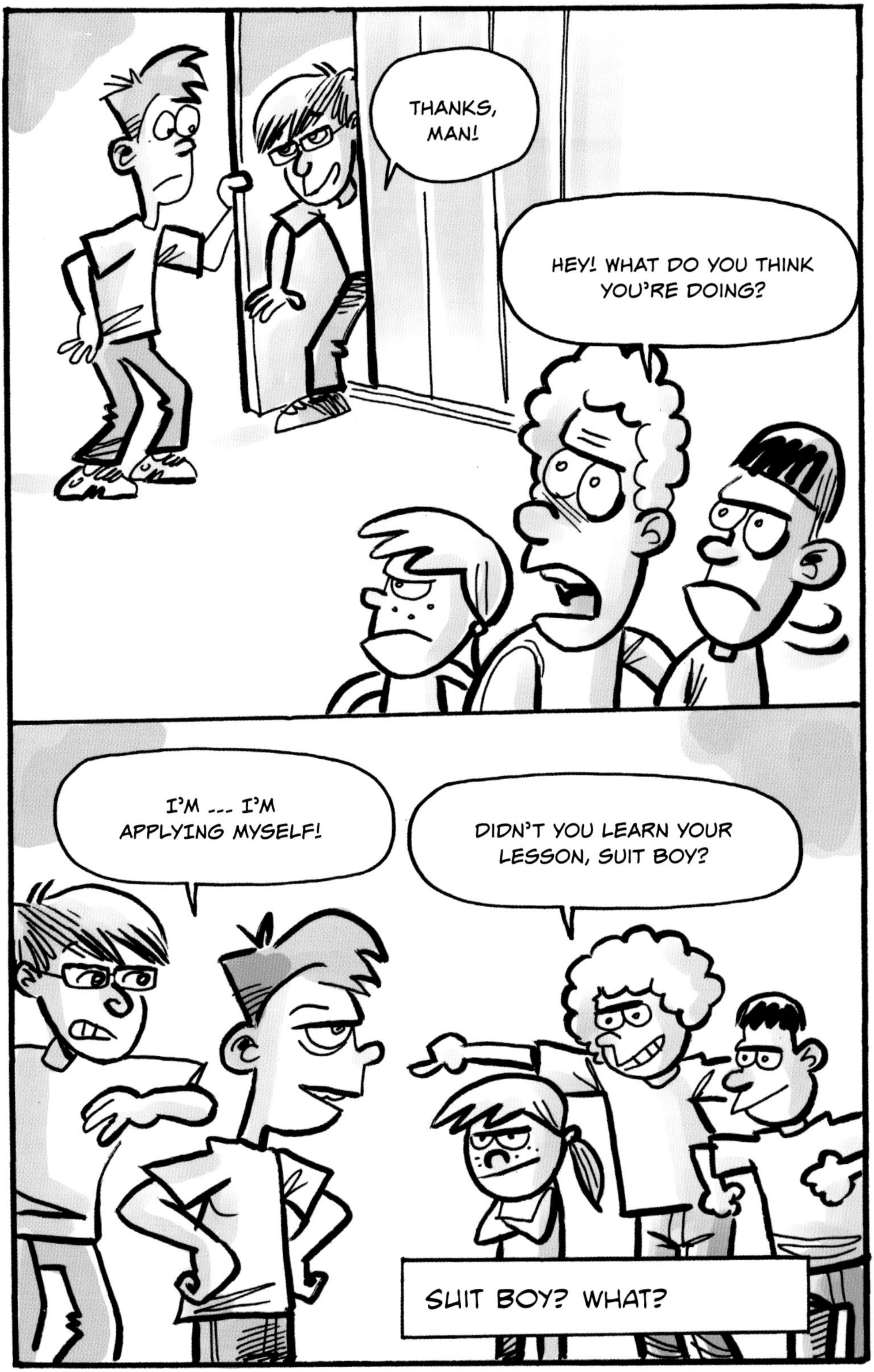
THANKS, MAN!
HEY! WHAT DO YOU THINK YOU'RE DOING?
I'M --- I'M APPLYING MYSELF!
DIDN'T YOU LEARN YOUR LESSON, SUIT BOY?
SUIT BOY? WHAT?

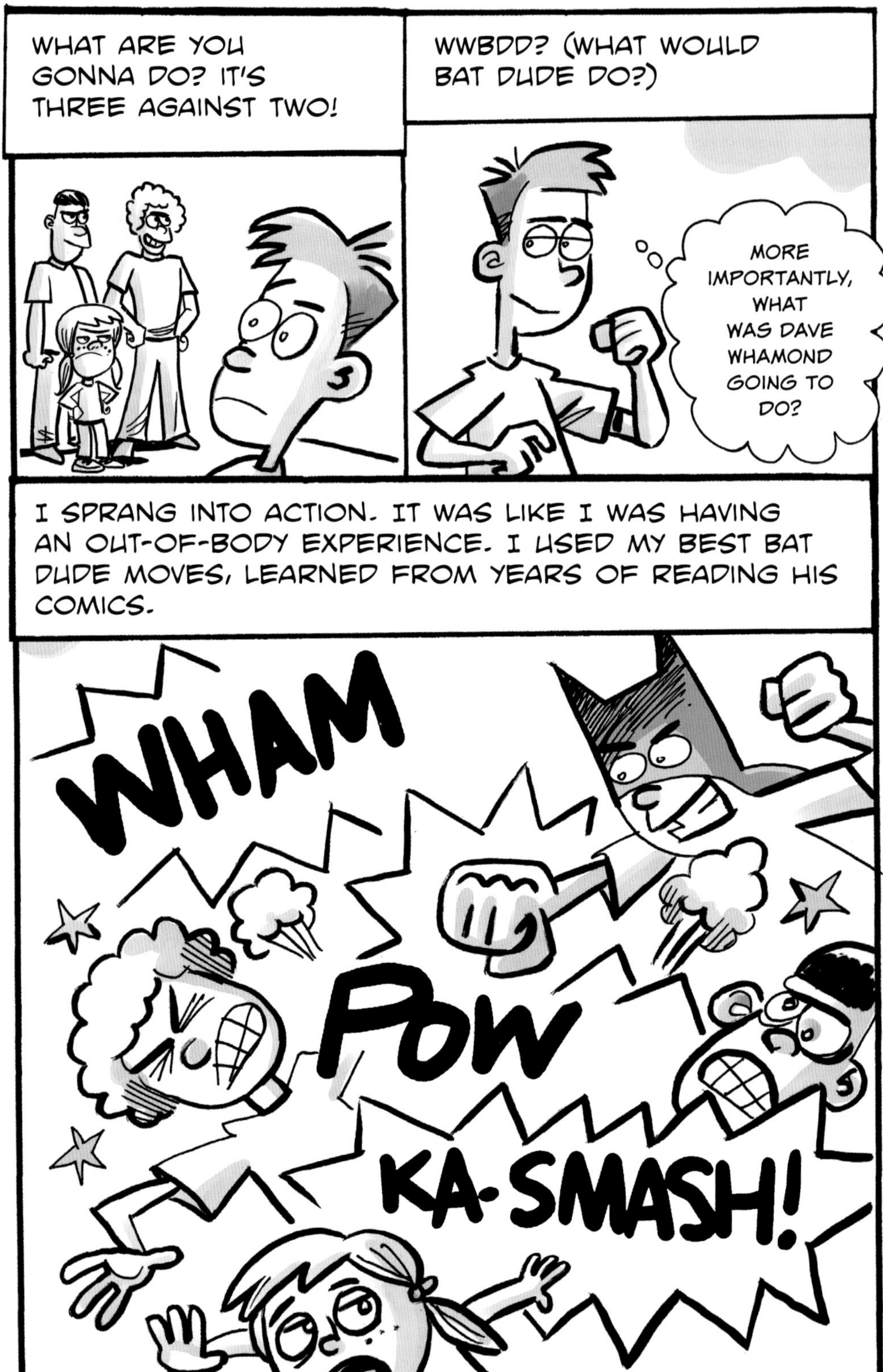
WHAT ARE YOU GONNA DO? IT'S THREE AGAINST TWO!
WWBDD? (WHAT WOULD BAT DUDE DO?)
MORE IMPORTANTLY, WHAT WAS DAVE WHAMOND GOING TO DO?
I SPRANG INTO ACTION. IT WAS LIKE I WAS HAVING AN OUT-OF-BODY EXPERIENCE. I USED MY BEST BAT DUDE MOVES, LEARNED FROM YEARS OF READING HIS COMICS.
WHAM
POW
KA-SMASH!

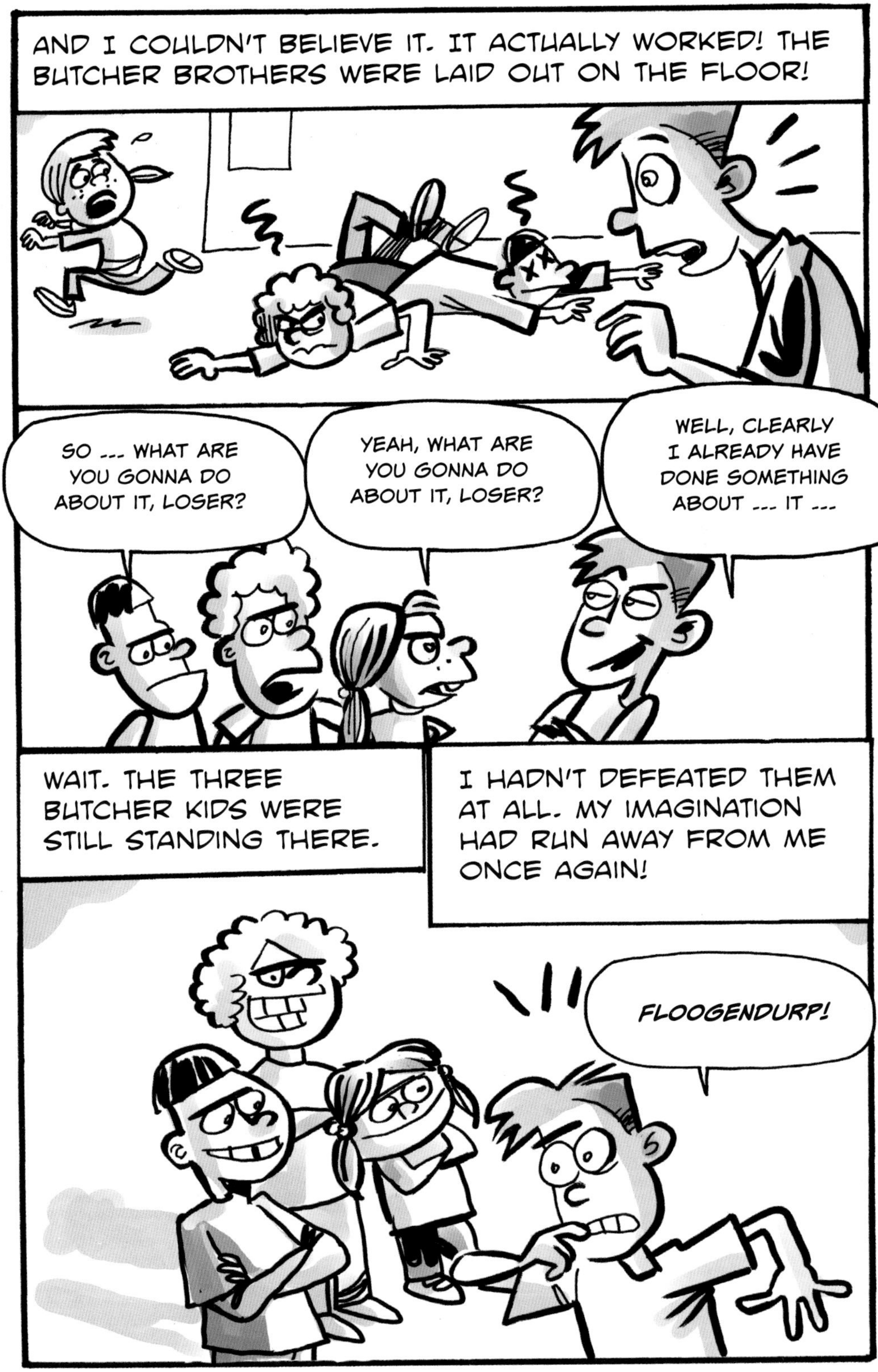
AND I COULDN'T BELIEVE IT. IT ACTUALLY WORKED! THE BUTCHER BROTHERS WERE LAID OUT ON THE FLOOR!
SO --- WHAT ARE YOU GONNA DO ABOUT IT, LOSER?
YEAH, WHAT ARE YOU GONNA DO ABOUT IT, LOSER?
WELL, CLEARLY I ALREADY HAVE DONE SOMETHING ABOUT --- IT ---
WAIT. THE THREE BUTCHER KIDS WERE STILL STANDING THERE.
I HADN'T DEFEATED THEM AT ALL. MY IMAGINATION HAD RUN AWAY FROM ME ONCE AGAIN!
FLOOGENDURP!

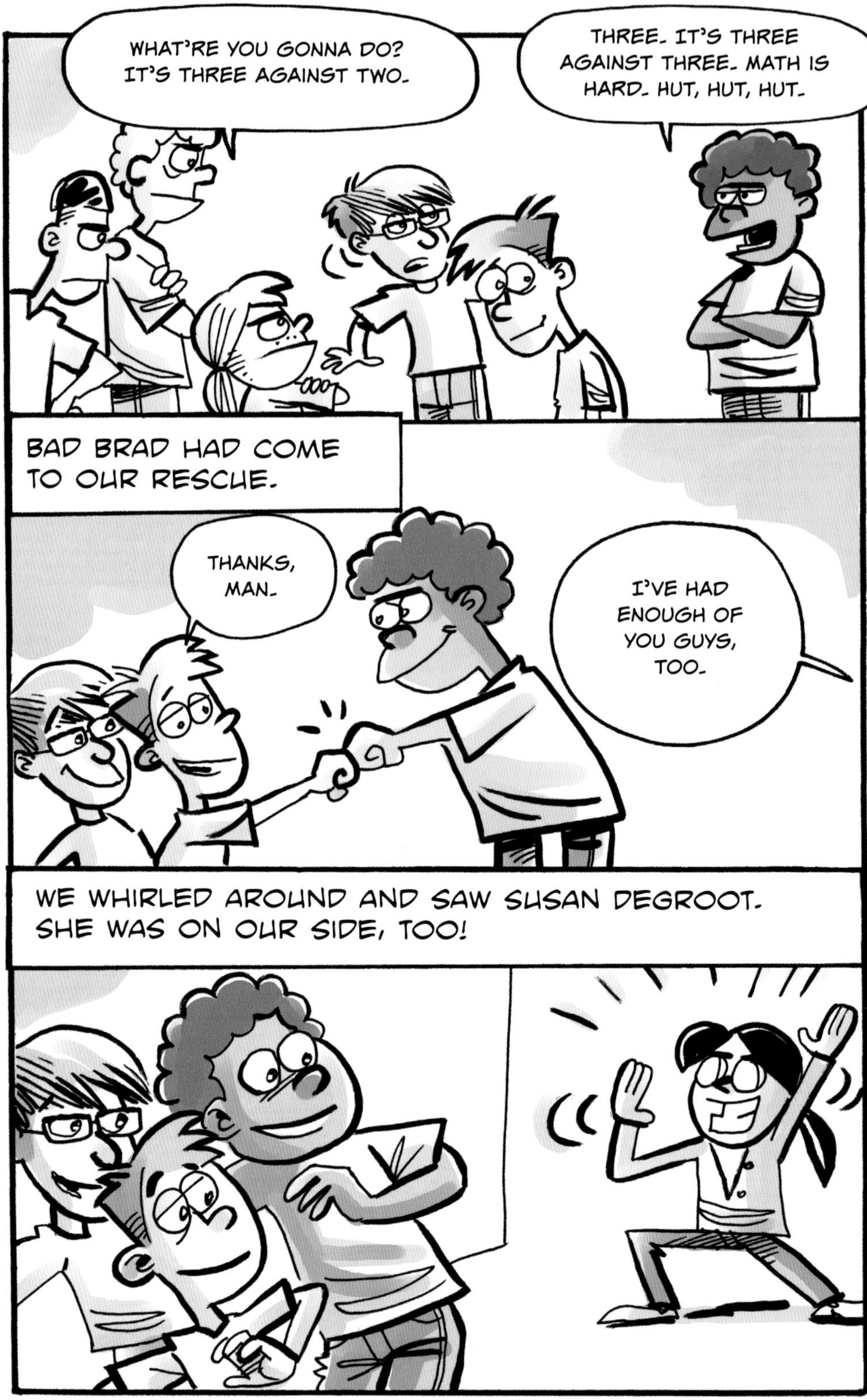
WHAT'RE YOU GONNA DO? IT'S THREE AGAINST TWO.
THREE. IT'S THREE AGAINST THREE. MATH IS HARD. HUT, HUT, HUT.
BAD BRAD HAD COME TO OUR RESCUE.
THANKS, MAN.
I'VE HAD ENOUGH OF YOU GUYS, TOO.
WE WHIRLED AROUND AND SAW SUSAN DEGROOT. SHE WAS ON OUR SIDE, TOO!

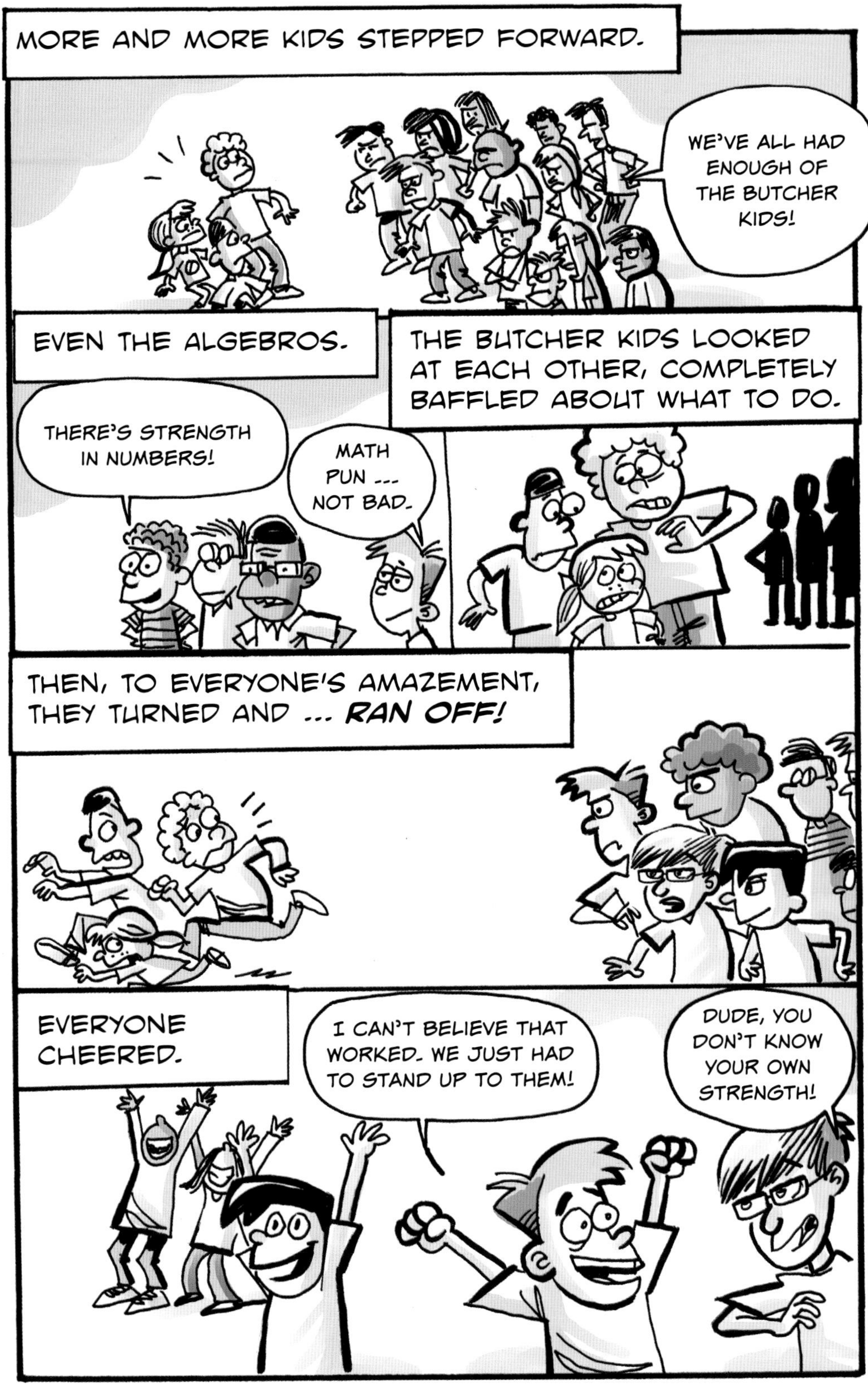
MORE AND MORE KIDS STEPPED FORWARD.
WE'VE ALL HAD ENOUGH OF THE BUTCHER KIDS!
EVEN THE ALGEBROS.
THERE'S STRENGTH IN NUMBERS!
MATH PUN --- NOT BAD.
THE BUTCHER KIDS LOOKED AT EACH OTHER, COMPLETELY BAFFLED ABOUT WHAT TO DO.
THEN, TO EVERYONE'S AMAZEMENT, THEY TURNED AND ... RAN OFF!
EVERYONE CHEERED.
I CAN'T BELIEVE THAT WORKED. WE JUST HAD TO STAND UP TO THEM!
DUDE, YOU DON'T KNOW YOUR OWN STRENGTH!

CHAPTER 10: IT'S ABOUT TIME!

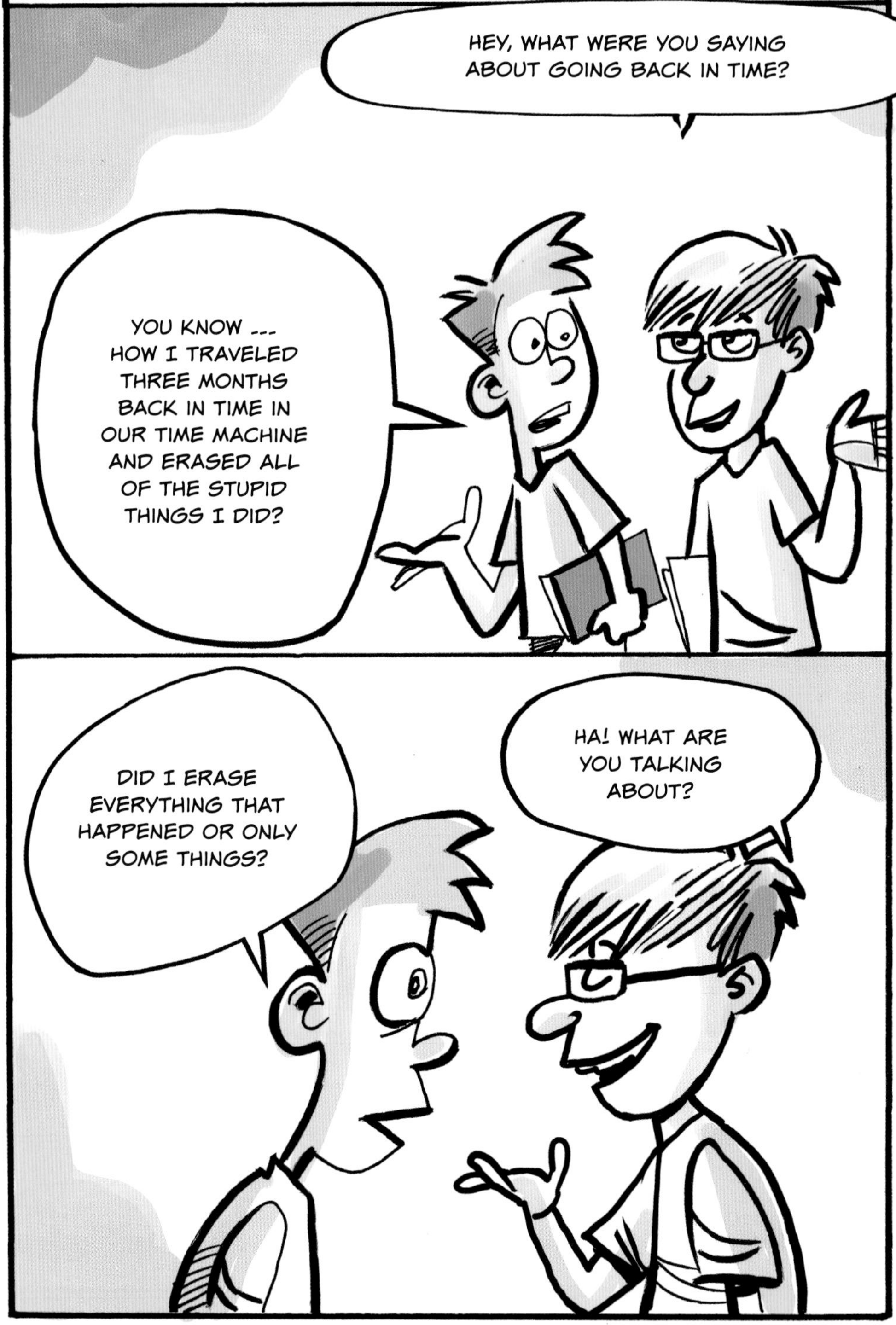
HEY, WHAT WERE YOU SAYING ABOUT GOING BACK IN TIME?
YOU KNOW --- HOW I TRAVELED THREE MONTHS BACK IN TIME IN OUR TIME MACHINE AND ERASED ALL OF THE STUPID THINGS I DID?
HA! WHAT ARE YOU TALKING ABOUT?
DID I ERASE EVERYTHING THAT HAPPENED OR ONLY SOME THINGS?

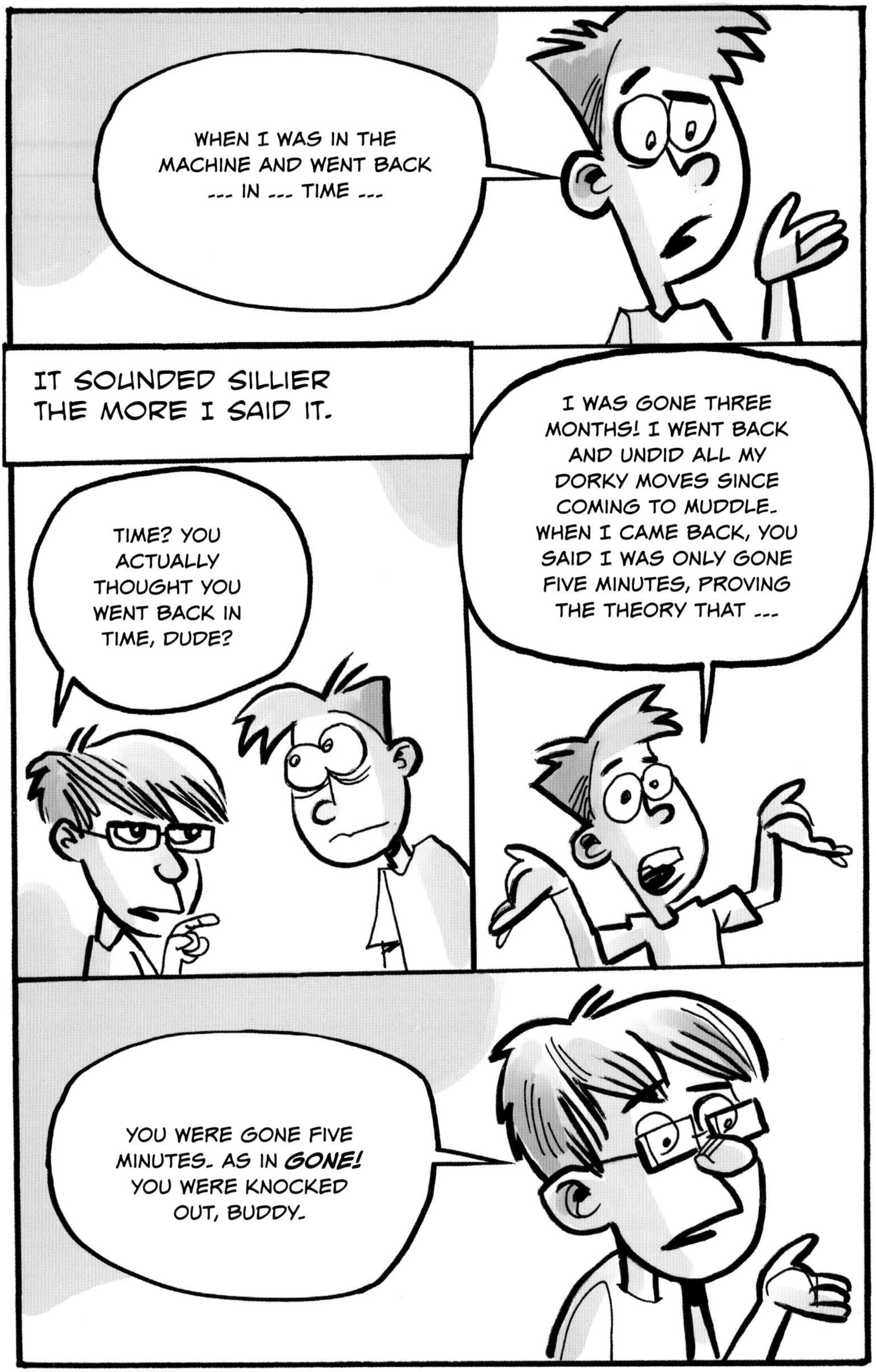
WHEN I WAS IN THE MACHINE AND WENT BACK --- IN --- TIME ---
IT SOUNDED SILLIER THE MORE I SAID IT.
TIME? YOU ACTUALLY THOUGHT YOU WENT BACK IN TIME, DUDE?
I WAS GONE THREE MONTHS! I WENT BACK AND UNDID ALL MY DORKY MOVES SINCE COMING TO MUDDLE. WHEN I CAME BACK, YOU SAID I WAS ONLY GONE FIVE MINUTES, PROVING THE THEORY THAT ---
YOU WERE GONE FIVE MINUTES. AS IN ***GONE!*** YOU WERE KNOCKED OUT, BUDDY.

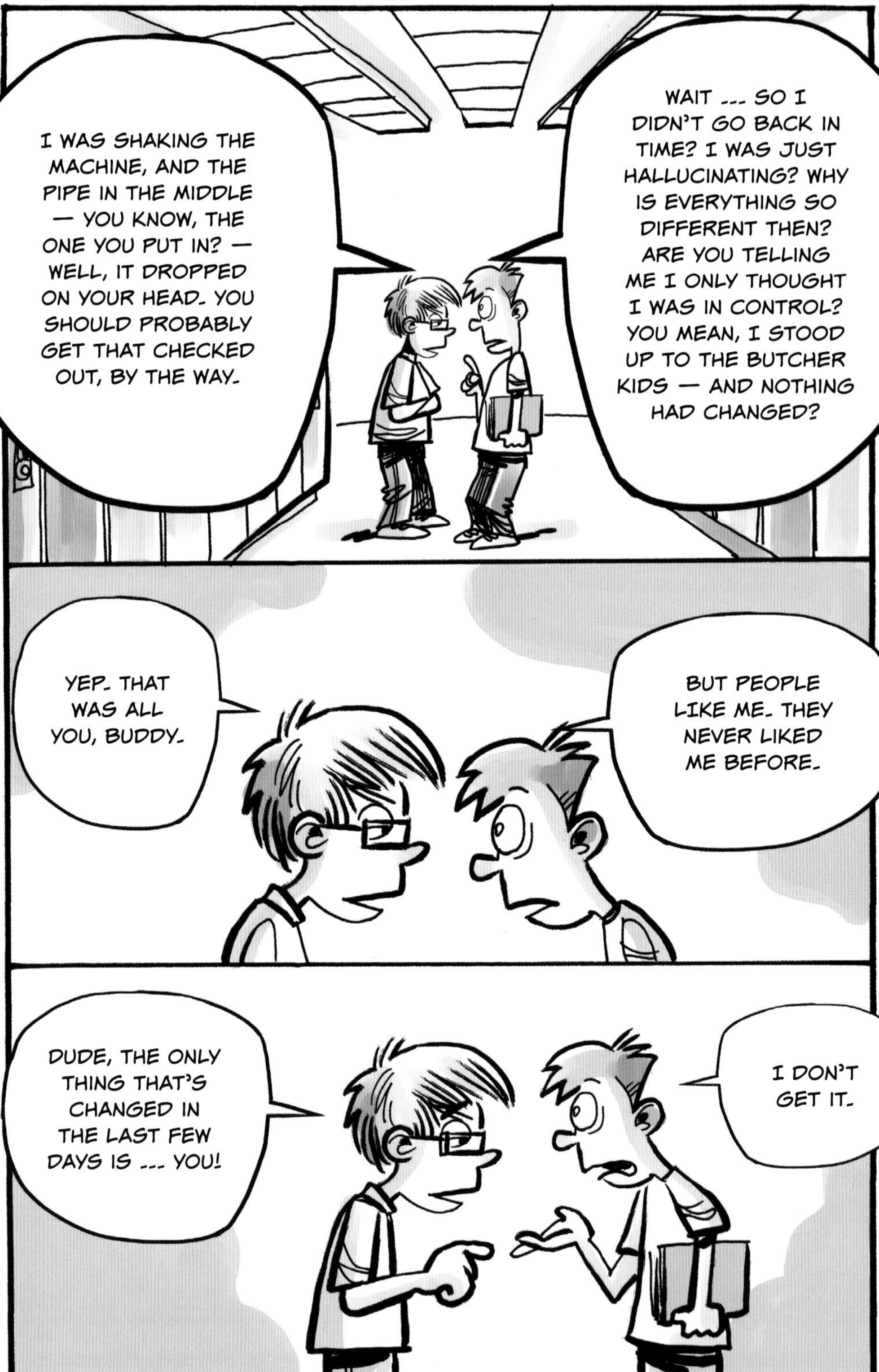
I WAS SHAKING THE MACHINE, AND THE PIPE IN THE MIDDLE — YOU KNOW, THE ONE YOU PUT IN? — WELL, IT DROPPED ON YOUR HEAD. YOU SHOULD PROBABLY GET THAT CHECKED OUT, BY THE WAY.
WAIT ... SO I DIDN'T GO BACK IN TIME? I WAS JUST HALLUCINATING? WHY IS EVERYTHING SO DIFFERENT THEN? ARE YOU TELLING ME I ONLY THOUGHT I WAS IN CONTROL? YOU MEAN, I STOOD UP TO THE BUTCHER KIDS — AND NOTHING HAD CHANGED?
YEP. THAT WAS ALL YOU, BUDDY.
BUT PEOPLE LIKE ME. THEY NEVER LIKED ME BEFORE.
DUDE, THE ONLY THING THAT'S CHANGED IN THE LAST FEW DAYS IS ... YOU!
I DON'T GET IT.

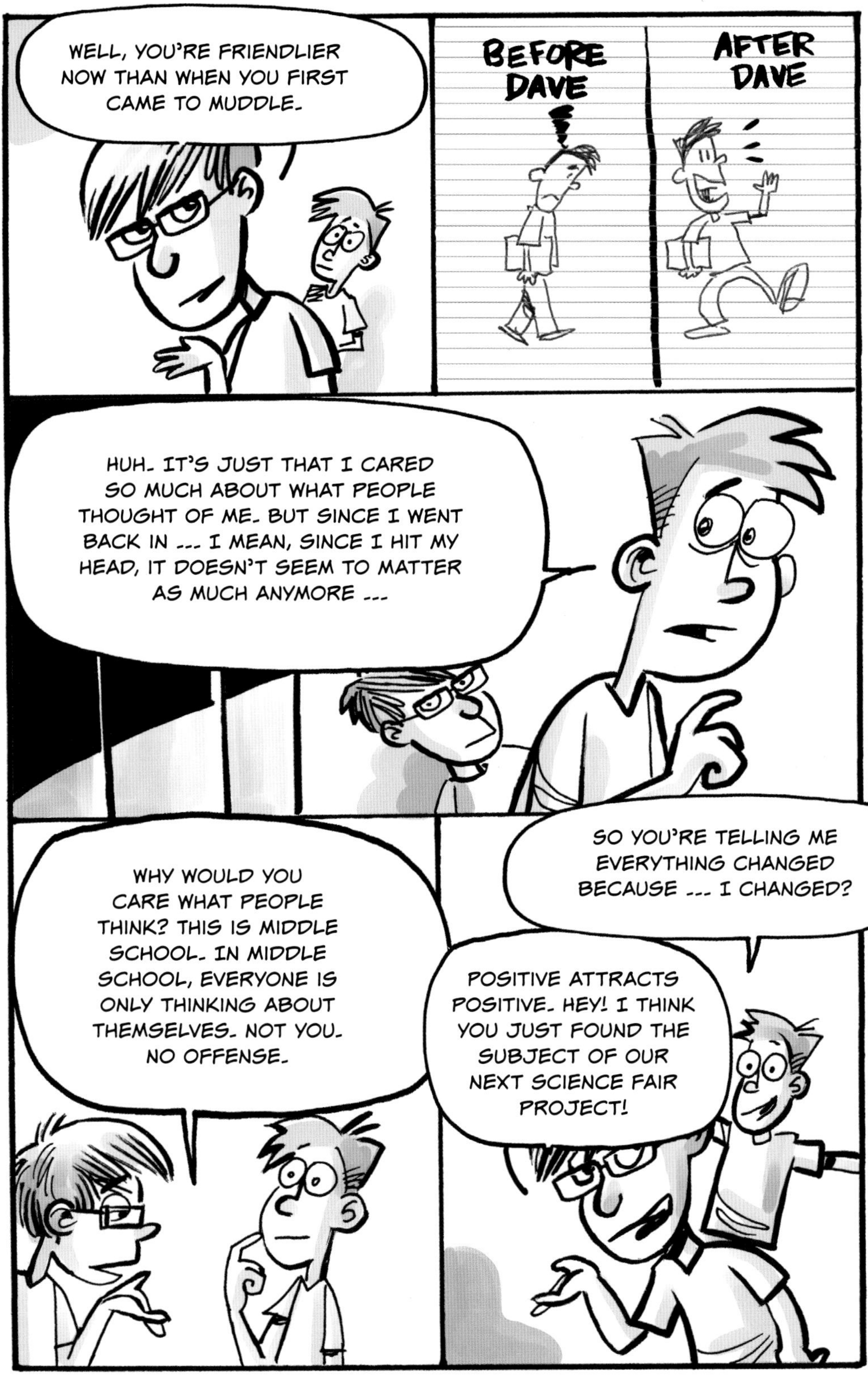
WELL, YOU'RE FRIENDLIER NOW THAN WHEN YOU FIRST CAME TO MUDDLE.
BEFORE DAVE
AFTER DAVE
HUH. IT'S JUST THAT I CARED SO MUCH ABOUT WHAT PEOPLE THOUGHT OF ME. BUT SINCE I WENT BACK IN ... I MEAN, SINCE I HIT MY HEAD, IT DOESN'T SEEM TO MATTER AS MUCH ANYMORE ...
WHY WOULD YOU CARE WHAT PEOPLE THINK? THIS IS MIDDLE SCHOOL. IN MIDDLE SCHOOL, EVERYONE IS ONLY THINKING ABOUT THEMSELVES. NOT YOU. NO OFFENSE.
SO YOU'RE TELLING ME EVERYTHING CHANGED BECAUSE ... I CHANGED?
POSITIVE ATTRACTS POSITIVE. HEY! I THINK YOU JUST FOUND THE SUBJECT OF OUR NEXT SCIENCE FAIR PROJECT!

CHAPTER 11: EVERYTHING IS AWESOME!

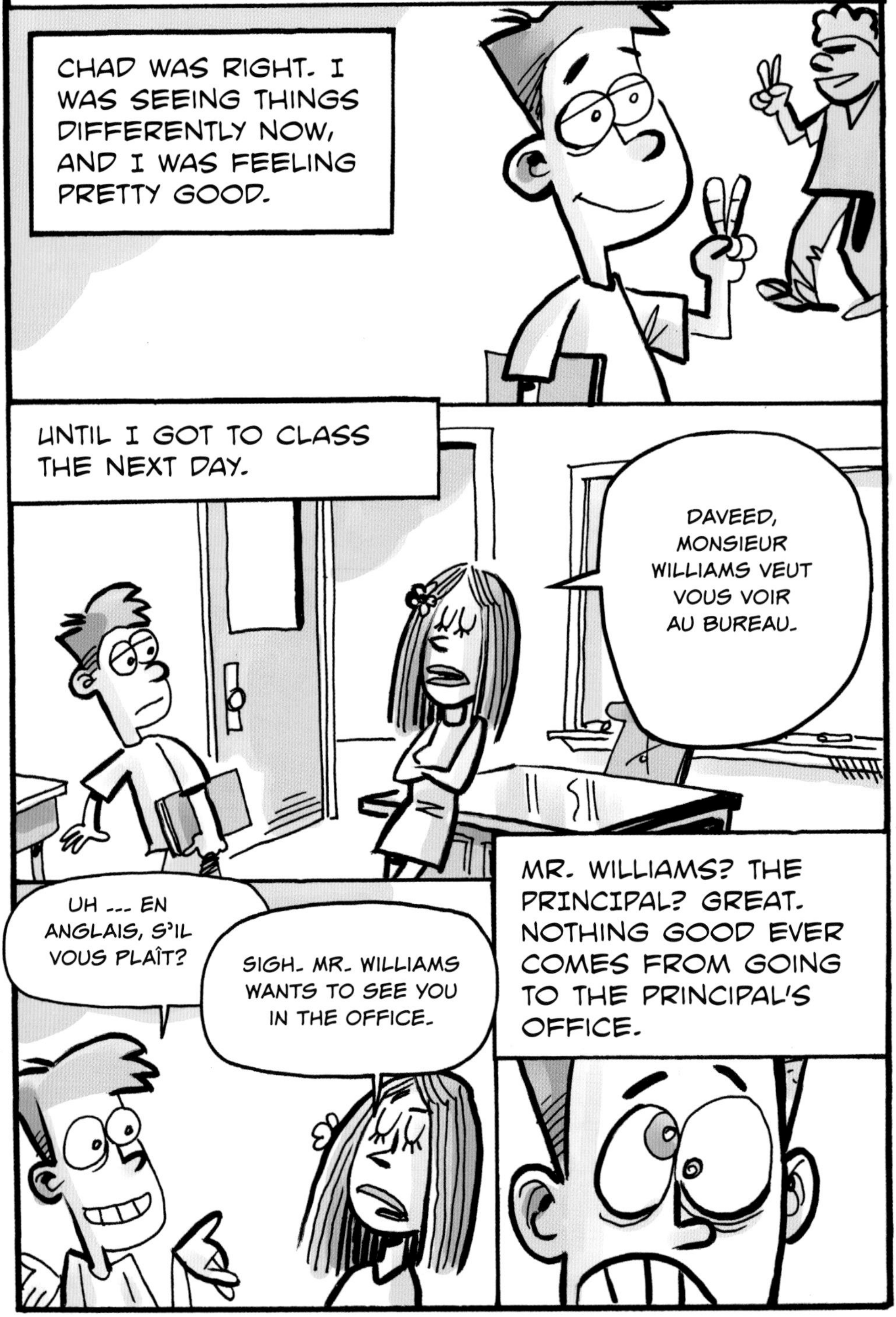
CHAD WAS RIGHT. I WAS SEEING THINGS DIFFERENTLY NOW, AND I WAS FEELING PRETTY GOOD.
UNTIL I GOT TO CLASS THE NEXT DAY.
DAVEED, MONSIEUR WILLIAMS VEUT VOUS VOIR AU BUREAU.
UH ... EN ANGLAIS, S'IL VOUS PLAÎT?
SIGH. MR. WILLIAMS WANTS TO SEE YOU IN THE OFFICE.
MR. WILLIAMS? THE PRINCIPAL? GREAT. NOTHING GOOD EVER COMES FROM GOING TO THE PRINCIPAL'S OFFICE.

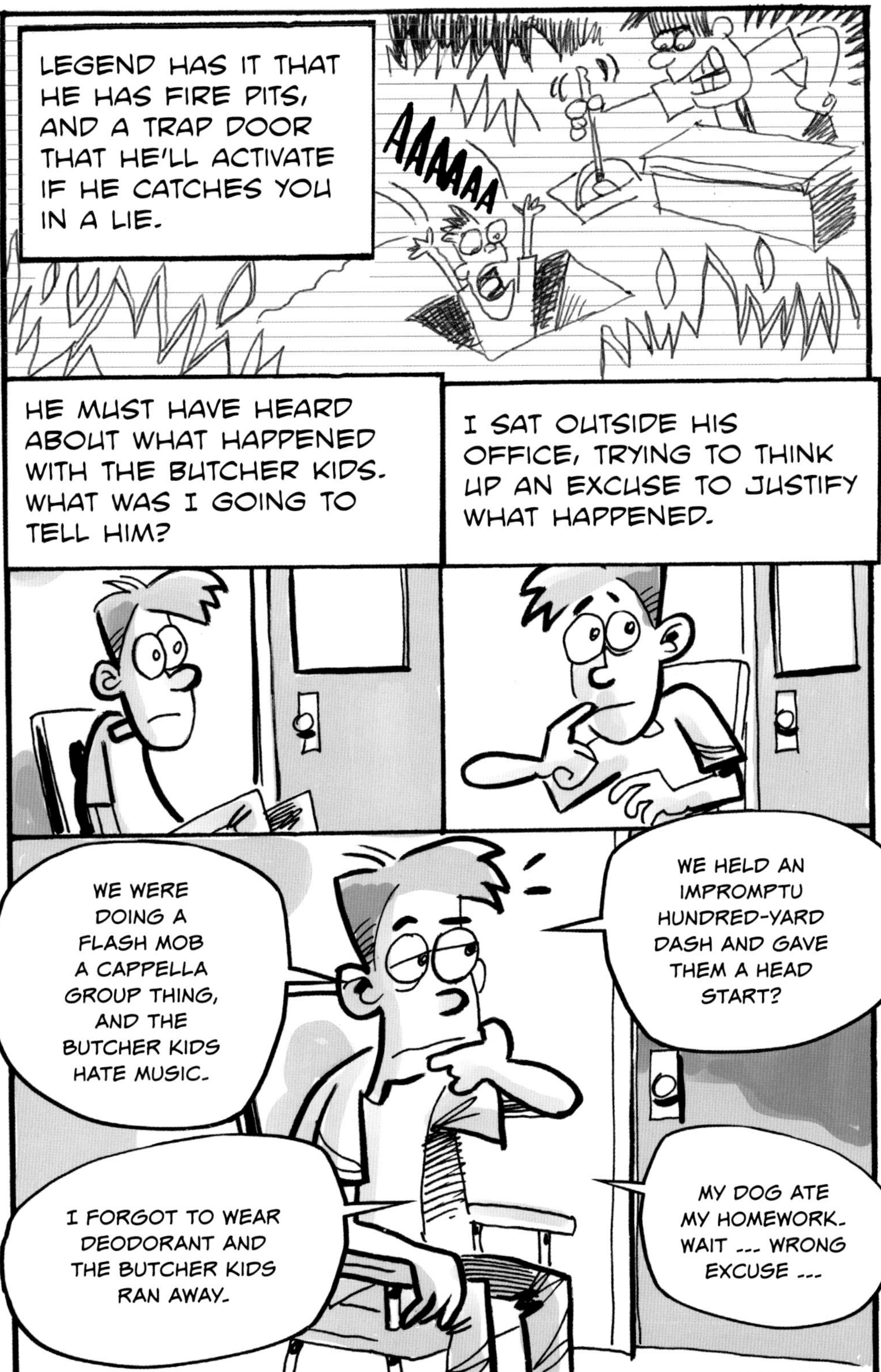
LEGEND HAS IT THAT HE HAS FIRE PITS, AND A TRAP DOOR THAT HE'LL ACTIVATE IF HE CATCHES YOU IN A LIE.
AAAAAAA
HE MUST HAVE HEARD ABOUT WHAT HAPPENED WITH THE BUTCHER KIDS. WHAT WAS I GOING TO TELL HIM?
I SAT OUTSIDE HIS OFFICE, TRYING TO THINK UP AN EXCUSE TO JUSTIFY WHAT HAPPENED.
WE WERE DOING A FLASH MOB A CAPPELLA GROUP THING, AND THE BUTCHER KIDS HATE MUSIC.
WE HELD AN IMPROMPTU HUNDRED-YARD DASH AND GAVE THEM A HEAD START?
I FORGOT TO WEAR DEODORANT AND THE BUTCHER KIDS RAN AWAY.
MY DOG ATE MY HOMEWORK. WAIT ... WRONG EXCUSE ...

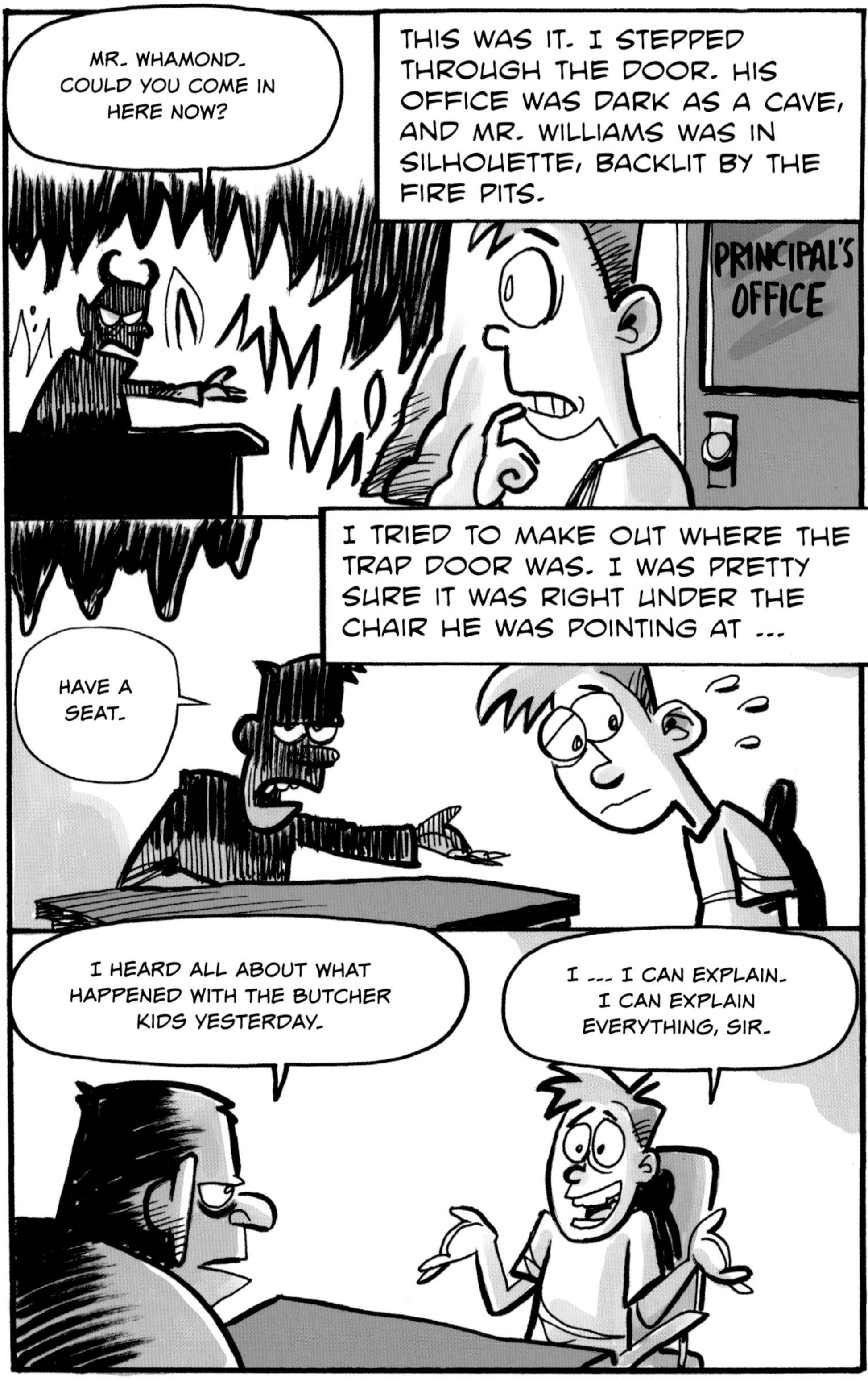
MR. WHAMOND. COULD YOU COME IN HERE NOW?
THIS WAS IT. I STEPPED THROUGH THE DOOR. HIS OFFICE WAS DARK AS A CAVE, AND MR. WILLIAMS WAS IN SILHOUETTE, BACKLIT BY THE FIRE PITS.
PRINCIPAL'S OFFICE
I TRIED TO MAKE OUT WHERE THE TRAP DOOR WAS. I WAS PRETTY SURE IT WAS RIGHT UNDER THE CHAIR HE WAS POINTING AT ...
HAVE A SEAT.
I HEARD ALL ABOUT WHAT HAPPENED WITH THE BUTCHER KIDS YESTERDAY.
I ... I CAN EXPLAIN. I CAN EXPLAIN EVERYTHING, SIR.

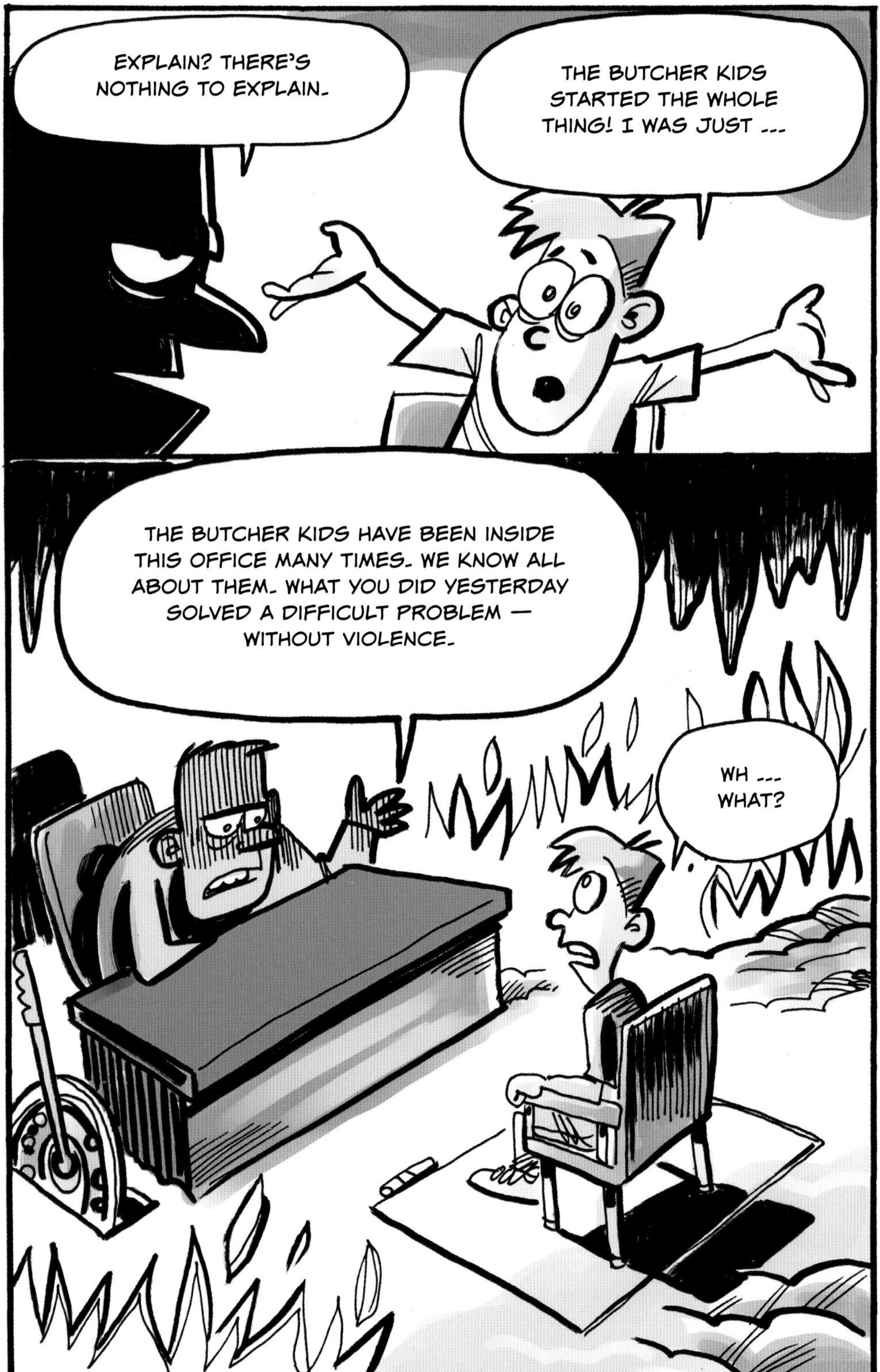
EXPLAIN? THERE'S NOTHING TO EXPLAIN.
THE BUTCHER KIDS STARTED THE WHOLE THING! I WAS JUST ...
THE BUTCHER KIDS HAVE BEEN INSIDE THIS OFFICE MANY TIMES. WE KNOW ALL ABOUT THEM. WHAT YOU DID YESTERDAY SOLVED A DIFFICULT PROBLEM — WITHOUT VIOLENCE.
WH ... WHAT?

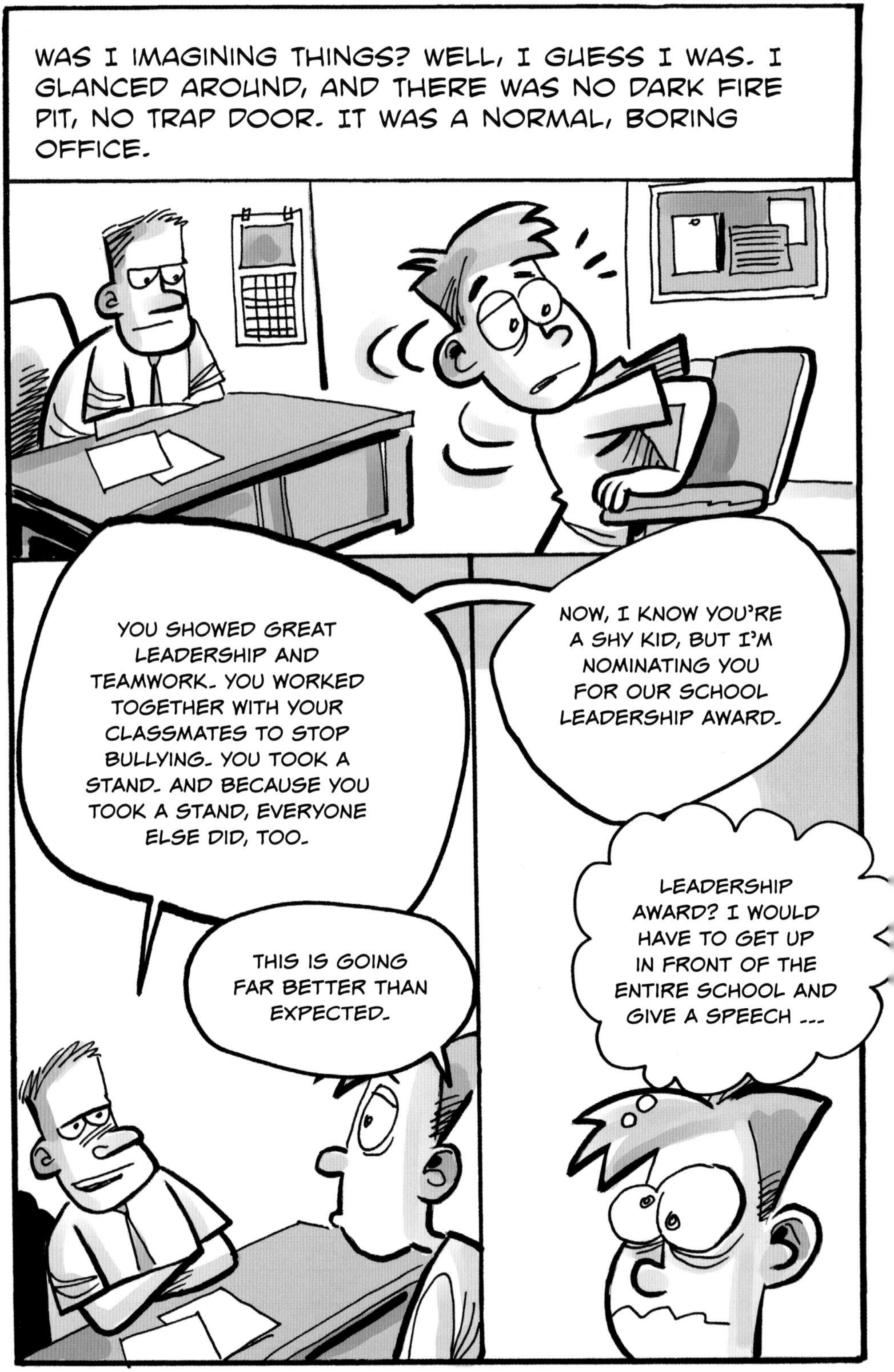
WAS I IMAGINING THINGS? WELL, I GUESS I WAS. I GLANCED AROUND, AND THERE WAS NO DARK FIRE PIT, NO TRAP DOOR. IT WAS A NORMAL, BORING OFFICE.
YOU SHOWED GREAT LEADERSHIP AND TEAMWORK. YOU WORKED TOGETHER WITH YOUR CLASSMATES TO STOP BULLYING. YOU TOOK A STAND. AND BECAUSE YOU TOOK A STAND, EVERYONE ELSE DID, TOO.
THIS IS GOING FAR BETTER THAN EXPECTED.
NOW, I KNOW YOU'RE A SHY KID, BUT I'M NOMINATING YOU FOR OUR SCHOOL LEADERSHIP AWARD.
LEADERSHIP AWARD? I WOULD HAVE TO GET UP IN FRONT OF THE ENTIRE SCHOOL AND GIVE A SPEECH ...

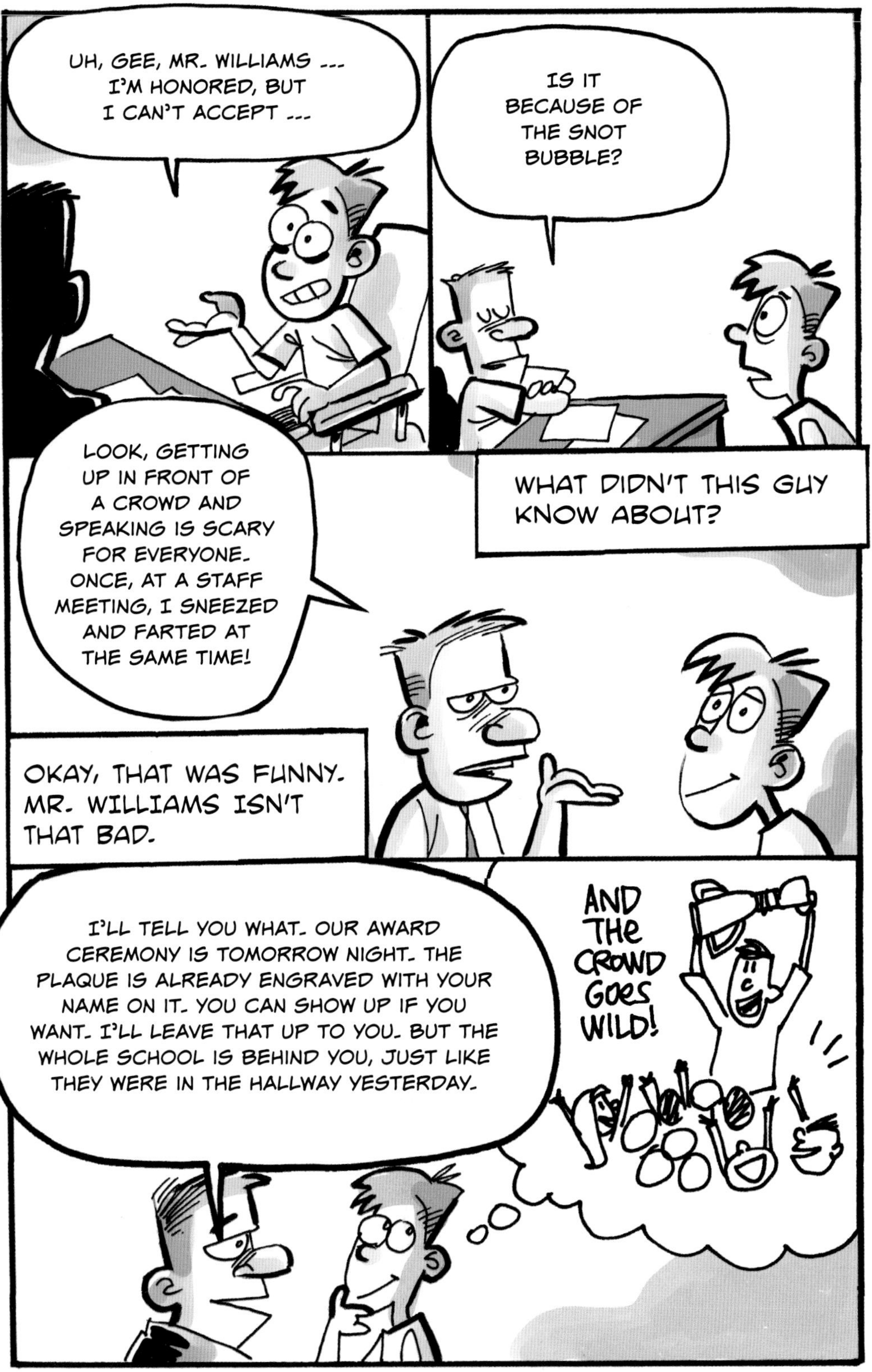
UH, GEE, MR. WILLIAMS ... I'M HONORED, BUT I CAN'T ACCEPT ...
IS IT BECAUSE OF THE SNOT BUBBLE?
LOOK, GETTING UP IN FRONT OF A CROWD AND SPEAKING IS SCARY FOR EVERYONE. ONCE, AT A STAFF MEETING, I SNEEZED AND FARTED AT THE SAME TIME!
WHAT DIDN'T THIS GUY KNOW ABOUT?
OKAY, THAT WAS FUNNY. MR. WILLIAMS ISN'T THAT BAD.
I'LL TELL YOU WHAT. OUR AWARD CEREMONY IS TOMORROW NIGHT. THE PLAQUE IS ALREADY ENGRAVED WITH YOUR NAME ON IT. YOU CAN SHOW UP IF YOU WANT. I'LL LEAVE THAT UP TO YOU. BUT THE WHOLE SCHOOL IS BEHIND YOU, JUST LIKE THEY WERE IN THE HALLWAY YESTERDAY.
AND THE CROWD GOES WILD!

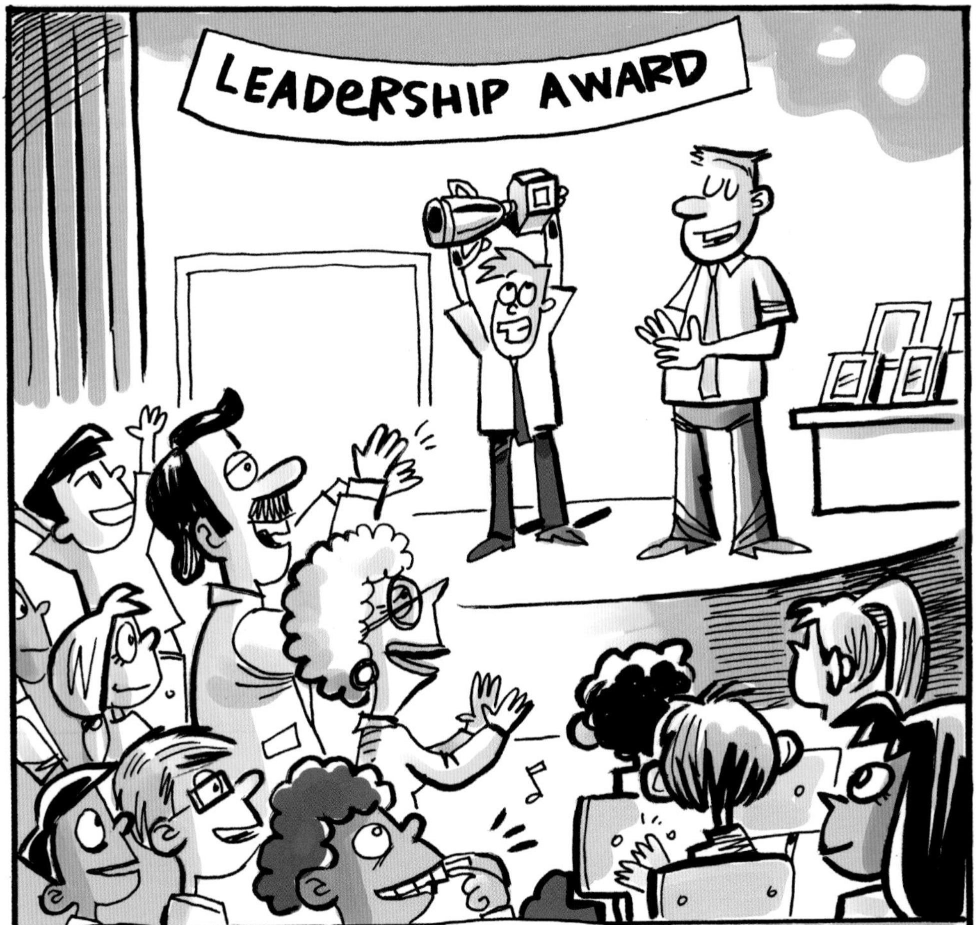
LEADERSHIP AWARD

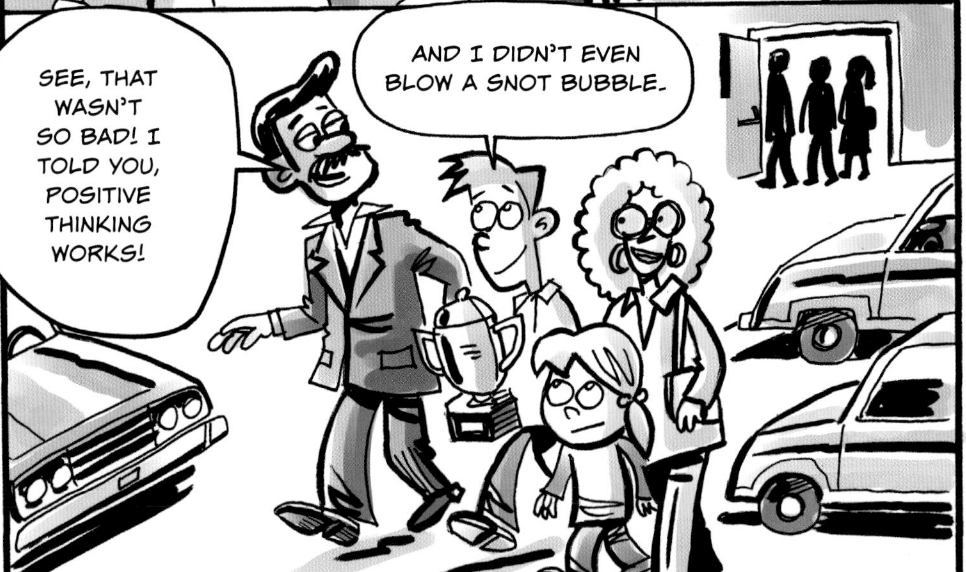
SEE, THAT WASN'T SO BAD! I TOLD YOU, POSITIVE THINKING WORKS!
AND I DIDN'T EVEN BLOW A SNOT BUBBLE.

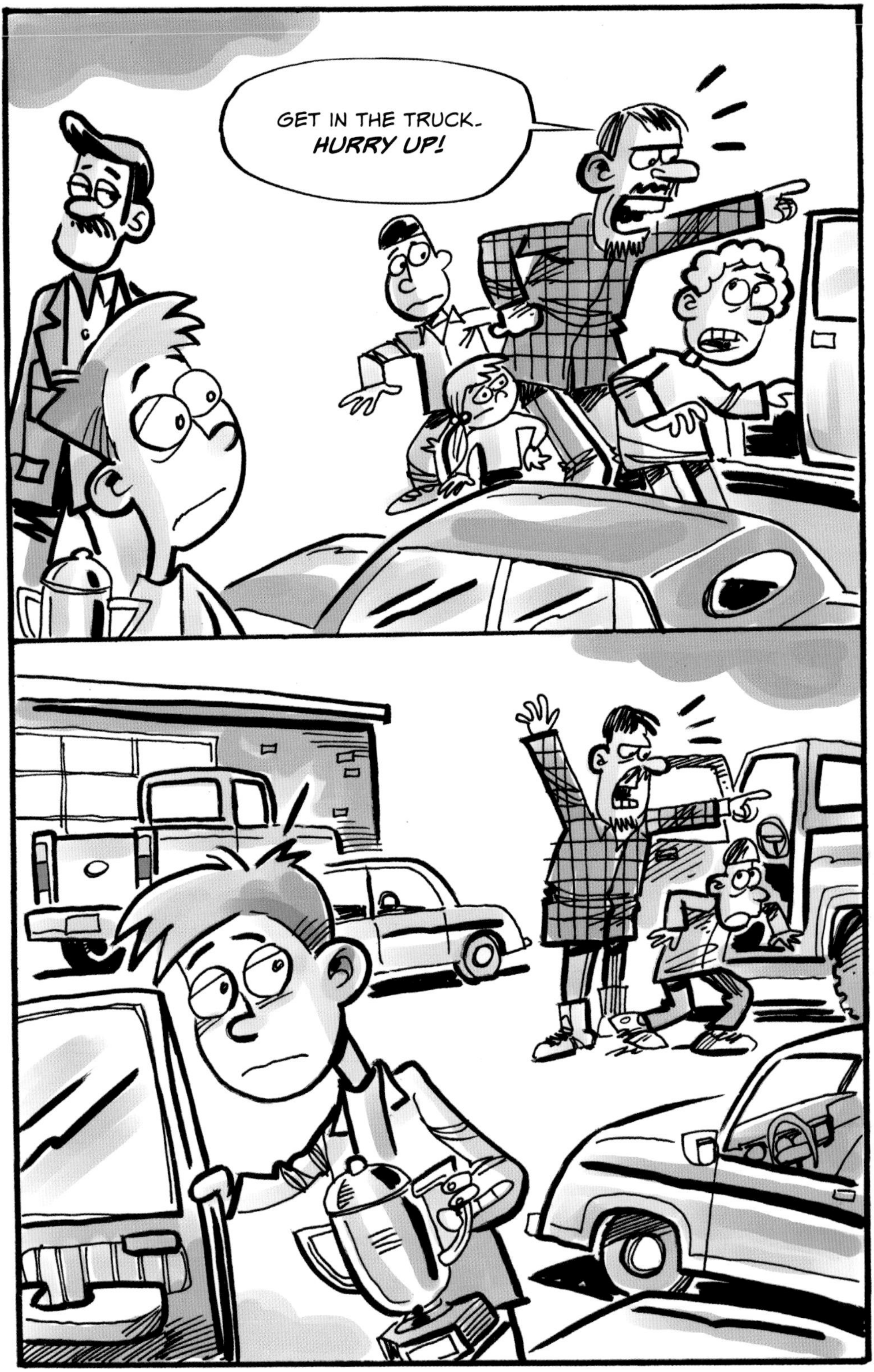
GET IN THE TRUCK. *HURRY UP!*

CHAPTER 12: REDEMPTION!

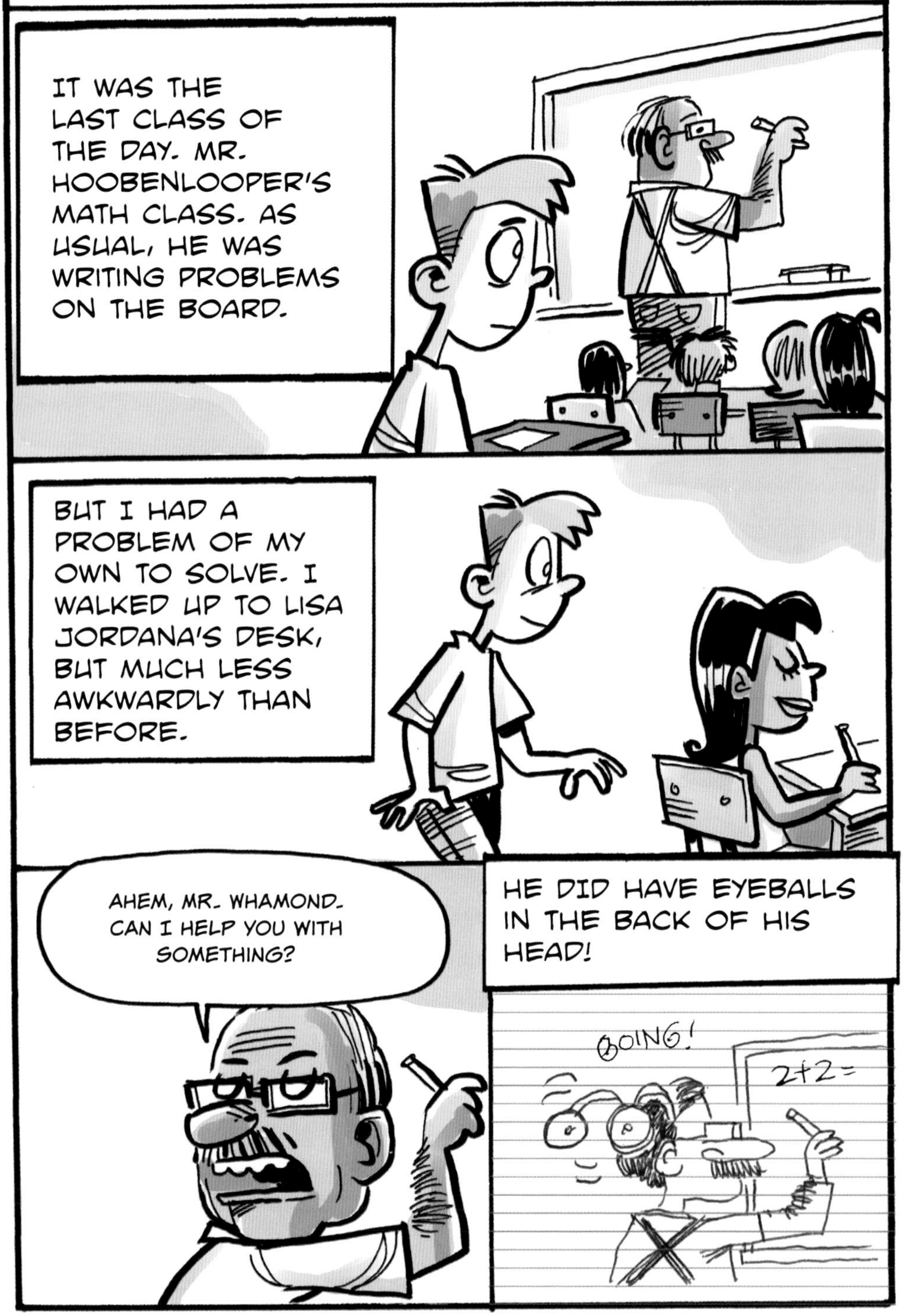
IT WAS THE LAST CLASS OF THE DAY. MR. HOOBENLOOPER'S MATH CLASS. AS USUAL, HE WAS WRITING PROBLEMS ON THE BOARD.
BUT I HAD A PROBLEM OF MY OWN TO SOLVE. I WALKED UP TO LISA JORDANA'S DESK, BUT MUCH LESS AWKWARDLY THAN BEFORE.
AHEM, MR. WHAMOND. CAN I HELP YOU WITH SOMETHING?
HE DID HAVE EYEBALLS IN THE BACK OF HIS HEAD!
BOING!
2+2=

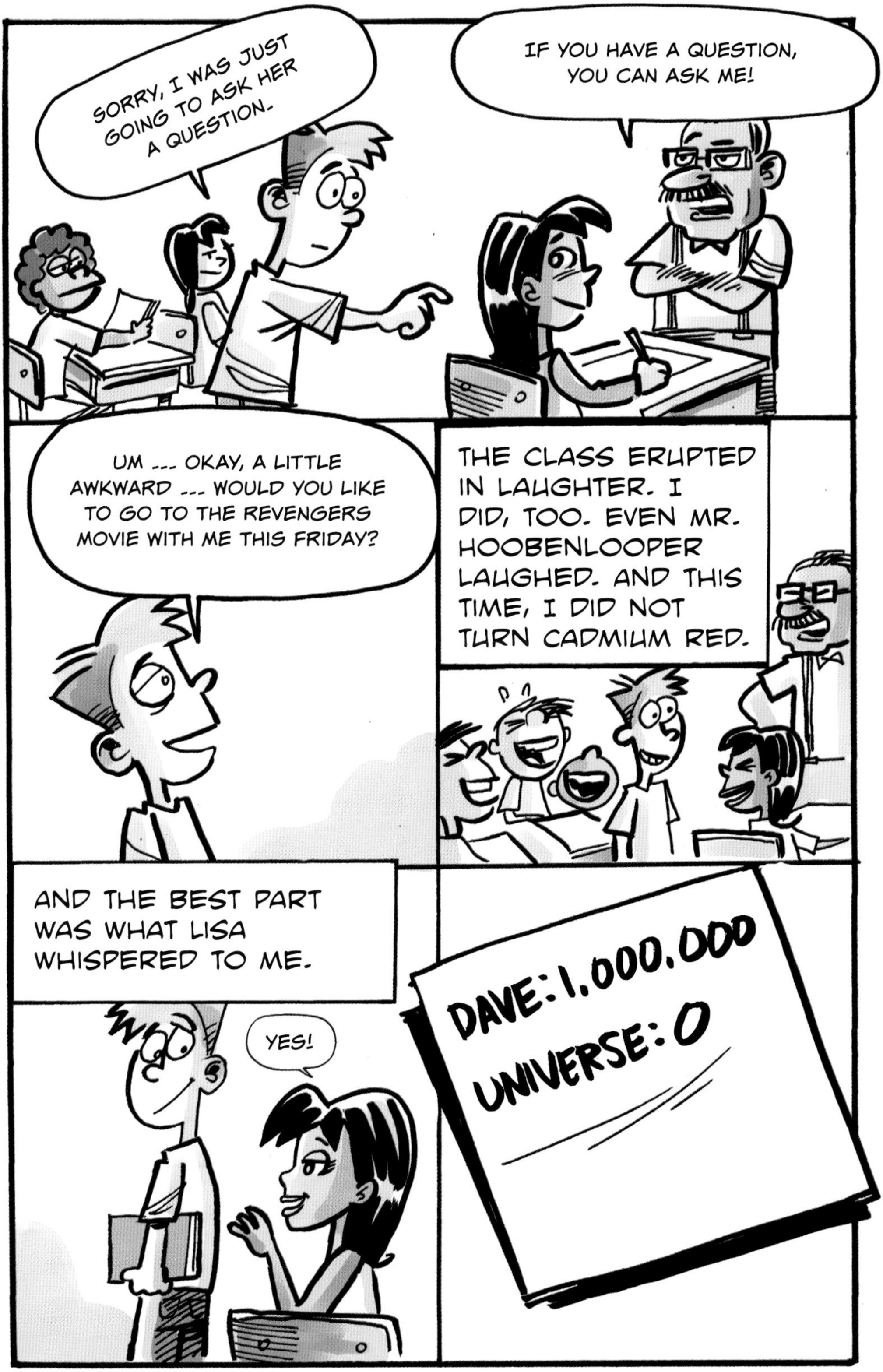
SORRY, I WAS JUST GOING TO ASK HER A QUESTION.
IF YOU HAVE A QUESTION, YOU CAN ASK ME!
UM --- OKAY, A LITTLE AWKWARD --- WOULD YOU LIKE TO GO TO THE REVENGERS MOVIE WITH ME THIS FRIDAY?
THE CLASS ERUPTED IN LAUGHTER. I DID, TOO. EVEN MR. HOOBENLOOPER LAUGHED. AND THIS TIME, I DID NOT TURN CADMIUM RED.
AND THE BEST PART WAS WHAT LISA WHISPERED TO ME.
YES!
DAVE: 1.000.000
UNIVERSE: 0

CHAPTER 13: AIN'T NOTHING GONNA BREAK MY STRIDE!

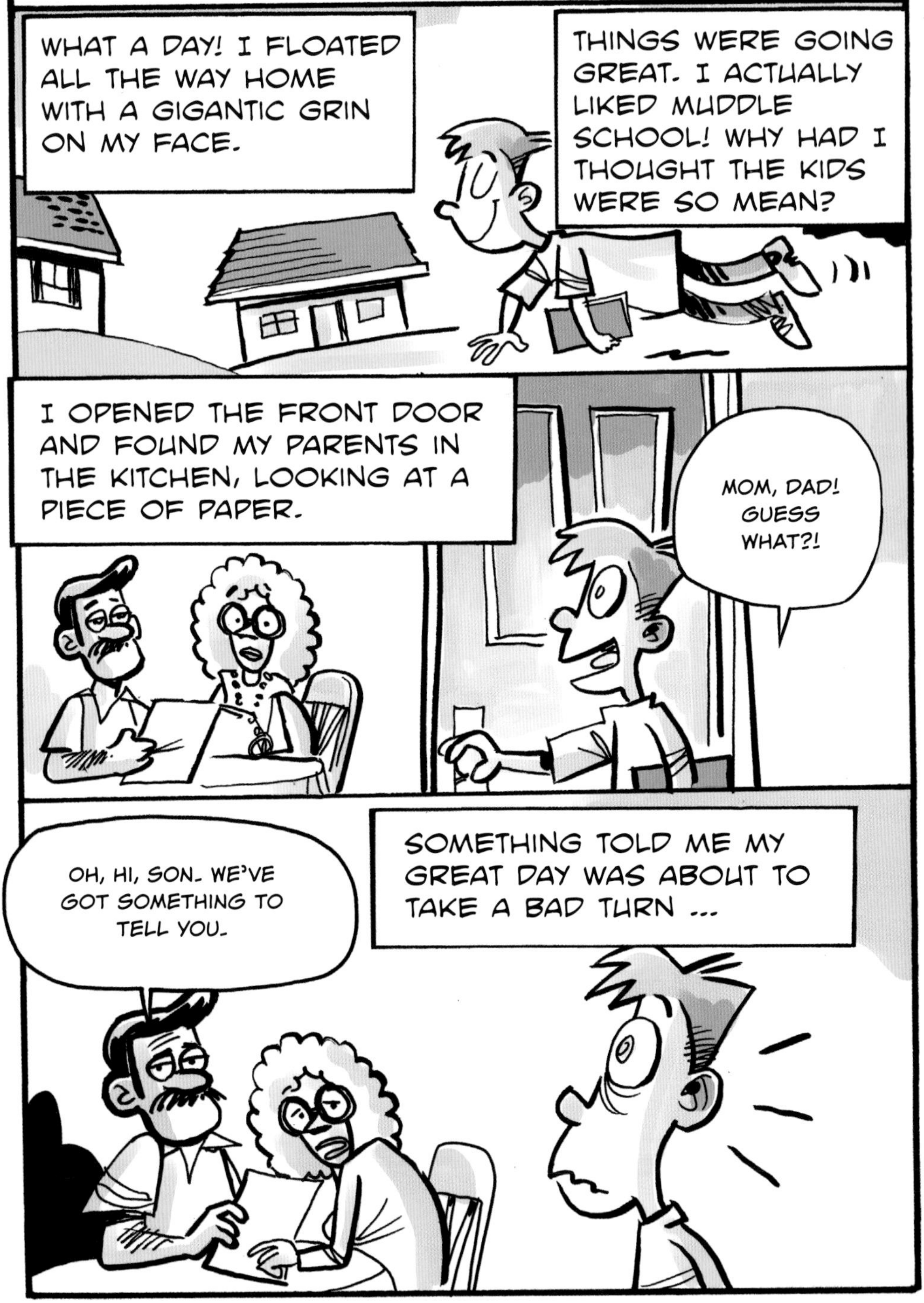
WHAT A DAY! I FLOATED ALL THE WAY HOME WITH A GIGANTIC GRIN ON MY FACE.
THINGS WERE GOING GREAT. I ACTUALLY LIKED MUDDLE SCHOOL! WHY HAD I THOUGHT THE KIDS WERE SO MEAN?
I OPENED THE FRONT DOOR AND FOUND MY PARENTS IN THE KITCHEN, LOOKING AT A PIECE OF PAPER.
MOM, DAD! GUESS WHAT?!
OH, HI, SON. WE'VE GOT SOMETHING TO TELL YOU.
SOMETHING TOLD ME MY GREAT DAY WAS ABOUT TO TAKE A BAD TURN ...

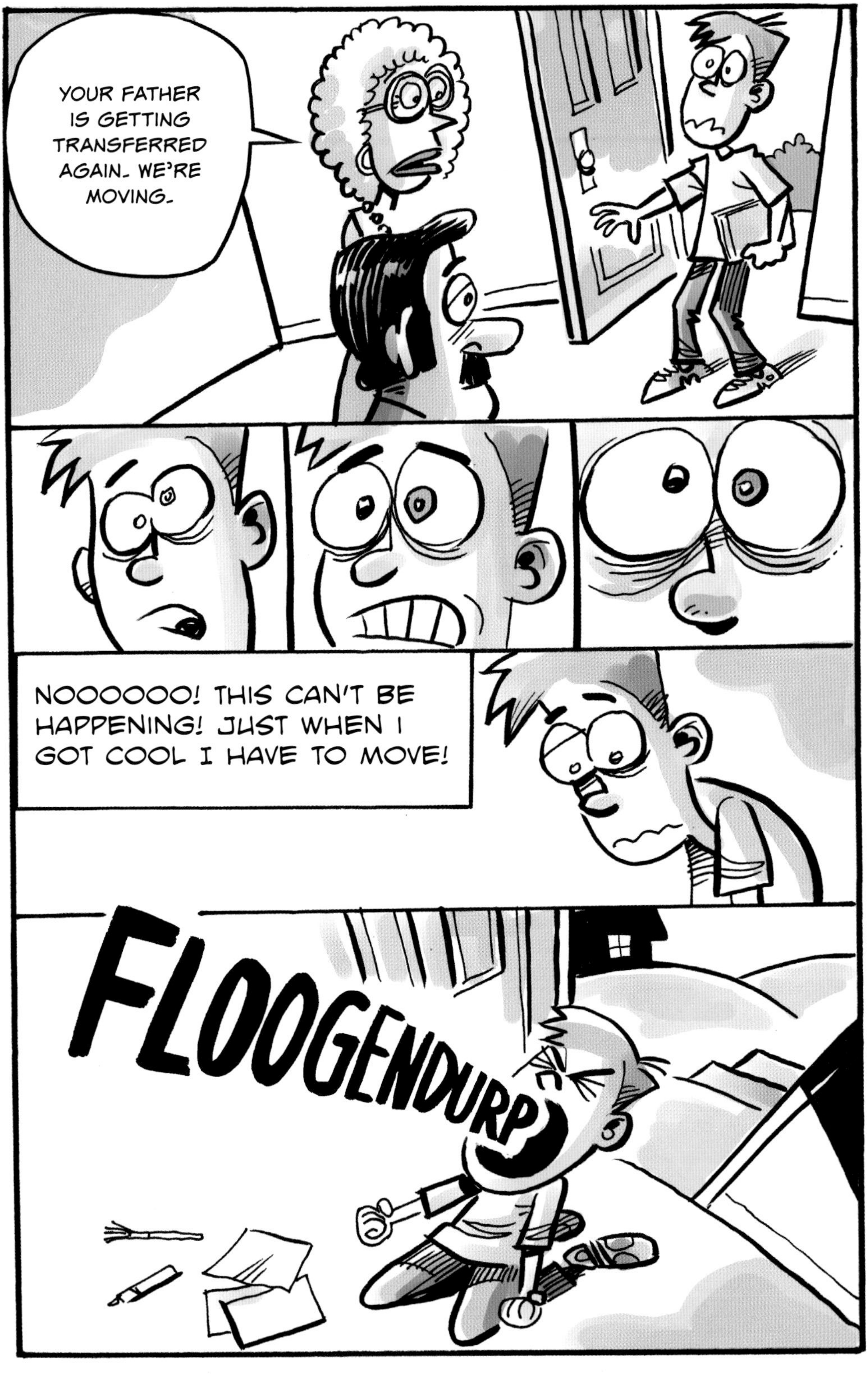
YOUR FATHER IS GETTING TRANSFERRED AGAIN. WE'RE MOVING.
NOOOOOO! THIS CAN'T BE HAPPENING! JUST WHEN I GOT COOL I HAVE TO MOVE!
FLOOGENDURP

CHAPTER 14: THE BIG DATE

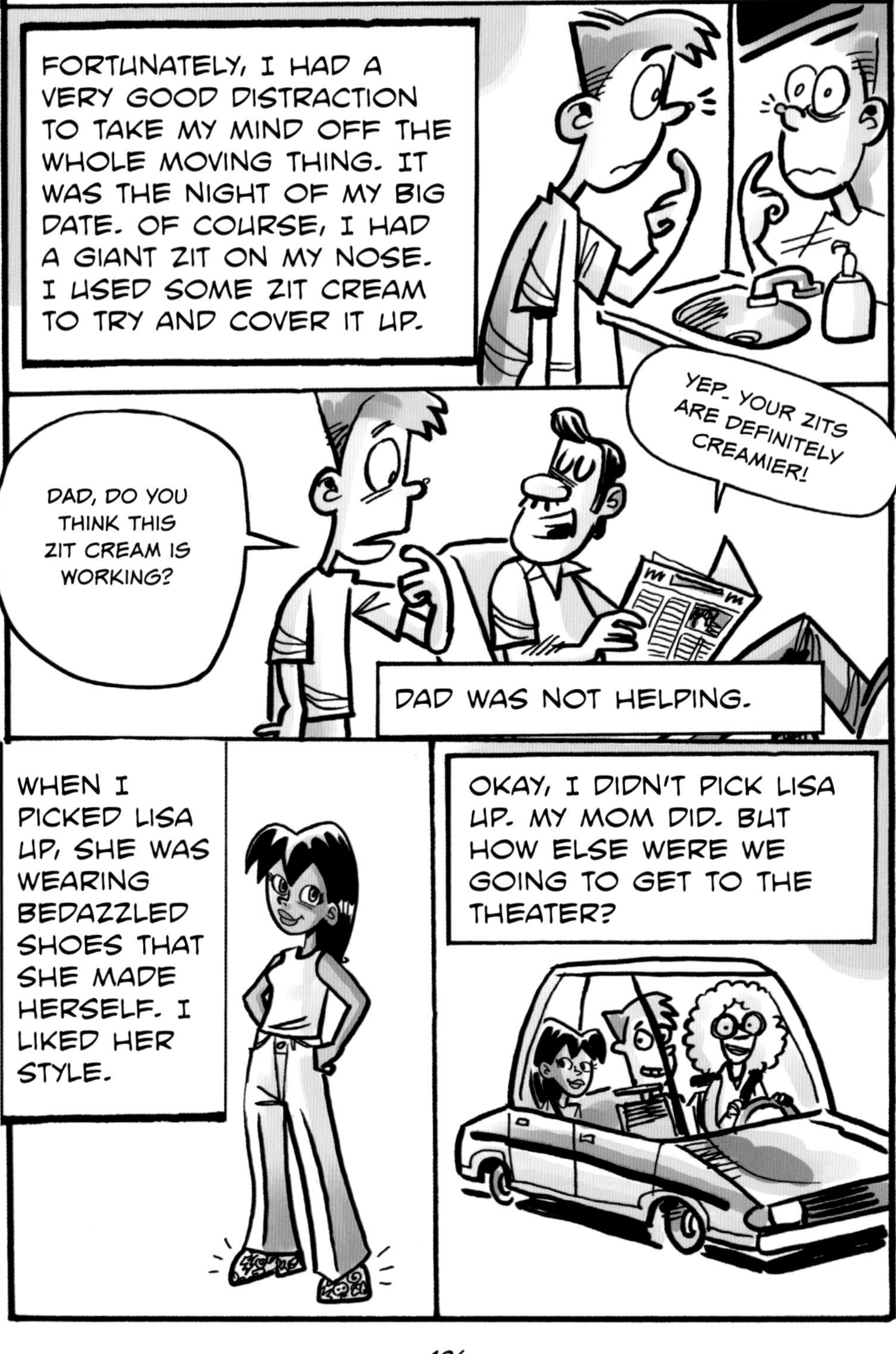

FORTUNATELY, I HAD A VERY GOOD DISTRACTION TO TAKE MY MIND OFF THE WHOLE MOVING THING. IT WAS THE NIGHT OF MY BIG DATE. OF COURSE, I HAD A GIANT ZIT ON MY NOSE. I USED SOME ZIT CREAM TO TRY AND COVER IT UP.
DAD, DO YOU THINK THIS ZIT CREAM IS WORKING?
YEP. YOUR ZITS ARE DEFINITELY CREAMIER!
DAD WAS NOT HELPING.
WHEN I PICKED LISA UP, SHE WAS WEARING BEDAZZLED SHOES THAT SHE MADE HERSELF. I LIKED HER STYLE.
OKAY, I DIDN'T PICK LISA UP. MY MOM DID. BUT HOW ELSE WERE WE GOING TO GET TO THE THEATER?

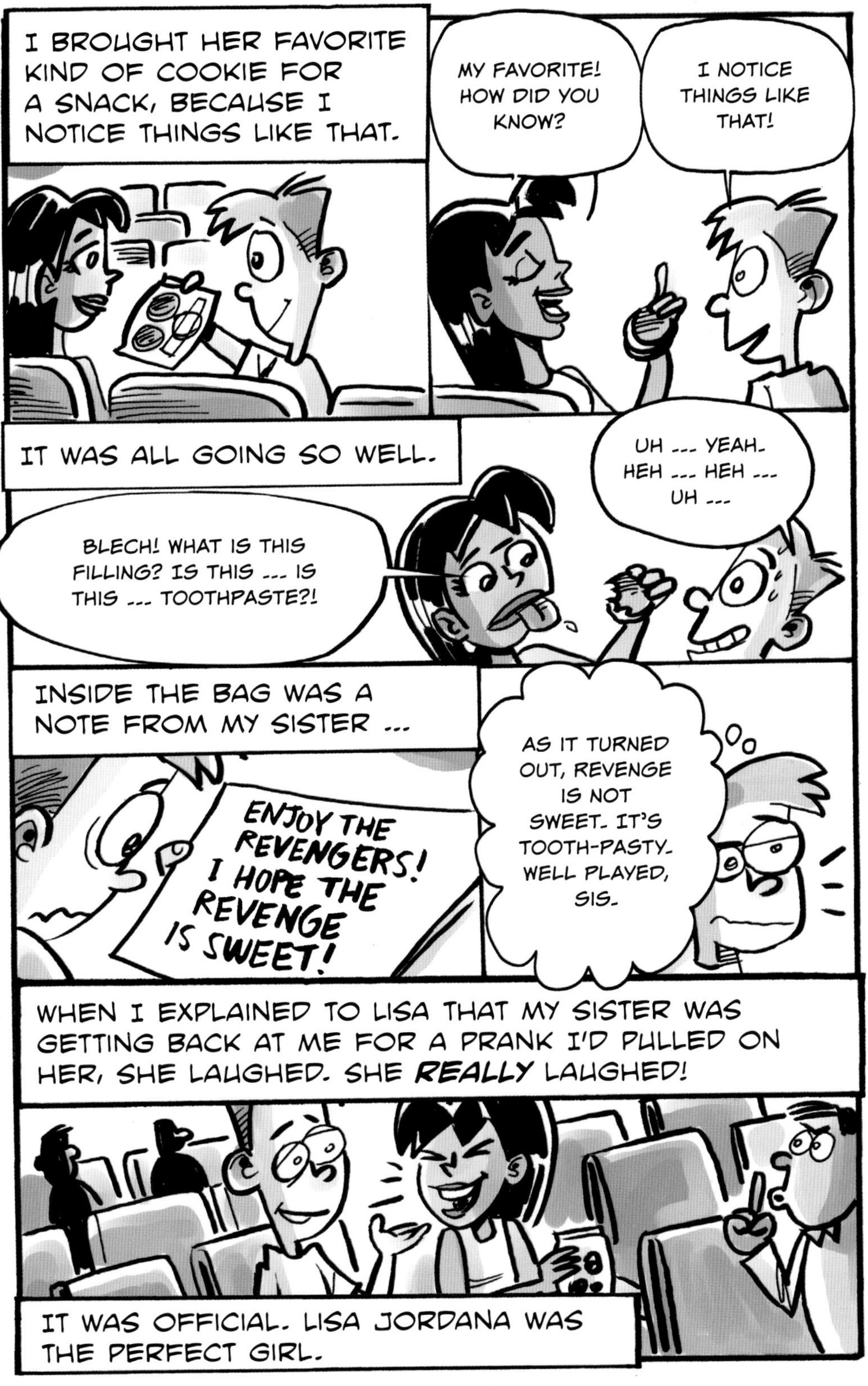

I BROUGHT HER FAVORITE KIND OF COOKIE FOR A SNACK, BECAUSE I NOTICE THINGS LIKE THAT.
MY FAVORITE! HOW DID YOU KNOW?
I NOTICE THINGS LIKE THAT!
IT WAS ALL GOING SO WELL.
BLECH! WHAT IS THIS FILLING? IS THIS ... IS THIS ... TOOTHPASTE?!
UH ... YEAH. HEH ... HEH ... UH ...
INSIDE THE BAG WAS A NOTE FROM MY SISTER ...
ENJOY THE REVENGERS! I HOPE THE REVENGE IS SWEET!
AS IT TURNED OUT, REVENGE IS NOT SWEET. IT'S TOOTH-PASTY. WELL PLAYED, SIS.
WHEN I EXPLAINED TO LISA THAT MY SISTER WAS GETTING BACK AT ME FOR A PRANK I'D PULLED ON HER, SHE LAUGHED. SHE REALLY LAUGHED!
IT WAS OFFICIAL. LISA JORDANA WAS THE PERFECT GIRL.

CHAPTER 15: GOODBYE

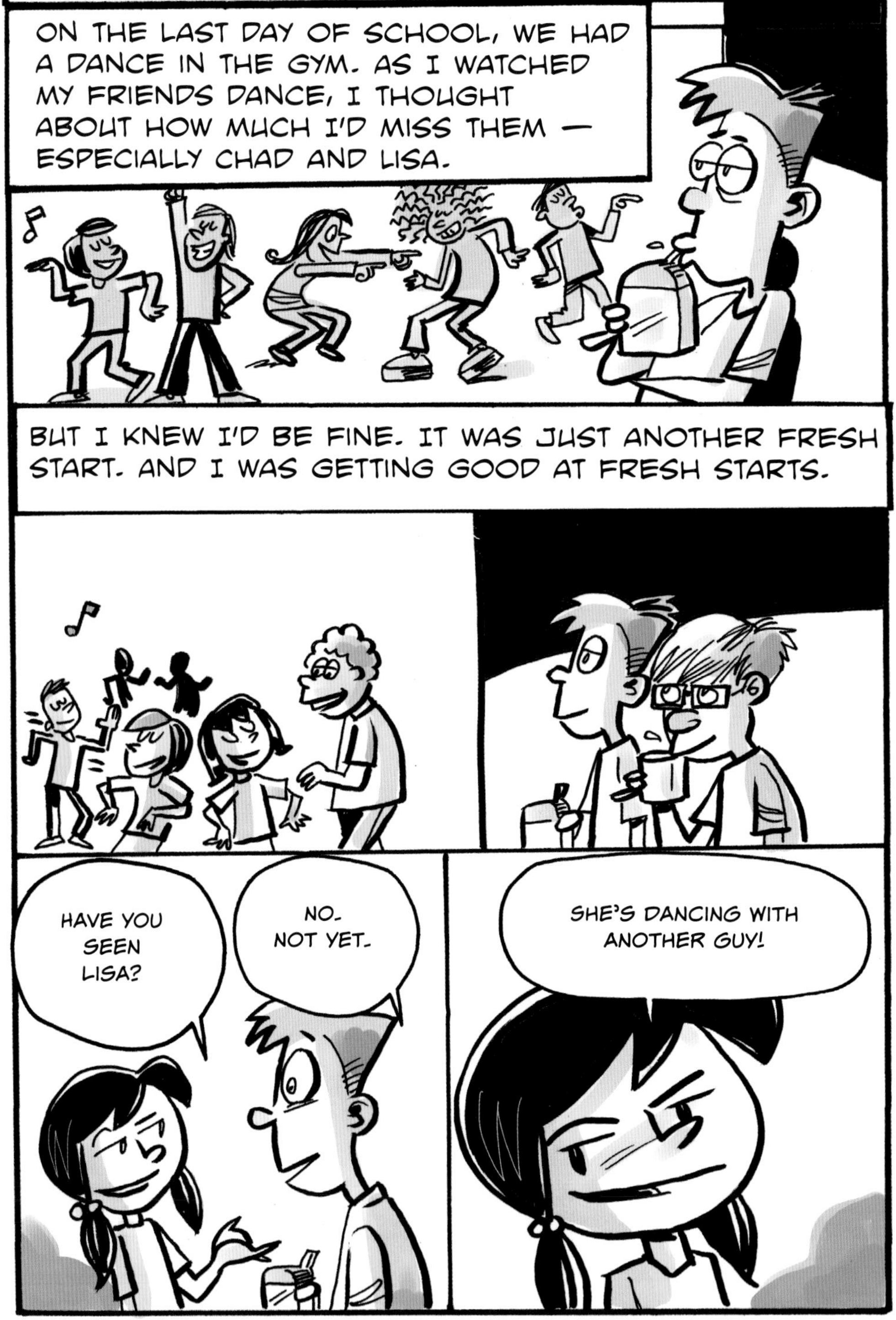
ON THE LAST DAY OF SCHOOL, WE HAD A DANCE IN THE GYM. AS I WATCHED MY FRIENDS DANCE, I THOUGHT ABOUT HOW MUCH I'D MISS THEM — ESPECIALLY CHAD AND LISA.
BUT I KNEW I'D BE FINE. IT WAS JUST ANOTHER FRESH START. AND I WAS GETTING GOOD AT FRESH STARTS.
HAVE YOU SEEN LISA?
NO. NOT YET.
SHE'S DANCING WITH ANOTHER GUY!

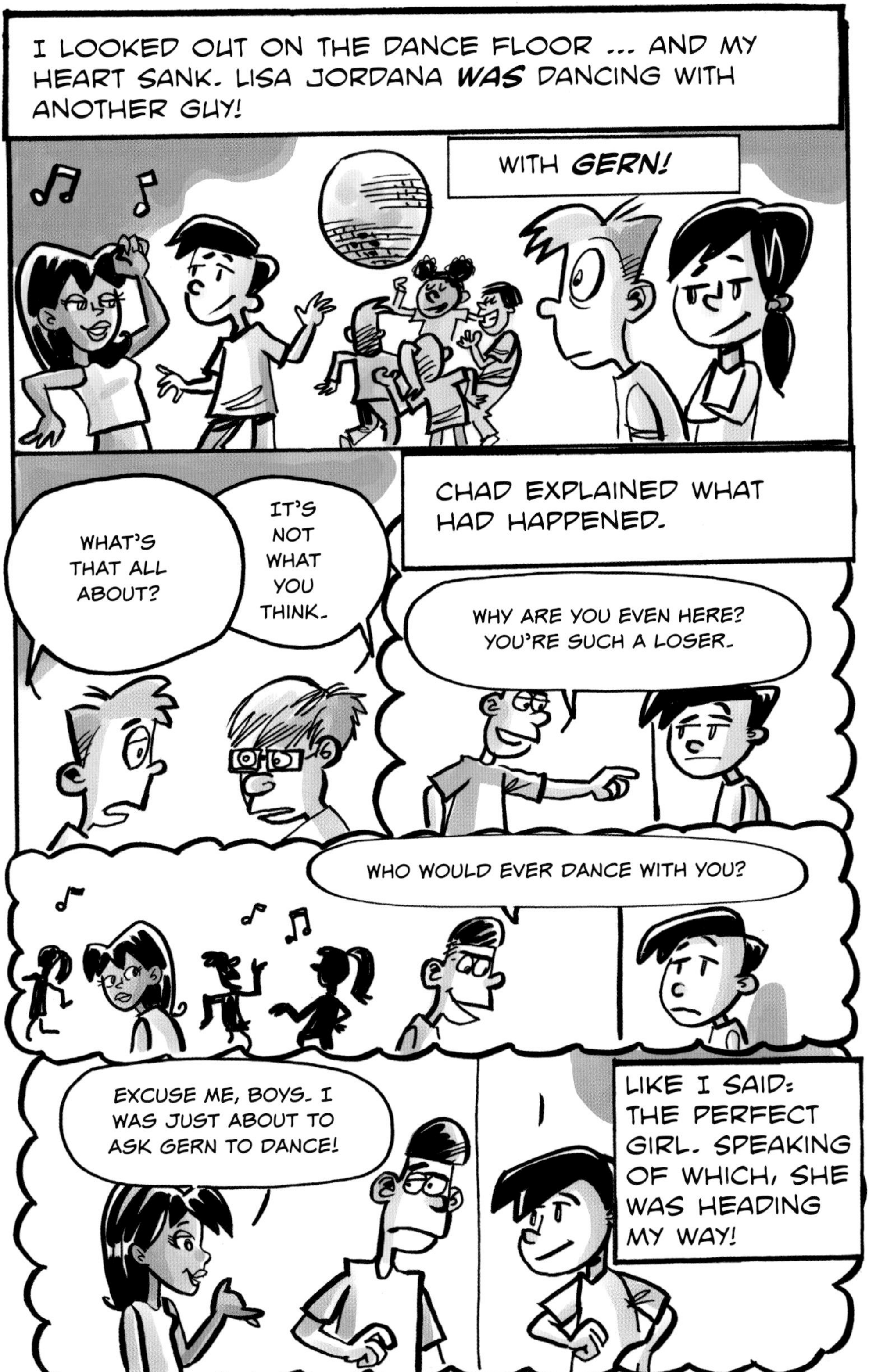
I LOOKED OUT ON THE DANCE FLOOR ... AND MY HEART SANK. LISA JORDANA *WAS* DANCING WITH ANOTHER GUY!
WITH *GERN!*
WHAT'S THAT ALL ABOUT?
IT'S NOT WHAT YOU THINK.
CHAD EXPLAINED WHAT HAD HAPPENED.
WHY ARE YOU EVEN HERE? YOU'RE SUCH A LOSER.
WHO WOULD EVER DANCE WITH YOU?
EXCUSE ME, BOYS. I WAS JUST ABOUT TO ASK GERN TO DANCE!
LIKE I SAID: THE PERFECT GIRL. SPEAKING OF WHICH, SHE WAS HEADING MY WAY!

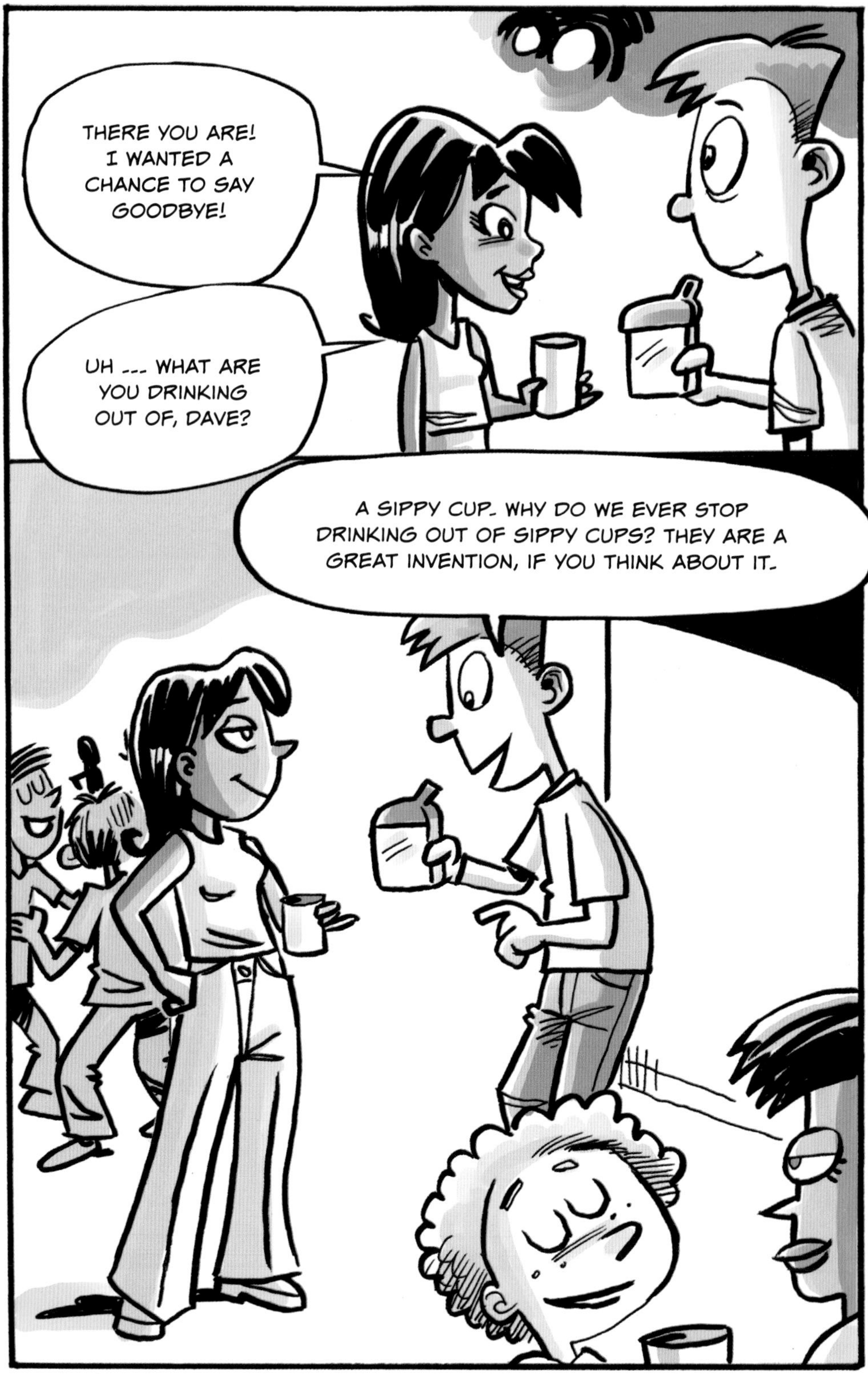
THERE YOU ARE! I WANTED A CHANCE TO SAY GOODBYE!
UH ... WHAT ARE YOU DRINKING OUT OF, DAVE?
A SIPPY CUP. WHY DO WE EVER STOP DRINKING OUT OF SIPPY CUPS? THEY ARE A GREAT INVENTION, IF YOU THINK ABOUT IT.

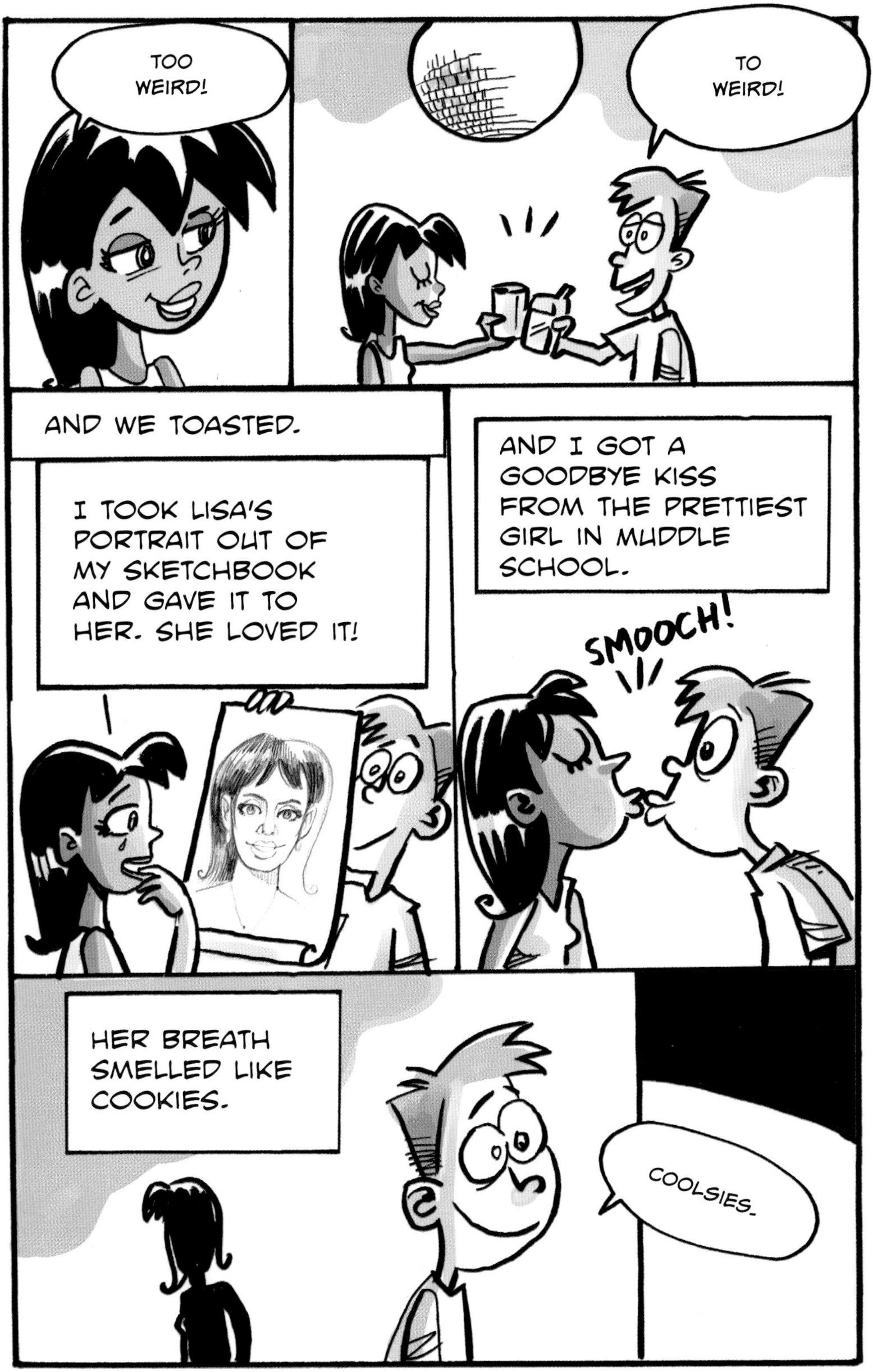
TOO WEIRD!
TO WEIRD!
AND WE TOASTED.
I TOOK LISA'S PORTRAIT OUT OF MY SKETCHBOOK AND GAVE IT TO HER. SHE LOVED IT!
AND I GOT A GOODBYE KISS FROM THE PRETTIEST GIRL IN MUDDLE SCHOOL.
SMOOCH!
HER BREATH SMELLED LIKE COOKIES.
COOLSIES.

CHAPTER 16: THE NEW KID ... AGAIN

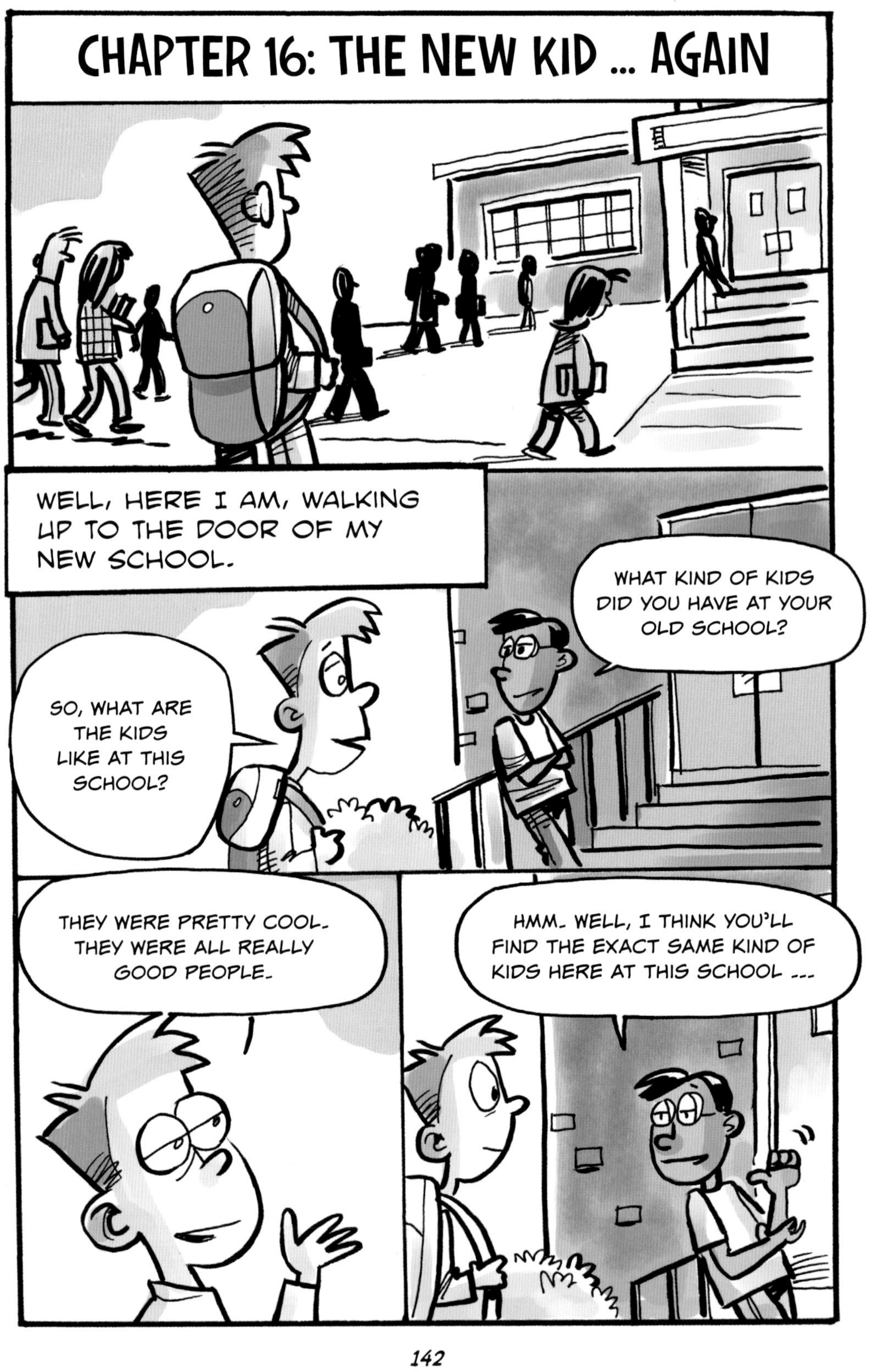

WELL, HERE I AM, WALKING UP TO THE DOOR OF MY NEW SCHOOL.
SO, WHAT ARE THE KIDS LIKE AT THIS SCHOOL?
WHAT KIND OF KIDS DID YOU HAVE AT YOUR OLD SCHOOL?
THEY WERE PRETTY COOL. THEY WERE ALL REALLY GOOD PEOPLE.
HMM. WELL, I THINK YOU'LL FIND THE EXACT SAME KIND OF KIDS HERE AT THIS SCHOOL ...

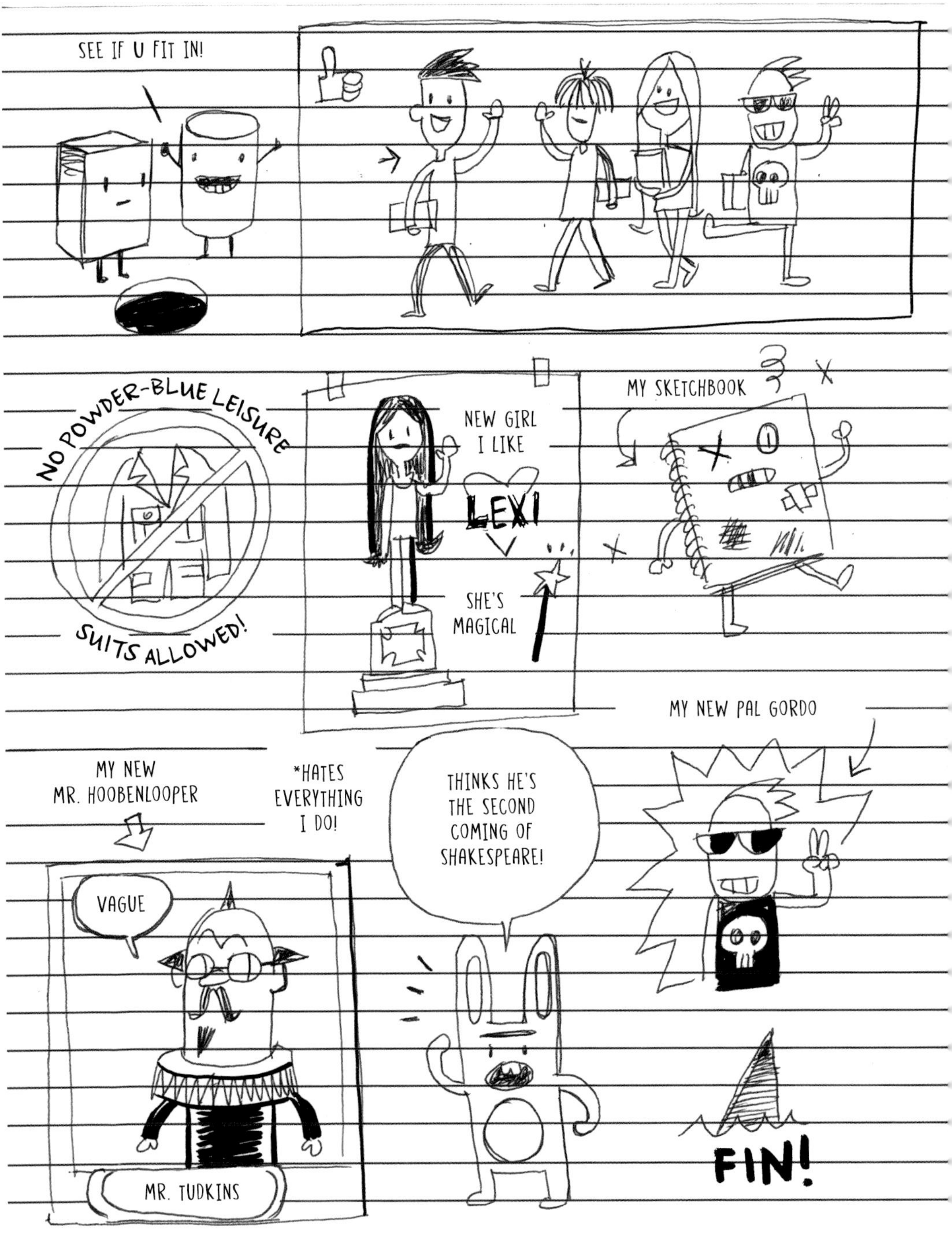
SEE IF U FIT IN!
NO POWDER-BLUE LEISURE SUITS ALLOWED!
NEW GIRL I LIKE
LEXI
SHE'S MAGICAL
MY SKETCHBOOK
MY NEW MR. HOOBENLOOPER
*HATES EVERYTHING I DO!
VAGUE
MR. TUDKINS
THINKS HE'S THE SECOND COMING OF SHAKESPEARE!
MY NEW PAL GORDO
FIN!

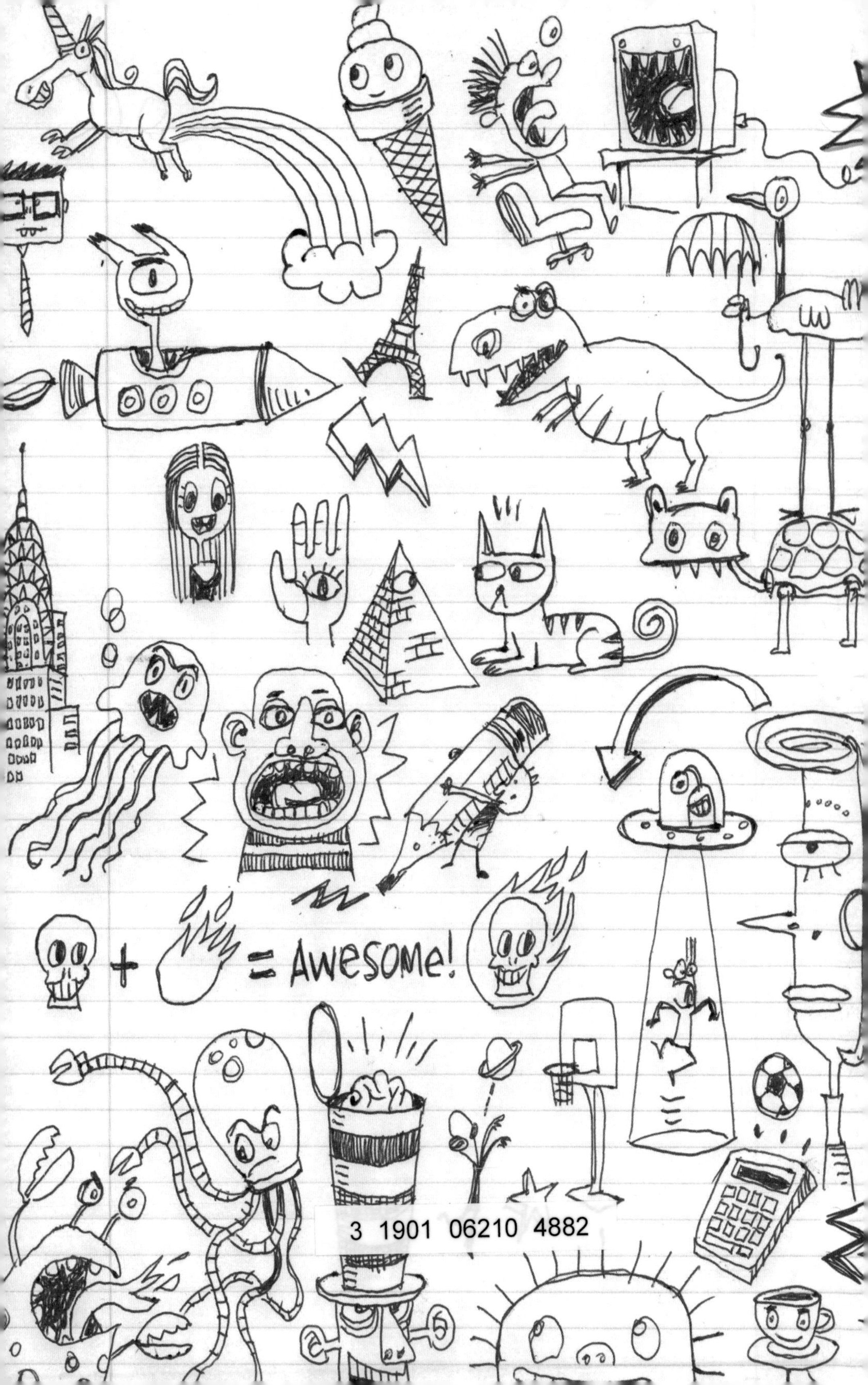
+ = Awesome!